THEY ATE, SITTING SIDE BY SIDE ON THE PILE OF HAY.

After they had finished, Evadne leaned against William, a glass of wine in her hand. He put his arm around her, holding her close as his lips brushed her cheek.

"Why don't you take that damned corset, or whatever you call it, off?" he suggested. He added quickly: "You will be able to sleep much more comfortably without it. I'll wait outside, if you like."

"In a minute." Evadne hesitated. "I am much too comfortable to move right now. Besides," she held up her glass, "I still have some wine left." She sipped it slowly, trying to make it last.

William put his glass in the basket and took her now-empty glass from her fingers. His lips sought hers as he lay back on the hay, pulling her gently with him.

The sleepiness that the wine had inspired in Evadne disappeared in the pounding of her blood. Lying so close to him, she felt a throbbing fire mounting in her veins until her whole body was burning with desire for him. Her mouth pressed hungrily to his.

Dear Reader:

We trust you will enjoy this Richard Gallen romance. We plan to bring you more of the best in both contemporary and historical romantic fiction with four exciting new titles each month.

We'd like your help.

We value your suggestions and opinions. They will help us to publish the kind of romances you want to read. Please send us your comments, or just let us know which Richard Gallen romances you have especially enjoyed. Write to the address below. We're looking forward to hearing from you!

Happy reading!

Judy Sullivan
Richard Gallen Books
8-10 West 36th St.
New York, N.Y. 10018

The Firebird

NICOLE NORMAN

PUBLISHED BY RICHARD GALLEN BOOKS
Distributed by POCKET BOOKS

Books by Nicole Norman

Heather Song
The Firebird

 A RICHARD GALLEN BOOKS *Original* publication

Distributed by
POCKET BOOKS, a Simon & Schuster division of
GULF & WESTERN CORPORATION
1230 Avenue of the Americas, New York, N.Y. 10020

ISBN: 0-671-43873-5

First Pocket Books printing October, 1981

10 9 8 7 6 5 4 3 2 1

RICHARD GALLEN and colophon are trademarks
of Simon & Schuster and Richard Gallen & Co., Inc.

Printed in the U.S.A.

The Firebird

was a senior. Else gathering, in fact, was in his hom...

1

Chapter I

"YOU MUSTN'T FORGET MY BIRTHDAY PARTY," EVADNE HARPER reminded her friends. "Remember, I'll be eighteen on December twenty-seventh."

Evadne was a tall, slender girl with a creamy complexion and hair the rich red shade of a Titian model. The green of her eyes was enhanced by the emerald color of her suit, which was the latest fashion. It was trimmed around the collar and down the front with the same black braid used for the frog closings. The full sleeves and short, fitted jacket with flared peplum emphasized her bosom and small waist, while the skirt molded snugly over slim hips and long legs. A small round-brimmed black patent leather hat with a pancake crown perched atop high-piled curls, accentuating the oval of her face and matching the patent leather handbag dangling from one wrist.

"Oh, Vad!" Lillie Dillard, a small blonde girl dressed in an equally fashionable blue suit, laughed. "How could we forget? You won't let us!"

Joining in her laughter were the two young men who made up the rest of the quartet of young people seated in the court of San Francisco's Palace Hotel. One was Lillie's brother Jack, home for the Christmas holidays from Yale, where he was a senior. The gathering, in fact, was in his honor. The

1

other young man was Paul Tyler, who had graduated from Yale the year before and now was working as an assistant to his father, the president of the Merchant and Seaman's Bank, one of San Francisco's largest financial institutions.

"You really should have arranged to have been born a few days later, Vad. Then you would have been a New Year's baby and we could have rung in 1906 with you," Jack declared with a grin. He was a stocky young man, a masculine version of his sister, with a turned up nose and round eyes that looked constantly surprised with the world around him.

"If she had been, it would mean one less party, and the more parties, the merrier, I say!" Paul's voice rang with enthusiasm. He was a tall, slender young man with dark hair and eyes, and he loved to dance.

"And *I* say that it's good to be home!" Jack looked appreciatively around him. "There's nothing like the Palace out East, is there, Paul?"

San Franciscans thought of the Palace Hotel as the eighth wonder of the world. Wonder or not, it was the largest and one of the world's finest. Opened in 1875, it was seven stories high and took up a full city block. Built of stone and brick, its facade featured the bay windows that San Francisco natives loved and used wherever possible on buildings large and small. The excuse given was that in a climate noted for its fogs, the windows permitted the maximum amount of light to enter rooms that would otherwise be dark during the day time. The outstanding feature of the hotel, however, was its immense central courtyard—called the Court of the Sun— with a circular drive more than wide enough for the largest stage coach to negotiate, in the days before automobiles, and discharge passengers under the protection of the court's glass roof. A good many of the hotel's 850 rooms looked out onto the court, which furnished them not only with a subdued daylight but also a view of the events going on.

The court was paved in marble except for the drive. At the western end it was encircled by Doric pillars, surmounted by copings of birds and flowers. Groupings of chairs, settees, and tables—accompanied discreetly by brass spittoons—were scattered about to provide intimate gathering spots for hotel guests and others, like the quartet of friends there to cele- brate Jack Dillard's return from the East.

Evadne, who had never been East, looked at surroundings that she took so for granted with new interest. "Is Jack right, that there is no place like the Palace in the East?" she asked Paul.

"Not in the East or in Europe that I know of," Paul said, gazing at her with admiration. "I tell you what, Vad. When we get married, I'll take you East and to Europe on our honeymoon, and you can see for yourself."

Evadne smiled. Their marriage was a long-standing joke between them—at least, it was a joke on her side. One reason was her height. At five feet, eight inches she was as tall as—and often taller than—most of the young men of her acquaintance. Paul, who topped six feet, was an exception.

"I know," she agreed amiably. "After all, I have to marry you. I don't want to lead in dancing the rest of my life, and who else do I know who is taller than I am?"

Unmentioned was the fact that the match was being encouraged by both Evadne's and Paul's parents, though this was no secret.

Lillie regarded the two jealously. She and Evadne were best friends and lived near one another, so Evadne could just as easily have seen Jack at the Dillard house. This gathering had been Lillie's idea, to give her an opportunity to invite Paul. Ever since she was twelve, Lillie had had a yearning for Paul—which Paul and Evadne knew only too well. Now, although it was Paul who had brought the subject up, Lillie scolded her friend. "Really, Vad, how can you talk about marriage? You're not even eighteen yet!"

As Evadne hesitated, sorry for the turn that the conversation had taken, Paul said, "She'll be eighteen in a week and as old as you, and I bet you don't think you are too young to get married."

His blunt statement irked Evadne, both because of Lillie, who had flushed in embarrassment, and because of herself, since she had no intention of marrying anyone just yet. When she married, it would be for love. Much as she liked Paul, she was not—and could never imagine herself to be—in love with him. She had told him so time and time again, but it only increased his insistence that sooner or later she would marry him.

Glaring at him, Evadne remarked sharply, "I do not mean to marry anyone until I am at least twenty-one. I want to see something of the world before I marry and—and settle down." She had been about to say "have babies," but that would have been risque in mixed company.

Paul laughed. "Seeing the world is for men, not women."

"That's what you think. Times are changing." Evadne leaned back casually in her chair, preparing to drop a piece of information she hoped would be shocking enough to jolt Paul out of his complacency. "By the way, Lillie, Papa, who is one of the trustees, told me Leland Stanford University has set aside five hundred places for women. Wouldn't it be fun to go there?"

"Don't tell me you're thinking of going to college?" Jack Dillard's eyes grew rounder at the idea.

"Why not?" Evadne tossed her head, her hat bouncing like a boat on the waves of her curls. Pleased with herself, she added, "What's wrong with girls getting the same education as boys?"

Her companions laughed so hard that a pair of elderly gentlemen, in cutaways and top hats, sitting nearby turned to stare at the group. Evadne, busy glaring at her friends, paid no attention. Her eyes flashed angrily. "I can't see what is so funny about wanting to go to college."

"It's not the idea of *college,* Vad," Paul said. "Why, if you want to go to college, there are plenty of schools for girls in the East. I met several girls from Mount Holyoke and Smith when I was at Yale. But you really don't think that girls are smart enough to attend the same university with boys, do you?"

"The next thing we know, Vad, you'll be telling us you're a suffragette," Jack put in, still laughing. "Tell me, do you want the vote too, Vad?" he teased.

Evadne had heard of the suffragist movement, although she wasn't exactly sure what it was. At the same time, she had too much pride to make such an admission.

"From what Papa says, I don't think a lot of men are smart enough to vote. Just look at the crooks they put into office." Although San Francisco's Mayor Eugene Schmitz was popular, almost everyone said the city officials under him and the Board of Supervisors could be bribed to do just about anything. "Oiling the skids" was the way to do business with City Hall.

Paul looked at her soberly, the laughter gone from his face. "Then you *do* think women should have the vote—just like men?"

Evadne hesitated, the idea appealing to her, new as it was. "Yes. Yes," she said firmly, "I do. I think women are just as smart as men—and maybe a lot more honest."

The flat statement shocked the others into stunned silence Evadne decided it might be an opportune time to leave. She stood, reaching for the black sealskin coat on the chair behind her. It was an early Christmas present from her parents, and she adored the look and feel of it, as soft and silky and luminous as the finest black velvet. It was the latest rage and made her feel very grown up and sophisticated, something she wanted very much at the moment.

The coat over her arm, she was about to announce that she had to leave to meet her mother—a lie she knew the others would not believe—when she noticed a man moving purposefully toward their table. Although he was wearing the same type of black suit with frock coat Paul and Jack were wearing, he wore it with a difference, his broad shoulders and deep chest filling out the coat as Paul's did not. His walk, too, was different; it was the stride of a man who knew where he was going and was in a hurry to get there. All this, Evadne noticed with a glance. What sent a tremor through her whole body and kept her eyes on him was his face. It was deeply tanned with a short, straight nose and a wide, firm mouth above which were the bluest eyes she had ever seen. His brown hair was as sun-streaked as his face was tanned. For an instant the ground seem to move under her feet. Her heart pounded and her knees felt rubbery when, to her surprise, he stopped at their table. What, she wondered, could he possibly want with them?

"Tyler," the stranger spoke to Paul in a deep, resonant voice. "Excuse me for interrupting. When I saw a familiar face here, I felt I had to say hello."

Paul rose quickly to his feet, holding out his hand. The two men were about the same height, although Paul seemed almost fragile next to the other man. "Frankly, you are a most welcome interruption, Hopkins," Paul said, with a glance at Evadne. "Let me introduce you to some friends of mine." He turned to the others. "This is William Hopkins. He's a distant relative of old Mark Hopkins, but his branch of the family went to Australia during the Gold Rush and so he's Australian, not American."

He introduced Lillie, who nodded at the introduction, and Evadne. Evadne, still standing, her coat over her left arm, held out her hand.

"Mr. Hopkins," she murmured, smiling with trembling lips, as he took her hand and held it in a strong grip.

"Evadne?" he said, still holding her hand. "That's an unusual name. I don't think I ever heard it before."

"It's a family name. I don't know where it came from." Her fingers closed on his.

"A family name?" His eyes held hers, seeming to drink in the pale oval face, the almond-shaped green eyes with their dark lashes and arched dark brows, the full lips, and the slightly acquiline nose. Reluctantly, he let her hand go to acknowledge the introduction to Jack.

"Won't you join us, Hopkins?" Paul asked politely.

The Australian's eyes returned to Evadne, who was still standing. "Weren't you leaving?"

She flushed slightly, the rosy color rising in her cheeks giving her an added loveliness. "I'm really in no hurry."

"In that case. . . ." Hopkins took her coat and put it over the back of her chair before holding the chair for her to sit down. After Evadne was seated, he drew up another chair for himself, placing it next to hers.

Lillie studied him with open curiosity. "If your family is related to Mark Hopkins, why did they go to Australia to strike it rich?"

"Well, though it's true Hopkins, Collis Huntington, Leland Stanford, and Charles Crocker—" he named the "big four" of San Francisco in the nineteenth century—"came west for the Gold Rush, actually they all made their money after that in what is now the Southern Pacific Railroad. My father didn't have much luck finding gold either. He had a promising claim jumped, and when he heard about the new strike in Australia, he decided to try his luck there."

"I take it that he was lucky?" Evadne asked, her voice husky. The presence of this stranger so close beside her stirred her in a way that she had never experienced before. She found herself longing for him to touch her again.

Hopkins looked at her, the sun lines at the corners of his eyes crinkling when he smiled. "Lucky enough to put the gold he found into land in Sydney and New South Wales. That land is why I'm here," he added.

"How did you meet Paul? What does land in Australia have to do with him?" Jack Dillard asked. "He's a banker."

Paul, who had been studying Evadne closely enough to notice her flushed cheeks, gave Hopkins no opportunity to answer. "The bank is handling Hopkins's letter of credit," he explained. "Rather, I am handling it," he added for Evadne's benefit.

The Australian smiled at Jack, who was obviously still puzzled. "I came to San Francisco because we're interested in starting a wine vineyard. Since the vineyards in the Sonoma Valley north of here have had a smashing success with European vines and our climate is similar, I'm here to investigate."

Evadne caught her breath in dismay. "Then you won't be staying in San Francisco?"

"I will for now." He turned to her again. "I will be here at least for the holidays, which are a bad time to do business."

"Of course, since Mark Hopkins was a relative, you must have family here whom you want to see . . . ?" offered Lillie.

"No," Hopkins answered. "My father was quite out of touch with anyone here. I am a friendless stranger and have taken a suite at the St. Francis. I was having luncheon alone in the Grill Room here. I spotted Tyler as I was leaving." He turned back to Evadne. "I fear my timing was poor, getting me here just before the holidays, although actually I didn't plan it that way. Storms in the South Pacific delayed my ship and made repairs necessary in Hawaii, which delayed us even longer. I tried to find another ship, but none was due to arrive any sooner. And so," he smiled, "instead of arriving in November, I find myself arriving here in mid-December."

"Oh, dear!" cried Lillie, who had missed little of the exchanges, both silent and spoken, between Evadne and Hopkins. She decided to turn their interest in one another to her advantage. She seized Paul's hand. "Paul, we must not let a stranger in our midst go friendless during the holiday season, must we?"

" 'We'?" Paul raised an eyebrow at her. Had Evadne said it, he would have welcomed the "we." He liked Lillie the way a brother likes a sister, which was understandable since the Tylers and the Dillards had built their houses next to one another on California Street, near the Crocker and Huntington homes on the southwestern corner of Nob Hill. "Lillie, dear," he said, gently removing his hand from her grasp, "I have already spoken to my father. If you had not happened to meet Mr. Hopkins today, you would have met him at the party we are giving the day after tomorrow. After that, I am sure he will not lack for invitations."

"Indeed, he will not," said Evadne, seizing the opportunity. "Mr. Hopkins, you must come to my birthday party on the twenty-seventh, for one thing. Papa will be very interested to hear what you have to say about Australia." Evadne's father, who had been a minority shareholder in the Southern Pacific, had invested heavily in shipping at the time of the Spanish-American War, seeing ships as the inevitable extension of the railroad across the Pacific.

Paul decided more than enough invitations had been issued. He took his watch out of his pocket and looked at it pointedly. "Well, children, I am a working man and I must get back to the bank."

Lillie sighed. "And you and I, Jack, must meet Mother at the City of Paris."

Jack groaned and got to his feet. Noting the puzzled look on Hopkins's face, Jack explained, "It's a department store. I am wanted, I am sure, merely to carry all the purchases that Mama and Lillie are certain to make."

"In that case," Hopkins rose to his feet and picked up Evadne's coat, "may I not escort you to wherever it is you must go, Miss Harper?"

"Thank you, Mr. Hopkins." Evadne smiled, deliberately pretending to catch her arm in the sleeve of her coat to allow the others to go ahead.

"Where might that be?" Hopkins asked again.

"Vad!" Jack called from the drive where a cab was pulling up. "Can we give you a lift?"

"Go ahead, Jack. You and Lillie had better hurry. You know how your mother is when you are late," she called back. As Jack and Lillie stepped into the cab, Evadne looked at Paul, who still lingered at the table. "I thought you had to get back to the bank?"

"I did—that is, I do. I thought I would get a cab for you first," he said stiffly. The bank was only a few blocks from the hotel.

"Mr. Hopkins has already offered to escort me, Paul," Evadne pointed out. She added wickedly: "You'd better be on your way, before your father locks the doors on you."

Paul flushed and nodded a quick goodbye to her and Hopkins. Despite what he had said about handling the Australian's letter of credit, as his father's assistant he had little responsibility at the bank, other than those simple matters his father decided to turn over to him, and Evadne knew it. He had gone into the bank only at his father's insistence after college and because he didn't know what else he wanted to do except paint—an idea that brought the full weight of his father's scorn down on him. Though the

Bohemian life of an artist appealed to Paul, starving in a garret did not.

As Paul left, Evadne, suddenly contrite, apologized to Hopkins. "I'm afraid I was a little sharp with him. I have a regrettable tendency sometimes to say too much."

"A redhead's temper?" The corners of his mouth twitched.

Evadne laughed ruefully. "I'm afraid so. My mother says it will be my undoing unless I learn to control it."

"There is nothing wrong with a temper as long as you are as quick to forgive as you are to show anger." He looked at her frankly, at the high, firm breasts pressing against the fabric of her jacket, at the small waist and the slender hips. "Temper, in fact, can be attractive in a woman," he added.

The blood seemed to pound in Evadne's temples. She wanted to ask him what he meant—and was afraid she knew the answer. "Really?" she murmured, trying to sound casual.

"Really." He smiled. "Now, Miss Evadne, since we are in a public place, where would you like to go . . . before I forget myself?"

Evadne flushed, then boldly suggested, "Why don't we walk to the St. Francis? It's only a few blocks from here and I can point out the sights along the way. Actually, I'm only going home and hardly need an escort," she added.

Hopkins bowed slightly, taking her arm to lead her out on Market Street. As he did, he laughed, white teeth flashing in his sun-bronzed face.

Evadne looked at him angrily, stopping short in the middle of the sidewalk. "Why are you laughing at me?" she demanded, her temper still short from the earlier confrontation with Paul and Jack. "And who gave you permission to call me by my first name?"

"I am not laughing at you," he said quickly. "I would never do that. I was laughing, because I was warned back home that Americans in the West are very . . . forthright—"

"Uncultured, you mean." Evadne's temper was rapidly approaching the boiling point.

"No, not uncultured. I was also told that San Francisco is a city that honors art, literature, music . . . shall I go on?"

"Then why did you laugh at me?" Evadne persisted stubbornly.

Hopkins waved his hand. "We are beginning to draw a crowd. Let's walk, shall we?"

Evadne blushed, aware then that people had paused to

gape at them and listen. She started forward quickly. "I still want to know—"

"I was laughing, my dear, because you seem to be the first true 'son' of the West I have met. Your friend, Tyler, for instance, and the others seem to talk in circles. Now are you mollified?" he asked, as they stopped at the intersection of Geary, Kearney, and Market Streets to let a cable car rumble by, clanging and swaying.

The intersection was one of the busiest in the city and notable for its fountain, an ornate, slender wedding cake with head-high water fountains around the base. It was called "Lotta's Fountain" after Lotta Crabtree, who had donated it to the city. To the north of Market was the financial heart of the city—at the Bay end—while Geary and Kearney led toward Union Square, around which were the best shops and stores, the theater district, and hotels as fine as the Palace, like the St. Francis. South of Market—also called south of the Slot because of the trench, or slot, between the cable car tracks—was given over to warehouses, factories, rooming houses, and frame homes where working men and their families lived.

Evadne, who should have been pointing out such things to Hopkins, a stranger here, was pondering his remarks. Calling her a true "son" of the West flattered and appeased her, but she was not yet ready to forgive and forget. "That still does not give you permission to call me by my first name," she insisted haughtily.

"You are quite right," Hopkins admitted, "and for that I beg your forgiveness." They had started across the intersection, but he stopped at the base of Lotta's Fountain to take off his hat and make Evadne a sweeping bow.

Her anger disappeared in a rush of laughter. She took his arm, urging him toward Geary Street. "As you guessed, Mr. Hopkins, I am quick to anger and quick to forgive. And we are both quick walkers. Up ahead is Union Square. We shall soon be at the St. Francis."

Hopkins stopped in front of the well-planned square, with its green grass and crosswalks and benches. Despite the chill of the December day, a few loungers were sitting on the benches reading newspapers or smoking cigars. In the center of the square was a tall column with a figure atop it, the figure of a woman standing on one foot who seemed to be running into the wind.

"What is that statue?" Hopkins asked.

"That's Victory. The monument is dedicated to Admiral Dewey and his defeat of the Spanish at Manila," Evadne explained, trying to think of something else to say to prolong the moment and keep him with her.

A chill wind arose suddenly, sending a few loose newspapers sailing, swooping and diving like the seagulls on the Bay. Despite the warmth of her coat, Evadne shivered.

Hopkins took advantage of the moment to put his arm around her. "I say, I can hardly send you home freezing in a cab. It was thoughtless of me to let you walk."

Evadne leaned against him, liking the feel of his arm around her. "It was my suggestion, Mr. Hopkins," she pointed out. "I like to walk when I have the chance."

"Even so, may I make amends by inviting you for a cup of tea at the St. Francis to warm you up?"

She raised her head to look into his face. He was very handsome. The tan gave him the dashing look of the outdoor man, a look rarely seen among the men Evadne knew. "That is most kind of you," she replied slowly, knowing she should go home. At the same time, there was really no hurry. Her father was at his office and her mother had a committee meeting that would keep her until it was time to dress for dinner.

"Then you accept?" He smiled. When she still hesitated, he added, "Please say yes and quickly, for if you are not cold in that fashionable fur of yours, I certainly am without an overcoat."

Evadne was overwhelmed by guilt. Surely he must have been cold long before now, and she had been so caught up with her own fancies that she had not even noticed that he had only the frock coat.

"Yes, I accept." She hurried him into the luxurious hotel with its crystal chandeliers and potted palms.

Once they were in the restaurant, seated discreetly at a table in the corner with tea ordered, William Hopkins leaned back in his chair, examining the girl opposite him. "Shall we make an exchange—a trade, so to speak?" he asked, a half smile on his face.

Evadne studied him before answering. The blue eyes were twinkling, and the corners of his mouth were twitching in a futile attempt to be serious. "An exchange?" she finally repeated.

He nodded. "An exchange. If you will let me call you Evadne—and it is a beautiful name, as beautiful as you are—I will let you call me William."

Once again, Evadne had to laugh. "You tricked me. I must say you are as forthright as you claim we Westerners are . . . William."

The not-quite-suppressed smile spread into a wide grin. "In that case, we shall make an agreeable couple."

"Except for my temper. Unless," she raised her eyebrows in mock horror, "unless you also have a temper. Do you?"

"Only when I am thoroughly aroused." The grin twitched at the corners of his mouth.

"Then I shall try not to arouse you." As soon as the words were out of her mouth, Evadne saw, by the amused expression on his face, that he had meant something quite different. She knew she should be embarrassed, but the rush of blood to her cheeks had little to do with embarrassment. It was time, high time, that she left this man.

To her relief, a waiter appeared with their tea. No sooner had he set the ornate silver teapot and two fragile cups and saucers down in front of them than another tail-coated waiter appeared with a cart laden with cakes and delicate French pastries, temptingly displayed on silver and crystal plates.

"Madam?" asked the waiter, holding in one hand a plate that matched the cups and saucers and a server in the other.

Evadne glanced from the array to William, who was watching her with that provoking half smile on his face. "Go ahead," he urged. "Have a sweet or two."

"Are you going to have something?" she asked.

"Does it matter? Pick out what you like," he said.

Evadne gave in to temptation, selecting a slice of chocolate cake and a cream-filled French pastry. William made the same selection, and Evadne poured their tea as the waiter wheeled the cart away.

This was not the first time that Evadne had been alone with a man, although the others had been boys like Jack and Paul whom she had known all her life, not men like William who must be several years older. She nibbled at her pastry and sipped her tea, suddenly at a loss as to what to say to an older man.

William Hopkins was not as sure of himself as he appeared. The girl sitting opposite him was obviously very well brought up and completely at home amid the elegance of the Palace and St. Francis, yet she was almost childishly high-spirited and willful. Recalling her invitation, he asked, "By the way, you said you were having a birthday party. How old will you be?"

Evadne paused, her mouth open to receive the fork with its bite of chocolate cake. As she put the fork down, she said, "Don't you know that a gentleman never asks a lady how old she is?"

"Then, being a gentleman, I withdraw the question." He regarded her speculatively as he polished off the last of the pastry on his plate and poured more tea for them both.

"Well, you'll find out at the party anyway. I'll be eighteen," she told him, watching his face to see his reaction.

"Eighteen," he said thoughtfully. "You look much older—all of twenty-one in that costume."

Evadne glowed at the compliment. The suit was new, and she had had an argument with her mother over whether or not it was too sophisticated for her. "Do I really?" she asked impetuously.

"Yes, really," he said, smiling.

"Say that again!"

William stared at her. "Say—what? That you look twenty-one?"

"No, silly." Evadne laughed. " 'Really'—I like the way you say it. It isn't *reely,* like Americans say it or *rawly,* like the English do. It's more like—" she paused, thinking—"like *relly.*"

"You are the most curious girl," he declared.

"Curious, yes," Evadne agreed, "but girl, no. I'll be a woman in a week, you know."

"There's more to being a woman than age, Evadne," William pointed out, amused.

"And more to being a man too?" Evadne asked with a smile, suddenly curious about William's age, especially since he had seemed to be surprised by hers.

He nodded. "I'm twenty-eight, ten years older than you, if that's what you want to know. But my father died when I was younger than you are and I had to grow up quite quickly." He paused. "Come to think of it, my mother was only your age when I was born."

"Then she was a woman, wasn't she? I mean, she was married, had a baby—" Evadne flushed. Having a baby was not something that a well-bred young lady discussed with a man, certainly not a man she had known for only a few hours. William, however, did not notice her embarrassment.

When he had invited Evadne to tea, he had assumed that she was at least nineteen or twenty, and he had had other intentions in mind. The revelation that she was only seventeen had taken him aback at first. Now, he decided that at seventeen she not only had the body of a woman but she was also a beautiful and a delightful companion. He pushed his plate aside, leaning across the table. "I say, what are you doing tomorrow?"

The question took Evadne totally by surprise. He was certainly very different from any man she had ever met. One moment he was the perfect gentleman. The next . . . ? Well, she was not quite sure what he was, but she did like the way he made her feel. No man—especially not Paul who vowed he loved her every time he could get her off alone—had ever made her feel so alive.

"What am I doing tomorrow?" she finally managed to say, stalling for time.

If it had been Paul or Jack or any of the other young men she knew, she would either have told the truth, which was that she had no plans, or pretended an appointment with the dressmaker or a girlfriend, depending on whether or not she wanted to see the young man or not—with her mother's permission of course. Not sure at all what this man had in mind, Evadne decided the best thing to do was to ask him.

"Did you have something special in mind?"

He chuckled. "If you like what I suggest, you'll be free, is that it? If not, well, there is always a girlfriend like Lillie to see. Or the dressmaker—"

"You are the most exasperating—" Evadne began, furious at the way he had read her mind.

"Temper, temper, Evadne," William warned with a laugh. "All right. I want to see a little of San Francisco as long as I am here and have the time, to get my bearings as the sailors say. Of course, I can hire a car with a driver to show me around, but I was thinking that you would make a much more charming guide, and no doubt know the city just as well—if not better. Will you be my guide, Evadne?" He reached across the table to take her hand.

Her heart leaped as her small hand was swallowed up by his larger one. She thought quickly: If she asked her parents' permission, as she was supposed to do, she knew that they would insist on meeting him first. Her mother would never let her go out with a stranger until her father had passed on him. The next day was a weekday, however, and her father would not stay home from the office simply to meet William. She looked into William's eyes, her heart beating faster as the warmth of his touch spread through her body. There was always a girlfriend to visit, she decided impulsively, realizing that it would be the first time that she had ever lied to her parents. She put that thought out of her mind, saying softly, "Yes, I'd like that."

"That's all right then. What time shall I pick you up? Is ten too early? We can have lunch somewhere," he suggested, as if anxious to settle everything at once.

Evadne's heart sank, almost skipping a beat. She had not thought beyond wanting to see him. If he came to the house, she would have to ask him in. Then he would have to meet her mother, who would refuse to let her go without his having met her father.

"No . . . I . . . I have to do an errand first. It . . . it won't take long. I'll meet you here, about ten-thirty. That would be best, William," she improvised.

He raised an eyebrow, indicating that he knew she was lying, but he made no objection. "I'll be in the lobby, waiting for you," he promised.

"And now, I must get home. It must be almost five." She had told her mother that she was meeting Lillie and Jack and might go shopping. Thus, if she arrived home a little late, her parents would not worry too much.

William understood without her having to say any more. He stood up quickly to hold her chair and help her with her coat. Telling the waiter that he was a guest of the hotel and would be back in a moment, he escorted Evadne to the front entrance where he put her into a motor cab.

"Will you be all right? Perhaps I should see you home . . . ?"

"Oh, no. I am quite used to getting home by myself at this hour," she said quickly. It would never do for him to take her home. Her parents would not understand. She would have to prepare them for William somehow.

"Very well. Until tomorrow." To her relief, he did not argue. He was half standing on the running board. Before Evadne, who was leaning toward him, could move, he gave her a quick kiss on the lips. Then he jumped off the running board, closing the door, and signaled the driver to go ahead.

Evadne sank back against the hard seat, automatically giving the driver the address of her family's home on Nob Hill. Her mind was reeling from William's kiss.

As the cab turned north on Taylor to start the painful chugging up the steep hill, Evadne tried to organize her thoughts. It would be best, she decided, to put William out of her mind for the present. Yet, she could not do that because of the invitation to her party; her parents would have to be told. Her heart sank. She had done a fine job of messing up her life, and all because of a handsome stranger. She smiled, an idea striking her. As far as the party was concerned, all she would have to say was that Paul had introduced William and that he was being sponsored by Mr. Tyler. For that reason— and because he was a stranger in town and it was the Christmas season—she had invited him to her party. Since her parents would be meeting him at the Tylers, they could withhold final permission until then.

Evadne sighed. Tomorrow would not be so easy to resolve. Giving up the search for a credible excuse, she looked about her at the houses. As always, they fascinated her, the way they grew grander and grander until they reached the crest of the hill and the turreted Hopkins house, opposite the new Fairmont Hotel that had been built on the site of the old Fair mansion by the daughter of James Fair, one of the owners of the famous Comstock mines.

She would have to show William the Hopkins house, Evadne thought with a smile. In fact, it would even be possible for her to take him inside, since it had been donated to the University of California many years before as an art school and gallery and contained a large collection of paintings and sculpture. Even though it was now properly known as the Mark Hopkins Institute of Art, Evadne always thought of it as the Hopkins house.

At her own house, she paid the driver and went straight inside, hurrying up the broad central staircase in the entrance hall to her own room. She had lingered too long over the tea and was beginning to wonder what her mother, who was surely home by now, would say. Luck was with her, however, because she reached her room without meeting anyone. With a sigh of relief, she closed the door before turning to her maid, who was waiting for her with a worried frown.

Grace Jones was twenty, the daughter of a Welsh immigrant who had come West as a laborer on the railroad. The railroad finished, he had stayed on, marrying the daughter of an Italian fisherman from Telegraph Hill. He had supported himself, his wife, and baby Grace by taking what jobs he could on the boats at Fisherman's Wharf and at the cannery nearby.

When Grace was twelve, her mother died trying to give birth to a son after several miscarriages. The baby died, too, and Grace's father turned to the saloons on the notorious Barbary Coast for comfort. Grace, young as she was, had learned the district well while searching for her father to bring him home. There was little of the worst of life that she had not seen by the time she was fifteen and found her father with a knife in his back, stabbed while trying to fight off the thugs attempting to rob him of the few cents he had on him.

Grace had gone to her mother's parents for help. They had taken her in grudgingly, never having forgiven their daughter for marrying a Welshman and a Protestant. An aunt who cooked for the Crockers heard that the Harpers were looking for a maid. With the aunt's recommendation, Grace had been hired, first to work in the kitchen and later as a housemaid before she became Evadne's personal maid as well as helping out wherever she was needed. The two girls, so close in age, had become friends, despite the vast difference in their backgrounds. It was from Grace, in fact, that Evadne had learned what little she knew about life.

"You're terrible late, Miss Vad," Grace told her. "I told your ma that you'd gone to meet Miss Lillie and Mr. Jack, and probably just got talking and forgot the time."

"Well, that's true . . . in a way." Evadne had taken her suit off and was standing in her camisole and petticoat. She lifted her arms, noting how her full breasts rose, and twirled in a waltz step. "Tell me, Grace, am I pretty?"

"Pretty?" Grace, who was short and plump with curly black hair, black eyes, and a round face, eyed her tall, redhaired mistress admiringly. "Miss Vad, you're beautiful!"

"Do you think a man would think so?" Evadne examined herself in the mirror, seeing only what she considered flaws. "My nose is too long and I have a big mouth."

Grace laughed. "Your nose is fine, and men like full lips."

"I'm really much too tall and skinny," Evadne went on, barely hearing what Grace had said.

The maid's curiosity was aroused now. "I ain't never seen you like this before, Miss Vad. Yale surely musta done something for Mr. Jack!"

"Jack Dillard? He's just a boy." Evadne dismissed him with an airy wave of her hand.

"Mr. Paul . . . was he there too?" Grace watched her.

"Paul Tyler can jump off the Call Building," Evadne said, referring to one of San Francisco's newest and tallest buildings and supposedly earthquake and fire proof. "Paul and Jack are *boys,* not *men.*"

"Well, you sure are pretty excited. Who is it then?" Grace demanded.

"Oh, Grace!" Evadne gave another waltz twirl before hugging the maid. "He's marvelous! His name is William Hopkins. When I saw him the ground shook under my feet like . . . like an earthquake."

"Miss Vad!" Grace was shocked. "You mustn't say things like that! It's terrible bad luck!" she shuddered.

"Don't be such a child, Grace," Evadne scolded. "Besides, don't you want to hear about William?"

"William, is it?" Grace's superstitious fancy was overwhelmed by her curiosity.

"He's tall—as tall as Paul—with magnificent broad shoulders, and, oh, he's so handsome! All tanned from the sun with glorious blue eyes and brown hair streaked with gold," Evadne rapturized. "He's a distant relative of some kind of Mark Hopkins, except he's from Australia," she concluded, sure that Grace would like the Mark Hopkins part.

But all Grace had heard was "Australia."

"A furriner? That ain't good, Miss Vad," she declared. Despite her immigrant heritage, she was suspicious of all foreigners, especially new arrivals whom she saw as usurpers. "Anyway, he don't speak English if he's from one of those European countries."

Evadne started to laugh and checked herself. It wasn't fair to poke fun at Grace, who had had little education. "Grace," she said gently, "I said Australia. You're thinking of Austria. Austria is in Europe and the Austrians speak German. Australia is . . . is somewhere in the South Pacific, and Australians speak English like you and me."

The explanation did little to reassure Grace, for whom Australia meant Shantytown, a rundown area of San Francisco also called "Sydneytown" because it was populated by gangs of Australians who rivaled the cutthroats and thieves of the Barbary Coast. "That's even worse, Miss Vad," she groaned. "The Barbary Coast ain't so bad so long as you mind your own business and know where you're going, but there ain't no women in Sydneytown."

This time Evadne did laugh, but she accompanied the laugh with another hug. "Now, Grace, don't get so upset. William is a gentleman, and—and Sydneytown is not really Australia," she added firmly, despite the fact that she knew as little about that continent as Grace did. Yet, Australia had to be cultured and civilized if William was from there, Evadne was certain.

"If you say so, Miss Vad." Grace still had her doubts, but she knew if anything more was said on the subject it would only make Evadne more stubborn. But as Evadne described her meeting with William and his invitation to tea, Grace's doubts grew stronger. For a gentleman and lady to call each other by their first names so soon after meeting was not at all proper, she was sure. At the same time, Evadne's tale had a romantic aura that was irresistible to Grace's own romantic nature. She sighed, saying, "It's like a storybook, one of them fairy tales Pa used to read me when I was little."

"It is, isn't it?" Evadne threw herself on the bed, stretching luxuriously, careless of the dress that Grace had laid out for her to wear for dinner.

"The only problem is, Miss Vad, you probably won't never see him again," Grace said hopefully.

"Oh, but I will—" Evadne bit her tongue to keep from telling Grace about the next day, knowing the maid would disapprove. She said quickly, "First of all, he is going to be at the Tylers for dinner the day after tomorrow. You know he *has* to be respectable," Evadne giggled, "for Mr. Tyler to invite him to his house. And, I invited him to my birthday party."

"Miss Vad!" Grace was shocked. "You can't do that! Your ma and pa'll have a fit—you inviting a man they ain't even met to the house. It ain't proper."

"Don't be a goose! Didn't you hear me say that he'll be at the Tylers? They'll meet William there, and I'm sure they'll invite him themselves." Evadne hesitated. She longed to tell Grace about tomorrow, but considering the girl's reactions to what she had already told her, that might not be a good idea. She would have to lie to Grace, too, which would be even more difficult than lying to her parents.

An idea came to her suddenly. She would tell Grace and her parents that she was meeting Jerusha Wilson for lunch. Jerusha was a school friend, married and in the last weeks of pregnancy, who rarely went out these days and most certainly would not be at the Tylers for dinner where she might accidentally say something that would catch Evadne out in the lie.

There was no time at the moment to say anything more to Grace, in any case. Evadne's father had come home—she could hear his booming voice coming from her parents' room down the hall—and she must dress for dinner.

Evadne paid extra attention to her toilette and did not complain about the dress Grace had laid out for her. Evadne considered it a schoolgirl's frock—the neckline was much too high, the skirt much too wide, and the waist was barely nipped in. The rusty brown did show off her hair to advantage, however, and a string of pearls and pearl bobs in her ears helped her feel better as she went downstairs.

Both Evadne and her mother thought the dining room the dreariest room in the house. Nathaniel Harper had permitted his wife to decorate all the other rooms as she pleased, but when it came to the dining room, he had insisted that he could not eat sitting on the fragile Queen Anne chairs that were in vogue. The consequence was a baronial room paneled in heavy oak which the elegant crystal chandelier did little to lighten. In addition, chairs and table seemed more appropriate to a castle in the Middle Ages than a modern San Francisco mansion. The table was oak and long enough to sit thirty more than comfortably, but it was the oak chairs with their black leather seats and backs that were the bane of the ladies' existence. They were so heavy that the ladies needed help to sit down or rise.

As her father helped her mother with her chair, Evadne managed to slip her slender figure between table and chair and seat herself opposite her mother. She looked at her parents, hoping to see in their faces that they had had a good day and were each in a good mood.

Nathaniel Harper was a tall man, well over six feet. In his youth, he had been slender, but the passing of years had added weight to his frame and face. His hair, once as red as Evadne's, had darkened with age and was streaked with gray, although it was still as thick as it had been in his youth. His wife, Evadne Sarah Harper, had been called Sally from birth. She, too, was tall, not quite as tall as her daughter but almost as youthful looking. It was from her mother that Evadne had inherited her fine features and green eyes.

Tonight, both parents were smiling, looking at one another with shining eyes, seeming more like a young couple in love than a pair who had been married for twenty years. The marriage had been for love and was a happy one, one that most of Evadne's friends—and Evadne herself—envied. She had always told herself that she would never marry unless she were as much in love as her parents. Yet she had often wondered whether she would, or could, be as much in love after twenty years with the man she chose as her mother was with her father. She would be, she thought now, if that husband were William. Thinking of William reminded her that she would have to tell her parents about the birthday party invitation. She put her own musings aside to pay attention to what her parents were discussing.

To her surprise, they were talking about New York. "New York," her mother was saying. "We went there on our honeymoon, Nathaniel. You always promised that we would go back."

"And I always keep my promises," Nathaniel Harper boomed. It was true; Evadne's father had brought her up never to give her word unless she meant to keep it—and never to go back on it once given. "If business goes as planned, I must go to New York to speak to the bankers about financing some new ships, which is going to mean a new stock issue. I thought we would make it a second honeymoon, my dear, that is, if Evadne would not mind. What do you say?"

"Do you have to ask?" Sally laughed. "But Evadne is still too young to be left alone," she said, sobering quickly.

"I have already taken that into account. You know, Auntie would be only too happy for an excuse to visit," Evadne's father replied, to the girl's dismay.

Auntie was her paternal grandfather's youngest sister. Her name was actually Jezebel, although no one had called her anything but Auntie for as long as Evadne could remember. Evadne's grandfather had been a stern, righteous man who did his duty as he saw it. His duty to his sister, who came under his care after their parents' death, was to protect her from the evils of the world. As a result, she had never had a suitor when she was young. By the time her brother died, she was a confirmed spinster. Even though she was a wealthy woman and there was more than one man who would have been happy to marry her, she had refused all offers, turning to philanthropy for solace. Evadne was still a little girl when Auntie decided that San Francisco had far too much noise and bustle for her and moved across the Bay to the growing village of Sausalito. The truth was that Auntie was growing deaf, and her deafness prevented her from enjoying music as she once had and limited her social life. She still came to San Francisco, however, to shop and was always happy to care for Evadne when her parents took one of their infrequent trips.

"Oh, Papa, not Auntie! I'm almost eighteen now—old enough to care for myself. Besides, there are the servants," Evadne protested.

"Evadne," Sally Harper looked pained, "I have never left you in the care of servants in your life."

"I had governesses when I was little!"

"To teach you, my dear. I have never gone along with the idea that a paid person can take the place of a parent, fashionable as the English idea is among so many of our friends. If people do not want children, they should not marry. It is my sorrow that we have only you. I am afraid, Evadne, it is either Auntie, or I shall have to stay home."

Evadne, thinking about William, was torn between thoughts of being with him . . . and being stuck with Auntie. She hesitated, finally saying, "I could go with you. You have always promised—"

"Not this time, Vad," her father said gently. "April is your mother's and my twentieth anniversary." He smiled lovingly at his wife. "There will be another time."

Evadne gave in, knowing that further argument was useless. Her father's mind was made up, and he was as stubborn as she was once he made his mind up. "Very well, Papa. Auntie can come here." Now that she thought about it, having Auntie here might not be so bad. Poor Auntie was now deaf as a post and thoroughly set in her habit of "early to bed and early to rise." Evadne might well have more freedom with her in the house than with her parents. "When are you leaving?" she asked.

"The end of March," her father told her. "We shall probably stay through May. That is a lovely time in the East, and I would like to go to Boston to see where my parents lived."

Evadne nodded. Her grandfather had been the captain of a Yankee clipper. He had made the trip around the Horn to China several times. On one trip he had had to put into San Francisco for repairs. The opportunities and the climate had so impressed him that on his next voyage he had brought his wife and family, settling in San Francisco when it was still governed by the Mexican alcaldes. It had been here that her father had been born, in 1846, the same year that California declared its independence from Mexico and the American flag was raised in the state. Her grandfather had made a fortune during the gold rush, all of which he had invested in the railroad when it was built, which provided the basis for her father's fortune and his reinvestment in ships and shipping.

"You do understand?" her mother asked anxiously. "I know we will miss you and you will miss us, but . . . ?"

Evadne looked at her parents. They were holding hands as they watched her anxiously. How very lucky she was to have them for parents instead of people like the Tylers for instance. Once again, William came into her mind. Now, she decided, was the time to bring up the party.

"Of course, I understand," she assured them, noting the smiles that broke out on their faces. "At least, you are not leaving on the twentieth of this month."

"The twentieth?" Sally Harper's smile turned into a puzzled frown. "That's the night of the Tylers' dinner, isn't it? What is so special about dinner at the Tylers?"

"Because there will be a special guest!" declared Evadne triumphantly. Quickly, she explained about meeting Lillie and the others and Paul's introduction of William Hopkins. She giggled. "You know if Mr. Tyler approves of him enough to let Paul establish his credit, he has to be eminently respectable."

Nathaniel Harper's laughter boomed throughout the dining room. Henry Tyler was the epitome of a banker in his estimation, a fussy, cantankerous man who saw life as a balance sheet, his mind constantly tallying up everyone—from business associates to old friends—in terms of assets and debits, like a Chinese merchant clicking away at his abacus.

"I must say, Vad, that you are not as respectful as you should be, but you do have a point. This gentleman must certainly have his—ahem—assets."

"Then you don't mind that I invited him to my birthday party? I know I should have waited for you to meet him and invite him yourselves," Evadne added with false modesty as she told the white lie, "but with everyone talking about my party, it seemed the polite thing to do."

Her father, who could rarely say "no" to her, smiled indulgently. "I hardly think one more person is going to matter, do you, Sally?"

Evadne's mother, although lenient according to her

friends, was stricter than her husband with her daughter. Now she said, "I do wish Evadne had waited until you had met him. You are a far better judge of character than Henry, who only sees a person's net worth—whatever that is."

"Come, come, Sally." Nathaniel was in too good a mood to want to let anything spoil it. "We will be meeting this young man in a day or so. As far as the party goes, Evadne is much too popular and there are going to be far too many people here for any one of her beaux to monopolize her. If I don't like what I see, if I feel he is unsuitable in any way, you can be sure that I will keep an eagle eye on him and make it clear that he is not welcome to come calling."

"Very well. Just remember, Evadne, that this is an exception. You are never again to invite anyone to our house without first getting my permission—and your father's." Sally looked at her nubile young daughter, and began to wonder if an extended trip to the East was a good idea. For a moment, she considered staying home or insisting that Evadne go with them, but she could not disappoint her husband whom she loved so much and who had planned the trip to coincide with their wedding anniversary. With a sigh, she said, "When we are away, you must behave with Auntie just as if we were here."

"Yes, Mama," Evadne agreed, completely the dutiful daughter.

All the while that they had been talking, no one had paid much attention to the dinner they were eating. Now, Evadne concentrated on the food on her plate. Her mind, however, was already on the next day. Yes, she would have to use Jerusha as an excuse. Her mother would understand only too well Jerusha's hunger for news of the world and company at that particular time and would think nothing of it if Evadne were gone for the day.

And so, as dessert was served, Evadne told the lie. Her parents only nodded. Relieved, she let her mind drift to William. How handsome he was, and how she hoped he would kiss her again!

Chapter II

When Evadne told Grace the next morning about visiting Jerusha, the maid was not fooled for a moment. She smiled knowingly.

"Miss Vad, I know you too well—better'n your ma in a lot of ways, I guess. You can't fool me," Grace said, standing with her hands on her hips, looking like one of the pugnacious Italian wives on Telegraph Hill.

Evadne glared at her. "Are you accusing me of—of lying?" Her voice rose in pretended outrage.

"I guess you could call it that, although maybe it's only a fib," the maid suggested cheerfully. "You're just not telling the whole truth, Miss Vad, and I'll tell you how I know. You love that green suit you wore yesterday. If you were going to see Miss Jerusha, like you say, you'd be wanting to wear that. But, you say you wore it yesterday and can't think what to wear today."

Evadne tossed her head and stamped her foot. "I told you—I don't want to wear the suit out."

"And so you can't decide what you do want to put on instead? Honest, Miss Vad, if you was just going to spend the day with Miss Jerusha, you wouldn't care what you wore, now would you?" the maid said smugly.

Evadne sat down on her bed, studying Grace and wondering how much to tell her. "What I do," she finally said in what she hoped was a lofty manner, "is none of your business."

"True enough." Grace hesitated, knowing she had gone too far. The trouble was that she genuinely cared for Evadne, who had always treated her kindly and with affection. Grace had had far too little kindness and affection in her young life. Because she cared, moreover, she wanted to protect her mistress from what she saw as the evils of life. "All right, Miss Vad," she said. "I won't say another word, but you can't stop me from thinkin'—and I think you're up to something."

Evadne uncharacteristically let that statement pass. If she did not hurry, she would be late for her appointment with William. Being late normally did not bother her. Her friends, in fact, usually expected her to arrive a little past the agreed upon hour. Today was different, however. Today, she did not want to miss a single moment of the time she would have with William.

She gazed at the gowns and ensembles in her armoire, trying to make up her mind not only what to wear but also where she would take William. She thought about Golden Gate Park and lunch in the Japanese Tea Garden that had been built for the 1894 midwinter fair. But the day was too overcast for that to be pleasant, although she knew that the clouds could break any moment. It might be better to go to Cliff House, a smart restaurant on the Pacific side of the peninsula that sheltered San Francisco Bay.

Regretfully, Evadne decided that it would have to be the green suit after all, despite William's having seen it on her yesterday. The suit was both warm and fashionable. The other choices might be comfortable, but they did not have the up-to-the-minute stylishness of the suit. The argument with Grace had been in vain.

She got grimly to her feet, picking up the corselet that she would wear over her thin chemise. "You will be happy to know, Grace, that I have decided to wear the green suit after all—to make you happy," she added as an afterthought, hoping to allay Grace's suspicions.

"Yes, Miss Vad." Grace adjusted the corselet, following Evadne's instructions to tie the strings tighter without her usual protest. After she had helped her mistress on with the skirt and then the blouse and jacket, Grace said quietly, "Miss Vad, I just hope you know what you're doin'. It's not like you to . . . to fib."

"Don't you worry about me, Grace. I'm all grown up

now," Evadne declared, studying her reflection in the pier glass. Her hair, instead of being piled high on her head, was drawn back in a simple knot at the nape of her neck, a precaution in case the winds for which San Francisco was known at that time of year were blowing.

When Evadne left the house, she realized immediately that her choice of hair style had been a wise one. The wind was blowing. She pulled the sealskin coat closer around her with one hand and, with the other hand, held on to her hat. Unfortunately, she would have to walk to Powell Street and then take the cable car to Union Square. Since Jerusha lived only a few blocks away, she had little excuse to ask one of the servants to get her a cab, which would have raised Grace's suspicions, not to mention her mother's if she found out about it.

At the corner of Powell, Evadne waited impatiently. Although she still had plenty of time, each passing moment seemed an hour long. Besides, she was getting cold waiting in the wind that buffeted her from every direction at the top of the hill.

The clanging, swaying car finally appeared. Evadne climbed gratefully aboard, going inside instead of hanging on to the platform as she usually did, not only because of the wind but also to avoid being seen by anyone she knew. Bells ringing to warn other traffic, the cable car careened down Powell Street, stopping here and there with a neck-snapping jerk to let off and take on passengers.

How the cable cars ever managed to stop once they started the headlong descent down the sheer sides of the San Francisco hills was a constant amazement to Evadne, to whom all machinery was a source of wonder, though one of her dreams was to learn how to drive an automobile. When she had suggested to her father that the chauffeur who drove the family's Packard teach her to drive, her father had only smiled at her indulgently. Evadne had not mentioned her desire to her mother, who would have been horrified at the idea of a woman just wanting to drive, never mind actually driving, an automobile. Women might be able to handle horses—which was different because it was the hands that counted with horses, not brute strength, and both Evadne and her mother were excellent horsewomen—but an automobile?

The cable car had reached Union Square. Evadne glanced at the watch pinned to her jacket. She still had five minutes to get to the St. Francis, which was more than enough time—enough, in fact, for her to change her mind about meeting William.

All of a sudden, the lies she had told began to fill her with doubt. She was not used to lying, and the reasons for the lies—that she wanted to see William again and that she knew her parents would refuse her permission to go for a drive alone with him even if they *had* met and approved of him—made her feel especially deceitful. Oh, she had told lies before, but they had been little ones, what Grace called fibs. For a moment, Evadne thought about getting on another cable car and actually going to see Jerusha, who would be only too happy to have company. Then she thought about William. What would he think of her and what might he say to her at the Tylers, in front of everybody, if she did not keep her appointment? She would never be able to face him again.

Aside from that, she was here. The more she thought about William, the greater the desire to see him again grew within her—to find out whether what she had felt yesterday had been genuine, or the result of an overactive imagination.

Well, the lies were already told. She was here, and she would not really be alone with him. He had mentioned hiring a car and driver. With a quick step, Evadne headed for the St. Francis, only to be assailed by another fear: Suppose he had changed his mind. What would she do if he wasn't in the lobby? Should she wait? Leave immediately? It was a decision she had never had to make with the friends with whom she had grown up. For one thing, she had never met a man alone before. There was always a group, girls and boys, as on the day before.

Evadne smiled to herself. She had never had tea alone with a man before yesterday either, and that had been fine. In a way, she wished that Lillie or Jerusha could see her. How envious they would be—and shocked too. What had William said, that there was more to being a woman than age? Well, she would prove to him—and everyone else—that she really was a woman now. After all, a mere girl would hardly have the courage to meet a man who was almost a stranger in a hotel lobby.

Feeling very daring and holding her head high, Evadne entered the lobby of St. Francis, where her bravery immediately faltered. It was so *big.* She would never find William here, and she did not know where to begin looking among the clusters of settees and chairs half-hidden by potted palms. She could hardly wander around. Innocent as she was in many respects, she knew that was not something any decent woman did. Once again, she was tempted to flee, but she hesitated, taking comfort in the smartness of her chic suit and the costly black seal coat.

"Evadne!" William's voice burst through the darkness of her thoughts like a ray of sunshine. He had been standing in the lobby where he could see the doors, smoking a cigarette. Dropping it now in a handy brass spittoon, he hurried toward her where she stood just inside the hotel's main entrance.

"My dear, I should never have let you talk me into meeting me here," he said, as if guessing her innermost thoughts.

Evadne was so happy and relieved to see him that she laughed nervously. Only her careful upbringing prevented her from throwing herself into his arms out of sheer delight at the sight of him. She gazed up at him, her green eyes feasting on his face and meeting his blue ones.

"We cannot stand here," William murmured. "We are blocking the entrance and people are beginning to stare at us."

"Not again!" Evadne who had begun to recover her composure lost it again.

"Again," he affirmed, taking her arm. "I hired a Packard touring car, by the way. It's parked around the corner."

She nodded, letting him lead the way. "I'm glad to see that you are wearing an overcoat today. You may need it," she added, smiling.

He laughed. "It was an oversight yesterday, although if I had worn one, I wonder if you would have accepted my invitation to tea?"

"Maybe, maybe not. Now you will never know, will you?" Evadne teased, starting to relax.

William did not answer. They had stopped by a big black car and he was busy unlocking the door.

Evadne looked around. "Where is the chauffeur?"

"Right here." William pointed to himself.

"You—you know how to drive?" Her heart sank at the realization that there would be no chaperone. She drew back in confusion as he started to help her into the car.

"Evadne, we have moved out of the horse and buggy age in Australia, just as you have here in the United States. It is a big country, fully as large as yours, and automobiles are becoming essential. Most of my friends drive and have their own cars, as I do," William explained.

"I see." She spoke slowly, trying to think of how to explain to him that going for a drive alone with him was not quite the same as having tea in a hotel restaurant with him.

William tapped his foot impatiently, his impatience gradually giving way to tenderness as he saw the vulnerable young girl that Evadne still was behind the fashionable facade. He knew that he should put her in a cab and send her home, but her innocence attracted him as much as her beauty.

"My dear," he said gently, "I might add that I am a better chaperone as a driver than any chauffeur. This way, with me as the driver, you will get only half my attention."

Evadne giggled, his words reassuring her with their obvious truth. She seated herself in the Packard. "Let's go then," she announced, the outing having a new excitement to it. Although both Paul and Jack knew how to drive, neither had his own car, and rarely had a chance to get the family car long enough to show off their driving skills.

"Now, where shall we go?" William asked. "Remember, I am a stranger in the city and you will have to direct me."

Evadne told him about her plan to drive first to Golden Gate Park and from there to Cliff House. The plan was actually sounder now than when she had first thought of it, for the clouds had broken and a weak winter sun was shining.

William was more than amenable. Regardless of his assurance to Evadne about his driving, he had not been overly eager to spend a day driving on the roller coaster of San Francisco's hills. As it was, the worst hill that he had to drive up was on Geary Street. By the time they reached Van Ness Street, a long street that ran north and south and formed the border between San Francisco proper and the Western Addition, Evadne's directions took them over comparatively level ground to the park.

They stopped near Stow Lake for William to see the Japanese Tea Garden with its rock gardens, bonsai trees, and half-circle bridges. There were hardly any other visitors due to the uncertain weather and the fact that it was a weekday.

At the top of the bridge by the rock garden, Evadne stopped, pointing out the carp swimming sluggishly in the chill waters below. The wintry sun did little to dispel the coolness of the breeze that fanned their faces, turning Evadne's cheeks a becoming rosy pink.

"They don't look like goldfish very much, do they," she said, "although that is what carp really are."

"Hardly," William agreed, his attention riveted on the girl and not the fish. "Evadne. . . ."

Her eyes met his. She knew she should look away, should lower her eyes. Yet, the intensity of his gaze held her until she seemed to be swimming in the blue depths of his eyes. Her body was suffused by a warm glow that had nothing to do with the weak winter sun. A longing she had never known before filled her. She yearned for his touch, his lips on hers. . . .

"Evadne," William murmured again. Her coat had fallen open, and his arms encircled her waist, holding her close as his lips brushed hers.

The kiss was light, a mere touch, but it was enough to tempt Evadne into embracing him, her arms going around his neck as her lips pressed eagerly against his for another kiss. His tongue parted her lips, as he held her with one arm, the other hand gently stroking her back. The two were totally lost in one another, oblivious to their surroundings, the weather, and to the woman and her little boy approaching the bridge.

The sound of a ball being bounced rapidly on the path only echoed the beating of their hearts until the little boy cried out: "Mama, look at that lady and that man. What are they doing? Are they trying to keep warm?"

Evadne blushed furiously, drawing quickly away from William, who only smiled.

"Hush, child," said the mother, her eyes bright with curiosity at the sight of the well-dressed couple. "It's not polite to talk about people, friends or strangers."

"But it is cold, Mama," said the little boy. "Why don't you hold me and keep me warm, like the pretty lady—?"

It was his mother's turn to blush furiously. She grabbed her son by the arm, hurrying him quickly off, his short legs running and pumping to keep up with her.

A burst of laughter exploded from William. Even Evadne, embarrassed as she was, had to smile, her blush fading to a becoming pink. William took her arm with the utmost courtesy, saying, "You are more than a 'pretty lady,' my dear, you are beautiful—and you certainly do keep me warm."

"William!" Evadne blushed a deep pink again, assailed anew by doubts about the wisdom of the drive. "I think perhaps—"

"We should hasten to Cliff House," William finished, giving her no opportunity to express a wish for him to take her home. "Indeed, all this fresh air has given me quite an appetite. I am sure that you must be hungry too."

They had almost reached the car. Though Evadne knew she should insist on going home after what had happened, she did not. Instead, she found herself saying, "I *am* hungry. We should hurry, for even at this time of year it may be crowded, because of holiday parties." She took comfort in the thought that there would be plenty of people around at the restaurant. William would certainly be the perfect gentleman in company, as he had been yesterday, she told herself. And in the car, he would be much too busy driving to pay her much attention.

All the same, the closer they drew to Cliff House, the more apprehensive she became. It was not William who worried her now, but the fear that someone she or her parents knew might be there. Although an older woman might very well meet a gentleman alone there, girls her age went there in party groups. Still, what could be more innocent? It was broad daylight, after all, and once luncheon was over she would insist that they return immediately to San Francisco. Such a short trip was hardly the stuff of scandal, Evadne told herself.

"I can see why it is called Cliff House," remarked William. The restaurant was built on a promontory that dropped sharply into the ocean and resembled a seventeenth-century French chateau, with its ornate gingerbread towers and mansard roof. Behind it rose another steep cliff.

Evadne nodded. "The cliff behind it is Sutro Heights. It's named after the man who built the house there. He also built Cliff House—this one that is. The first one burned down. He built the baths next door to Cliff House too. You can see them under the glass roof. There are three pools, all at different temperatures, in which hundreds can bathe."

"Not in this weather!" exclaimed William.

"Maybe not." Evadne laughed. William had parked the car and was helping her out. "Let's hurry. We will want to reserve a table and then go for a walk," she told him mysteriously, pleased with the surprised look on his face and quickening her step.

William did not question her. After he had reserved a table, he let Evadne lead him outside to the enclosed balcony that circled the building.

"Look at those rocks out there," she said, indicating two

huge rocks that reared out of the ocean and were washed by the breaking waves. "They are called Seal Rocks."

William, gazing out, suddenly noticed the sleek, wet black bodies of the seals. One lay sunning itself, appearing to be almost a part of the rock on which it lay, ignoring three other seals that were cavorting nearby. They dived into the waves only to surface and clamber awkwardly back to their perches. William chuckled, partly in amusement at the gamboling seals and partly because of Evadne's childlike pleasure. "I do believe that under that fashionable green suit beats the heart of a child," he said with a smile.

"Really? Oh, dear, and here I thought I was being very casual about the seals." Evadne sighed, pouting a little. "But I do like to watch them, especially in summer when the windows are open. Then you can hear them barking at one another, almost like puppies."

William's smile broadened and he took her small hand in his. "Don't pout, Evadne. If you were as bored as those ladies," he indicated a group of distinctly elegant and blasé young women standing with their equally stuffy companions, "I would never have gone to your table to speak to Tyler."

"You mean, Paul was not the reason you came over?" Her eyes widened in surprise. "I thought you were lonely and glad of a friendly face—"

"Did you really think that?" William shook his head. "It was an introduction to you I wanted. I saw you from across the court and what I saw drew me like a moth to a flame, Evadne."

She flushed, withdrawing her hand. "You must not say such things, William. It's true that I am young, but I am old enough to know when a man is simply flattering me." But her heart was beating quickly again, as she recalled how she had been ready to leave when she saw him approaching the table.

"Tell me," he went on, "didn't you feel it too? A kind of electricity between us?"

"You are being very impertinent," Evadne declared, not knowing what else to say. She had no intention of answering the question or making an admission of any kind. "We had better order before the restaurant stops serving."

William smiled and bowed as Evadne swept by him toward the dining room. They were seated promptly, the waiter handing each of them menus and giving the wine list to William. William looked it over, saying, "I suppose I should order a California wine. After all, your wines are what I'm here to investigate." With a shrug, he laid the wine list aside. "I have a better idea. I think we shall have a good French champagne—to celebrate your birthday. Would that be agreeable, Evadne?"

Evadne, who was more used to *apollinaris* water, could only nod. Her self-confidence was returning. William must consider her an adult if he ordered champagne, and she glowed at the unspoken compliment.

"Good enough. Champagne it is." William picked up the menu, studying the flamboyant script with a frown. "Oysters to start, I think, followed by squab and a salad, and we can order dessert later . . . or would you like a meat course, too?" He raised his eyebrows questioningly at her.

She had picked up the menu and had been thinking in terms of consommé and a chop. Evadne smiled, setting her menu aside. "Oysters and squab do seem to go with champagne, don't they?"

Once more, she was reassured by his manner as he gave the order for the champagne to the wine steward, asking that it be brought to the table first, then ordered their meal from the waiter. She put out of her mind the recurring thought that no real gentleman would have kissed her on a first meeting, or have held her the way William had in the Japanese Tea Garden . . . or have asked her the questions he had asked on the balcony. Then there was the way he looked at her, the light that came into his blue eyes and the directness of his gaze. He was a most disconcerting man—and an exciting one. She wondered what would come next.

Over lunch, including the fruit and cheese and coffee for her and coffee and a brandy for him that followed, William kept the conversation impersonal, asking her about the dinner party at the Tylers and who would be there. Even later, when they took another brisk walk along the balcony for a last look at the seals, he kept his distance, taking her arm in a formal manner.

Only when they were back in the Packard and he was driving with a daredevil lack of regard for the road and other traffic did he exhibit again the less than proper side of his character. "What a marvelous girl you are, Evadne!"

She stared at him in surprise. "I—I beg your pardon?"

Despite the fact that the car was careening along the road, he took one hand off the wheel to reach over and draw her close to him, close enough so he could again drive with both hands on the wheel.

"Because you have shown me a side of this lovely city of yours that I would never have known about."

Evadne was torn between struggling against the arm that embraced her and the fear of causing an accident at the speed at which he was driving.

"William," she said, sounding more timid that she liked, "hadn't you better watch the road?"

"I am—and I am keeping both hands on the wheel," he added with a grin. "But I am not being the proper gentleman, is that what you mean?"

"Well. . . ." She hesitated, desire for him struggling with propriety.

"I will let you in on a secret, my dear Evadne." He turned his head to give her a quick kiss on the cheek that sent her blood racing. "I sometimes find it a dreadful bore to be a gentleman—just as I suspect you sometimes get a little tired of being a proper lady."

"William, that—that isn't fair." She tried to struggle against him, succeeding only in finding herself held even tighter.

"I will let you go, if that is what you really want." In fact, he did remove his hand from the wheel to permit her to move away. The suddenness of his action surprised her so that at first she could not move. Then she found that she did not want to. William, therefore, put his arm back around her, holding her closer than before.

"You see, my dear, you are only partly the proper lady."

"And the other part?" Evadne demanded, not sure of what she would hear or that she would like it.

"A desirable, passionate woman eager to taste all the joys and delights that life has to offer," he told her.

"Part Nob Hill and part Barbary Coast, is that what you mean?" Evadne was troubled by the connection more than she would admit.

"In a way. Tell me, Evadne, are you not curious about this Barbary Coast of yours, about the ladies and the gentlemen, where they meet and live?"

Evadne recalled what Grace had told her and shivered slightly. "It's a dreadful place," she said, not answering him directly, "where men get drunk and the women do things that no lady would do."

William's arm tightened around her. "You *are* an innocent," he declared. "Is that why you attract me so?"

Evadne gazed up into his face, at the eyes watching the road, at the thin and gentle line of his mouth, the straight nose, and the well-sculptured strong chin. "I am not as innocent as you make me sound," she protested, not sure what he meant and wanting him to like her.

He glanced down at her, frowning. "My dear, those . . . things, as you call them, what do you think happens between a man and a woman when they love one another? What do you think happened between your mother and your father before you were born, for that matter?"

Her face grew hot with embarrassment at the thought of her parents being compared to the likes of those on the Barbary Coast. At the same time she longed to know what William meant. Shocked yet tantalized, she realized suddenly that they had reached the outskirts of the city and were approaching Van Ness. This time, when she pulled away, William let her go.

"Now, you had better tell me where you live," he told her, "for if I take you back to the St. Francis, I will not let you go as readily as I did yesterday."

Her mind spun crazily at his words. She could not go home in the confused state she was in. Her mother would surely guess that she had not been at Jerusha's even if she did not notice the strange car stopping in front of the house and Evadne getting out of it.

"You must let me off at the corner of California and Taylor streets," she said, and gave him the directions.

He nodded, following her directions without further comment. At the corner, however, he put his hand on her arm to prevent her from scrambling out of the car. "Evadne . . ." He spoke softly but there was no mistaking the firmness in his tone. "I will do as you wish today, because I do not believe you have told your parents about this. Tomorrow is another matter. You must introduce me to your parents and after that I will pick you up and take you home, as is proper for Nob Hill—not the Barbary Coast."

"William. . . ." Evadne's voice shook with an emotion she did not understand and could not explain to herself, much less to him.

He put his hand under her chin, raising her face until she had to meet his eyes. "Don't be ashamed of what you feel, at least if it is what I think it is." He kissed her, his mouth hot and sweet on her lips. "Go now, my beautiful Evadne. I will see you tomorrow night."

Evadne was trembling as she hurriedly left the car. She did not know what to think. All she knew was what she felt. She glanced back. He was sitting in the car, watching her.

Chapter III

DURING THE TWENTY-FOUR HOURS BEFORE THE TYLER PARTY, Evadne kept her thoughts to herself, trying to solve the puzzle that William had planted in her mind. What did her parents have to do with what went on on the Barbary Coast, she asked herself? The question disturbed her, and she preferred to take refuge in the memory of William calling her his beautiful Evadne.

As she bathed, preparing for the party, she studied her body with new eyes, trying to see it as William might. She raised one long, slender leg out of the water, noticing the curve of the calf and the firmness of the thigh. She studied her torso, from the soft, curly thatch of red hair between her thighs to her breasts, firm and well-shaped, not needing the corselet to push them up into full rounded mounds. Although her shoulders were a little broad, they set off the smallness of her waist and her slender neck. As far as her red hair was concerned, it accentuated the creamy tone of her complexion.

Evadne sighed, standing up to step out of the relaxing warm water and towel herself dry before Grace washed her hair. Grace's short, strong fingers massaged Evadne's scalp vigorously, soaping and rinsing the long red hair, taking a towel to squeeze out the excess moisture.

"Miss Vad," Grace said, brushing the hair with long

strokes. "You seem awful quiet for just before a party. Usually you're wriggling around so much, you don't hardly give me a chance to dry your hair proper."

"I've been thinking, Grace," Evadne said, which was certainly true.

Grace nodded wisely. "This gentleman of yours, he'll be at the party tonight? Don't tell me, you and him have had a fight already."

Evadne glared at her. "What gentleman? I told you I was seeing Jerusha yesterday."

"Yes, Miss Vad," Grace replied meekly. "And you told me it was none of my business what you did too."

"Then—?" Evadne wrenched her hair free of the brush and flung herself off the dressing table bench into the little maid's arms. "Oh, Grace!" she cried. "What am I to do?"

"I don't rightly know, and I can't say unless you tell me what's bothering you," Grace said, patting the girl's head. "Now, you get yourself back on that bench and tell me what it's all about while I finish your hair."

"You won't say a word to Mama, will you, Grace?" Evadne asked anxiously.

"Have I ever? Miss Vad, you know I'm true blue when it comes to you." Grace gave Evadne's hair an extra firm stroke of the brush to emphasize her words.

"I know, Grace, but—well, when I told you about William. . . ." Evadne began tentatively, her eyes on Grace's face in the mirror.

"I shoulda known. It's that furriner. You know how I feel about them," Grace stated primly.

"Grace, he's not what you're thinking, not like anybody on Fisherman's Wharf and Telegraph Hill. Remember, he does speak English. He's Australian—not Austrian," Evadne added with a giggle.

"I know, Miss Vad. I looked it up on the big globe in your Pa's library. Australia's awful far away, and he ain't an American like Mr. Paul and Mr. Jack." She hesitated. "So, it was him you were out with? And without asking your Ma and Pa's permission either!"

"They'll meet him tonight," Evadne said in what she hoped was a casual tone. "And I know they will like him. *Anyone* would," she added pointedly.

She gave Grace a carefully edited version of yesterday's excursion to Golden Gate Park and Cliff House. Grace listened, her youthful face wrinkling into an old woman's scowl of disapproval that relaxed only when Evadne concluded her story by saying, "So, you see, we were in the public eye all the time, Grace."

"He didn't touch you?" Grace demanded.

Evadne forced herself to laugh. "How . . . how could he? There were always people around—a woman with a little boy in the park," she said quickly, "the other diners at Cliff House. And in the car, he needed both hands to drive."

"Sure, Miss Vad, but where there's a will, there's a way," declared Grace. "It don't keep him from suggesting things, either."

"Oh, Grace," Evadne protested, on the defensive now. "William's a gentleman."

"Sure." Grace studied her thoughtfully. "But it wasn't yesterday you wanted to talk to me about, was it, Miss Vad?" she said shrewdly. "Was it?"

Evadne hesitated. It was the Barbary Coast she wanted to ask Grace about, a subject that always brought out the maid's stern disapproval, the curious mixture of peasant Catholicism and evangelical Protestantism that was her heritage.

"No," Evadne answered slowly. "Oh, Grace," she said impulsively, "what happens on the Barbary Coast? Not the drinking, but the—the—"

"Them ladies and the men who go there to see them? Fine men, even gentlemen, some of 'em." Grace sniffed. "I saw it. What are you so interested in that for, Miss Vad? It's not for the likes of you."

"But Mama and Papa did *that* too, didn't they?" Evadne asked, only vaguely understanding what "that" was. "I mean, otherwise I wouldn't be here, would I?"

Grace laughed and picked up a comb. "You want your hair high up on your head or low on your neck?" She knew Evadne, conscious of her height, often decided on her hair style on the basis of whom she hoped to see or dance with.

"High," Evadne answered, without a second thought. "You did not answer my question, Grace."

"Well, Miss Vad, I ain't had that much experience. I mean," she looked at Evadne, wondering whether to tell her about the young sailor who had come off the whaling ship, who had promised to return and marry her but never had.

"I mean," Grace took a deep breath, "it depends on the man and the woman," she said carefully. "Some women, well, they don't much like the idea of a man getting into their beds. Some of those women on the Barbary Coast ain't much different, but that's all they got—their bodies—and they gotta live. Others, they kinda like it. Maybe it depends mostly on the man."

"Is it—is it fun, exciting?" asked Evadne, more curious than ever after what Grace had said.

"I told you, Miss Vad, it depends on the man."

"Then, you—!" Evadne studied Grace with new eyes.

"Me?" Grace giggled nervously. "I ain't sayin' nothin' more."

All the while Grace was finishing dressing Evadne's hair into a high tumble of curls, with one long curl down her back, Evadne thought about what the maid had said. It was actually little different from what William had told her.

Grace, too, was thinking, remembering the sailor and the delights that he had shown her. She had thought that Ethan Morgan loved her. She had only been fifteen when she had met him in a saloon where she had gone searching for her father and found him in a drunken stupor in the arms of an old witch with dyed red hair and wattled cheeks. Ethan had helped her take her father back to the shack on Russian Hill where they were living and had stayed the night, helping her watch over him. After that, he had returned again and again, to help Grace search for her father and to comfort her, delighting in the big plates of spaghetti and fruit and cheese that Grace set before him. It had been only natural for Grace to fall in love with the young New Englander, who had overcome all her defenses.

He had sailed away, promising to return as soon as possible, to get a job on one of the fishing boats and marry her. Grace had waited for him, counting the days at first, until her father had died and she had come to work for the Harpers. Gradually, she had lost hope, preferring to believe that Ethan had died at sea, not wanting to believe that he had lied to her. Only rarely these days did she think of him, and the memories Evadne had brought back swamped her now with the loveliness of the moments they had shared in that rude shack on Russian Hill, with Ethan fondling her breasts as his manhood grew strong until he had to plunge it deep inside her, eliciting her cry of pleasure and desire.

Grace sighed, putting those thoughts out of her mind. She picked up the dress Evadne would be wearing. Like the green suit, it had been chosen especially to celebrate her eighteenth birthday. First, however, came the corselet that Evadne insisted must be laced as tightly as possible, forcing her breasts into high, seductive mounds. Then came the petticoat that did little to conceal the shapely thighs. Over that came the elegant gown, of creamy satin, cut so low that it barely covered the corselet and supported by ripples of satin, like narrow bracelets, around her upper arms. The skirt gave the appearance of being tight, although it was actually cleverly made with the slightest of bustles to give it enough fullness for dancing. Around Evadne's neck went a double strand of perfectly matched pearls that had been her father's gift on her sixteenth birthday, with matching pearl bobs for her ears.

The result was an alluring portrait of virginity that made Grace gasp. "There ain't no young gentleman—or old one, for that matter—who's going to be able to resist you tonight, Miss Vad."

Evadne smiled, her hands smoothing the gown over her hips. "Do you really think so, Grace? Are you sure that I look . . . beautiful?"

Grace nodded, pleased with her handiwork. "You're more than beautiful, you're—" she searched for the right word "—you're *grand!*"

Evadne smiled with pleasure. "I hope William thinks so!" She twirled around in front of the pier glass, examining the curve of her breasts and the expanse of creamy white back that the gown showed to perfection.

Grace shook her head. "Don't you worry, Miss Vad."

Evadne laughed, delighted. Quickly, she kissed Grace on the cheek and picked up her gloves. "Well, I had better go and see what Mama and Papa think."

Her parents smiled at her, especially her father. Her mother, on the other hand, wondered whether the gown was not more daring than what she had originally planned. She would have to keep an eye on her daughter, she decided, confused at what had happened to turn her impulsive, innocent child into a seductive, lovely woman. Sally Harper herself had never been plain and had had her share of admirers, but some combination of herself and her husband had resulted in this glorious creature whom Sally could barely recognize.

The impression that Evadne made at the Tylers more than equaled Grace's prediction and fulfilled her mother's fears. Every eye in the grand salon turned to look at Evadne, who was immediately surrounded by admirers of all ages. To her mother's relief, the first to take her arm was Paul Tyler, and

Sally Harper relinquished her watchdog role with a sigh, knowing Paul's feelings for her daughter. As the son of an old friend, he did not represent a threat in Sally's mind.

Evadne's smile for Paul, however, was perfunctory. Even his compliments did not hold her attention as she glanced about the room, searching for William Hopkins. Finally, she looked back at Paul.

"I don't see Lillie and Jack . . . or that Mr. Hopkins we met the other day," she said casually.

Paul frowned in annoyance at her obvious lack of interest in him. He took a glass of wine from a tray being offered by a waiter and handed it to her.

"Lillie and Jack arrived with their parents a short time ago. Mother has spirited them off to the conservatory to admire her orchids." His curt tone revealed his displeasure with Evadne.

She smiled. Mrs. Tyler was noted for her flowers, though the orchids were new. The house had been built to incorporate a huge conservatory filled with palms, roses, lilies, and other flowers that bloomed year round to grace the Tyler mansion. Tonight the salon, for example, displayed silver urns filled with roses on the heavy oak tables, and Evadne was sure that roses would also be on the dining table, which was large enough to seat a hundred guests, a number that seemed to be exceeded on this occasion.

"And Mr. Hopkins?" Evadne persisted. "Where is he?"

Paul ignored the question, having no intention of sharing her with anyone. "You are quite the young lady tonight, Vad. I have never seen you looking more beautiful, more desirable—"

"Do you really think so?" She looked at him with wide eyes. The memory of how he had laughed at the idea of her going to Stanford made her say tauntingly, "It is good to know that an old childhood playmate can recognize that I am a woman now."

"You are quite the most beautiful woman here, of any age," Paul responded, unaware that she was teasing. "Just wait until Lillie sees you—and Jack."

Evadne smiled, gazing about the room again and suddenly catching sight of a man in tails just entering the salon. It was William. Old Mr. Tyler hurried toward him as if the young Australian were an honored guest.

"Vad!" Before Evadne could move, Lillie came rushing

toward her. "What a marvelous gown, and how did you get your mother to agree to that neckline?" Lillie looked down at her own gown, equally close fitting but with a much more decorous bodice. She took Paul's arm, peering up into his face. "Don't you think Evadne's gown is quite daring, Paul?" she asked.

"Well. . . ." Paul looked at the two girls he had known all his life, realizing whatever he said would hurt one or the other, finally saying awkwardly, "I find it exceptionally charming. By the way, where is Jack?"

At the change of subject, Lillie wrinkled her nose. "Your mother has him and Mama enthralled, explaining how to grow roses in midwinter."

"Lillie, Jack has always loved the country, you know that," Evadne protested at the sarcastic note in Lillie's voice.

"I know." The other girl sighed. "I do think that Yale is an utter waste. He will probably end up growing grapes or raising horses in Sonoma, or some such thing."

"We all had good times on that ranch your father used to have," Paul pointed out. "You and Jack, and Evadne and me."

Lillie did not miss his emphasis on Evadne and himself. Smiling sweetly, she corrected him. "You mean, Evadne and Jack. They were the ones who used to go riding while we sat around under the trees."

"I always liked horses, just as much as Evadne." Paul freed his arm and turned belligerently toward Lillie.

Evadne took advantage of the argument to slip away and tried to walk casually over to where Mr. Tyler was standing with William, who had obviously noticed her. His eyes watched her admiringly, though his head was bent to listen to Mr. Tyler.

"Mr. Hopkins, how good to see you again," Evadne said. "Mr. Tyler, I hope I'm not interrupting, but Paul introduced Mr. Hopkins to us the other day, and I could not resist welcoming a stranger to our midst."

"You are a most gracious girl, Evadne. Indeed, instead of monopolizing him, I should have been introducing him around." Mr. Tyler's eyes fastened appreciatively on Evadne's bosom.

"Perhaps I might have the honor of introducing him to my parents?" she asked, anxious to get away from Tyler's scrutiny. It was one thing for Paul or Jack or William to find her attractive, but she was embarrassed at the same admiration coming from a man as old as her father!

"Please do, my dear." Mr. Tyler tore his eyes away from her. "I must find my wife, who seems to be neglecting our guests."

"She is in the conservatory with Mrs. Dillard and Jack," Evadne told him with a smile.

"Those damned roses," Mr. Tyler muttered, walking off.

"You are an angel in disguise, my dear," whispered William, raising her gloved hand to his lips.

"Am I?" Evadne met his eyes, seeing the twinkle in them.

"Indeed you are, although I hope you are not angelic by nature." He took her arm, adding, "Have you thought about what I said?"

"Yes." The girl nodded, all innocence and totally noncommittal. "Did you not say that you were anxious to meet my parents, to—to be able to pick me up and take me home?"

"Minx," he whispered.

Without further comment he let her lead him to where her parents were standing. Nathaniel and Sally Harper were charmed by William, to Evadne's relief, giving her a chance to collect her thoughts. She knew only too well to what William had been referring, though her conversation with Grace had done little to clarify her confusion. All that was clear to her was that from the moment she had entered the Tyler house, she had thought about no one but William. Just the sight of him had been enough to set her tingling and fill her with the longing for him to touch her.

She glanced at William, who was being the soul of politeness. He had shaken her father's hand with a grip firm enough to satisfy that man and had kissed her mother's hand with the grace of a true gentleman. Now, he was smiling and saying, "I hope you will permit me to call on your daughter and that you will allow her to show a stranger your fair city."

Evadne, looking at him, wondered what he was thinking. "Yes, Mama, Papa," she put in demurely, "it would be such a pleasure to act as a guide for . . . Mr. Hopkins." She had been about to say William, and she hoped the pause had not been noticed.

"It is agreeable to me, as long as Evadne is willing," replied Nathaniel Harper heartily. "In fact, my daughter has told me that she has already invited you to her birthday party?"

"That she has, sir, although it is my hope that the invitation will be matched by yours?" answered William with a slight smile at Evadne.

"It is indeed, is it not, Sally?" He turned to his wife who was regarding William Hopkins with a mixture of suspicion and pleasure at the company of such an attractive man.

"Of course, Nathaniel." Evadne's mother was properly courteous. Yet, for the first time she felt old enough to be the mother of an eighteen-year-old daughter. The second honeymoon East was just what she needed, Sally Harper decided, although she was not sure that she liked the idea of this man being around her daughter. The idea of leaving Evadne unprotected—for Sally had few illusions about Auntie's guardianship, well-intentioned though it might be—with this very attractive man in attendance made her uneasy. She asked, "How long will you be with us, Mr. Hopkins?"

"I am not sure, Madam." William turned to her politely, unable to conceal the twinkle in his blue eyes. "It depends on how long it will take me to finish my business in San Francisco."

"Business is business," Nathaniel agreed. "It must come first. Do I understand, however, that you are quite without relatives in the city?"

Once again, William explained about being only a distant relative of Mark Hopkins, adding, "I am afraid that years and distance have taken their toll. There is no one left who remembers my father, and no one to whom my name means anything."

Nathaniel nudged his wife's arm gently, and Sally Harper smiled at the young man. Against her better judgment, she said, "In that case, we would consider it an honor if you would join us for Christmas dinner. It is only a small affair, no party. We prefer it that way."

"You will join us, won't you?" Evadne said eagerly.

"I accept, in the face of such feminine beauty." William's smile included Evadne's mother.

Paul's arrival at Evadne's elbow brought the conversation around to what William should see while he was in San Francisco. Paul managed to murmur to Evadne, "You are enchanting this evening, and I will not let you neglect me as you have done."

"Poor Paul!" Evadne's lips curled in a faint smile. "You did not appear neglected when I last saw you, with Lillie on your arm."

"Vad, Lillie is like a sister to me," Paul protested. "We grew up together, playing cowboys and Indians in the backyard!"

"How well I know!" Evadne teased him.

Paul colored. With a malicious glance at her, he said, "Hopkins, I don't think you have met everyone here. Let me take care of that now . . . and introduce you to some people your own age."

Evadne managed to suppress a giggle. In the past six months, Paul's attentions had become oppressive, despite all she did to dampen his enthusiasm. Paul was fine as a friend, but Evadne knew that Lillie had been in love with him for years—and Lillie's friendship meant more to her than Paul. Her teasing him unfortunately only encouraged him, but she could not resist saying softly now: "I still think women should have the vote."

Paul glowered and walked quickly away with William. Sally Harper looked at her daughter in bewilderment. "What is wrong with Paul? He seemed almost rude, the way he stalked away."

"Nothing, Mama." Evadne smiled innocently. "We were talking the other day about whether or not women should have the vote. I said we could do no worse than men have."

Her mother's brow cleared, and she smiled. "I must agree with you, Evadne, although you are much too young to think about such things."

"Women vote? Not in my lifetime!" Nathaniel took his wife's arm to lead her away. "I will not have you encouraging such ideas."

The two women smiled at one another. As Evadne looked around for Lillie, she thought with amazement about what her mother had said. It had surprised her. She began to wonder about those meetings her mother was always going to. Perhaps they did not have to do with the art collection being brought together at the gallery in Golden Gate Park after all.

Lillie was sipping a glass of wine when Evadne found her, Jack at her side. From the expression on her friend's face, Evadne knew she had seen Paul join her and she sighed. Evadne would have liked nothing better than for Paul to take an interest in Lillie.

An idea struck her. Had her parents not agreed to let her show the city to William? That would be a perfect opportunity for her to invite Lillie and Paul along. Once Paul saw that she was interested in William and not in him, Evadne was sure he would eventually turn to Lillie. Of course, she thought, she would not invite them every time—she wanted William to herself. But it would do no harm to have company once in a while, and it would help Lillie too.

"Come, Lillie." Evadne squeezed her friend's arm. "You look much too solemn. Let's enjoy the party, shall we?"

Lillie looked at her wistfully, noting the contented smile and sparkling emerald eyes. "You look beautiful, Vad, so grown up. That dress! If only Mama—"

"See? There are Paul and that Mr. Hopkins," Evadne interrupted her. "Let's join them, shall we? And you," she smiled at Lillie, "you leave Mr. Hopkins to me while you talk to Paul."

"Oh, Vad!" Lillie mourned. "I love him so, and he hardly even talks to me some times."

"He will tonight. You'll see," Evadne promised. As they approached the two men she saw William watching her with that faint smile that always made her heart beat faster. "Why, Mr. Hopkins," she said, as if caught by surprise. "What are you and Paul doing here all by yourselves when I am sure all the women here are panting for your company?"

"There is only one whose company interests me," William replied gallantly.

Paul had opened his mouth to add his assurance to William's when dinner was announced. Since William immediately offered to escort Evadne, Paul had to offer his arm to Lillie. When, at the table, Evadne found herself seated between William and Paul and Lillie seated between William and her brother Jack, she suggested that she and Lillie change places. Lillie was only too happy to oblige, and Jack also found the seating more to his liking. The only one unhappy was Paul, who found Lillie and William between Evadne and himself, but he could not object.

Once seated, Evadne had William to herself. A girl who was going East to college the next fall had been seated next to Jack and she monopolized his attention in her eagerness to find out what to expect.

"Clever girl," William murmured in Evadne's ear.

"Am I?" She was flustered by the remark, and even more flustered when William's leg pressed purposefully against hers, sending her blood pounding. Quickly, she unfolded her napkin to place it in her lap. As she did, William unfolded his, his hand brushing hers and giving it a quick squeeze. The boldness of his actions amid the formality of the occasion and in the presence of others made Evadne catch her breath. What kind of man was this? Her heart beat faster at the nearness of him.

Chapter IV

THE NEXT FEW MONTHS WERE THE HAPPIEST EVADNE HAD EVER known in her eighteen years. Her eighteenth birthday party—which she had expected to be the climax of the season, with even New Year's Eve an anticlimax—was only one of the events that made the winter memorable.

To begin with, there was Christmas. William had arrived at the Harpers laden down with gifts—cigars and brandy for Mr. Harper and candy and flowers for Evadne and her mother. At dinner, he had spoken knowledgeably about the cultivation of grapes for wine, calling it properly "viniculture." Evadne's father had been impressed, finding him far more sensible than Paul Tyler and the other young men who called on Evadne and took her to parties. Because of Sally Harper's respect for her husband's judgment, William had won her too.

His major accomplishment, however, was getting Grace's approval, but it didn't happen right away. Grace had regarded the young man with a sharp eye at the Christmas dinner and the birthday party, where she had helped serve. She had reserved approval at Christmas.

The birthday party lasted until two in the morning, with William among the last to leave. Afterward, as she helped Evadne undress, Grace said, "Well, Miss Vad, for a furriner, he's a gentleman."

Evadne, who was sitting in front of the mirror in her chemise while Grace took her hair down, smiled. "Mama and Papa think so, too, Grace."

"He's enough to make any girl's heart flutter." Grace sighed. "Them broad shoulders and that big chest . . . and those blue eyes! My, he's a handsome gent."

"Yes, he is, isn't he?" Evadne giggled. "Did you see the way the other girls looked at him?"

"Except Miss Lillie," Grace said. "You don't have to worry about her. She has eyes for no one but Mr. Paul."

"I know. Poor Lillie. If only Paul would pay more attention to her." Evadne rose from the bench. She removed her chemise and slipped into the voluminous nightgown, with its high neckline and long sleeves, that Grace held out for her. "I do everything I can," Evadne said, "to bring them together."

"Well, Miss Vad," Grace shook her head, "you can't change nature, and Mr. Paul's nature is to go after you—especially the more you try to push him and Miss Lillie together."

"In other words, I shouldn't play matchmaker!" Evadne laughed. "I'll think about it tomorrow." She stretched and slipped into her bed, snuggling under the covers. "William is taking me to lunch at the Palace tomorrow—today, I mean—with Mama and Papa's permission."

That lunch with William had been the first of many occasions when her parents permitted her to go out alone with him. The fact that he was older helped; Evadne's father saw him as more responsible, a more suitable escort for his young daughter than her usual beaux. Since her mother was more and more impressed by William, Evadne was no longer forced to lie about her whereabouts.

Another factor that Evadne used to her advantage was her parents' impending trip East. As she pointed out to them, wasn't it better to give her more responsibility while they were still there to observe her and could approve or disapprove than to leave it for Auntie's arrival? Her mother, after some hesitation, had finally agreed, knowing that Auntie was really a token chaperone. For that reason, when Emma Dillard criticized her for allowing her daughter to go out unchaperoned with an older man, Sally Harper came home in a thoughtful mood. That afternoon, Evadne and Lillie were visiting Jerusha and her new baby daughter, but that evening, Evadne was going to the Orpheum Theatre with William.

She came home from Jerusha's marveling at motherhood

and the miracle of birth. When Grace told her that her
mother wanted to see her in her sitting room, Evadne's first
thought was that her mother had changed her mind about
permitting her to go to the theater with William. She entered
the cozy room filled with anxiety.

Her mother's sitting room, next door to the master bedroom, was one of Evadne's favorite rooms. Unlike the formal
rooms on the main floor which were furnished in a stiff, stilted
style that was a mixture of Queen Anne and Georgian, both
equally uncomfortable, this room was simple and comfortable. The pale blue wallpaper was set off by an overstuffed
sofa and matching chairs in bright, flowered chintz. The
tables, on which stood oil lamps although gas lighting was
used throughout the house, were white and gold to match the
escritoire in the corner. Evadne's favorite spot was the
enormous bay window. Its seat, luxuriously upholstered with
plump pillows, reminding her of pictures she had seen of a
Turkish harem.

Her mother, still in her afternoon dress, was seated in a
chair by the escritoire, going through the mail.

"Good afternoon, Mama. Grace said you wanted to see
me?"

"Yes, Evadne." Her mother laid the letters down on the
desk, surveying her daughter. Only a few months ago,
Evadne had still seemed a child. Now she looked and carried
herself like a woman in the rust suit she was wearing that was
similar to her favorite green one, except this one was simpler
with no trimming. The sight made Sally Harper feel both old
and proud—and at the same time glad for the weeks she
would have alone with her husband.

"Mama?" Evadne was puzzled by her mother's silence and
the expression on her face. Her fear that her mother was
going to forbid her to go the theater—perhaps she had heard
that a few of the skits were risque?—grew.

"Sit down. I want to talk to you, Evadne." Sally Harper
took a deep breath, wondering how to begin. "As you know,
your father and I will be leaving shortly—" she managed to
say.

"I know, Mama, and Auntie is arriving next week. William
and I are to going to meet her at the ferry and bring her and her
luggage to the house," Evadne said in a rush. "While you are
gone, I am to obey her as I would you."

"Emma Dillard has suggested that it is unwise of me to

allow you as much freedom as I have the past few months,"
Sally Harper told her frankly. "She also feels that it is not
entirely sensible for me to leave you in deaf, old Auntie's
care, as I did when you were younger. She proposes that you
go and stay with them, since you and Lillie are such friends."

"Oh, Mama!" Evadne cried, rising from the window seat
where she had been sitting and going to her mother. She sat
on the footstool at her mother's feet, saying, "You surely do
not propose that I move in with Lillie, much as I like her!"
She thought quickly. "Or to close up the house! What will the
servants do? And Auntie will be so disappointed. You know
she is looking forward to seeing her old friends."

"I know." Her mother had to smile at her daughter's
vehemence. "Although I did not know that you were so
interested in Auntie's welfare, I quite agree with you that it is
much too late to change our plans. Still, Emma does have a
point. . . . Perhaps it is unwise for you to see so much of
William without a chaperone."

Evadne was silent, wondering what was going to come next
and trying to think of something to say. "Surely, Mama," she
ventured, "I have proven these past few months that . . . that
I am to be trusted."

"Yes, my dear, you have. It is only—" Sally Harper sighed.
"We live in society, Evadne. It is of you I am thinking. I
would not have people—our friends—think the less of you. If
Emma thought it necessary to speak to me, others are
undoubtedly thinking much the same thing. You must behave
with the utmost propriety, you and William both, to avoid
even the slightest hint of . . . of . . ." Her mother stopped,
unable to find the right words for what she wanted to say.

Evadne frowned. "Of scandal? Is that what you mean,
Mama?" she asked, chafing at the idea of any restraints on
her. What a silly, proper world it was.

"That, I suppose, but I was thinking more of . . . of . . ."
Again her mother hesitated. Finally, she took her daughter's
hands in hers. "Evadne," she said firmly, "it is of you and
your happiness I am thinking. You are still very young, with
your life ahead of you, and you are innocent of the ways of
the world. It is one thing for you and William to go out in
public. I must say that I feel Emma is overreacting about the
necessity for you to be chaperoned wherever you go. But it is
another thing for you to be alone—quite alone—with him.
Men are men, regardless of their age and background. The

rules of society being what they are, it is up to you to see that you do not encourage him to . . . to take liberties." Sally Harper looked helplessly into her daughter's eyes.

"Liberties, Mama?" Evadne had been listening to her mother with only half her mind. The other half had been on a conversation she had had that day with Lillie and Jerusha. Jerusha had been only too eager to relate the agonies she had endured during childbirth, but it had been only with difficulty that Lillie and Evadne had been able to get her to discuss a few of the joys of the marriage bed. When they did, Jerusha had avowed that such joys were highly overrated. Those private moments with her husband had been painful and brief, over almost before she had known what had happened.

Sally Harper took a firm grip on herself. She had always known that she would have to have this conversation with her daughter someday, although she had not expected it so soon, thinking the night before Evadne's wedding would be time enough.

"Child," she said gently, "what I mean by 'liberties' are the pleasures that . . . that a man and a woman enjoy together after they are married."

Evadne looked at her mother in surprise. Sally Harper's face was suffused with happiness, as if the . . . the *thing* that happened was a cause of joy and not pain as Jerusha had claimed.

"One of these days," her mother was saying, "you will know what I mean. Until then, you must guard against letting your feelings—your emotions—carry you away. Do not let him embrace you or touch you familiarly. Certain parts of a woman's body—" Sally Harper sighed and stood up, walking to the bay window where the afternoon fog could be seen rolling in great billows across the Bay to embrace the city.

Evadne, still sitting on the footstool, watched her mother with wide eyes and flushed cheeks. She could not tell her that William had already embraced her—and ardently—had brushed her breasts, which she was sure were one of the parts of her body that her mother meant, that his hands had caressed her back, that his thigh had pressed urgently against hers. Why had her mother not spoken to her earlier? she wondered. Was she a "fallen woman," a subject for scandal, before she was barely a woman? "Mama—"

Her mother did not look at her, having found the conversation embarrassing—for more than one reason. To begin with,

Sally Harper could not find the words to explain to her daughter the beauty of the act that had conceived her. For another, she felt a certain amount of guilt about having enjoyed—and still enjoying—the act of love between herself and her husband. It was a feeling she knew Emma Dillard and others of her friends did not share. All too often she had heard them speaking of marital "duty"—not pleasure. Yet, one of the reasons that Sally had agreed so willingly to leave Evadne home in San Francisco was to have her husband to herself, to relive the ecstasy she knew and that he had taught her on their first honeymoon. Thus, Emma Dillard's criticism had struck at the very heart of her life, making her feel as if she must sacrifice either her husband or her daughter. Given such a Solomon's choice, she had faced it the only way she could—by warning her daughter, hopefully in strong enough terms, about the weakness of the flesh. It was, moreover, one decision she could not discuss with her husband.

"That will be all, Evadne. If you are going to the theater with William, it is time for you to change. I will have Grace bring you an early supper in your room. You will not have time to dine with us."

Sally Harper dismissed her daughter with a heavy heart, wanting to say so much more, yet fearing that she may already have said too much. The last thing she wanted to do was tempt Evadne into pursuing the pleasures of the flesh, or experimenting with her body.

Evadne left the sitting room trying to reconcile what her mother had said with the intensity of her mother's feelings. At the same time, she resolved to keep her distance from William from now on, to give him no chance to tempt her into the response her mother seemed to fear. Yet, she was confused by the differences of opinion expressed by her mother and Jerusha, and she was eager to see William and explore her own feelings more deeply.

To her dismay, William was late. He arrived with a car only in time to greet Evadne's parents briefly before they had to leave for the Orpheum. At the theater he was unusually quiet and a little restless, as if the acts bored him. When the intermission came, he suggested that they go outside for a walk.

Although he had taken her arm with his usual courtesy, he seemed somehow distant. Finally, Evadne asked timidly, "Is anything wrong, William?"

"I'm sorry, Evadne," he quickly apologized. "First, I was late meeting you and now I'm not paying you much attention, am I?"

She smiled hesitantly, not sure how to answer. Her emerald eyes were dark with worry, and she bit her lip nervously.

"Oh, my dear." William smiled, the laughter lines at the corners of his eyes crinkling. "It is not you, if that is what is worrying you. I have been trying to think of a way to tell you that I must go to Sonoma tomorrow for a few days."

"Tomorrow!" Evadne looked at him in alarm. She had always known that sooner or later he would leave San Francisco, but she had put it out of her mind.

"It is rather unexpected, but it will only be for a few days. A vintner from the Valley has been staying at the St. Francis, and we met in the bar." His eyes glinted in amusement. "I assume that he has, shall we say, checked me out with Mr. Tyler, whom he knows, for today he invited me to travel home with him and see his vineyards. He is one of the biggest growers," William added hurriedly, "which means the opportunity is too good to miss. Do you understand, my dear?" At her reluctant nod, he went on. "Don't worry. I have promised to go with you to pick up Auntie, and I promise I will be back in plenty of time to meet the old girl."

Evadne tried to disguise her disappointment with a brave smile. "I will miss you!"

"And I, you." William took her hands, looking into her eyes.

Evadne flushed, her heart beating faster at the touch of his hands. She was oblivious to the sound of the bell announcing the end of the intermission, conscious only of William.

"Do you wish to go back?" William asked, not missing the pulse beating in her breast. "We could go to Marchand's—" he mentioned the famous restaurant nearby, on Stockton Street "—for a light supper."

"To Marchand's," agreed Evadne eagerly, wanting to be with him where she could see him and not in the darkness of the theater. "I am sure you are planning to leave early in the morning," she added.

"I am." As he helped her with the sealskin coat that she had only draped across her shoulders, wrapping it around her, his hands brushed her breasts, lingering.

Evadne's pounding blood reminded her of her mother's warning. She raised her own hands to take his, less from wanting to obey her mother than because they were standing on the street. It would not do for a scandal to arise before her parents left town!

William grinned, freeing his hands to put on his own coat and taking her arm. "I am sure you will not be lonely, Evadne. Paul Tyler will be only too glad to escort you wherever you wish."

"Paul!" Evadne wrinkled her nose. "He is such a boy, although Lillie does not think so." She sighed. "I *will* miss you."

Squeezing her arm, William chuckled. "You are sure about that?"

"Oh, yes!" She sighed. "How I wish I were going with you. It will be quite warm there, even at this time of year. The sun would feel so good after this long, damp, cloudy winter."

"I quite agree. I miss the sun, although you more than make up for it, my dear," he added.

"I do?" The unexpected compliment took her unawares.

"You do, and the next time I go to the Valley, I promise you shall go with me. Would you like that?" William asked, serious now.

"Of course." She tried not to think about what Mama or Auntie would say. If William did ask her, she would have to find some way of accompanying him, come what may.

The restaurant was still filled with late diners, but the headwaiter managed to find them a table in the corner after William slipped him a bill. As soon as they were seated, a wine steward arrived. William ordered champagne, then picked up the menu. He insisted that they have oysters, a crabmeat mousse, and filet of beef, despite Evadne's protests that she was not that hungry. Conversation was difficult in the crowded restaurant, giving them little opportunity for more than pleasantries, to Evadne's annoyance.

She toyed with her food, her mother's warnings fading as she observed the features of the handsome man across the table from her. She ached to be somewhere alone with him, her head against his broad shoulder and his strong arms around her as his lips brushed her cheek and mouth. The thought of not seeing him for a week was unbearable.

William, as usual, ordered coffee for Evadne and coffee and brandy for himself. As he lit a cigar, he said softly, "Yes, next time you must come with me. I shall be thinking of you often."

"I know you must go." Evadne sighed. "A week, though, seems terribly long, and you make it sound so . . . so *final*."

"It is far from final, and the time will go more quickly than you think. Besides, it will give you a chance to spend some time with your parents before they leave for the East," William pointed out.

"True, but Auntie will soon be here and," Evadne grimaced, "wait until you meet her. Still," she brightened, "though Auntie never married, I have noticed that she likes a gentleman's company. I am sure you will quite charm her." She laughed. "As long as you talk loud enough!"

William laughed, too, motioning for the waiter to bring the check. Since he had left the car near the St. Francis, they walked slowly toward Union Square. At the corner, before they reached the hotel, he drew her inside the park where an overhanging bush shielded them from the street. Taking her in his arms, he murmured, "I have been wanting to do this all evening, to give you something so that you will not forget me."

His lips crushed hers. His hands slipped inside the coat to caress her body. One hand touched her hips, fondling them, sending tingles of joy rippling through her body. His other hand hesitated at her breast before retreating to take her hand and guide it to a spot between his legs.

"If you think I can forget you, feel what you do to me, my dear," he whispered before his lips sought hers again, his tongue gently parting her lips.

Evadne trembled as she felt his member seem to swell under her touch. She tried to pull her hand away, but William pressed it against him, forcing her fingers to explore the longing that filled him with a pulsing desire for her. Curiosity and her own desire urged her on. As she caressed him, willingly now, he removed his hand from hers to feel her breast, seeking out the nipple that hid just below her corselet. Her free hand circled his neck, drawing him closer to her, as waves of longing swept over her, making her forget time and place.

The sound of wood slapping against the palm of a hand and a loud "Ahem" startled them. They drew apart hastily, Evadne wrapping the sealskin coat tightly about her quivering body, to stare at the policeman whose nightstick continued its ominous tattoo.

"Now, now," the policeman scolded, not missing the well-cut expensive clothing the pair wore. "It's not for the likes of you to be lingering in a public park."

Evadne stared at him dumbly, her face bright red with humiliation as she remembered her mother's warnings about her reputation. Her first thought was that he would take them to the police station. The scandal would force her parents to cancel their trip!

"Officer," William began. "We—"

"I see what I see. I should be taking the two of you in for loitering," the officer remarked.

"Oh, God!" cried Evadne, turning as white as she had been red before.

"The young lady is blameless," William replied in his most courteous manner. "We were walking to my car from Marchand's, and I am afraid that I was carried away by the night and the stars . . . and her beauty." He added the last with a rueful smile.

"Well, 'tis a lovely evening, and the young lady is beautiful—" The policeman hesitated, eyeing Evadne again and noting the expensive fur coat. He obviously had little taste for doing his duty and possibly bringing down on his head the wrath of a wealthy family which undoubtedly had friends at City Hall. "I'll tell you what: I'll let you go—with a warning. Union Square at night is no place for ladies and gentlemen."

"Thank you, Officer. You may be assured that this will not happen again and that I will take the young lady home promptly." William took Evadne's arm.

"You do that, Boyo. I see you here again, I won't be so easy on you," warned the policeman, stepping aside to let them pass and slamming his nightstick one last time against the palm of his hand.

"Thank you, Officer," Evadne murmured in a shaking voice.

Although she felt like running out of shame, William's hand on her arm kept them moving at a sedately steady pace. He glanced down at her, seeing the trembling mouth and the tears sparkling at the corners of her eyes in the light of a street lamp. When they reached his car, he helped her in more gently than ever.

The tears that Evadne had been holding back burst in a torrent from her eyes. She huddled in a corner of the seat, as far away from William as possible.

"Oh, William," she wept, "what am I going to do?"

"First of all, you must forget what happened. Evadne," he took out his handkerchief to hand it to her and put his arm around her. "It was entirely my fault. I apologize, and I hope you will not think the less of me. As I told the officer, the night and the stars, your beauty—"

Her tears stopped. She turned to William, saying honestly and utterly miserable at the admission, "It was my fault too, I . . . I wanted you to . . . to kiss me—"

"Then, wipe your eyes. You do not want anyone to see that you have been crying," he advised. He tried to pull her closer to him, but Evadne held herself too stiffly, and he sighed. "Are you all right now? I have to get out of the car to crank it."

Evadne nodded. During the few moments that it took him to start the car, she composed herself. He would be away for several days, perhaps as long as a week, after which she would have to be careful not to put herself in such a position again. She did not even consider the possibility of not seeing him again—that was unthinkable. As William got back in the car and started to drive slowly up the street, all Evadne could think about was how much she would miss him. For all of her resolve, her body yearned for his touch, for the nearness of him. Watching him drive, she recalled again the feel of his manhood swelling under her fingers, recalled his desire. If they had not already reached the drive in front of her home, she would have touched him again. As it was, their arrival flooded her with relief that the temptation would not be repeated—at least, not that evening.

William escorted her to the front door and the butler let them in. Her parents were waiting for them in the library, as usual. Even so, Evadne's heart sank. Guiltily, she wondered whether the policeman had recognized her and called her parents. She struggled to compose herself.

William greeted her parents in his normal manner. When Nathaniel Harper offered him a cigar and a glass of brandy, he hesitated, glancing at Evadne as he helped her off with her coat.

Evadne spoke quickly, not wanting to be alone with her parents. "Please stay, William. After all," she added, thinking quickly, "you will not have much of a chance to talk to Mama and Papa before they leave since you are going to Sonoma tomorrow."

Sally Harper smiled. She had noticed that her daughter seemed agitated and now she thought she knew why. "In that case, you must stay a moment, William. Isn't this trip rather sudden?"

"It is, Mrs. Harper." William accepted the cigar, taking his time to light it, before sitting down, brandy in hand. He explained, as he had to Evadne, about the chance meeting in the bar and the invitation to go to the vineyard. "The gentleman's name is Mario Di Corso, sir." He turned toward Nathaniel Harper. "I understand he owns one of the finest vineyards in the Sonoma Valley."

"You are quite right. The family is very respected in the Bay area. A cousin, in fact, is president of one of our larger banks," Evadne's father said.

"Then I can assume that I have been thoroughly investigated by the cousin through Mr. Tyler," William said thoughtfully, studying the end of his cigar.

"*And* approved," agreed Mr. Harper with a smile.

William smiled apologetically. "I am afraid, sir, that in conversation I also mentioned your name. I hope that was not presumptuous of me?"

"William, if my wife and I did not think highly of you, you can be sure that we would not permit our daughter to go out with you." Evadne's father leaned forward anxiously. "Since you and I will have little time to talk before Mrs. Harper and I leave, perhaps now is a good time to say that we rely upon your discretion and sense of responsibility where our daughter is concerned while we are gone."

"Yes, William." Sally Harper glanced at Evadne, whose cheeks flushed at the last statement. "Of course, Auntie—Miss Harper—will be here, but we shall still worry."

"Oh, Mama!" Evadne said. "William will get on quite famously with Auntie."

Evadne's mother smiled. "Speaking of Auntie reminds me, William, that you and Evadne planned to meet her at the ferry. Does your trip mean—?"

"I promised I would perform that duty to give you time for any last-minute chores. I always keep my promises," declared William, smiling at Mr. Harper. "I will be back at least a day before she is due, if I must swim the Golden Gate!"

"I doubt that will be necessary." Sally Harper smiled and stood up. "Come, Evadne. Say goodnight to William, and let us leave him and your father to their brandy and cigars."

"Yes, Mama." Evadne rose to her feet and picked up her coat. She kissed her father goodnight before pausing in front of William, who had stood up as soon as her mother had risen to her feet. "Thank you for a lovely evening. Do enjoy your trip."

William took her hand. "The time will pass quickly. I'll be back before you know it."

She smiled at him and followed her mother, hoping that her mother did not want another private chat with her. To her relief, her mother left her at her bedroom door, kissing her cheek and telling her to get a good night's sleep.

Chapter V

THE DAY THAT WILLIAM LEFT FOR SONOMA, THE HARPERS WERE
expected at the Tylers for dinner. Mrs. Tyler had wanted to
give a gala farewell party for Sally and Nathaniel, one of her
grand affairs—with one hundred people invited for dinner
and more for a dance afterward. But Sally had politely talked
her out of the idea, on the grounds that such a party would be
too much for her and Nathaniel, with all the other things they
had to do before they left. Dinner, however, was unavoid-
able.

Evadne was not looking forward to the evening. Over the
last three months she had spent more and more time with
William. In fact, although Paul had often asked her out, the
only times she had seen him had been at parties. She had seen
more of Lillie, because the two girls often went shopping
together or met for lunch or tea. Though Lillie found William
attractive, her mind was, as always, on Paul, who, since
Evadne was busy with William, paid Lillie more attention
than he ever had before. Evadne suspected he was trying to
make her jealous. As a result, she greeted Paul at the Tylers
with some reservation.

While their parents talked, Paul offered to show Evadne
the orchids his mother had recently acquired from Hawaii for
her conservatory. When Evadne hesitated, not wanting to be

alone with him, her mother, who had seen the orchids, urged her to go. "They are exquisite, Evadne, truly lovely."

Reluctantly, Evadne accompanied Paul to the glass-enclosed tropical garden that was Mrs. Tyler's pride and joy. The conservatory, large as it was, had a closed, sultry atmosphere that Evadne found distasteful. She had never been able to appreciate the passion so many San Franciscans had for conservatories, a passion that, fortunately, her mother did not share.

"Where are the orchids, Paul?" Evadne asked, anxious to leave.

"Over here." Paul took her hand to pull her close to him so they could walk side by side on the gravel path.

Evadne grimaced and pulled free. His touch did not repel her, but last night's episode with William had been too recent. Then, too, Paul was—Paul, a good friend from childhood. He was not William.

"Paul—"

"Evadne." His arms slipped around her waist and drew her close, his lips searching for hers as she twisted her head away. "You never used to mind a kiss," Paul said angrily.

"That was when we were dancing, or with others. Here, in this place—" She struggled against him. "It's much too hot in here. Please let me go."

"Give me a kiss first," Paul insisted, his mouth against her cheek. He was breathing heavily, and one hand was groping for her breasts. "Don't be such a tease, Vad. You know what happens to teasers."

"A tease!" Her hands pushed against him, trying to push him away from her. "What do you think *you* are, acting like this?"

"I love you, Vad. I always have. When I see you with that fellow Hopkins, it's all I can do to keep from strangling him. Why are you trying to make me jealous?"

"Make . . . you . . . jealous!" Evadne was so surprised that she stopped struggling to stare at him.

Paul took advantage of the moment to hold her even closer and press his cheek against hers. "Of course. Why else would you be paying so much attention to Hopkins? After all," Paul said sneeringly, "what do you have in common? What do you know about him? He is far too old for you, and he could be a scoundrel—he probably is."

. At Paul's condescending tone, anger rose in Evadne as

quickly as passion had the previous evening. When Paul's lips found hers, his urgency increasing with every moment as he held her, she bit him hard, and slapped his face with all the strength she could muster.

He stepped back in shock. "What the hell!"

"Don't you dare swear at me, Paul Tyler. You asked for it—and I thought we were friends!" She glared at him.

"Damn it, Vad, what has gotten into you? You know someday we're going to be married!" Paul licked the blood off his lower lip and rubbed his stinging cheek.

"I *don't* know! Oh, come on, Paul. We've joked about it, yes, but surely you never took it seriously. All that talk about my height. . . ."

Now it was Paul's turn to feel outraged. "You've been teasing me all the time! Why, you're no better than the girls on the Barbary Coast," he said, wanting to hurt her.

"I never meant to tease. And . . . and what do you mean by the girls on the Barbary Coast? What do you know about them?" she demanded, curiosity mixed with her anger.

"Don't be as stupid as Lillie, Vad. Where do you think men go when they want . . . want a little fun? You and Lillie don't know what you are missing." He gave a short laugh. Taking his handkerchief out, he touched it to his lip. The sight of the blood on it added to his anger. "You two, all you know how to do is tease a man. You make us go there."

"I think we had better rejoin our parents, Paul." Evadne had heard enough. Disdainfully picking up her skirt, she moved to the glass double doors that Paul had shut behind them. "Aren't you coming with me?"

"How can I? My lip is still bleeding." The bleeding had actually stopped, but he was determined not to let her escape so easily. "Besides, you haven't seen the orchids."

Evadne shrugged indifferently. "I have seen orchids before, and your mother knows I am an ignoramus when it comes to plants." She opened the door and stepped across the sill, not waiting for him to follow.

When he saw he couldn't detain her, Paul hurried to catch up with her. "Vad, I'm sorry. I know I shouldn't have . . . well . . . done what I did, or said those things, but you've been driving me mad these past few months. Paying no attention—"

"You seem to find solace in Lillie." Thinking about Lillie, she turned impulsively to face him. "Can't we just be friends?

I mean, who knows what may happen—" She had meant to say between him and Lillie, but he gave her no chance to finish.

"You're teasing again, Vad," he said. "Maybe you can get away with it with me, but I wonder what Hopkins thinks? Or maybe—" Paul looked at her and laughed harshly. "Maybe you are not as innocent as—"

"You—you—" Words failed her in her anger. She raised her hands and began to beat him on the chest with her fists.

Paul grabbed her wrists, smiling at her fury and pleased with himself. "What will our parents think, seeing you like this?" he jeered at her.

"Let me go!" Her breasts heaving, Evadne twisted her wrists, trying to free herself.

Paul released her. The two stood there attempting to regain their composure. Neither moved nor spoke until a maid arrived to tell them that dinner was about to be served.

Somehow, Evadne managed to get through the seemingly endless dinner. Mrs. Tyler, denied the pleasure of a party, had made up for it with a dinner of numerous courses and wines. Evadne barely touched any of it. To make matters worse, she was seated across from Paul, which meant that every time she looked up from her place her eyes met his watching her. As a result, she kept her gaze down on the plates that seemed to be constantly changing in front of her.

The conversation was, fortunately, one that did not require her participation. The newspapers that day had been filled with news about the eruption of Mount Vesuvius, the worst eruption, it was said, since the one that had buried Pompeii. Thousands had been sent fleeing as lava and ash covered their homes and despoiled their fields and olive groves.

"How can people live in such a place, at the mercy of nature?" Mr. Tyler said, shaking his head.

Nathaniel Harper smiled. "Remember, Henry, we have had our earthquakes, and we stay."

Tyler brushed that aside. "Small ones, only small ones. We have not had more than a quiver since 1868. What is an earthquake in comparison with Vesuvius, or with the hurricanes, tornadoes—even the blizzards—other parts of this country get?"

"Maybe so," Harper agreed, but he did not look convinced.

Mrs. Tyler sighed. "Can't you two think of a more pleasant

topic? Still, I suppose that we have to raise some money for those poor people. It is our duty, and it will be a good opportunity to donate any clothes we want to be rid of, won't it, Sally?"

Evadne only half listened, noting with relief that her dessert plate was being removed. She knew that there would now be a respite, since Mrs. Tyler preferred the English custom of leaving the men to their cigars and port while the ladies retired to the salon.

As they left the dining room, Sally Harper squeezed her daughter's arm. "Don't worry, we'll be going home early. You do look terribly tired tonight. Perhaps you have been trying to do too much."

"Oh, no, Mama," Evadne said quickly. "It was all that food. It does seem such a waste, doesn't it? Twelve courses for only the six of us!"

"Shhh, Mrs. Tyler might hear you." Her mother squeezed her arm again. "I quite agree with you, however." She glanced at her daughter. "You must promise me that you will not overdo this social life you have been leading while we are away. I fear—"

"Mama," Evadne smiled at her. "I promise that I will behave with Auntie exactly as I do with you." As she said this, Evadne felt her heart skip a beat, knowing that her mother would not have approved of some of her actions of the past few months—from the first drive with William to the Cliff House to what had happened in the park the night before.

Growing up, becoming a woman, Evadne decided, was terribly, terribly difficult. Yet, Lillie, even Jerusha, did not seem to be undergoing such agonies as she was. But then, they had not known the ecstasy of such a love as she felt for William. How could they? Jerusha had married her childhood sweetheart, and it was Lillie's childhood love who consumed her thoughts. Evadne was different. Despite Paul's accusations, she had never dreamed of marrying him. She had always felt that somewhere, somehow, there had to be a better, more exciting and fulfilling life than the one she knew and that all her friends led.

She wished that she could discuss some of these feelings, as she wished she could discuss William, with her mother. But that was impossible. The conversation with her mother just yesterday, before she had gone to the Orpheum, had shown her that she must rely on herself. Still, Grace might understand. . . . Evadne had a sudden yearning to talk to her. Grace might be overly protective, but Evadne could talk to her as she could not to her mother, or to her friends. Yes, after what Paul had said about her being a tease and the Barbary Coast, she must talk to Grace.

Her reverie was interrupted by the arrival of the men. Paul promptly seated himself on the arm of the settee where Evadne was sitting. He seemed to have recovered from the scene in the conservatory.

"I won't give up easily, Vad," he whispered under cover of the others' conversation. "I intend to marry you, and I do not intend to lose you to any damned foreigner—no matter how romantic you think he is."

"And I," Evadne declared softly, her voice firm, "intend to marry the man of my choice. To me, you are—were—a friend, that is all."

"We'll see about that. If I can't have you, Hopkins won't either." Paul rose from the settee, giving her no chance to reply.

Evadne looked after the young man thoughtfully. Something in his voice told her to take the threat seriously. Paul was up to something that boded no good for William, of that she was sure. He was not only jealous of the way the Australian had monopolized her attention, but also envious of the place William had assumed so quickly in San Francisco society. More than ever, Evadne was anxious for the evening to be over and to be home.

Her parents, to her relief, showed no inclination to linger. Her father seemed as eager as she was to leave. On the short walk home—the Tylers lived only a few blocks away— Nathaniel Harper was unusually silent. Only once did he speak and that was to mutter, "Tyler may be a good banker, but he knows nothing about shipping. I need ships. We must go to New York, Sally."

The remark, answered only by Sally Harper's taking her husband's hand, added to the uneasiness that had been growing in Evadne all evening. Oh, how she wished that William had not gone to Sonoma! Still, he had been right about one thing: his absence would give her more time to spend with her parents. She was glad of that because the evening and her father's remark had impressed on her that they would soon be leaving.

During the next week, however, Evadne had reason to become even more uneasy. First, there was a question Lillie asked over lunch with Jerusha. Her father was a realtor, deeply involved in both business and residential real estate in the Bay area.

"Do you know how much your house is worth, Vad?" Lillie asked.

Evadne stared at her. It had never occurred to her to think of her home in terms of money. "What do you mean, Lillie?"

"Well, I heard Papa telling Mama that your house would bring two hundred and fifty thousand dollars on the market." She laughed. "Just think! Two hundred and fifty thousand dollars! Doesn't that sound like a lot of money?"

Evadne laughed too. "It's more money than I can even imagine."

She dismissed the conversation until she arrived home a little later. Hearing her parents' voices coming from the library, she started to go in, and was stopped by what her father was saying. "It might be better for Vad to go to the Dillards, or even to Sausalito to stay with Auntie, Sally."

"Oh no, Nathaniel!" Sally responded. "This is her home. What would people think if we were to bundle Evadne off and close up the house for a few months? If it comes to that, she must come with us."

"Yes, appearances do count—you are right about that. And I cannot afford to have anyone in the business community think that—that—" Her father's voice broke.

"We have been through difficult times before." Her mother's voice was firm. "This is no different, and you have always had good dealings with the New York bankers. They know how important the East is to us."

Evadne's father laughed. "Sometimes you surprise me with how much you understand, Sally. It is one of the things I love about you."

"It is settled then." Her mother's voice was muted, as if she had turned her back. "Evadne will stay here, and Auntie will come as planned."

Evadne, slipping past the door to go upstairs, glanced inside. Her mother was sitting on her father's lap, her head against his shoulder. Softly, Evadne pulled the door shut before thoughtfully mounting the stairs to her room.

Something had to be very wrong. Yet, what could it be? There was the sealskin coat and all the new clothes that her mother had bought her for the holidays, and no expense had been spared on her party. During the past few months, she had noticed no changes in the way money was spent on her or on running the house.

She entered her room to find Grace waiting for her. Evadne attempted a smile.

Grace was not fooled. "What's wrong, Miss Vad? Did those girls tease you about where Mr. William is?"

"What? Oh, no." Evadne did smile now. The remark, however, reminded her of what Paul had said in the conservatory. "Am I a tease, Grace?"

"A tease, Miss Vad?" Grace's eyes widened. "Who called you a tease?"

"Paul Tyler, the other night. I wouldn't kiss him, and he called me a tease. He said . . . other things too," Evadne added evasively.

"That Mr. Paul!" Grace snorted in disgust. "He's just jealous because of Mr. William. He used to take you to the parties and things before Mr. William."

"Does that make me a tease?" asked Evadne.

"No, Miss Vad, a tease is . . . well . . . a girl who leads men on, makes them think that she's goin' to—" Grace looked at her young mistress, not sure how much more to say.

"That she's going to . . . to give them her body?" Evadne finished quickly. "Like the girls on the Barbary Coast?"

Grace colored. "I guess you could put it that way, Miss Vad. I mean, when Pa was alive, I saw lots o' women teasing them poor drunken fools—getting them to buy drinks, showing them a leg or a . . . a bosom, then maybe robbing them and having them thrown out in the street. Now, *that's* what I call teasing," Grace declared. "You ain't no tease."

But Grace's assurance did little to lighten Evadne's mood, not when she thought about what had happened between her and William. Yet, she had not deliberately offered her mouth or her body to William. Even so, she had let him caress her, and she had enjoyed the feeling that had warmed her through and through. Once more, Evadne resolved to keep her distance from William when he returned.

"Miss Vad, you all right?" The young girl's silence disturbed Grace, who did not know just what had happened to draw Paul Tyler's accusation.

"Yes," Evadne said, and managed a smile. "You're right, Paul was most likely just jealous."

"Good." Grace nodded with satisfaction. "Now, when is

Mr. William coming back? I think you miss him, even if he is a furriner."

Evadne laughed. "Soon, I hope. Probably tomorrow—if he keeps his word." She sat down abruptly on her bed, afraid suddenly that William might not keep his word, that she might not see him again. She said as much to Grace.

It was the maid's turn to sigh. Evadne's moods were beyond her understanding. "Now, Miss Vad, don't be looking for problems. Problems enough will find you without you looking for them."

"You're right, Grace." Evadne stood up and gave her a hug. She did not tell Grace about the conversation she had overheard between her parents, that one problem may have already found her. Tomorrow, though, Evadne tried to convince herself, everything would be fine, because William would be back. At the thought, her heart beat faster. It would be so good to see him again, to feel his arms. . . .

No, she might let him kiss her on the cheek, but that would be all she would allow—no matter how much her body longed for the touch of his hands.

William's return the following afternoon drove Evadne's other concerns out of her mind. At the sound of his voice on the telephone, shivers of joy raced up her spine. He told her how much he had missed her and that he would pick her up at one o'clock the next afternoon, in plenty of time to meet Auntie at the ferry.

Evadne's obvious pleasure and eagerness both relieved and worried her mother. The relief was due to the fact that Evadne had been uncharacteristically subdued all week. Unaware of what had happened between her daughter and Paul Tyler, Sally Harper had decided that Evadne's mood had to do with their going away so soon and for such a long time. Now she realized that it had been due to William's absence and began to worry again about the wisdom of leaving the girl in Auntie's charge. Even though Nathaniel had had a talk with William, and reminded him of Evadne's youth and innocence and vulnerability, her daughter's change in mood worried Sally. She wished that her husband could have another talk with William, but that was impossible. The next day was filled with appointments for the two of them, one of the reasons they had been happy to accept William's offer to meet Auntie.

The appointments meant that Evadne was alone in the

library at one o'clock, waiting for William. As soon as she saw him and the butler had left them, closing the door behind him, all of Evadne's good intentions faded.

She rushed into his arms with a hunger that surprised him. "William!" she cried. "I am so glad to see you."

"And I am glad to see you," William replied with a smile, holding her close, his lips brushing her mouth and eyes. "I missed you, Evadne, more than I dreamed I would—busy as I was."

"Did you really?" she asked, her heart beating quickly at his words. "How I missed you too." Her face was flushed with emotion, and suddenly she recalled her resolve. She drew away from him. "How—how was your trip?" she asked.

"I'll tell you about it on our way to the ferry," he said.

They were not going to the main ferry building, with its tall clock tower, at the foot of Market Street, but to another pier on Powell Street. Here ferries left for and arrived from Marin County. During the drive, William talked of what he had learned on his trip, of the different grapes he had found growing in the valley—the Chardonnays, Gewurztraminers, Rieslings, and Chenin Blancs that went into white wines, and the Cabernet Sauvignons, Zinfandels, and Pinot Noirs that were made into reds. The names meant nothing to Evadne, but she reveled in his enthusiasm.

At the pier, William left her in the automobile while he went to check on Auntie's ferry. The day was cold and gusty, the waters of the harbor surging with white-capped gray waves. Poor Auntie, thought Evadne, hoping the old lady would not arrive seasick.

William returned. "The ferry won't arrive for an hour. Would you like to wait here, or shall we go for a drive?"

Evadne hesitated. It was too windy to wait in the open, and the waiting room would surely be overheated and crowded. "Let's go for a drive," she told him. It was broad daylight, and he was sure to behave, with Auntie due so soon.

"Fine." William cranked the car and joined her, driving south along East Street toward Broadway and Pacific Street, at the foot of which was the area known as the Barbary Coast. Even that early in the afternoon, the streets here were filled with drifters and with sailors from the many ships riding at anchor in the harbor, wandering from one garish saloon and dance hall to another.

Evadne looked curiously at the men—and at the women

with them. Although she had been born in the city, this was the first time she had ever been here. What she saw made her shudder, remembering what Paul had said to her. The Barbary Coast women were of all ages. Many had dyed red hair, and there were ebony blacks and brassy blondes with faces heavily made up, like painted dolls, with caked face powder and bright red rouge and lipstick. A few sported expensive fur coats; these were generally the younger, more attractive women. Most of them were slatternly and dressed in cheap cotton housedresses or sometimes garish satin gowns with thin shawls covering their shoulders. Evadne's face grew hot with embarrassment and anger that Paul Tyler could compare her to such women.

William, still rapturizing about wines and grapes, had barely noticed where they were until Evadne's silence made him look at her. Seeing her expression, he looked around him.

"My dear, I am sorry," he apologized earnestly. "I should have paid more attention to where we were going. This is no place for you."

He stopped the car, preparing to put it in reverse and back up to a place where he could turn around. As he did, an older man, his gray-streaked hair wild under a blue-knit fisherman's cap and his cheeks grimy with dirt and a scraggly beard, staggered against the car. He knocked on Evadne's window.

"You, Mish . . . Missy," he called. "How 'bout a drink? I know a place," he winked a bloodshot eye. "Jush the place, nice and private. . . ."

"William," Evadne whimpered, as the drunk's hand fumbled for the door handle.

William hurriedly reached over and locked her door. The man staggered onto the running board. Hanging onto the door handle with one hand, he pounded his fist against the window.

"Damn him," William muttered. Taking the car out of reverse and putting it forward, he stepped on the gas. The car lurched ahead, the motion sending the drunk reeling off the running board. At the entrance to a nearby pier, William turned the car around. Heading north toward the Sausalito ferry, he drove as fast as he could on a street crowded with drays and trucks and at last they were out of the Barbary Coast.

Slowing down, William glanced down at Evadne, who was

huddled against him, as far away from the window as she could get. "Evadne," he said, "I *am* sorry. What can I say? It was all my fault."

Now she was safe, Evadne smiled. "Don't blame yourself, William. I should have been paying attention too. I admit I was frightened when I thought that awful man was going to get into the car." She shuddered. To think that Grace had wandered the area alone, searching for her father. "What a terrible place!"

"You saw the worst of the area, near the piers where the sailors hang out," William said.

"How do you know?" Evadne stared at him. "Have you been there?"

"Does that shock you, my dear? Yes, I have. You would be surprised at the number of gentlemen who go there," he added.

Grace had said the same thing, and Paul. . . . "Did Paul take you there?"

William looked startled. "How did you know that?"

Evadne gave a short laugh. "I guessed . . . from something he said."

"As far as what I did," William told her, "I had a few drinks in a place called the Little Silver Dollar, but I didn't stay long. I didn't go there to be shanghaied."

"Shanghaied?" Evadne was puzzled.

"The place is built over the water. It's said it has a trapdoor. Unsuspecting chaps have a few drinks too many, and before they know what's happening, the trapdoor has opened, dropping them into the water or into a boat that takes them to a ship short of hands for its crew. When the chaps wake up, they have left the Golden Gate behind."

"How awful!" Evadne was horrified. "And I always thought San Francisco was so . . . so civilized."

"That has nothing to do with it, my dear. The term 'shanghaied' may have originated here, because of the China trade, but press gangs do the same sort of thing in other parts of the world. Even the British Navy resorted to the practice not too long ago," William said grimly. "Now, let's forget about that. You want a smile on your face to greet Auntie." He stopped at the ferry building, parking off to one side.

Though her fear had dissipated by now, Evadne remained snuggled against William, taking comfort—and pleasure—in the strength of his body. He smiled down at her, into the beautiful face so close to his. William put an arm around her, holding her even closer as he kissed her gently on the tip of her nose.

She kissed his chin. "We mustn't keep Auntie waiting," she murmured.

William nodded, releasing her and getting out of the car. After he had helped her out, the two of them walked through the building to a gate where a sign had been put up indicating the arrival of the ferry from Sausalito. The ferry itself was just nosing into the pier. Sailors on deck stood ready to drop heavy hemp lines over the mooring posts. Shortly afterward, the throng of passengers began to move down the gangplank onto the pier.

"Come along." Evadne took William's hand, weaving her way among the disembarking passengers. "Auntie will be waiting for us to find her," she explained.

They found the little old lady, sitting upright on a trunk, surrounded by a variety of bundles and valises. Despite her age, as soon as she saw Evadne, she sprang lightly to her feet.

"Evadne!" she exclaimed. "How grown up you are! You have become quite the young lady." She looked at William. "And who is this gentleman?"

Evadne made the introductions, noticing how Auntie beamed at William, despite probably only half hearing what was said. William, in his turn, beamed just as broadly, taking off his hat with a flourish as he kissed Auntie's hand. He was obviously surprised by what he saw. From what Evadne had said, he had expected a big-bosomed female version of her father. Instead, Auntie was tiny—barely five feet tall—and birdlike, with a smooth, unlined face and red hair only slightly grayer than her nephew's.

The introductions over, William surveyed the luggage, hoping it would all fit into the car.

"Wait here, Evadne . . . Miss Harper," he shouted to make Auntie hear him, "while I get a couple of porters."

Evadne, too, was wondering how everything would be squeezed into the car, but she was sure that William would manage. If not, a dray could be hired for fifty cents or a dollar, at most, to bring the luggage, though that might cause a problem because Auntie would insist on accompanying it.

William, however, fulfilled Evadne's expectations. With the help of two porters, he managed to get everything either into or tied on top of the automobile. Auntie was squeezed in among her valises, not seeming to mind at all, while Evadne had a bundle at her feet and balanced another on her lap. It was fortunate that William had hired a big touring car, for the heavily laden vehicle had to struggle under the weight it carried to make the steep grade to the top of Nob Hill. At the Harper house, the car seemed to groan with relief as William drew to a stop.

William, with the help of the butler and the gardener, managed to get the trunk into the hall and up the stairs to the room that Auntie would use during her stay, while Grace helped Evadne unload the valises and bundles.

"Goodness," Grace whispered, "is she staying a year? Even your Ma and Pa together ain't takin' this much stuff East!"

Evadne giggled. "You know you don't have to whisper, Grace. Auntie can't hear you unless you shout in her ear. And you know that she *always* travels this way—she did the last time she came to visit."

"I know." Grace sighed. "I was hoping it was my imagination."

Tugging the last valise into the hall, Evadne said, "We can leave everything in the hall for now. I hope cook has tea ready. I know Auntie will want it as soon as she has freshened up. Go tell cook, please, Grace, to be sure."

"Yes, Miss Vad." Grace hurried off just as William came back downstairs with the gardener and the butler. All three men were mopping their brows.

"She must have packed that trunk with gold bullion, from the weight of it," William declared. "What about these things?" he asked, eyeing the valises.

"Grace and the butler can take them upstairs later. As soon as Auntie comes down, we'll have some tea."

Evadne took his arm, and they went into the library. "Thank you, William. I should have warned you about the luggage, but I hoped that this time she might travel light." She chuckled. "Come to think of it, she did. Last time, she was only here for two weeks—and she had *two* trunks!"

Chapter VI

TWO DAYS AFTER AUNTIE'S ARRIVAL, WILLIAM AND EVADNE drove Mr. and Mrs. Harper to their ferry. This time the destination was the main Ferry Building, at the foot of Market Street, from which ferries connected with the East-bound trains at Oakland, across the Bay. Even though a dray had been hired to go ahead with the luggage and there was plenty of room in the car for Auntie, she had insisted on saying her goodbyes at the house. Automobiles might be as practical as young people insisted, she said, but to her they were untrustworthy and uncomfortable, and journeys in them to be undertaken only under duress. In fact, if it had been her nephew who had met her, she would have insisted on a horse and carriage. But William had seemed such a nice young man, and she had not wanted to hurt his feelings.

At the Ferry Building, William left to see to the dray, which would go on the ferry on the lower deck, while the passengers rode on the deck above. Mrs. Harper took advantage of his absence to say to Evadne, "Now, dear, I want you to be considerate of Auntie while we are gone. You must be obedient to her wishes—even though they may not be the same as ours. Remember, she is an old lady. You are not to worry her in any way."

"Yes, Mama." Evadne smiled, though she knew that her

mother meant that Auntie would probably be much stricter—especially in regard to Evadne's relationship with William. "I shall miss you." She sighed.

"And we will miss you, dear." Sally Harper hesitated. "Also, Evadne, I wish you would see more of the other young men you know, like Paul Tyler. For a girl your age, you are seeing far too much of one man. I should have spoken about this before, but time just seemed to fly."

"Paul?" Evadne wrinkled her nose. "Mama, Paul is becoming a bore, now that he is working for his father."

"Still—"

"Sally," Nathaniel Harper interrupted his wife, "Auntie will take good care of our daughter." He kissed Evadne on the cheek, and she threw her arms around his neck.

"Oh, Papa, I *am* going to miss you and Mama! But have a good trip, and don't worry about me. I promise to listen to Auntie," she declared. Listening to Auntie was a promise she knew she could keep; obeying her old-fashioned wishes might be another matter, though. For the moment, anyway, Auntie seemed to be quite enchanted with William.

William came back now to say that the dray had been taken care of and passengers were now getting ready to board the ferry. Evadne kissed her parents again, and William shook hands with them. Now the moment for leaving was there. Sally dismissed her fears, turning to her husband and taking his arm. To Evadne, they looked like a honeymoon couple as they stepped on the ferry, arm in arm, to find a spot on the deck where they could wave goodbye. Within seconds, the ferry whistle blasted shrilly four times, indicating it was backing into the Bay. Evadne spotted her parents waving their handkerchiefs at her and waved her own in return until the ferry was swallowed up by the fog rolling into the Bay from the ocean beyond the Golden Gate.

She looked at William with tears in her eyes. "It will seem strange to have them gone for so long—at least two months!"

"The time will pass before you know it." William smiled at her, putting his arm around her. "Let's go back to the car. It's getting cold here."

Evadne nodded and wiped her eyes. "We had better go home and let Auntie know that they got off all right, or she will worry. You'll stay for tea, won't you, William?" she begged, not wanting to be alone with Auntie at the moment.

"I will do better than that. I will ask Auntie if she will let me take you to dinner at Marchand's this evening, to cheer you up. How would that suit you?" he asked, kissing her cheek.

Evadne snuggled against him, shivering in a sudden blast of cold wind from the Bay. "Very much—if you promise that we will not stop in Union Square," she added with a giggle.

William laughed too. "I have something else to ask Auntie," he said mysteriously.

"What? Tell me, William!" she looked at him, her eyes sparkling. "Why didn't you ask Mama and Papa before they left?"

"They had their minds on too many other things," he replied logically. "But I guess I should ask you first." He seated her in the car before going to the front to crank it and then getting in behind the wheel.

"Tell me!" Evadne begged. "You are being a dreadful tease!"

"Di Corso has invited me to Sonoma for Easter," he said. "He wants to show me the Buena Vista vineyard, where the original cuttings were planted after being brought from Europe."

"Oh, no! Now you are leaving me too," Evadne moaned in dismay.

"Let me finish!" William laughed. "I was going to ask you to come with me. As your father said, the family is eminently respectable, and Di Corso is most eager to meet you. In fact, when I told him your parents were leaving for the East, he immediately suggested that I bring you."

Evadne looked at him with rising excitement. Then, her face fell. "Auntie would never agree to my going on such a trip alone with a man. Neither would Mama or Papa, if they were here. After all, it would be for at least overnight." She sighed. "It would have been such fun too."

William was not easily discouraged. "I have already thought of that, Evadne. Do you think Auntie would object if Grace came along?"

Evadne's face lightened. "No, I don't think so. She likes Grace. I think—"

Suddenly, Evadne was almost thrown against the windshield as the car came to an abrupt halt. William was driving up California Street. At the intersection of Sansome Street, a dray pulled out in front of him. It was overloaded and swayed dangerously from side to side. A group of Chinese men with long pigtails and satin coats ran alongside, trying to keep it from tilting over on the hilly street.

"Oh, look at them!" cried Evadne. "Those poor people!"

The bony horse struggled with the weight of the load, head hanging almost to the ground as it fought to maintain its footing and pull the cart. This area was the heart of China-town, a rabbit warren of alleys and buildings filled with the shops and homes of the Chinese laborers who had been brought to San Francisco to help build the transcontinental railroad and had stayed on. Nearby, lined up against a building looking on, were several women, teetering on their bound feet and shivering in the thin cotton-quilted robes they wore.

The horse finally managed to pull its load, assisted by the men accompanying it, past the intersection, and William drove on.

"There must be thousands of Chinese living inside a few blocks," he observed. "How do they make a living?"

"Some work in restaurants, others in private homes. Several people I know have Chinese servants . . . I—I really don't know what else they do." Evadne frowned. The ques-tion had never occurred to her anymore than it did to most San Franciscans. As long as the Chinese stayed where they belonged—in the few blocks dubbed Chinatown—no one cared.

Evadne forgot about the Chinese when they reached the house where Auntie was waiting anxiously for them. Evadne tried to explain why they had been delayed, but Auntie only nodded brightly, saying, "Don't shout, child. I can hear you."

Evadne glanced at William and smiled.

As they had their tea, which Auntie had waiting for them, William requested permission for Evadne to have dinner with him that night. Auntie agreed willingly, saying it would be good for Evadne to get out of the house. The proposal to visit Sonoma, which Evadne promptly made, in view of Auntie's good mood, was greeted less warmly.

"I cannot make such a trip in an auto. I am too old," the old lady objected.

Evadne smiled at her aunt. "Auntie, I had intended to ask Grace to accompany me. You know how well Mama thinks of her."

"Grace would be a fine chaperone." Auntie nodded. "And she could do with some fresh air. She is looking much too pale. It is time for my nap, Evadne. I will sleep on it," she announced.

As soon as she left them, William asked, "What do you think?"

"Oh, she will let me go. I'll see to that," Evadne said firmly. "In a little while, she will begin to think it was her idea. You heard what she said about Grace? She will say the same about me."

Evadne's prediction would prove right before the week was out. There was a problem, though, and it was Grace.

When Evadne came home from dinner at Marchand's with William that night, she found a radiant Grace waiting for her. The little maid was bright-eyed, her normally sallow complexion flushed and rosily becoming. "Miss Vad," she bubbled, "my Ethan's back!"

"Your—who?" It was the first time Evadne had heard Grace mention anyone other than her parents.

Almost too excited to talk, Grace finally managed to explain to her young mistress about the sailor whom she had not seen in five years. "He said he's been lookin' for me for days. Finally, he found someone on Telegraph Hill who told him where I was, and he came here right off—just after you and Mr. William went out!" exclaimed Grace. "We been talking until just before you got back."

"A sailor, Grace! He'll go away again!" Evadne warned her, saying the first thing that came into her mind.

Grace shook her head. "Not this time. He's saved his money, and he says we'll rent a little place and he'll work on the fishing boats and we'll save for a boat of our own," she said proudly. "He ain't no drinking man, like some, not with him being from New England and all."

Evadne stared at Grace with a sinking heart. She wanted to be happy for her, but all she could think of was her own thwarted wishes.

Grace, who as yet knew nothing about the trip to Sonoma, saw the expression on Evadne's face and immediately associated it with something else. "Don't you worry, Miss Vad. I ain't leaving you right off, least ways, not till your Ma and Pa come home. I couldn't do that."

Evadne's spirits rose, and she told Grace quickly about the planned excursion. But Grace, to her consternation, firmly shook her head. "No, I ain't going nowhere—not with my Ethan just back. I'm sorry, Miss Vad, I couldn't—not even if you order me—'cause then I'd have to leave."

After much discussion and argument and pleading on

Evadne's part, the two young women finally came to an agreement. Grace would not say "no," if Auntie should say anything to her. She would merely nod noncommittally, and give Evadne a chance to think of something else.

The "something" came to Evadne suddenly one evening while Grace was impatiently helping her get dressed for a party at the Dillards. The only time that Grace had free to see Ethan was in the evening, in the few hours between the time when she helped Evadne dress for the evening's social occasion until Evadne came home again and she helped her prepare for bed. During the day, the cook and Auntie kept Grace busy around the house. Except for those few hours in the evening, she only had Sundays—after dinner at noon—free.

"Grace," Evadne said slowly, "you'd like more time to spend with Ethan, wouldn't you?"

" 'Course I would, Miss Vad. You know that!" Grace looked at her. "You got an idea for getting your Auntie and cook to give me some time off?"

"I do!" Evadne spun around and seized Grace's hands. "This is what we will do. You agree to go to Sonoma with me—"

"Miss Vad, no! I told you—!"

Evadne shook her head. "Hear me out, Grace. I said, you agree to go with me. We'll pack as if we were both going. Then we both drive to the ferry to Sausalito, but you—"

"Oh, Miss Vad! You've got a naughty mind—if you're thinkin' what I think you are. You mean, Ethan meets me there and we go off and have a few days together while you and Mr. William go off by yourselves, is that it?"

"That is exactly what I mean. What is so naughty about it? The Di Corsos are very respectable. I would be as safe—if not safer—in their care as I am here at home with deaf old Auntie."

"What if your Auntie finds out? I'd lose my job." Grace's expression was a mixture of hope and fear.

"She is not going to find out. No one will know except William and me and you and Ethan, and none of us is going to tell her. You meet Ethan at the ferry the day we leave and be at the ferry the day we are scheduled to return. It will be the same as if we were away together all the time," argued Evadne.

"Miss Vad, do you really think it would work?" Grace was imagining three days spent with Ethan, cooking for him as she used to do, going to sleep in his arms, sharing again the joys they had known together that so far had been limited to ardent kissing and touching.

"I know it will if you do as I say." Evadne stood up. "Think about it, Grace. You must make up your mind by tomorrow, because by then we will have to pack. Auntie *does* think you are going with me, you know."

"I'll talk it over with Ethan tonight," promised Grace. "Now, you'd better hurry. That Mr. Tyler don't like to let that auto of his idle, wasting gas."

Evadne laughed and picked up her coat. She was not looking forward to the evening. For one thing, William had not been invited. For another, the dinner party consisted of the Dillards, the Tylers, and a few other Nob Hill families. The only young people who would be there would be Lillie, Paul, herself, and a young Easterner who was visiting the city and in whose honor the dinner was being held.

After Evadne had left, stopping to give her aunt a good-night kiss, Grace assisted Miss Harper with her evening toilette, leaving the old lady, finally, propped up against a pile of pillows, reading. Grace went downstairs to the servants' quarters. Ethan was waiting for her in the kitchen with the cook. At the sight of her, he stood up eagerly.

Ethan Morgan was a solidly built young man with pale blue eyes and a shock of red hair. He was heavily freckled from his years at sea, and his large hands were rough-skinned. Yet, something about him, perhaps it was his Welsh ancestry, reminded Grace of the more tender and loving side of her own father.

Grace nodded to the cook and took her heavy coat from the hook behind the door. The only place that Ethan and she had to be alone was on the streets, and they took long evening walks, usually toward the construction site of the new Fairmont Hotel. Actually, the building was completed and it was due to open April 19th, the Thursday after Easter Sunday. Still, at night, no one was around, and the couple had the building to themselves. They had found a little niche, out of sight of the street and out of the cold winds that often swept the hill. It was here they shared their only moments of privacy.

This evening, they headed straight for their secret place. As soon as they reached it, Ethan took Grace in his arms, kissing her hungrily. "Oh, Love, how much longer are we going to have to meet like this?" He sighed. "Don't you know what it does to me—not to be able to hold you right, not even to be able to touch that lovely body of yours?"

"I know, Ethan. I want you, too, as much as you do me. I think of you so often in that room of yours, wondering if maybe you—well, you're not going to places like . . . like—"

"The Eye Wink Dance Hall?" he suggested. "It's you I want, Grace. If I just wanted any girl, well, I wouldn't have come looking for you like I did, would I?"

"I know, Ethan." Grace snuggled closer to him, remembering how warm and tender he had been in bed, the way his hands had touched her all over, rousing and filling her with such passion as he caressed her breasts and the soft muff of hair between her legs. What joy it had been for her to touch him, too, to feel his manhood growing so strong before he plunged it into her. "But I got an idea. Rather, Miss Vad has."

Ethan did not have to think twice about Evadne's plan. To him, it was the perfect—the only—solution, in view of the fact that Grace refused to leave her mistress until Mr. and Mrs. Harper returned. He chuckled. "I'd say that's one clever girl, Love. I don't know why you even had to think about it. It's her idea, so you can't get into any trouble. You just tell her yes, and we'll have three beautiful days together." As if to tempt her and banish any lingering doubts, he slipped his hands inside her coat to touch her breasts, searching out the tender nipples that hardened immediately under his fondling.

"Oh, Ethan!" Grace clutched him to her. "I'll do it. Yes, I'll tell Miss Vad tonight. Just think, three whole days and two nights together. Just you and me. It will be heaven."

If Grace was happy, Evadne was happier. She could hardly wait to tell William, who seemed even more pleased than he had been originally. Actually, he had suggested that Grace go with them, knowing that it was the only way. He was delighted to learn he was to have Evadne to himself.

The weather seemed to smile on the excursion too. The Saturday before Easter dawned warm and sunny. William arrived in his rented automobile at ten. Evadne and William and Grace packed the car, taking along a picnic lunch since William did not think they would arrive at the Di Corsos until almost dinner time.

Evadne promised Auntie that she would return on the afternoon of the sixteenth, in time for the opening performance of New York's Metropolitan Opera Company in *Queen of Sheba* at the Grand Opera House. Although the famous tenor, Enrico Caruso, was not appearing as Don José in *Carmen* until the following day, when Madame Olive Fremsted was to make her debut in the title role, Evadne wanted to attend both events. Though her parents' always had season tickets to the opera, this was to be Evadne's first season opening. She was as excited about going to the event with William, in fact, as she was about the excursion to Sonoma. William, who was not fond of opera, could not refuse her request to accompany her, especially since Auntie would not go because of her poor hearing.

Thus reassured, Auntie stood on the steps of the house fluttering a lace handkerchief after them. She, too, had been looking forward to the excursion. She had found San Francisco dirtier and noisier than she had remembered and Evadne a bigger responsibility than she had realized. She yearned for a few days of peace and quiet.

William glanced at Evadne sitting beside him. "We're off! No second thoughts?"

"Of course not. I am ever so happy, William." She squeezed his arm, keeping a respectable distance between them, mindful of Grace watching from the back seat.

At the ferry, Grace peered anxiously into the crowd of people taking advantage of the lovely day. "Ethan!" she called, spotting him as he ran toward the car. There was little time for introductions. Ethan had all he could do to take Grace's valise and help her out of the car before William drove onto the ferry, maneuvering carefully among other cars and horse-drawn drays.

After the car was parked, William and Evadne went to the upper deck. Evadne's green eyes were sparkling. Under the sunlight, the promontories called the Golden Gate that marked the entrance to the bay did gleam like gold. It must have been on just such a day that John C. Fremont, on a geographical survey, first saw them and gave them the classic Greek name "Chrysopylae," or golden gate.

Evadne took off her sealskin coat, holding it over her arm as she basked in the sunshine. How at home William looked, with the sun making his face appear even more bronzed and heightening the blond streaks in his hair. She smiled at him, her heart beating faster and her blood pounding excitedly at the thought of the three days ahead.

For Evadne, who had lived all her life on Nob Hill, the drive from Sausalito through the countryside was a constant marvel. The winding dirt road led over rolling hills, on whose rich grass cattle browsed lazily. At a place where willow trees provided a green dell of shade by a creek, William drew to a stop.

"Shall we picnic here?" he asked. "We can wash our hands afterward in the spring, if need be."

"What a lovely spot!" Evadne leaped out of the car. She felt like a little girl stealing an afternoon off from school.

William laughed at her pleasure, as he followed with the basket. Evadne spread a cloth, placing on it the cold chicken and cheese that cook had provided and pouring hot coffee from a jug into cups. "We should have wine," she remarked.

"There will be plenty of that later." William took his watch out of his pocket. "Remember, we have to be at the Di Corsos' by four at the latest, and we will be eating a monstrous feast then—if what I had there before was any example."

"Oh, William!" Evadne moved closer to him. "Can't we stay here for a while? It is so lovely." She kissed his cheek.

William gazed at her longingly, drawing her close to kiss her lips and wanting nothing more than to stay. "This is an Eden for an Adam and Eve," he declared.

Evadne flushed at the mention of Adam and Eve, thinking of them naked in Eden. What would William look like, playing Adam, she wondered? And would he like her Eve . . . ? "William," she murmured softly.

"Don't tempt me, Vad," he said, using her nickname for the first time. He took her hand and held it between his thighs. "Feel that. You know we should not linger."

"I'm sorry." Evadne abruptly pulled away to sit demurely on the other side of the cloth. She had let herself get carried away, and yet . . . and yet she had to admit to herself that had William done more than kiss her, she would have given in to whatever he wanted. She smiled tremulously at him. "I did not mean to tease you."

"My dear, don't you know by now that you do not have to do anything to tease me? There has been nothing that I wanted more, since the first time I saw you, than to take you in my arms and make you mine."

Evadne looked down at the remains of their lunch and began quickly to pack it carefully into the basket, not knowing what to say. His words had excited her, but they had also left a question in her mind. If William did indeed want her so much, why had he never said that he loved her?

The question nagged her the rest of the drive, making her barely aware when they entered the valley. Here the road was bordered by eucalyptus trees. William's remark that they had been imported from his native Australia made her momentarily pay attention to her surroundings.

The town of Sonoma itself was more Spanish than American. It had been one of the first capitals of the territory under Spanish and Mexican rule. It was here that the flag with the bear insignia was first raised by the Americans and their Mexican colleagues who had declared California free and asked the United States to accept it as a state. The town was centered around a plaza and had probably changed little since those days. It was mostly adobe; its whitewashed buildings had small windows, to keep the inside cool under the hot valley sun, and verandas that extended over the sidewalks to provide welcome shade.

Where Evadne and William were going was just beyond the town. William had to stop to open a wooden gate before proceeding along a twisting dirt road that led through a virgin forest into a clearing at the foot of a hill. Straight ahead was the winery, which actually consisted of caves dug into the hillside and protected by heavy wooden doors. Halfway up the hill was an elaborate house, resembling a Spanish fort, that overlooked the valley.

Mario Di Corso, having heard the car, came out to greet them, shaking William's hand and kissing Evadne's with a European flourish. "Come," he said, "the family is waiting. I will send someone down for your luggage."

Evadne was never able to straighten out all the names of the large family, which consisted of Di Corso's wife Maria, three sons, two daughters, and innumerable aunts, uncles, and cousins who wandered in and out. Fortunately, the daughters—Lucia and Marina—one a year older and one a year younger, took Evadne in hand. They led her immediately to their room, which she was to share with them, chattering gaily and asking about San Francisco while Evadne freshened up. They even helped her change from her green suit into a lightweight cotton dress with short puffed sleeves and a low, round neckline that they said was more suitable for the heat of the day. Evadne was glad that Grace, whose feelings would surely have been hurt, was not there.

The dinner was even more plentiful than William had suggested. Plates of pasta were followed by broiled brook trout from the family's own stream. Then came a whole roast lamb accompanied by more vegetables than Evadne had ever seen, after which came a splendidly rich Easter cake.

All during the dinner, the women of the family were constantly jumping up and down to clear the table and serve the next dishes, as well as pour the wine that flowed copiously, a different one with each course. After the table was cleared one last time, platters of fruit and cheese and a bottle of brandy were set out.

"Come, Evadne," Lucia whispered to her. "Let us leave the men to their talk. We will go to the kitchen."

In the kitchen, the women prepared to wash the dishes, and Evadne discovered that not only had they served the meal, they had cooked it. Mrs. Di Corso said, "Papa keeps after me to have servants, but just look at all the help I have! Besides, I think every girl should know how to cook. It is an art that can always come in handy."

"It looks like fun," Evadne told her, a little enviously. The extent of her own cooking was to put the water on to boil for tea on Sundays, when the servants had the afternoon off. A cold supper, even then, was always already prepared and ready to be served.

Once the dishes were put away, the women retired to the garden. Unlike the formal gardens Evadne was familiar with, this one was a riot of color. Roses and other flowers bloomed in masses, lending their fragrance to the air, and herbs and vegetables were planted among them. At the lower edge of the garden, which sloped toward a pool on which ducks and geese were swimming, were several tables set under a grape arbor where the family usually ate, weather permitting.

The men joined them shortly afterward, but to her dismay, Evadne had no chance to be alone with William. Perhaps the next day, she thought, for she and William were to go to the Buena Vista Vineyards.

The Di Corsos, however, were determined to provide the daughter of Nathaniel Harper with the proper chaperonage due a Nob Hill debutante. When the big car set out the next day, it was filled to overflowing. William and Di Corso had the front seat to themselves. In the back were Evadne, the two daughters, and a pair of six-year-old twin cousins.

Amid all the chattering and with the twin boys scrambling from lap to lap, Evadne had a hard time hearing Di Corso explain how the Buena Vista vineyards had been started by a

Hungarian—a Count Agoston Haraszethy—who had heard about this magnificent wine land from General Mariano Guadalupe Vallejo, after whom a street in San Francisco had been named. The count settled in the valley in 1857, but the local grapes did not appeal to his European palate. As a result, he went to Europe on a commission for the state government, which never compensated him, to collect some one hundred thousand cuttings of the three hundred best varieties of European grapes. On his return, regardless of the fact that he was not compensated, he had shared the cuttings generously with other vintners in the valley. Most of the vineyards—including Di Corso's—owed their existence to the count, for whom the viniculture soon lost its appeal. He left California for Nicaragua, to grow sugar cane.

Back at the Di Corso house again, William and his host disappeared into the wine caves, leaving Evadne with the women. She had little opportunity to be bored as she helped prepare dinner under the tutelage of Maria Di Corso. That evening, they ate under the grape arbor. Then it was early to bed, since Evadne and William planned to leave after breakfast the next morning.

In the morning, however, the car refused to start. One of the Di Corso sons, a master mechanic according to his proud father, buried his head under the car's hood but had little luck. Another son was sent into Sonoma to fetch a mechanic from the garage there. As a result, it was well into the afternoon by the time Evadne and William managed to get away. William had wanted to stay another night, but Evadne had insisted on going home—though the last part of the trip would be made in darkness—not only for the opera, but because of Auntie, who would worry, and Grace, at the ferry.

William reluctantly gave in. The entire Di Corso family gathered to wave goodbye and wish them a good journey. Once they were on the main road to Sonoma, William speeded up the car, barely slowing down to go through the town and driving almost recklessly as the road began to twist over the rolling hills beyond the valley, trying to take as much advantage of the remaining daylight as he could. Evadne kept to her side of the seat, forced to cling to the dashboard as the car took the curves without slowing down. The onset of darkness, when he had to turn on the headlamps, slowed William down.

"Vad," he said, speaking for the first time. "I hope you

realize that we will never get back before Auntie goes to bed. It would have been far better to have Di Corso send her a wire from Sonoma."

"I should have listened to you, William," Evadne admitted, a little frightened by the dark road and the loneliness of the countryside. "But it did not seem such a distance when we drove out here."

"Well, we will just have to—"

William's voice was drowned out by what sounded like an explosion at the rear of the car. The vehicle careened crazily toward a ditch, which William managed to avoid only by swerving the car to the opposite side of the road. He drew to a halt on the shoulder.

"Damn it!" he swore.

"What—what happened?" Evadne was huddled against the door where she had been thrown when the car swerved.

"A flat tire, I'm afraid." William turned off the ignition and pulled the hand brake. "I hope I'll be able to change it. At least the moon is out." He glanced up into the clear sky where bright stars twinkled and the moon cast a silvery glow over the hills.

"Is there anything I can do to help?" asked Evadne, feeling guilty.

"Not for now. Wait here," William told her, "while I see what I can do."

He was back shortly, looking worried. "My dear, I am afraid we have no choice but to spend the night here. Both rear tires have blown, and I have only one spare tire. Unless someone is on the road at this hour, we are quite stuck for the night."

Evadne stared at him, her mind not comprehending fully what he had said. "We could go back to Sonoma—"

"How? Walk? It is a good twenty miles, about as far, I would guess, as we are from the ferry. Have you any idea," he asked, forcing a smile, "how long that would take to walk in daylight, never mind at night with only the moon and the stars to guide us?"

Evadne got out of the car to look around. Now that night had fallen and they had left the Valley, the air was cool. A chill breeze made her shiver. "It's all my fault," she said dejectedly, determined not to cry, even though that was how she felt.

William smiled again, genuinely this time. He took Evadne into the shelter of his arms. "No, my dear. I knew you felt we must get back today, and I could understand the reasons. Besides, how could anyone expect to have *two* flat tires? We must have hit something I did not see on the road."

"What will we do?" Evadne nestled against him, her fear of what Auntie would say or think and her concern for Grace assuaged by the comfort of being close to him.

"Spend the night in the car, I suppose. Wait." He thought for a moment. "I remember seeing a building of some sort just as we rounded that last curve. Do you want to wait here? I'll investigate—"

"No! Don't leave me alone. I'll go with you," Evadne cried. The empty countryside and the night sounds of the crickets and the wind in the trees filled her with more fear than the Barbary Coast had.

William tried to protest, saying he would only be gone a few moments, finally giving in when he realized the extent of Evadne's fear. "Very well." He locked the car, first taking out of it their coats and a blanket that was in the trunk.

The building, which was where he had remembered seeing it, was actually a shed used to store tools. Still, it offered more comforts than the car, since one corner had a stack of hay that had been stored there when the field around it was mowed. There was also a lantern, which William lit.

"What do you say?" he asked. "We can spread the blanket over the hay. With your coat to cover you, you should be quite comfortable . . . more so than in the car."

Evadne nodded, the walls and the light from the lantern giving her more of a feeling of security than the car. "We forgot the picnic basket," she recalled suddenly. "The Di Corsos packed us some lunch and wine."

"I'll get it, if you promise to wait here. Those flimsy slippers of yours—" he looked down at the thin kid pumps, already scratched from the short walk "—are not made for walking country roads."

Evadne agreed reluctantly. She watched him leave, standing in the doorway until his figure disappeared into the darkness. The moon, so bright before, had hidden itself behind a cloud. To keep from thinking about her predicament, she examined the hut. With a sigh, she pushed the hay into a mound and draped the blanket over it to form a rude bed. As she stepped back to survey her work, she realized uneasily that there was no place for William to sleep except on the floor.

The sound of footsteps crunching on the ground outside

made her jump. One hand pressed against her pounding heart, she backed into a corner, sure that William could not have returned in such a short time. A whimper escaped from her as the steps drew closer.

"Evadne!" The soft call penetrated the roaring waves of fear that had filled her ears like surf on a beach.

"William!" She ran to embrace him. "I was so afraid that it might not be you!"

"Who else would be fool enough to be on the road at this hour?" He put his free arm around her. "Don't worry, my love. We will be quite safe here until morning."

Evadne gazed into his eyes, dark and mysterious in the lantern light. He had called her his love!

"Yes, of course." She took the basket from him, opening it. "Do you know, I am quite hungry," she exclaimed in surprise.

The Di Corso's had provided them with a more than adequate supper. There were thick sandwiches of crusty home-baked bread filled with cold lamb and home-smoked ham, several slabs of cheese, fresh fruit, and two bottles of their finest wine. Even glasses had been provided, the thick glasses used by the Italian families on Telegraph Hill and not the fine crystal used on the Di Corso table.

They ate, sitting side by side on the pile of hay. After they had finished, Evadne leaned against William, a glass of wine in her hand. He put his arm around her, holding her close as his lips brushed her cheek.

"Why don't you take that damned corset, or whatever you call it, off?" he suggested. He added quickly: "You will be able to sleep much more comfortably without it. I'll wait outside, if you like."

"In a minute." Evadne hesitated. "I am much too comfortable to move right now. Besides," she held up her glass, "I still have some wine left." She sipped it slowly, trying to make it last.

William put his glass in the basket and took her now-empty glass from her fingers. His lips sought hers as he lay back on the hay, pulling her gently with him.

The sleepiness that the wine had inspired in Evadne disappeared in the pounding of her blood. Lying so close to him, his hands gently exploring her breasts, she felt a throbbing fire mounting in her veins until her whole body was burning with desire for him. Her mouth pressed hungrily to his, she gave herself up to the pleasure his hands excited in her. She had left the jacket of her suit off, and William was undoing the buttons of her blouse, seeking the ties to the corselet.

"William, no!" She tried to protest, but the protest was unconvincing even to her own ears. All the desire she had felt in his presence since the first day they had met seemed to build up to the moment that she felt his hands on her naked breasts. Her body arched in longing. His lips touched her breasts. Her nipples hardened with pleasure, a pleasure she had never before known, and she moaned with joy, protesting now as William stood still holding her close.

"Shall I help you, my love?" he asked, caressing her body.

Evadne knew what he meant, what he wanted, knew, too, that she should resist him with all her might—but her mother's teachings and cautions were overwhelmed by his presence. With quick fingers, she finished the undressing he had started, all the while watching him as he took off his own clothes. His deep chest was as bronzed as his face, the curly hair as mixed with golden lights as the hair on his head. His lower body was pale, the hair between his thighs a dark shadow as she forced herself to look at his manhood.

William gave her no chance to examine him further. His eyes had taken in the loveliness of the strong young body that he caressed with practiced hands. He picked her up, laying her down lightly on the makeshift bed, his hands fondling her thighs as his mouth sought out her breasts once more. Evadne kissed his head, her own hands tentatively touching his body, feeling the strength of the broad shoulders and gradually reaching out for the rest of him. He turned on his side, one of his hands slipping between her legs to touch her most intimate parts, his other hand enclosing one of her hands around his manhood, helping her massage it.

William made no attempt to force her. When he heard her breath coming faster between her parted lips, he asked softly: "Do you want me now, my love?"

Any will to resist him had vanished long ago under his touch. "Yes," she whispered eagerly, not knowing what to expect, what was to come. "Yes . . . I want all of you."

William kneeled over her, half crouching, one hand on his manhood as he slowly guided it into her. The sharp pain of his entry sent a shiver through her body, and she tried to pull away. It was too late. He had plunged deep inside her. Holding her close, his body atop hers, he drove again and again into her, gently and slowly, until gradually her pain gave way to ecstasy. Filled with passion, her breath coming faster and faster, Evadne's body rose to meet his. Their bodies were locked together, their hips moving as one, their breathing quickening until William moaned. He gave a last urgent drive deep inside her, his motion quickening and then, still holding her close, his body gradually relaxed.

At first, Evadne thought he had gone to sleep. "William? William," she whispered. "I . . . I love you."

He rolled off of her, raising himself on one elbow to look at her face glowing in the lantern light. "I know. I love you too."

"Tell me, tell me again." Sudden awareness of what she had done flooded her. Tears formed in the corners of her eyes.

"Evadne, my love, I love you. Didn't I tell you that the very first time I saw you? I—"

"You said you *wanted* me," Evadne finished. "Wanting is not the same as loving, is it?"

"In a way. But, all right." He kissed her mouth, her eyes, her nose, her breasts. "I love you, darling, and as soon as your parents come back, I will ask your father's permission to marry you. I wanted to before he left, but there was so little time." He paused, seeing the startled expression on her face. "Don't you want to marry me?"

Evadne laughed, flinging her arms around his neck. "I think you should ask me first, but yes, yes, I want to marry you."

The door of the hut banged open in a sudden gust of wind that brought with it the chill night air. Evadne shivered, nestling closer to the warmth of his body. William managed to slide the blanket from under them, to cover them. Evadne smiled sleepily, unaware of the hay tickling her skin or the sweetness of its scent. She fell asleep, aware only of William's arms around her.

The sound of birds singing awakened her. She stretched lazily, reaching out for William . . . but he was gone. Wide awake and frightened, she sat up, calling: "William, William!"

He appeared, dressed in his trousers and shirt, in the doorway. "Good morning, my love. How do you feel?"

"Fine!" She stretched again, and was suddenly aware of a soreness between her legs. "A little . . . little—" She stopped, not sure whether it was proper to tell him and not wanting to hurt his feelings—not when he had told her he loved her and wanted to marry her.

"A little sore? Don't worry. It's only natural the first time." William sat down beside her on the hay. She noticed then that he was holding a wine bottle. "I went to see if there was any water near by, but I am afraid we will have to use this other bottle of wine."

"The wine?" She did not understand, for a moment, what he meant.

"You were a virgin, my darling," he reminded her, with a grin. "Of course, it should be champagne."

Evadne blushed, suddenly ashamed, and covered her body with the blanket as William opened the wine. He took a napkin from the basket.

"You have nothing to be ashamed of. Here." He pulled the blanket back. "You are so beautiful, my love."

With hands tender and loving, he gently washed the stains from her body, washing her with the wine and drying her with the napkin. "Now you have been properly christened," he told her, bending down to kiss her thighs.

"Darling!" Evadne clasped him to her, her body warming with desire from his touch.

He disentangled himself, smiling at her, and stood reluctantly. "You had better dress, or I will not be able to resist you. We must get back to the car and see what we can do. Perhaps we can catch someone passing by."

Chapter VII

DAWN HAD JUST BROKEN WHEN THEY ARRIVED BACK AT THE car—along with a farmer astride a huge Belgian plow horse. He looked at them in surprise until he saw the flat tires, and then he understood their predicament. Because of the distance of his farm from town, he kept a reserve spare tire for his own car in his barn, and he offered to sell it to William. While William prepared to change one tire on the car, using his own spare, the farmer set off for the barn, which was next to the farmhouse. The high hill behind the hut where they'd spent the night had kept William and Evadne from seeing the lights of the farmhouse the night before.

By the time the first tire was changed, the farmer was back. With his help, the second tire was changed in no time.

As the farmer waved goodbye and they started on their way again, Evadne turned to William, her worries of the night before returning with greater intensity. "What are we going to tell Auntie?"

"The truth—that the car broke down. There is no sense in lying about it. As to where we spent the night—" He smiled reassuringly. "You slept on the back seat and I, in the front. That is all there is to it," he declared.

"Will she—anyone—believe it?" Evadne shifted uneasily, watching the hills unfold ahead of the car. "Oh, William!

Poor Auntie must be out of her mind with worry. Grace, too," she added. "I wonder what she did when we did not return?"

"Darling, I will be with you," William reassured her. "We can only take things as they come. Anticipating the worst is not going to help."

Evadne had to agree. Yet, the closer they got to Sausalito, which turned out to be nearer than they had thought, the more apprehensive Evadne became. All too soon they were on the ferry, then across the Bay and climbing the last street to Nob Hill. Evadne was filled with dread when she saw Grace standing outside the house, obviously—and anxiously—waiting for them. To Evadne's relief, Grace was wearing her uniform. At least Auntie hadn't dismissed her.

"Miss Vad!" she wailed, her eyes red and her mouth trembling. "Thank the Lord you're home and all right."

The statement for some reason filled Evadne with dread. She stared at Grace. "The car . . ." she began to explain and stopped.

"It's awful," Grace cried. "Absolutely terrible."

Evadne looked at William, who took her hand. Grace's agitation seemed extreme, and she did not seem to be interested in what had happened to Evadne.

When the maid broke into tears, William said firmly, "Pull yourself together, Grace. What is it?"

"Old Mr. Tyler! He's been waiting over an hour," she sobbed.

"Mr. Tyler!" Fear rose in Evadne's throat, almost choking her. What was Paul's father doing here? "Oh, William!" She ran toward the front door, leaving William and Grace to follow.

Henry Tyler was in the library. His eyes were bloodshot with weariness and he was unshaven. He looked at Evadne, opening his mouth to say something and then shutting it when he saw William. Finally, as Evadne stood watching him, too afraid to speak, he said, "Please . . . come here and sit down, Evadne."

"William . . . ?" she stood her ground, appealing to William for support.

As William put his arm around Evadne, Tyler grimaced. "Very well," he said. "I don't know how to tell you this. I had a wire early this morning and came here at once. You were . . . were not here." Before Evadne could open her mouth to explain, he went on brusquely, as if unable to stop now that he had begun talking. "I am afraid it was bad news about . . . about your parents. They . . . they are dead, killed in an automobile accident—"

William caught Evadne as she staggered against him, picking her up and carrying her to the couch. The news had shocked him, too, as had the way Tyler had presented it. He looked at the banker, who was standing there as if he had something else to say.

"Is that all?" William demanded.

Tyler set his jaw, an angry glint in his eyes at the way William seemed to have taken over. "I had better come back later, after she has recovered, when we can talk."

Evadne, stunned and numb, heard him and started to sit up. "Mama and Papa . . . both of them?" she asked unbelievingly.

"I am afraid so." Tyler glanced at William. "There is . . . more, but I can return later," he suggested again.

"More?" Evadne laughed harshly. "What more could there be?"

Tyler told her, but Evadne only half understood what he was saying. Too numb to cry, she held William's hand, trying to comprehend what the banker was saying, but the words seemed to glance off of her. Her father, according to Tyler, had been heavily in debt. The major reason for the trip East had been to try to borrow money from New York bankers, since the San Francisco banks had refused to lend him any more. As soon as word of his death became public, as it surely would once the newspapers heard of it, the banks—including Tyler's—would be forced to call in their notes. In short, Evadne was destitute. Even the house would have to be sold to cover her father's debts.

Evadne, who had not as yet absorbed the news about her parents, was bewildered by the suggestion that she would not even have a home. Tyler was no help; his voice went on and on, enumerating her father's losses and grating on her with its insensitivity to her loss.

"Mr. Tyler!" Evadne's voice was sharp, covering her inner turmoil. "Please . . . please leave now."

"Yes, yes." The man broke off abruptly. "I must get to the bank to see what can be done to save something for the bank. My wife or son will stop by later to see to you."

He left hurriedly, eager to be gone. William put his arms around Evadne. "My dearest . . ."

"Auntie," she whispered, her hand taking his and holding it tightly. "Grace, what about Auntie?"

"Miss Vad, after the last ferry yesterday, I come back here, thinking maybe I . . . I'd missed you. Anyhow, I told Miss Harper that we was late and you'd gone directly to the opera. I thought she'd guess then, but she didn't notice. Then, this morning, when Mr. Tyler came, he wouldn't speak to anyone but you."

"I must see her . . . tell her." Evadne rubbed her eyes. As yet, she hadn't shed a tear.

"Do you want me to go with you, my love?" William offered.

"No, I must do it myself." Evadne looked at him, her eyes tender and filled with love.

"Do you want me to stay?"

"Oh, William! I don't know—" She rested her head against his shoulder.

"Then let me go back to my hotel and have a bath and change. Perhaps there is something I can do." He turned to Grace. "Draw a hot bath for your mistress, Grace, and try to get her to lie down as soon as she has spoken to her aunt."

Grace nodded, hurrying off. When they were alone again, William drew Evadne into his arms, kissing her lightly. "Do not worry about anything, my love. If need be, I will take care of Tyler for you."

"Thank you, William. You . . . you will come back?" she asked again, wanting to hear him say it.

He tried to reassure her as much as he could before Grace returned to say that Auntie was asking to see her. Kissing William goodbye, Evadne climbed the stairs with a heavy heart.

Auntie had just finished breakfast and was sitting by the bay window, fully clothed in her usual neat black dress with its white lace collar. "What is the matter, Evadne? Please don't tell me nothing is—why did cook bring my breakfast instead of Grace? Why is everyone whispering and tiptoeing around? I can hear well enough when I want to," she added. "And I can smell well enough to smell bad news in the air."

Evadne went to her aunt, sitting herself on the window seat and taking her aunt's hands in hers. Briefly, as gently as she could, she told the little old lady about the tragic accident.

"Poor child!" Auntie reached out to embrace her. "You have never known what it is to lose someone you love, and now you have lost both your parents at once. I would it had been me instead, for I am old, but God's will is God's will, Evadne."

The words and her aunt's sympathy evoked the tears that the girl had been unable to shed. She had thought that she would be comforting Auntie, not that Auntie would be comforting her.

"Oh, Auntie!" Evadne buried her face in the old woman's shoulder.

"There, there, child. They are together in Heaven, which is what they would have wanted," the old lady soothed her. "At least you are well taken care of—"

Evadne shook her head. "There is nothing left." Haltingly, she told the rest of the story as best she could.

"What a nasty man that Mr. Tyler is!" exclaimed the old lady. "Surely he could have waited! But you need not worry, child. I have money, more than enough for my needs, and it will go to you now instead of charity as I had planned. Oh why—why didn't Nathaniel come to me?" Still holding Evadne, the woman glanced up at Grace, who had timidly entered the room.

"Grace, take Evadne to her room. Let her have a nice hot bath and lie down."

"Yes, Mum," Grace agreed, having already prepared the bath. "I'll bring her some hot tea, too."

"Good girl," Auntie nodded. "Now, when that horrible Mr. Tyler comes back, Grace, I want you to send him to me. He is not to bother the poor child again. In fact, she is not to be disturbed. . . ." Auntie paused. "That nice young man of hers, I think it would help if he were to come here this afternoon. Will you get a message to him?"

Grace nodded. There was no need to tell Auntie that William already knew, or that Evadne had been with him all night. "Come, Miss Vad," Grace urged. "Take that bath now."

Evadne went to her room. She let Grace help her undress and then sank gratefully into the hot tub, taking no pleasure in the sight of her body as she had in the past. How she wished William were here now, to caress her until her fears fell away.

Only when the water cooled did Evadne leave the bath, but she was to have no rest. Grace told her that Paul Tyler was downstairs, insisting on seeing her.

"What does he want?" Evadne sank down on the bed.

Paul, of all people, was the last person she wanted to see.

"I don't know, Miss Vad, but he says it's important and that he'll wait till you do see him." Grace looked at her mistress anxiously, sure that Paul's visit meant more bad news to come.

"Can't you tell him I'm resting?" Evadne pleaded.

"I did that already. He said to wake you, or he'd sit there and wait all day," replied the maid helplessly.

"Oh well!" Evadne got up. "I might as well get it over with. Get me the black dress."

Evadne had only one black dress that she wore rarely. Mrs. Harper had insisted that black was not suitable for young girls, though it might be fashionable.

She dressed quickly, buttoning the front of the dress while Grace brushed her hair, tying it back simply with a black ribbon.

"Grace," Evadne said quietly, "you are to stay with me, regardless of what Mr. Paul says. I will not be left alone with him for a single second. Do you understand?"

Grace did not understand at all. Evadne and Paul had been friends for years and the request was incomprehensible, but Grace agreed. It must, she thought, have something to do with what old Mr. Tyler had said that morning.

As a result, Evadne entered the library with Grace close on her heels. When Evadne sat down on a chair near the fireplace, the maid took her place behind her.

Paul, who was standing by the windows, glared at Grace before going to Evadne. He looked down at her, at the set face and the hands clasped tightly in her lap. "I am sorry about your parents. The rest—"

Evadne would not let him continue. "Thank you for your sympathy, Paul. If that is all, would you please go? I really want to be alone," the girl answered.

He held out his hand to touch her cheek, but she turned her head away. The gesture aroused his anger. Gritting his teeth, he took a chair opposite her, where she had to look at him. "Would you leave us alone, Grace?" he asked.

"I have asked Grace to stay with me, Paul." Evadne's green eyes flashed in the paleness of her face. "Now, what is so important that you insist on seeing me at such a time?"

He hesitated, glowering at Grace, then looked at Evadne. "You know how I feel about you. I thought you might want me here. I don't want you hurt—"

"Paul, for heaven's sake, haven't I been through enough? Say what you have to say," Evadne demanded. "If you have come to propose . . . at such a time—"

"Very well." Paul's fair skin flushed with anger. "It's about that Hopkins fellow."

"William?" Whatever Evadne had expected might be on Paul's mind, the last thing was William. The name struck her sharply, driving like a knife into her heart. Fear rose in her throat.

"Yes." Paul noted the shock in her face with satisfaction. "I have been doing a little research, you might say. The Hall of Records here and at Sacramento are quite complete. There is no record of any kind of a John Hopkins—William's father—in either place, much less any listing of him among the relatives of old Mark Hopkins. We have all been taken in. William Hopkins is an impostor, to put it bluntly. Oh, the letter of credit is good enough, at least for the present. . . ."

Evadne stared at him, feeling faint but refusing to show any sign of weakness before Paul. "I am sure there must be some mistake."

"No, there isn't, Vad. I have checked and rechecked. I even," he added with relish, "talked to some of those fellows down in Sydneytown—the Australians. They know about a John Hopkins, all right. It seems he was accused of murder and . . . various other crimes in the Australian goldfields. He was acquitted and later disappeared, but he had quite a reputation as a confidence man, always ready to turn a fast dollar. In short, this William Hopkins is a cad, trading on the Hopkins name, and probably a fortune hunter. Once he hears that you are no longer a wealthy heiress, but a—"

"An impoverished lady of quality?" finished Evadne. Her mind was reeling. In desperation, she reached for the memory of William's declaration of love, for those precious moments of ecstasy in which their bodies had been joined. Surely, if he did not love her, he could never have acted with such loving tenderness and desire.

"You put it more delicately than I had intended to." Paul was taking a perverse delight in giving her his news. "At any rate, you can be sure that you have seen the last of him, for I have made sure he knows everything. Before coming here, I left a note for him at his hotel."

Evadne glared at him. "And you call yourself my friend! You say you love me! Yet, at such a time, when I need all those who truly care about me, you insist on bringing me such news."

Paul shrugged. "I agree that it might have waited. But, I hoped that hearing the story first from me would soften the blow that will come when this Hopkins disappears . . . perhaps is even arrested for misrepresenting himself."

Evadne wanted to stand up, but her knees felt weak. She clasped her hands more tightly in her lap, the knife in her heart turning again. From the depths of her, she summoned a strength that she had not known she had. "This is still my house, Paul. Now, I ask you to leave—as I had to ask your father to leave. Get out!" she said firmly, color rising in her pale cheeks.

"Very well." Paul did not argue. "I will leave for now, but I will be back once you have had the chance to come to your senses." He picked up the hat and coat that were lying over the arm of a sofa. "Like it or not, Vad, you are going to need me to take care of you."

The words stung Evadne, and her pride came to the fore. "I can take care of myself, and I will prove it. Grace," she appealed to the maid who was still standing behind the chair, "show Mr. Paul out."

"There is no need for that." Paul went to the door of the room, pausing to glance once more at Evadne before leaving.

"Oh, Miss Vad!" Grace came around the chair, wringing her hands. "Do you think it's true? Mr. William seemed, I mean, he will be back, won't he?"

"Yes, I . . . I know he will." Evadne struggled to her feet. "I am going to lie down now, Grace. Please tell the staff that I will not be disturbed for anyone—except Mr. William. As soon as he arrives . . ."

"I'll come and tell you, Miss Vad," the maid promised, her face wrinkled with worry as Evadne left the room.

Evadne maintained her composure until she was alone in her room. Then she sank down on the floor next to the bed, cradling her head in her arms. This time the tears poured from her eyes. William, William! she cried silently. Please hurry back to me!

She struggled to her feet to take off the black dress and put on a soft, silk lounge robe. There was no sense in lying down; her mind would not let her rest. She was more filled with guilt at being alive when her parents were dead than with grief. She wandered about her room, touching a music box that had been a present from them and opening it. The strains of the "Toreador Song" from *Carmen* tinkled forth, and she hurriedly closed the box. That was the opera she had been so eager to see with William. What did the opera or Caruso mean now?

When the doorbell rang, her heart leaped. She put her ear against the door, listening for William's voice. It was old Mr. Tyler, however, and she heard her aunt talking to him.

Finally, Evadne lay down on the bed, closing her eyes. Grace found her there, crying into her pillow.

"Miss Vad!" The maid sat down on the edge of the bed, patting her mistress's shoulder. "Don't cry so. It's going to be all right. Your Auntie—"

"First Mama and Papa, now William," Evadne gasped through her tears. "It cannot be true—what Paul said!"

"You gotta be brave, like you were with Mr. Tyler—and Mr. Paul. Huh," Grace sneered, "I didn't think Mr. Paul was as sneaky as that."

"Mr. Tyler!" Evadne's tears stopped. "He was here again. What did Auntie say to him?"

Grace had to giggle in spite of her sorrow and pity for the girl. "You should have heard her, wouldn't hardly let the old bast—buzzard get a word in edgewise. Told him he was a cruel, money-grubbing thief, that he should have come to her first, not you, so she could have softened the blow of such terrible news. Then, she told him she was going to take care of everything, and he better get the facts and figures to her and her lawyers afore he did anything else."

Evadne smiled. How wrong she had been to consider Auntie a vague little old lady. "Where is she now?"

"In her room, writing to her lawyers in Sausalito. It's kinda funny, in the library, talking to old man Tyler, she was sharp as anything," Grace mused. "But she had to ask me the date. She didn't even know it was Tuesday, much less April seventeenth."

"I guess, at Auntie's age, days of the week and dates don't mean much, Grace," Evadne pointed out. She sat up, recalling again that Caruso was to debut that night, and immediately forgetting it when she saw the concern in Grace's face. She tried to smile, wanting to take the maid's mind off all that had happened . . . to stop thinking about it herself.

"Tell me, Grace, you and your Ethan . . . ?"

"Miss Vad, it was paradise." The little maid sighed, the

worry lines vanishing. "Three days in his arms, us loving one another, me cooking and caring for him—"

Grace stopped as the bell rang and hurried to the door, her face eager as she pressed her ear to a panel. Almost immediately, her face fell, telling Evadne better than words that the caller was not William. "It's Mrs. Dillard and Miss Lillie," she said. "Do you want to—?"

"No." Evadne shook her head firmly. "I know they mean well, but I cannot listen to any more today, about . . . about my parents or . . . or William," she managed to say. "I don't think Auntie should be bothered either. Ask her, although you can easily tell them that we are resting."

Grace nodded and left the room. Alone, Evadne gave up any pretense of fortitude. Where, oh where, was William, her heart cried. What was it he had said about always keeping his promises? Surely nothing could have happened to him too! She had to know. If he could not or would not come to her, she must go to him.

Grace returned to tell her that the Dillards had gone, after asking Grace to extend their sympathy and their hospitality to Evadne.

"You are sure that there has been no word from William?" Evadne asked.

"No, Miss Vad. You know I'd tell you," the girl said reproachfully. "Do you want me to send a message?"

Evadne shook her head. "Go to my mother's room, Grace. She has a black suit, similar to my green one, that I know she did not take with her. Bring me that and her big hat with the blackbird wings and veil."

"Miss Vad! What are you up to now?" Grace stared at her mistress, her eyes wide with apprehension.

"I intend to put the suit on later. I will go to Auntie's room for an early supper. If William has not come by then and there has been no word from him, call the chauffeur and tell him to have the car ready," Evadne ordered.

Despite Grace's protests, Evadne stuck to her decision. She and Auntie both did their best to eat and comfort one another. Then, while Auntie was preparing for bed, Evadne dressed herself in her mother's clothes. The two women had been close enough in build so the fit was good. The black of the suit and the hat made Evadne seem much older, especially when she dropped the veil. Grace had to admit that even a close friend would have difficulty recognizing her mistress.

Once she was in the car, Evadne's confidence began to fade. Telling herself not to give in to panic or even to admit that William might already have abandoned San Francisco and her, she instructed the chauffeur to take the route to the St. Francis she knew William always took, to avoid missing him. To be safe, she had told Grace that if William arrived while she was gone or there was word from him, he was to be informed that she was waiting for him at the St. Francis.

Refusing to think any further, Evadne got out of the car at the hotel, sending the chauffeur back to the house in case he was needed there. Then, head held high, Evadne entered the lobby, going straight to the desk.

"Mr. William Hopkins, please," she told the desk clerk. He looked at her with a practiced eye, measuring her respectability. The combination of the black suit, her sealskin coat, and the hat, plus Evadne's haughty bearing, impressed him.

"Mr. Hopkins is in the men's bar, I believe," he said.

"In that case, I would like to have someone take him a message." She took the piece of stationery and the pen the clerk offered her. Thinking quickly, she wrote, "William, I am in the lobby. Evadne." Folding the paper, she put it in an envelope and handed it to a bellboy the desk clerk had summoned.

There was nothing more she could do now, except wait. Her knees were beginning to shake from fear and relief, and she looked around for a chair, finding one far enough from the reception desk so the clerk could not see her, yet near enough so she could see anyone approaching the desk, for she had no idea where the men's bar was. Each moment seemed an hour, as she surveyed the lobby, waiting and wondering whether William could have gone out without saying anything to the clerk, whether he would come to her.

Then she saw him. Her note in his hand, he was moving in the direction of the desk. She got to her feet, hurrying toward him. "William!" she called.

He turned. His eyes found her, passed by, swung back in startled recognition. "Evadne!" He came to her, taking her hands. "What are you doing here? Didn't I say—?"

"But you didn't come, and Paul—" She stopped, unable to go on, the tears choking her.

"Paul. I see." William regarded her thoughtfully. "So you came here to talk to me?"

"I had to know if it were true . . . to hear it from you."
Evadne began to tremble with emotion, a mixture of love and
fear and longing.

"Oh, my dear!" William glanced around, looking for a
place where they could talk quietly. It was the dinner hour,
however, and the lobby was crowded. "We cannot talk here."

"Can't we go to your room?" Evadne suggested, desperate, now that she was with him, for his reassurance.

"We could, but—" William looked at her, at the green eyes
frightened behind the security of the veil and the quivering
lips. "The hell with respectability," he muttered. He took her
arm and led her leisurely toward the elevators, as if they were
man and wife.

Once they were in his suite, he closed the door into the
bedroom before helping her off with her coat. "Evadne, I will
tell you everything you want to know, if you will be patient a
little longer. I must return to the bar for a few moments and
then I will be back. Do you trust me?"

Evadne nodded, and he squeezed her hands. After he had
gone, she glanced about the room. It was elegantly but stiffly
furnished, comfortable in an impersonal way. Too restless to
sit down, she walked toward the mirror to take off her hat and
smooth her hair. Noting how pale she was, she pinched her
cheeks trying to give herself a little color. She was turning
from the mirror when William returned.

He smiled. "Fashionable as that hat is," he nodded toward
it, "I am glad that I do not have to talk to a veil. Come here."
He sat down on a settee, patting the place beside him. As
soon as she was seated, he took her in his arms, kissing her
gently. "Dear, dear girl. I am sorry for keeping you waiting,
but I did not realize the time."

Evadne's body quivered at his touch. She forgot everything
in the longing rising in her. "William . . . my darling." Her
arms went around his neck and she kissed him with utter
abandon.

It was William who drew away. "First, I think you had
better tell me what it was Paul said that brought you here."

She told him quickly, watching his face, noting the wry
smile when she spoke about his father. "Then—then Paul said
that you were a fortune hunter, a confidence man. That you
were . . . were after my money and that I would never see
you again now that I am . . . destitute."

"Is that all?" William gave a short laugh. He got up and

went to a table where there was a brandy decanter and several glasses. Pouring the liquor into two glasses, he came back to her, handing her a glass. "I think you need this right now."

"But . . . is it true?" she asked, taking the brandy.

"Yes and no," William admitted. "First, as to your money, I never gave it a thought. Regardless of what Paul said, or may think, I do have plenty of my own, though I am not in the same class as some of the Nob Hill nabobs." He took her hands. "I love you, Evadne. I love you just as much now—more, in fact—as I did yesterday. If I had my way, we would be married tonight, so I could protect you better over the next few weeks. As to the rest. . . ." William put his hand under her chin to raise her face until their eyes met. "I fear Paul is more or less correct."

"You lied?" Evadne looked at him, puzzled.

"Not exactly. My father was . . . well, you would have had to know him to understand. He left England after running through a fortune from *his* father and came to California to recoup. I am afraid that he did pass himself off as a relative of Mark Hopkins, who then had a successful hardware business in Sacramento, to get credit. Hopkins, however, caught up with him, and my father decided it would be politic to go to Australia. He did strike gold there, just as I told you. There was no murder charge, but mining camps are rough places, and there was a brawl in which a man was killed—an Irishman. My father, being English, was not particularly popular. He was never charged with any crime, however. As far as his 'disappearing' goes," William chuckled, "good old Dad simply decided he was wasting his talents in the gold-fields—he never did like hard labor. He took his gold and went into business in Sydney, as J. W. Hopkins, buying up land from farmers who wanted to go after gold. Whether it was all honorable or not, he was not the only one, and land was one thing he did know something about."

Evadne nodded thoughtfully. "But you did tell Mr. Tyler that you were related to Mark Hopkins."

"No. He assumed it, because of the name, and I—well, I let it ride, thinking it would not hurt anyone. Besides, he was such a pompous ass about it. But it was his idea, not mine." William smiled at her.

Evadne had to smile back. "Then you would have come back?"

"Naturally. I had hoped—" He took her hands. "I am sorry, my love. What I have been doing today had nothing to do with me. I called that banker cousin of Mario Di Corso's, trying to get more information about your father. His bank will not call in its loan, at least not until we know exactly where matters stand with the estate. I had a little luck with some of the other bankers, too, although Tyler—" William's mouth twisted "—had gotten to them first. Your home is safe for now, however."

"There is Auntie, too," Evadne said.

"I had forgotten about her!" William exclaimed. "How is the old girl taking it?"

"She has been marvelous." Evadne related what the old lady had said and done, finishing with, "Grace told me Mr. Tyler did not waste any time leaving."

"Good for Auntie! But now that you know everything, Vad, tell me: Were you really so worried that you threw all caution to the winds to come here to find me?" A teasing smile lighted his eyes.

She nodded. "I suppose it was silly, but . . . but—" Tears came to her eyes. "I was so frightened. If I had lost you, too. . . ." She put down her glass and threw herself in his arms. "Hold me, William . . . hold me close and make me feel alive again. I feel as if a part of me had—had. . . ."

"Evadne . . . my beautiful girl." His arms embraced her as his hands caressed her body. In her hurry to dress and because her mother's suit was slightly large on her, she had left off her corselet. Her body offered no resistance to his touch.

He touched her breast, rousing her nipple through the fabric of her blouse and thin chemise. Memory of the passion he had stirred in her—was it only the night before?—made her shiver.

"It seems like a year ago, darling William," she murmured.

"Last night?" he asked, understanding at once, marveling at the desire in the girl. Her green eyes were emerald dark and sparkling with the longing filling her.

"William . . . don't leave me tonight. I don't want to be alone," Evadne begged.

"Vad," William's hand left her breast. "Do you know what you are doing? You have been through hell today—"

"And I, I want—" Evadne hesitated, recalling Grace's description of her three days with Ethan. "I want . . . paradise tonight."

William looked into her face, wanting her, yet not wanting to take advantage of her. "You are sure?"

In answer, her arms circled his neck, pressing him close to her. She kissed him, her tongue parting his lips. William needed to know no more. He picked her up, carrying her toward the bedroom. He opened the door with one hand and carried her inside to the bed.

"We shall have a proper bed tonight, my love," he whispered, beginning to undress her.

When she lay naked before him, he took off his own clothes, almost ripping them off in his hunger for her. Despite his eagerness, he did not immediately plunge into her. First, he kissed her—her mouth, the mounds of her breasts, the pink nipples that grew red and hard between his lips. As she moaned with joy, he leaned down to kiss the softness inside her thighs, including the most intimate parts of her.

"William!" she cried. "My love, my darling!" She drew him up to lie beside her, fondling him, admiring the strength of his body, of the manhood now swollen between his thighs.

Her thighs parted and her hips rose, inviting him to enter her. She cried out when he did, satiating herself in the ecstasy of their union; her body moving up to meet his with every stroke. If she had been aroused the night before, she was now completely immersed in the need to fulfill that desire. Her hands pressed against his hips as her body arched upward. His motions grew faster until he could no longer hold back. . . .

Evadne held him close, refusing to release him until his manhood, soft and small now, slipped from inside her. Even then, she nestled against him, clinging to the protection of his body. Her eyes opened, and she smiled at him.

"I love you, my darling."

"I love you, too, my sweet, sweet girl." His mouth twitched in a half smile. "I loved you before, and now I love you so much more. You are a mad, passionate creature." He chuckled. "Poor Paul."

"Poor Paul!" She sat up, picking up a pillow to beat him. "How can you think of him at a time like this!"

William laughed and pulled her close again. "You are even more exciting when you are angry. Be careful or you will have me aroused again before you know it!"

"I think I would like that," she said complacently.

"I do believe that you are insatiable," he said, kissing her mouth to stop her from answering. When she was quiet in his arms, he said, "Now I had better get you home."

"Not yet," Evadne pleaded. "Let me stay with you a while longer. Grace knows where I am, and Auntie went to bed hours ago." She was afraid of being alone again, of losing William in some catastrophe as she had lost her parents.

He hesitated. "I am thinking of you, Vad. For you to be seen leaving the hotel at midnight or later—"

She giggled. "In that hat and veil? You yourself did not recognize me at first." Then, she remembered what had brought her there and sobered. "Oh, William, hold me for just a little while longer."

"For a little while," he agreed, taking her in his arms again.

Evadne stretched her body against his, feeling the strength of him, the hair on his chest tickling her breasts and nipples.

"How fantastic you are," she murmured as she fell asleep.

Chapter VIII

THUNDER ROLLED, CRASHING IN THE DISTANCE. EVADNE, LYING in William's arms, stirred—and awakened with a gasp. It was not thunder but a roaring, grinding crescendo of noise, like a giant locomotive rushing down on the room.

The room itself was a ship, rising and dancing as if swept upon the crest of a tidal wave, then dropped to the bottom of a trough only to rise again, higher, then drop even lower. The roar subsided in the wild ringing of church bells, sounding like every belfry in the city gone mad.

As the room came to rest, Evadne held frantically to William. "William—! William—it's an earthquake!"

He had no time to answer. The world came alive again, the room shaking and dancing to the accompaniment of a cacophony of creaking, rasping sounds. The magnificent hotel had taken on a life of its own. Its windows shattered. Its cornices —and those of adjoining buildings—and chimneys fell in an explosive succession of crashing masonry. Gradually the undulations and the noise ceased, leaving silence—a silence so complete that it seemed like the end of the world.

William stumbled from the bed to draw the curtains. Dawn had broken, and the rising sun showed the destruction outside. Across the square, a brick facade had fallen into the street. All around were tumbled piles of brick and stone.

Evadne joined him at the window. Her eyes found the Victory of the Dewey Monument, still proud and free on its pillar. Other than that, it was a Union Square she did not know. Despite the fallen facades, most of the buildings were still standing, although all the distinguishing cornices and chimneys were scattered on the streets, resembling the wild disarray of a willful child's toys. Evadne drew closer to William. Together, they surveyed the room.

A pier mirror, gold-frame and glass, lay in a pile of shattered and splintered fragments. Toiletries that had been set out on a chest had smashed to the floor, along with a pitcher of water and its glasses. Even a Queen Anne chair at the desk had been shaken into an unrecognizable stack of kindling.

The floor undulated again with an aftershock. "We must get out of here," Evadne whispered. William nodded agreement.

Evadne had never known how quickly she could dress. Within seconds she was in her skirt, her blouse half buttoned, her coat over her shoulders. William had pulled on his trousers and a shirt.

As Evadne started to leave, he stopped her, looking at her feet. "For God's sake, put on your shoes, my love."

Evadne found her shoes filled with splinters of glass from the windows. William took them from her, shaking them out and running his hand inside to make sure there were no glass fragments left. His own shoes had been far enough from the windows to avoid the same problem. Still only half dressed, they hurried into the sitting room. It, too, looked as if it had been picked up and shaken. William unlocked the door, turning the handle. The door refused to budge, until he pulled it. Then it opened with a protesting groan.

The corridor was filled with people. Some were rushing toward the elevators, others dashed for the stairs. No one was screaming and everyone was so intent on getting out of the building that they were not even talking to one another. If either William or Evadne gave a thought to her presence being noticed, the worry was in vain. In the silence, which in its way was as terrible as the noise of the earthquake, all anyone cared about was his own safety. Most of the hotel guests were still in their nightclothes and barefooted.

In the suite next to William's someone was pounding on the door and shouting. The muffled cries sounded somehow out of place.

"Wait a minute, Vad," William said. "The quake must have jammed the door. Let me see if I can open it."

She nodded, her fear beginning to recede. She would stay with William to the end, she told herself, watching as he threw himself against the door, his effort merely causing it to shudder.

"Damn," he muttered, looking around for something to use to pry the door open. Seeing nothing, he put his shoulder to the door again. This time it gave way.

A frightened couple rushed from the room, not even stopping to thank William in their relief at being freed. Evadne reached for his hand and saw blood on it.

"William—you're hurt!" she cried.

"It's nothing." He put his arm around her as the floor heaved under their feet again. "We must get out of here."

"There is no sense in trying to take the elevator," Evadne observed, seeing the crowd waiting. "We are only on the fourth floor. Where are the stairs?"

William led the way to the stairs. Other guests had had the same idea. They joined the line winding down, Evadne holding tightly to William's hand. The lobby, to their surprise, had survived. It looked normal except for the half-clothed people fleeing into the street. The chandeliers were tinkling slightly, but the furniture was in place. The glass of the entrance doors had shattered, however, and Evadne was grateful for the shoes that William had made her put on.

Union Square was crowded with people, some standing still in shock and others milling around. A horse pulling a dray past the hotel had fallen to its knees, and was neighing wildly. The delivery wagon had evidently contained milk, for milk was spilled whitely on the street. The driver was whipping the horse, trying to get it to stand.

William put his arm around Evadne, leading her into the park. The crowd here seemed numbed into a stunned silence. A few women were crying, others moved their lips in silent prayer. Only one voice was heard from a man running around asking for the time. Finally, another man, a waistcoat on over his nightdress, pulled out his watch. "It's 5:30," he announced, to no one in particular. The man asking for the time had vanished.

"Oh, my God!" someone cried. "Look!" He was pointing toward the Bay front and Market Street where smoke was rising in several scattered columns into the clear blue sky.

"The gas mains must have broken," William observed at

the sight of the fires. Around the square itself, all was peaceful, however. "I think the worst is over for now. We must get you back to Nob Hill," he told Evadne.

"Like this?" She looked down at her disheveled clothing, suddenly aware of how she looked. She was not alone. Others, too, were becoming conscious of their appearance— of nightdresses covered by shawls or blankets. Now that the earth was quiet, embarrassed smiles began to be seen as people hurried back toward their hotels.

"The others are going back. It's safe enough, I suppose." William smiled, realizing that his shirt was not buttoned, or even tucked into his trousers. "I admit that it would not look too well for me to escort you home dressed like this, and besides, I don't have the car keys." He hesitated, studying her. "Are you sure you are all right?"

"I—I think so. For a while there. . . ." Evadne shivered. "It was like the end of the world, but it's over now," she added, with more assurance than she felt.

William did not answer for a moment. His eyes were on the rising pillars of smoke. "I hope so. San Francisco, after all, is supposed to have one of the finest fire departments—"

"Fire departments?" Evadne was surprised: her mind was still on the earthquake. "Oh, the smoke?" She smiled. "Those will be put out any moment now."

As she spoke, a man came toward them from the bar of the St. Francis with an armful of water bottles. "Better get some," he advised William. "There is no water in the hotel."

Evadne did not believe him. Expecting the man to leave the hotel, she was surprised when he crossed the lobby and began to climb the stairs with them. "No water?" she asked.

"Not that I know of. Of course," he added, "it could just be here at the hotel."

Evadne put the thought out of her mind as she and William reached the suite. As the day grew brighter, the extent of the damage was more apparent. If it was this bad here, what must it be like on Nob Hill, she wondered. "William, I must get home. Poor Auntie and the servants—"

"I agree." William looked around. The telephone was still standing on the desk. "Do you want to telephone?"

Evadne hesitated, thinking of what the servants would say about her not being home all night. But they knew that already. She would have to face them sooner or later—and there was Auntie to consider. "Yes, I think I had better."

William had already picked up the receiver and was jiggling

the hook. "It's not working," he said finally. "The lines must be out, although it could simply be that no one is at the switchboard. We had better dress and drive there as soon as possible."

Both had to undress again to dress properly. In that moment of nakedness, Evadne looked at William, relishing the sight of him in the full light of day. How masculine he was with his broad shoulders, the golden brown hair on his deep chest, his narrow waist, the powerful thighs. . . .

William, holding his trousers in one hand while he reached for his underclothing with the other, paused to laugh. "At a time like this, you should not be thinking about such things," he teased her.

"Why not? It's not the end of the world," she retorted. "But I guess I *am* a—a brazen hussy. Is that the right term?" In spite of the lightness of her tone, she was dressing swiftly.

"I am not an expert on brazen hussies, but you may well qualify." William finished dressing. Picking up his watch, he glanced at it. To his amazement, it was only six o'clock. He put the car keys in his pocket, hesitated, then opened a drawer and took out a sheaf of papers that he folded and placed in his breast pocket.

"What are the papers for?" Evadne asked, feeling uneasy again.

William shrugged. "Business. I'm taking them just in case I shouldn't get back to the hotel soon. Who knows who may be looking around? The doors can't be locked—or even shut."

"Looters, you mean?" Evadne frowned. "Not in the St. Francis!"

"I am sure it is safe," he assured her. "Still, it is best to have the papers with me."

The faint tremor of another aftershock emphasized his words. "Let's hurry," Evadne said quickly. "I want to get home."

Once again, they found their way down the stairs. The elevators had obviously been damaged during the first giant quake, and no one was trying to use them.

In front of William and Evadne were two men, obviously in high spirits and looking forward to any adventure they might encounter. One was laughing as he said to his companion, "When I came in from the square, I thought I might as well see if the grill was open. Only the chef was there. He informed me that he is not cooking this morning. What he meant was not for me, because Caruso was there, just starting to eat an enormous breakfast."

"He must have come over from the Palace Hotel, that's where he's staying," said the other man. "I wonder why he couldn't get anything to eat there . . . ?"

If Caruso was still at the St. Francis he was not lingering in the lobby, which was crowded with guests trying to leave or find out what arrangements they could make to get out of the city. Evadne ignored them, walking proudly beside William toward the street. Here the crowd was larger than before. William took her arm to protect her and guide her over the broken masonry and bricks.

The milk wagon was gone, but other drays were hard at work. Some were loaded crazily with furniture and clothing. A guest from the St. Francis brushed past William tugging frantically at a trunk while he waved at a passing dray. The driver stopped, looking down at the man.

"Take me to the Ferry Building," the man said. "It's worth a dollar."

The driver laughed. "It's worth fifty dollars, Mister."

"Fifty dollars! Are you out of your mind?" the man demanded.

"I got that just for takin' some stuff from Market Street to Powell. It's fifty bucks, or you can carry it yourself." The driver raised his whip to urge his horse forward.

"You got it! You got it!" the hotel guest screamed.

"Lemme see it," insisted the driver, taking no chances.

"Come along, Love." William guided Evadne around the trunk, which was blocking their way. Ahead of them, the street had heaved up and the cable car tracks were twisted and bent into giant metal bows. "Dear God," William murmured.

Evadne shuddered, her anxiety about what she would find when she got home increasing. To her relief, William's hired car was safe, not even a window broken. William cranked it into life and got in beside her. He drove carefully, using the utmost caution to avoid the huge cracks in the pavement and the hillocks where the pavement had heaved up as if in agony.

Evadne moaned at what she saw around her. The entire front of one brick house had fallen, dropping to the street like a falling curtain and baring the home's contents. It reminded her of a doll's house, complete on three sides, except that the rooms were so untidy. A few wooden houses were askew, leaning against one another the way a house of cards was balanced. Still, the wooden structures had survived better than the brick and stone homes, all of which seemed to be missing some of their parts.

In spite of the early hour, the streets were filled with people. Some were fully—even elegantly—clothed; others were still in nightclothes, covered by blankets. All were staring toward Market Street and the Bay, and the billowing smoke that was increasing by the minute. A few men were walking purposefully toward the business district. Traffic, too, was starting to move in that direction.

The higher William and Evadne drove up the San Francisco hills, the greater the crowd of spectators, as well as businessmen in cars and on foot hurrying toward their shops and offices. Nob Hill was no different. Evadne had to smile at the sight of some of her mother's elegant friends, on the street dressed in a variety of garments that, heretofore, no one—neither husband nor personal maid—had ever seen them wear.

Nob Hill itself had escaped most of the brutal force of the quake, since its stone mansions were solidly rooted in rock. Still, most of the windows were broken, and masonry and sculpture adorning the mansions had crashed to the ground and shattered. As William pulled into the drive in front of her home, Evadne noticed that it had escaped with little damage, probably because it was less ornate than its neighbors. The staff was standing outside, and Evadne scrambled out of the car to run to them, her eyes searching for Grace and Auntie.

"Cook!" she cried. "Where is Grace—and Aunt—Miss Harper?"

"Upstairs, Mum." The cook looked at her numbly, not seeming to care where Evadne had been. The others servants, too, paid no attention to her.

With William following, Evadne ran through the open front door and up the stairs. "Grace, Grace!" she called.

The maid came out of Evadne's room. She was carrying a bottle of water. As Evadne and William approached, she sprinkled them with it.

"It's Holy Water, Miss Vad," she explained. "You'll be safe now."

Evadne, who not so very long ago would have been amused by Grace's behavior, was exasperated. "Oh, Grace, forget that nonsense. Where is Auntie? Is she—?"

At the question, Grace sank to her knees, covering her face with her hands. "Miss Vad! Oh, Miss Vad!" she wailed.

"William . . . ?" Evadne looked from Grace to William in confusion.

He shook his head and pulled Grace to her feet. When she continued to wail, he slapped her sharply to stop the rising hysteria. "I'm sorry, Grace," he apologized, "but where is Miss Harper?"

"With . . . with—" Grace gulped, swallowing new tears. "She is with . . . with *them*—with Mr. and Mrs. Harper."

Evadne looked at her uncomprehending. "What do you mean? What are you talking about, Grace?"

"She . . . she passed away, Miss Vad. During the night," Grace said.

As Evadne started toward her aunt's room, William stopped her. "Let me go. You stay with Grace."

William needed only one look. The little old lady was sitting upright in bed, propped against her pillows. In front of her was a breakfast tray spread with papers on which she had evidently been working. He picked the top one up. It was a new will, still unsigned, leaving all her property to Evadne.

As William came out of the room, Evadne looked at him, fear in her face. "Grace was right, Vad," he told her. "She seems to have passed away long before the quake. She was writing this." He handed the will to her. "I don't know how good it is, since she did not sign it, but you had best hold on to it."

"William—" Before Evadne could say more, she was interrupted by a loud cry from the street, the echoing sound of many voices raised as one.

The three rushed downstairs and outside. Where smoke had been rising to the east, the whole sky was now alight with a flaming dawn of fire from south of the Slot toward Telegraph Hill.

Awesome as the sight was, Evadne forgot it as the Tyler family car chugged to a stop in front of the house. Paul was driving with Mr. Tyler beside him.

"Evadne!" Paul stumbled out of the car and to her side, totally ignoring William. "Thank goodness, you're all right. Your aunt . . . how is—?"

Evadne shook her head. "She passed away sometime during the night. The news about Mama and Papa must have been just too much for her. At least, she was spared this." She waved her hand, indicating the surrounding chaos.

"You can't stay here alone." Paul turned to his father. "Hadn't we better take her home, Father?"

"Paul," the old man grumbled testily, "we have no time for her. We must get to the bank. Get back in the car," he ordered.

"But—Vad. . . ." Paul wavered between the girl and his father. "Father, you heard what General Funston said."

"General Funston?" Evadne asked, puzzled at his mentioning the acting commanding general of the Army's Pacific Division, headquartered at the Presidio, the large Army base that fronted on the Bay, just inside Golden Gate.

"We saw him just a little while ago," Paul explained. "He had already been downtown, and he has ordered the troops out from the Presidio and Fort Mason to help the firemen and to assist the police in keeping order."

"I don't give a damn about the troops. What are they going to do—shoot looters?" bellowed Tyler, his face an apoplectic red.

"If they have to. You heard Funston say that, Father." Paul gave a short laugh. "No one is going to get into the bank, Father, maybe not even us."

"Dammit, Paul, forget that girl!" Tyler roared in fury. "Hopkins can see to her. Take her to our house and leave her there," Tyler ordered, using the same tone to William he used speaking to his son. "You—Paul—get back in the car."

"Go ahead, Paul, go with your father," Evadne said, her voice cold. "I will be quite all right. William," she stressed his name, "will see to everything."

William took advantage of the other young man's confusion. "Your father is waiting, Paul. If you do not get moving, the bank may burn down before you make up your mind."

"Damn you! I'll take care of you later." Paul glared at him.

"Paul, what is the matter with you? Didn't I tell you to get in the car? The bank!" Tyler was losing what little reason he had left.

Paul grimaced, getting back into the car and driving off. The car descended the hill, narrowly avoiding a troop of soldiers, bayonets fixed on their rifles, marching toward the center of the city.

"That's what comes of being a bank president," William observed. "But Paul is right—you cannot stay here, my love."

"The servants—" Evadne looked around, expecting to see

the cook and the rest standing where she had left them. They were gone. "Where . . . ?"

"They have families of their own, Vad," William said quietly. "Now the worst is over, for the moment, and with those fires . . . they are probably gone to look after their own."

Evadne nodded, recalling how she had thought first of herself and then of Auntie. "I understand." She turned to Grace, who was standing with her hands clasped as if praying. "And you, Grace, what about you?"

"My Ethan!" Tears welled in the little maid's eyes. "I ain't got nobody else, Miss Vad. I want to go find him. Something must have happened or he'd be here by now, looking for me. Oh, Miss Vad!" she cried, her heart torn between loyalty and love. "I want my Ethan, but I can't leave you alone here like this. Mr. William," she appealed to him, "what . . . ?"

"I should go and see if there is anything I can do to help," William said, actually eager to discover what was happening for himself. The sight of the columns of smoke and the flames, the crumpled streets, even the recollection of the twisting, heaving, grinding horror of the earthquake made his eyes sparkle with the desire to be part of the event. As Grace had appealed to him, he now appealed to Evadne. "Evadne—?"

Evadne felt as if she had aged ten years in the twenty-four hours that had just passed. There were so many decisions to be made, and she felt so terribly alone. If William were to leave her, along with Grace, she would have no one—and she had never really been alone or called upon to make a serious decision in her life. She wanted to ask William to stay with her. Yet, looking at his face, seeing his eyes sparkling and his face flushed with excitement, she could not.

"Vad!" It was Lillie, dressed in a quaint combination of clothing, a skirt pulled over her nightgown and her fur coat over all. She dashed up to Evadne and threw her arms around her. "I told Mama I had to find you. Are you all right?"

Evadne nodded. "Your parents?"

"We are all still frightened to death—especially Mama. She is having hysterics in cook's arms. The others are gone."

"Your . . . father?" Evadne had trouble saying the word.

"Gone to the office, of course. The minute the earth stopped shaking," Lillie added contemptuously.

"Then you had better go back to your mother," Evadne said quickly. "She is certain to need you."

"Come home with me, Vad," Lillie suggested. "You cannot stay here alone," she added, having forgotten all about Auntie.

"No, Lillie, I can't." Evadne shook her head. As good a friend as Lillie was, Evadne did not want to be with her at that moment. Sooner or later, Lillie would mention Evadne's parents—as would Mrs. Dillard—and she would be swamped with sympathy. Mrs. Dillard was noted for her tear-shedding.

"Yes, you can, Vad." Lillie took her hands, pleading with her. "I don't want to be alone. Mama will be glad—"

The word "alone" was all Evadne needed to hear. Lillie did not know what it was to be alone—really alone. "No." She pulled her hands away and moved to William's side. "You had best go home, Lillie. Your mother needs you, and you don't know how long your cook will stay. Ours is already gone."

Lillie's jealousy rose at the refusal. "Paul wants you to go there, is that it?"

"Paul has nothing to do with it. I told him no, too," Evadne declared firmly.

"Then he did stop by! I saw him after—after. . . . We all ran into the street. He was worried about you," Lillie said coldly.

"Wait a moment." William interceded now between the two old friends. "I think you *should* go to the Dillards, Evadne. You will be safe there, and I—"

"No," Evadne insisted stubbornly. "There is Auntie. I must . . . see to her." An idea suddenly struck her that offered a solution to Grace's problem as well as her own—and William's. "William, you can drive Grace and me downtown. Where is Ethan staying, Grace?"

"The Brunswick Hotel, on Mission Street. Oh, Mr. William! Could you do that?" begged Grace.

Lillie's jaw dropped. "You're not going into that . . . that inferno?"

"What inferno?" Evadne laughed, dismissing the columns of smoke and the flames that were shooting higher all the time. "Besides, we can always come home again, and—"

"I cannot do that!" William was horrified. "It isn't safe for you there—either of you." He gave Grace a hard look. "Grace, you will never find him the way people are rushing about. It is far better for you to wait here where he can find you."

"I can't, Mr. William. I gotta find him," Grace said, her mind made up, "if I gotta go alone."

"And I, William, must see to . . . to what can be done about Auntie," Evadne managed to say.

"You're crazy!" Lillie stared from one to the other. "All of you. Nob Hill is safe. You should stay here . . . where you belong."

Evadne ignored her. She raised her head, her eyes meeting William's. "If you do not take me, I will go with Grace, or go alone, if I must."

"Very well." William gave up arguing with her, realizing that anything he said would only make her more stubborn. "Then I suggest we hurry."

"I'll get dressed." Grace, still in her nightie and robe, ran off.

Grace's departure reminded Lillie of what she was wearing. "Oh, just look at me! What will people think?" Once more she turned to Evadne. "Please, Vad . . . ?"

When Evadne refused her again, Lillie hurried away leaving William and Evadne staring at one another.

"You will not wait here and let me take care of Auntie later?" he asked.

"I must do it myself, William. Besides, I will not leave you. They would have to pull you away from me."

"No one could do that," William reassured her, putting his arms around her. "We must be sensible though." He paused thoughtfully. "Where is your car, Evadne? I am sure it has more gas than this one. I did not have time to fill the tank after we came back from Sonoma, or to replace the spare tire."

Evadne showed him the way to the small garage that had replaced the stable at the back of the house. The big Packard was sitting there, fortunately left behind by the chauffeur. William checked the car over with satisfaction, noting that the gas tank was full. To his relief, too, the keys were in the car. Quickly, he started it, backing it out into the drive where Grace was now waiting for them.

Chapter IX

WILLIAM CHOSE POWELL STREET AS THE BEST ROUTE TO UNION Square. As they drove along, Evadne noticed a group of Chinese, rarely seen this far west of Chinatown, seated on boxes, impassively watching the flames and smoke in the distance. Where, twenty-four hours earlier, the owner of the house in front of which the Chinese were sitting would have quickly and irately chased them away, today no one paid them any attention.

Farther along Powell, a Chinese family was climbing the hill, as if out on a Sunday outing. The husband walked in front holding the hand of his son who was dressed in a Buster Brown outfit. The short pants and jacket, the round-collared white shirt and tie, and the broad-brimmed hat looked incongruous paired with the pigtail hanging down the boy's back. A few paces behind the two came the wife and a young girl, probably the couple's daughter, both in black silk pants and quilted jackets. They walked with short, mincing steps on stilted lily-style shoes that made it appear as if their feet were bound. Their eyes were modestly downcast.

Although Evadne had never seen so many Chinese on Nob Hill in her life, she took the sight as much for granted as everyone else that incredible day. So, apparently, did Grace, who normally would have sniffed in disdain.

124

At the corner of Union Square, William had to stop the car. The street and the square were filled with people. These were not the same people who had emptied into the Square earlier that day after the first violent quake, but refugees fleeing from the fires who had no place else to go. There were women in nightclothes and shawls, others in cotton house-dresses, even some in the revealing gowns of the Barbary Coast. There were men in rough work clothes, others in business suits and bowlers. Everyone wore the same look of resigned acceptance as they sat on trunks or cases on the ground, clutching the few belongings they had managed to save. At that moment, the refugees from expensive hotels, the Barbary Coast, and south of the Slot were equal—the equality of loss. Strangely, there were no voices to be heard, as if the refugees had also lost their tongues. The only sound was the rasping, grating noise of trunks being dragged across the pavement, announcing the arrival of more refugees to the island of safety the square represented.

"These poor people," Evadne said, and thought of the big empty house on Nob Hill. "Where will they go for the night?"

Grace did not hear her. She was peering into the crowd. "Do you see Ethan? Oh, where is he!"

"We'll find him, Grace, won't we, William?" Evadne said with more confidence than she felt at the sight of so many people.

William smiled grimly. Ethan would be only one face in the crowd, and that crowd would reach gigantic proportions soon if the stream of refugees from the eastern and southern areas of the city did not slow down.

"Vad," William said, more anxious for her than Grace, "where is it you want to go?"

"Around the corner. You can wait—"

"You!" a man's voice called. "You in the car!"

All three turned to see a soldier, bareheaded, his blue uniform streaked with ashes, standing by the car. His rifle was in his hands, the bayonet fixed, and around his shoulder was an ammunition belt with what seemed to be enough bullets to shoot a regiment. Behind him was an officer, his hand on his pistol holster. Evadne recalled what Paul had said about the Army being called in, with orders to shoot looters, and she shrank back against William.

"Yes, what is it?" William asked, his voice steady.

"I'm sorry, sir," the officer stepped forward, "but I am afraid we need your car—and you."

"What!" William's arm encircled Evadne protectively.

"You heard me—sir," the officer repeated. He was very young, with blond hair and blue eyes, and his second lieutenant's bar shone with newness. "We have orders to requisition all vehicles not being used for emergency service, along with their drivers."

"There are women here! I cannot just leave them," William protested.

The other soldier was older, a grizzled veteran with the chevrons of a sergeant and numerous hash marks, indicating his years of service, on his sleeve. He might well have seen action with General Funston in the Philippines a few years before, when the Army had been sent in to end the Filipino insurrection. At William's resistance, he raised his rifle, sliding off the safety bolt with an ominous click.

"Like the lieutenant says, we got our orders, Mister. Ladies," the sergeant went on, his tired bloodshot eyes barely noticing the age of the two girls, "I suggest that you get out of the car now."

William's arm gripped Evadne more tightly. "Lieutenant," he said in a soft, firm voice. "I appeal to you. If you must have the car, let me at least see these ladies to a place of safety."

"Safety!" snorted the sergeant, "there ain't none. By nightfall the whole city'll be in flames."

"That's enough, Sergeant," snapped the officer. He turned to William. "You must forgive him, sir. I am afraid that he is exaggerating and unnecessarily frightening the ladies. The fires, for the moment, are confined to the Market Street area and to the south. In the Mission District, many of the wooden buildings collapsed. The sergeant has been rescuing survivors just ahead of the flames and taking the injured to the Mechanics Pavilion, where a hospital has been set up. He has had a long day, and it's not yet ten o'clock. And now, sir, I must ask you again to relinquish your automobile."

Evadne looked at the two soldiers. Taking reassurance from the fact that this time the lieutenant had mentioned commandeering only the car, she said, "Let them have it, William. We can go on on foot."

At her words, the lieutenant moved swiftly around the car to help her out as she opened the door. Then he quickly helped Grace down. William started to get out on his side, but the sergeant barred his way with the rifle.

"Not you, pal. We need the car and you," he growled.

"What do you mean, me?" William started to shove the rifle out of his way.

"The lieutenant and me, we're cavalry—horse soldiers. You're the one who's gotta drive. Stay where you are." The sergeant emphasized his words by shoving William back in the car as the lieutenant got in beside William.

"Vad, for God's sake—go home!" William begged, hemmed in by the lieutenant sitting next to him and the sergeant now standing on the running board.

"William!" Evadne reached for the door handle, to try to get in the back seat, but Grace held her back, clinging to her arm.

The sergeant nudged William with the butt of his rifle. "Get going. We have to try to get to the Hall of Justice on Portsmouth Square. That's emergency headquarters—right, Lieutenant?"

"That's right." The lieutenant looked out the window at Evadne, and Grace clinging to her. "I—I'm sorry, ladies, but orders are orders, and we desperately need the car and this man to drive it."

"At least, let me take them home first," William suggested. "Come with us. Then I'll be glad to—"

"No time for that. Get going." The sergeant again nudged William, this time with the bayonet.

Evadne's fear for William was greater than her fear for herself at the sight of that bayonet. "You—you had better do what they say, William. We will be all right," she added bravely. But as the car moved forward to turn into Post Street, she started after it, calling: "William, I love you . . . !"

There was no sign that he heard as the car lurched on over the broken pavement.

"Miss Vad, what we gonna do?" cried Grace. "I just gotta find my Ethan. He might be hurt—or worse. I gotta know."

Evadne looked at the trembling girl, at the tears pouring down her face, and her heart went out to her. The living had to come before the dead at a time like this, she decided. "We will find him, Grace."

"What we gonna do?" the maid repeated, looking at her hopefully.

Evadne bit her lip, trying to think. The sergeant had said something about the Mechanics Pavilion, a building the size

of the block on which it stood that was often called the
Madison Square Garden of the West. "We'll go to the
Mechanics Pavilion, Grace, I think. If Ethan was injured, he
will be there. We will have to walk," she warned, "and it's a
distance to the Pavilion—it's opposite City Hall."

"Let's go." Grace swallowed her tears. "It's that Vesuvius," she declared suddenly.

"What?" Evadne was startled. She was leading Grace
along one side of the square, picking her way through the
rubble. "This is San Francisco and Mount Vesuvius is in Italy,
Grace, what are you talking about?"

"Cook said this happened because of that mountain—you
know how she's always reading the newspapers—it blew up
last week, didn't it? Now we're getting it."

"Oh, I don't think a volcano erupting half a world away
could possibly have anything to do with this." Evadne,
looking up from the ground, realized that they seemed to be
walking straight toward a fire, toward blue and violet and
purple flames shooting high into a reddened sky. She realized
that if Grace noticed, it would start her crying again. To
distract her, Evadne kept talking. "We have had earthquakes
before, and Vesuvius has erupted before without any harm to
us. Just think of the money we collected for those poor people
there, who were left with nothing!"

Evadne laughed grimly at the irony of that statement,
thinking of the homeless refugees in Union Square. "I guess
we need it just as much ourselves now," she added.

Grace did not hear the last statement. "I still say it's all that
Vesuvius's fault," she insisted.

Evadne let it pass, her attention caught by a piece of paper
tacked to the front of a building that had once been a store.
"Wait a minute, Grace," she said, stopping to read it. It was
a proclamation by the mayor that had been issued and posted
in the few hours since the quake. The words chilled the
girl:

"The Federal Troops, the members of the Regular Police Force
and all Special Police Officers have been authorized by me to
KILL any and all persons found engaged in Looting or in the
Commission of Any Other Crime. I have directed all the Gas and
Electric Lighting Co.'s not to turn on Gas or Electricity until I
order them to do so. You may therefore expect the city to remain
in darkness until daylight every night until order is restored. I
WARN all Citizens of the danger of fire from Damaged or

Destroyed Chimneys, Broken or Leaking Gas Pipes or Fixtures or any like cause."

The proclamation was signed E. E. Schmitz, Mayor. So, Paul had been right, thought Evadne.

"What is it?" Grace asked, tugging at her arm and paying little attention to the poster. "C'mon, Miss Vad, we gotta hurry and find my Ethan. It's—it's funny here."

Evadne decided now was not the time to tell her. Taking the maid's arm, she hurried her forward, her mind on William. Those soldiers could easily have shot William and taken the car, she was thinking. Still could if he balked at their orders. That sergeant had looked more than capable of shooting someone, and he could always claim William was a looter. She would have to put her trust in the lieutenant—and the fact that neither man could drive.

Ahead, at the end of the block, was City Hall. Both girls came to a stunned stop. The dome of the Hall of Records still reared proudly, but the Corinthian pillars that had surrounded the hall had toppled, one crashing into an apartment building across the street. Walls had collapsed or fallen, leaving the building—which had only recently been completed after twenty years of work—a skeletal ruin.

In the plaza in front of the building, people had gathered as they had in Union Square, but here the loss was more complete. Many were soot-blackened and wearing bandages. Few had managed to save enough to have anything to carry. The police and the Army were also present in large numbers.

Grace groaned in despair. Evadne took her firmly by the arm, saying, "We must look quickly for Ethan."

"Where? Just look at all them people!"

Evadne sighed, afraid the search was hopeless but not wanting to dash Grace's hopes. "Why don't you go that way and I'll go in the other direction? We can meet at the main entrance to the pavilion."

"You only seen Ethan that once at the ferry," Grace pointed out. "How are you goin' to recognize him?"

"The red hair—and I'll ask. You ask too. Maybe you can find someone who knows him." Evadne patted Grace's shoulder and set out on her mission. Hopeless or not, she had to help Grace, who was all she had left.

As Evadne went from group to group calling Ethan's name, people looked at her dully, no one moving or trying to stop her. All too soon, she was at the pavilion where Grace, standing alone, was waiting for her.

When Grace spotted Evadne, she ran toward her and clutched her hand. "Let's not separate again, Miss Vad. It took you so long, and I got so scared!"

"Don't worry. Nothing is going to happen to me," Evadne declared bravely, as much to give herself courage as to encourage Grace. "Now, let's try inside the pavilion."

At the entrance, however, a policeman barred their way. "Sorry," he told them, "I can't let anyone in unless they're injured. There are too many people—from the fires and from the Central Hospital. It nearly collapsed after the quake," he added.

"We're looking for someone who may be hurt. We could take him home with us," Evadne said.

"Orders is orders," he said to them. Unlike the soldiers who had said the same thing, the policeman relented, seeing how young they were and noting Evadne's fine clothes. "Still . . . there's a reception place just inside." He waved. "You go and ask."

A tired attendant listened to their story. At the mention of the Brunswick, he nodded. "We have some survivors from there, but I don't know who they are."

"Can't we see them?" pleaded Evadne. "We've come so far. To go home without knowing . . . ?"

"Miss—" the attendant started to shake his head.

"Oh, please," begged Evadne, seeing the tears rise in Grace's eyes. "If you had a loved one missing, wouldn't you want to know?"

The question struck the man sharply. "I do have, Miss, and I don't know." He got to his feet. "This way."

They followed him into the arena where only the night before a skating masked carnival had been held. Today, there were stretchers and people lying all over the huge floor. In one corner lay the survivors from the Brunswick, most of them wrapped in bandages. They looked at the two girls with vacant eyes, not even turning their heads when Grace asked about Ethan.

As they were about to leave, a man with an arm and a leg in splints tugged at Evadne's skirt. "I know Ethan Morgan," he whispered hoarsely. "I never seen him since last night. Maybe he got out afore the fire."

"The fire?" Evadne looked questioningly at the attendant.

"The hotel collapsed in the quake and caught fire before

everyone could get out, or anyone could get them out," he told her.

Grace's face crumbled, and Evadne took her arm, hurrying her away. Once outside the building, Grace could hold her tears back no longer. "Miss Vad, he's dead. I know he is! I'll never see my Ethan again—and I only just found him!" She covered her face with her hands, her whole body shaking as she wept helplessly.

It was probably true, Evadne thought, but she told the girl, "Don't give up hope. We must get home. Ethan may be there," she urged, trying to make Grace walk.

"He's gone, gone forever!" Grace wailed.

"Grace—please!" Evadne looked around for help.

To her horror, she saw a line of policemen and soldiers advancing through the crowd in front of City Hall. As they did, the people they passed struggled to their feet and began to walk—toward Union Square. Evadne had to pull Grace out of the way of a line of drays and ambulances. It stopped, and she saw that the vehicles were loaded with sick and wounded. There was no need to ask what was happening. Evadne suddenly became aware of an intense heat and then she saw the flames, only a block away from City Hall.

She drew a deep breath. Grace was still so lost in her grief she was oblivious to the danger sweeping toward them. Evadne called her name again, then raised her hand, slapping the maid's face as sharply as William had earlier.

The blow startled Grace into a blubbering awareness of her surroundings. "Miss Vad," she managed to say, "what we gonna do?"

"Get out of here." Evadne took her arm, trying to pull Grace back toward Union Square before she saw the fire and the smoke that was starting to gain on them and dissolved again into hysterics.

"My feet hurt," Grace said petulantly, standing her ground.

Evadne stared at her, too startled by the commonplace remark to move or speak. Her feet hurt, too, she realized, and she was even less used to walking than Grace. In addition, her shoes were not as sturdy; a hole had already been worn into the right sole from the ripped and uneven pavement.

"Oh, Grace, how can you think of your feet at a time like this?" Evadne felt close to tears herself.

"Maybe we can get a ride?" the maid suggested, looking at the line of vehicles in front of the pavilion.

"I doubt it. We still have our two feet, and we can walk. Others need a ride more." With that Evadne began to walk, saying over her shoulder, "Come with me this instant, Grace, or I will leave you here to fend for yourself."

"Don't leave me!" Grace ran after her. "I'll—I'll die if you leave me, Miss Vad."

Evadne took her hand. "Let's go back to Union Square, then. Maybe Ethan is there," she suggested, hating to raise false hopes yet knowing it was the only way to get Grace to move. She herself was sure that Ethan had not survived the collapse of the hotel and the fire.

The crowd swept them along, funneling them to a safer place. With the flames and the heat at their backs, men, women, and children moved steadily at a pace swift enough to soon have the two girls panting. At a corner, Evadne pulled Grace into a side street that was miraculously empty. Grace immediately crumpled to the ground, but Evadne rested her cheek on the cooling roughness of a brick building, wondering whether she could go any farther . . . until she thought of William. He would be expecting her to go to Nob Hill and would go there to look for her. Even so, Evadne had to rest for a moment. Not even the thought of William's arms around her could make her move, and then a shout drove everything out of her mind except fear.

"Hey, you!" A soldier was racing down the street toward them.

Evadne drew back in fright, almost falling over Grace, when she saw the rifle he held out in front of him. Huddling against the protection of the building, she wondered whether the soldier would shoot a woman. Her heart pounded in her throat at the idea that she and Grace might possibly look like looters because they had stopped to rest.

The soldier stopped, halfway to them. He raised his rifle and pointed it at a building in front of him. "You in there—come out!" he ordered.

A man came out then, his arms laden with clothing. There was an explosion and smoke rose from the rifle barrel. The man's body twisted, seeming to lift off the ground before he fell, his head resting on the stolen clothing, blood spilling redly over the calicos and silks. The soldier stood over him, his rifle raised.

Evadne jerked Grace to her feet, tugging the dead weight of the girl along back into the stream of humanity, which now seemed a haven. Ahead was Union Square with its refugees patiently still sitting there.

The sight of the square revived Grace. "Miss Vad, do you think my Ethan might be here? It wouldn't hurt to look or ask, would it?"

Between all that she had seen and what she had heard at the Mechanics Pavilion, Evadne was sure that Ethan was gone. The shooting she had just witnessed did not encourage her either. Perhaps other soldiers and the police were not so quick to pull the trigger, but Evadne could not put the sight of that raised rifle and the bleeding man on the ground out of her mind—or the memory of William driving off with the soldiers.

"Miss Vad?" Grace appealed to her again.

Evadne sighed, looking at the square. There was hardly room for one more person to stand inside it, and the crowds had spilled over onto the sidewalks and streets. Even so, it was growing by the moment as more people struggled up the hills from south of Market, accompanied by the squeak of wheels of buggies of all types. Doll buggies, baby buggies—anything that could be pushed or pulled was filled to overflowing with belongings. Mixed in with those escaping the fires were businessmen, solemn in black suits and bowlers or top hats, and even sightseers. The drays and a few automobiles, heavily laden with household goods or merchandise rescued from stores, lumbered through the crowds.

"Very well," Evadne said, "but we will have to split up. You take the upper half of the square and I'll take the lower. We will meet at the Dewey Monument."

Grace hesitated, not wanting to leave Evadne. Seeing the no nonsense look on her mistress's face, however, she did not argue. After Grace had darted across the street, Evadne paused, her eyes drawn by the faces in front of her and the odd look of patient resignation common to all of them, rich and poor alike.

At least, Nob Hill is safe, she thought, not considering the short distance that separated it from Market Street. The fires would surely be put out long before the flames reached there—before they reached Union Square, for that matter.

She stepped off the curb, stopping suddenly, raising her head at the sound of an explosion that boomed in the distance, bracing herself for the expected tremor of an aftershock. When it did not come, Evadne glanced around in bewilderment, wondering what had happened.

A man in a business suit had stopped beside her to catch his breath. With his gray hair and lined face, he looked like a prosperous merchant or banker. "They are dynamiting some of the buildings," he explained, his voice expressionless, "trying to stop the fire down on Market and at the end of California Street."

"Dynamiting?" Evadne shivered at the sound of another explosion.

"Trying to make a fire line—to keep the fire back. Without water—" the man shrugged "—that is all they can do. And hope it works."

"But some of the buildings are fireproof," Evadne protested. "The Call Building and the Hearst Building. . . ." These were two of the city's biggest and tallest, and housed its largest newspapers.

"Not the inside, Miss." The man gave a sad smile. "They're burning now. I know, I just came from there. The Palace is on fire too."

"The Palace Hotel!" Evadne felt weak, recalling the day she had first seen William. "Oh, no!" she sighed, barely aware of a garbage wagon coming up the street. On top, amidst trunks and a stack of what looked like gaily colored satin and velvet costumes, sat a heavy, dark-haired man whose face was far from expressionless. It had a petulant, unhappy look.

"Do you see that man?" asked the stranger, the sad smile still on his face.

"Yes?" Evadne looked up at the man on the garbage wagon. She thought he seemed vaguely familiar.

"That's the great Caruso. I saw him at the opera house last night." The man gave a shrug, tipping his hat. "At least he managed to save his belongings," he said, and went on his way.

Evadne stared after Caruso, wondering where he was going, as the wagon passed the square. How unimportant missing the opera now seemed—and she had more to think about than Caruso. First, she had to help Grace. Determinedly, despite the hole growing ever larger in the sole of her shoe, she made her way to the square.

Few people bothered to answer her question about Ethan. Most had their eyes on the smoke and distant flames, shivering convulsively when each new charge of dynamite went off. It was a useless quest, Evadne decided, and would take hours. The only thing to do was to return to Nob Hill and wait for Ethan to come there—if he was still alive—and for William to return. But hating to disappoint Grace, she determined to ask one more person.

It was a woman—a girl, actually, about Evadne's own age. She was sitting on a crate, staring at the ground. On her head was a flat-topped, small-brimmed hat similar to Evadne's own black patent one, except the leather was cracked on the drooping brim. Over her printed cotton dress, unbuttoned at the neck to bare the full curve of her bosom, was a tired black boa. Hearing Evadne's question, the girl raised her head. The mascara on her heavily made up eyes had smudged and only a rim of bright red lipstick remained on her lips. She gazed curiously at Evadne with coal black eyes.

"What's that name again?"

At the sign of interest Evadne's heart jumped. "Ethan Morgan," she said.

"He a beau of yours?"

"No, he's the fiancé of a—a friend," Evadne replied, not wanting to say that Grace was her maid, not to this girl who was so obviously from the Barbary Coast.

The girl smiled. "Don't know him, Miss. Matter of fact, I ain't seen anybody I knowed, male or female. But someone said there's a lotta folks going to Golden Gate Park, 'cause there sure ain't no more room here. Thought I might go there myself."

"Thank you." Evadne started to leave, but the girl caught her sleeve.

"I guess there's some gettin' rich, ain't they?" she asked.

"What do you mean?" Evadne looked at the girl again, realizing that she was no more than a child for all her makeup.

"I heard them soldiers shot a couple looters who were cutting the fingers off dead folks—to get their rings. But they can't shoot 'em all, can they?" she demanded with a bluntness that shocked Evadne.

She thought of the man she had seen shot, of the blood that had spurted on the pile of stolen garments. Had they been worth his life to him? Would human beings do what the girl suggested? Evadne shuddered.

"I can't believe . . . cutting fingers off—"

The other girl shrugged. "There's lotsa ghouls around. I

could tell you stories that'd raise the hair on your head." She lost interest in Evadne now as suddenly as she had found it. "Sure wish I had a drink," she muttered, more to herself than Evadne. "But them soldiers, first thing they did was dump all the booze, beer, and wine in the sewers. Said it was for our own good." She gave a short laugh.

Evadne gazed down at her, pity for the girl's plight filling her. "Miss," she said softly, "if you need a place to stay—?"

The girl shook her lowered head. "Thanks. That's real nice a you, but soon's I feel like walking some more, I think I'll just go to Golden Gate Park 'n' see if I can find someone I know." She looked up with a smile. "Hope you find your friend."

Evadne moved on. At the monument, she searched for Grace, locating her finally talking to a group of men who might be sailors, judging by their clothes. By the look on Grace's face, she knew the maid had had no more luck than she had. Evadne hurried toward her.

"Best thing you can do," a burly, thick-necked sailor was saying, "is go home, Miss. You ain't never gonna find nobody now. Folks is all over. Best get somewhere while you got time."

"I gotta find him," Grace insisted. "You don't understand—"

"Sure, I understand." The sailor nodded. "I'm just sayin', it ain't no use. If he was in the Brunswick—"

Grace's face crumpled. Evadne managed to reach her just before she sagged to the ground. "Grace!" she cried, wondering how she could possibly get the little maid home in this condition.

The sailor studied Evadne. "She a friend of yours?"

Evadne nodded. "Grace," she begged, "please look at me. We—we have to get home."

"Where's that?" the sailor asked. His voice was casual, but there was nothing casual about the way his narrowed eyes ogled Evadne.

Evadne bit her lip. Despite her concern for Grace, she had been aware of the sailor's scrutiny. For the first time, she thought about her own appearance—about the smartly expensive suit that had been her mother's and the well-made kid shoes, so in contrast with the calico dress and shawl and sturdy shoes that Grace was wearing.

The maid sagged against her until Evadne had to struggle to support her. She would never be able to get Grace home alone like this. Besides, she was so tired herself that she was close to collapse. All that was keeping her going was the hope that William would be waiting for her at Nob Hill.

The sailor was still looking at her. Seeming to read her thoughts, he reached out a huge, hairy hand to take Grace's other arm, relieving Evadne of the burden of the maid's entire weight.

"Where's home?" he asked again gruffly.

Evadne hesitated, still reluctant to tell him. He was a stranger, and all her life she had been warned about speaking to strange men. Yet, how ridiculous, what did that matter now? Hadn't she spoken to the man on the other side of the square and hadn't she been asking strangers all day about Ethan?

"Nob Hill," she managed to say, ashamed for the first time of where she lived, not so much because of what Nob Hill stood for but because it was safe from the fire.

"Tell you what," the sailor offered, "I'll give you a hand, if you want. I'm thinking of going to Golden Gate Park, and it's not far outta the way. A soldier was saying they got tents and a soup kitchen there. It's better'n waitin' for the fire to get here."

"Oh, the fire will be put out by then," Evadne gasped under Grace's weight.

"Miss, there's fires all over the place. They can't get one out afore another starts. I seen it myself," he told her.

"The dynamiting—that will work, won't it?" she asked.

"Who knows? I ain't takin' no chances." They were walking up Powell now, half dragging Grace between them. "I seen 'em dynamite one building. The explosion set some stuff afire, and you know what? That stuff was blown across the street and set another building afire. It's tricky stuff, 'specially with the wind blowin'. I don't mean to scare you, but you asked," he added, giving her a malicious grin.

Evadne was too busy struggling to hold Grace up and keep her moving to notice the grin. Starting the long climb up the hill, she began to wonder what she would find at home—and to worry about the sailor. She could only hope that William was there. She offered up a silent prayer in the hope it would be answered.

"My name's Matt," the sailor offered. "My ship was due to sail this afternoon."

"Then why are you still here?" Evadne asked.

"I wish I knew." He laughed. "First came that quake, and I

helped dig a couple fellas out of the place I was staying. By then, the fire had me cut off, and I couldn't get to the Bay. So, I wandered around, and finally went there." He nodded his head back toward Union Square. "I guess maybe a few others didn't make the ship either."

"I'm sorry." Perspiration was running down Evadne's face, but she didn't dare let go of Grace to wipe it.

"How far now, Miss?" the sailor asked.

"A few blocks." Evadne sighed as Grace's arm slipped from around her neck.

The sailor slowed, watching her. "A few blocks, huh? Tell you what, a couple blocks ain't far. I've carried heavier cargo than this." He picked Grace up in his arms. "You lead the way, Miss."

Evadne hurried ahead, forgetting about her aching feet and the hole in her shoe, concentrating entirely on willing William to be at the house waiting for her. At the last corner, she stopped, closing her eyes to give one more silent prayer. When she opened her eyes, her heartbeat quickened. No familiar figure stood there waiting. Blinking back her tears, she noticed that William's car was gone. Had he come back and left to search for her? That had to be what had happened —that or the car had been commandeered by the Army, just as the Packard had been.

She refused to listen to the voice inside her, a voice that echoed Paul's words about William being a fortune hunter. She did not believe it—not after what he had told her and all that had happened. William would not have come back and taken the car and simply driven away to safety—not after telling her that he loved her and wanted to marry her. Still . . . he *had* lied about the relationship with Mark Hopkins . . .

"Where now, Miss?" the sailor asked, standing beside her and shifting Grace's weight in his arms. "She's getting a little heavy."

"I'm sorry." Evadne firmly put William out of her mind, along with her suspicions. Before she could think about anyone or anything else, she must see to Grace.

When they reached the house, Evadne had the sailor put Grace on the sofa in the library. She couldn't bring herself to go upstairs. In a way, she was relieved that the house was empty and as she had left it. All the talk about looters had made her apprehensive.

The sailor looked around speculatively. "You all alone here?" he asked, eyeing Evadne.

Fear rose in her throat. Her gratitude to him gave way to panic, and she fought to get control of herself. "My . . . my husband should be here any moment," she said, trying to sound convincing and once more praying for William to come.

"Husband, huh?" Matt looked at her ringless left hand. "He must be mighty rich—or old—for you to live in a house like this." He picked up a heavy silver candelabrum from a sideboard. "Bet you got a lotta pretty stuff like this."

Evadne swallowed hard, wondering what to do, especially with Grace lying senseless on the couch. It would do no good to scream—there was no one around to hear her.

Matt put the candelabrum down to wander around the room, gazing at the books and the china and the crystal bric-a-brac on the tables, most of which had been shivered into glittering fragments by the earthquake. Finally, he turned his sharp eyes back to Evadne.

"Musta been mighty fancy here. It's a shame, ain't it?" He waved his arm toward a table that had collapsed, carrying with it a pair of Chinese figurines that now lay in fragments among the slivers of wood.

"Take . . . take what you want," Evadne said quickly. "My husband won't mind, I'm sure. You did help—" She backed away as his survey brought him close to her. "Please. . . ." She tried to lick her lips, but her mouth was too dry.

The sailor looked at her. He was a big man, not so much tall as broad, with enormous muscled arms on which tattoos played with every motion and huge hands, the left one with a finger missing.

"Miss," he said in his sandpaper voice, "none a this stuff is worth a thing to me. Who's gonna buy it?"

"Then, what . . . ?" Evadne croaked out, becoming aware of her body as she had not been since that morning with William. A hot flush rose into her face at the man's obvious scrutiny—and approval—of what he saw of her.

"You're sure gonna need a man around afore this night is over—to protect you, mind," he said with a laugh. "You're one very pretty lady."

"Get out!" Evadne blazed, anger overcoming her fear. Hadn't she been through enough without having to put up with this?

Matt grinned, raising his shoulders so that his short, thick neck disappeared. "Yes, you're one pretty lady, and you got spirit. Women with spirit are sure the ones to have in bed. This husband of yours," he went on, "he good to you? Treat you nice? Make that hot little—"

"How dare you say such things to me!" Evadne suddenly remembered the heavy candelabrum. She took a step backward, trying desperately to think of something to distract him. He had mentioned a ship. "Don't you have to get back to your ship?" she asked.

"There's time for that. I told ya, prob'ly there won't be a crew anyway." He took a step toward her.

Evadne backed up another step. As she did, the floor rose under her, the earth protesting the violent pressures caused by the quake with still another aftershock, this one the worst yet. Furniture jiggled in a dance, and a figurine that had remained on a shelf fell into a tinkling heap. Matt took his eyes off Evadne, looking around in fear. With what she thought had to be the last of her courage, Evadne stumbled toward the sideboard, managing to grab the candelabrum before it, too, fell to the floor. Brandishing it like a club, her back to the wall, Evadne faced Matt.

His fear had vanished as the tremor faded. At the sight of Evadne armed with the candelabrum, he lost his easy manner. "Why you—!" He started toward her.

Evadne raised her weapon. "Don't touch me or I'll—"

"You'll what?" he snarled. "Didn't I give you a hand? Well, now I'll take some payment." He held up one huge hand to protect himself and took another step.

He was breathing heavily and the sour stink of his breath made Evadne recoil. Just as he was about to grab the candelabrum, she swung it with all her strength. It grazed the side of his head, stunning him for a second and giving her a chance to raise it again. This time the weapon struck him full force, the weight of the silver adding to the force of the blow. He fell heavily to the floor, his hands twitching at the hem of her skirt.

Evadne stared down at him, too weak to move. Blood was flowing from a gash on his head where the edge of the candelabrum had caught him. The sight of the red stain on the floral Brussels carpet brought back to Evadne the full shock of the sight of the man the soldier had shot. A bitter taste filled her mouth and she swayed, sagging to the carpet.

"I've killed him," she whispered.

Matt grinned weakly at her. One huge hand snaked quickly out to grab the front of her suit. Evadne wrenched herself backward. Strong as his grip was, Matt was too stunned to do more than hold on. The fabric ripped, leaving Evadne free to scramble away on her hands and knees toward the door to the library. Gasping, she clung to the frame, and pulled herself to her feet. Her only thought was to get help. She stumbled out to the street, looking for a familiar face.

Three soldiers were coming toward her. She stared at them, and recognized the young lieutenant who had commandeered her car that morning. The sailor on the carpet, Grace, everything she had seen and heard, flew from her mind as the thought of William again possessed her.

"Lieutenant!" She ran to the officer, grabbing his arm, not seeing the fatigue that lined his face and made him look like an old man.

"Yes, Ma'am?" He stopped in his tracks, his eyes dull as he looked at her without recognition.

"William," she whispered, suddenly afraid—more afraid even than she had been when Matt had come at her. "This morning . . . the car—"

The lieutenant shook his head. "Ma'am, I—"

"This morning," she persisted. "You and that sergeant, you took my car with William—Mr. Hopkins—"

His eyes lit up. "Yes, Ma'am, I remember now. You got home all right, I see. . . ." He paused, noticing her torn jacket.

"William . . . where is he?" she asked desperately.

"He isn't here?" the officer asked. When she shook her head, he said, "Then I don't know. We drove, carried messages until the car ran out of gas. The last I saw of him was at Portsmouth Square, across from the Hall of Justice. The mayor's committee of safety moved there after the hall started to burn. Now we're all on our way to the Fairmont Hotel. That's the new headquarters."

"If the mayor is coming here, we must be safe," Evadne said, heaving a sigh of relief, momentarily distracted. But when the lieutenant started to leave, she thought of William again. "Wait! About William—"

"Ma'am," the lieutenant took off his cap, running his fingers through his hair, "your friend's probably on his way here now, but if he doesn't make it by dark, he may not make it at all this evening. There's a curfew from dusk to dawn, you know. It holds for you too."

Evadne shuddered, thinking of Grace and the sailor. "Lieutenant," she said firmly, "I need your help. There's a . . . a man inside. He tried to attack me. . . ."

Despite his fatigue, the lieutenant reacted immediately. "You!" He motioned to one of the men with him. "Come with me. Where is he, Ma'am?"

Evadne led the way inside and pointed to the door to the library. The soldier, holding his rifle in front of him, went inside, the lieutenant beside him, his pistol in hand. There was a loud click as the safety bolt on the rifle was drawn back.

Matt gave in without any resistance, not that he was capable of it. He staggered out of the library, blood still oozing from the cut on his head. When he tried to stop by Evadne, the soldier with the rifle prodded him forward.

"We'll take care of him, Ma'am," the lieutenant told her grimly. "What hit him?"

"I did—with a . . . a silver candlestick," Evadne admitted. "I was afraid I had killed him."

"It would take more than a knock on the head to kill the likes of him," the lieutenant assured her.

"Wait a minute!" Evadne called as he turned away. "You're not going to—shoot him, are you?"

"If he tries anything, we may have to." At Evadne's horrified gasp, the officer added, "We'll send him to the prison at the Presidio as soon as we have the chance. After that, it's up to them."

"I know he wanted . . . tried to. . . ." Evadne flushed with embarrassment. "Still, I wouldn't like to think that I—"

"It's all right, Ma'am, I understand. I have a sister . . . by the way," the lieutenant asked, "are you alone here?"

"There's my maid and—and William and—" Suddenly she remembered Auntie. With all that had happened, she had forgotten the original purpose of her venture into the disaster-struck city. "Lieutenant, I hate to ask another favor of you—"

"If you want me to post a soldier here, I wish I could," he interrupted her. "We don't have enough men now—"

"No, oh no! I will be all right. It's not that." She explained quickly about Auntie.

"I can take care of that, Ma'am. We have set up a morgue at the Presidio. As soon as more men arrive at the Fairmont, I'll send two around," the lieutenant promised, obviously relieved that the request was for something he could do.

"Thank you. I would appreciate that. I hate to be a bother," Evadne said with a tremulous smile.

He smiled in return. "I guess I owe you that, Ma'am. We did . . . well . . . steal your car and your friend, leaving you stranded and unprotected. I have to go now, but don't worry, I'll send those soldiers as soon as I can."

Chapter X

EVADNE STARED AFTER THE LIEUTENANT, HOPING THAT HE would keep his word as—she had to smile in spite of herself—as an officer and a gentleman. Although he had not behaved much like a gentleman, taking William away and leaving her unprotected, he had done what he could now. She would have to trust him; she had no other choice.

Looking out at the city, however, made any sense of security the lieutenant had given her vanish immediately. From the height of Nob Hill, the sight was awesome. From almost due north and extending to the south, enormous fingers of flame were clawing at the sky, reaching over a mile high in an eerie beauty. Purples, oranges, yellows, and reds vied to outdo one another in their vividness. It was futile, utterly hopeless, to believe that anything in their path could possibly survive. Yet, Nob Hill had to be safe. Hadn't the lieutenant said that the mayor was moving to the Fairmont? She would have to trust in Mayor Schmitz's judgment. If anyone knew what was happening, he would, surely. In the meantime, she herself must see to Grace.

The maid was still lying on the couch, her eyes shut. Evadne sank down on the floor beside her, too tired from all the walking to stand any longer. Her feet were swollen, and the muscles in her legs ached. How wonderful a hot bath would feel, she thought, closing her eyes and imagining longingly letting her body down into the water and lying there, as she had done only the day before. That seemed years ago now.

On impulse, she got up and climbed to the second floor to try the taps in the bathroom. Regardless of the water mains in the rest of the city, she could hope that water was still flowing on Nob Hill. The attempt was useless. Water trickled out only to dribble to nothing. It would do no good to think of the impossible, and she put the idea of a bath out of her mind. It would do no good either, she told herself as she went back to Grace, to think about William, holding her, caressing her. . . .

With a sigh, she picked up one of Grace's hands. It was cold, almost lifeless. Rubbing the hand between hers, Evadne whispered desperately, "Oh, Grace . . . Grace, please open your eyes! We did all we could."

Grace's eyelashes fluttered, and the pulse began to pound in her temple. Brandy might help. Evadne remembered the bottle that her father always kept in the sideboard. Although it was probably broken like everything else made of glass or china, it would do no harm to look. Avoiding the spot on the carpet that was still wet with Matt's blood, Evadne went to the sideboard, picking up the candelabrum from where she had dropped it and replacing it. The door on the sideboard was jammed shut. Tugging furiously, Evadne finally managed to open it wide enough to see the decanter leaning against the door. It hadn't broken. The glasses, too, were in one piece, kept from falling out when the door jammed.

She brought the decanter and two glasses back to the couch. After pouring the brandy into a glass, she raised Grace's head, trying to force a little of the liquor between the maid's pale lips.

Grace's eyelashes fluttered again and her mouth opened, permitting the liquor to dribble into her throat, making her cough. She pushed at the glass and Evadne sat back on her heels, relieved at this sign of life.

"Miss Vad . . . ?" Grace whispered, her glazed eyes opening. "We . . . we're home. How—?"

"It doesn't matter, Grace." Evadne did not want to think, much less tell Grace, about the sailor. "All that matters is that we are here and safe."

Grace sat up wearily, accepting the answer. "What now, Miss Vad? Is Mr. William . . . ?"

Evadne's lips tightened. "No, he is not here, Grace. I am afraid that we are alone."

The maid stared at her. "What are we ever gonna do?" she asked.

Evadne shook her head. She had had no time to think ahead. Too much had happened for her to make any plans. Fleetingly, she considered going to the Tylers and the Dillards.

A knock on the front door sent her hurrying into the hall, first stopping to pick up the heavy candelabrum. Holding it firmly, she opened the door. Two men in blue uniforms, carrying a stretcher, stood there. One was a grizzled veteran who reminded her of the sergeant who had prodded William with his bayonet, the other was a youngster. Evadne quickly led the way upstairs and pointed out the door to Auntie's room. The soldiers entered, came out again shortly carrying the stretcher on which now lay a tiny sheet-wrapped figure.

Evadne followed them downstairs, thanking them as she took the slip of paper with the address of the morgue in the Presidio the old soldier handed her. That left only Grace to worry about.

The maid was sitting sipping brandy, when Evadne returned. Noting the color in her cheeks, Evadne asked, "Are you feeling better?"

Grace nodded. But she asked again, "What we gonna do, Miss Vad?" putting the full burden of their welfare on her young mistress.

Evadne grimaced, looking longingly at a chair but afraid to sit down for fear she would not want to get up again. "First," she said, "I am going to find another pair of shoes and change my clothes. Then I will go to the Tylers and the Dillards—"

"Oh, Miss Vad!" Grace wailed. "I can't move! My feet—"

"I am not asking you to," Evadne said firmly. "Someone must wait here in case—in case William or Ethan come."

"But you can't leave me alone! I'm scared!" Grace trembled, the color leaving her face again.

"Oh, Grace!" Evadne, just as tired, perhaps more so, lost patience with her. "Do as you wish. I am going upstairs to change. In the meantime, make up your mind whether you'll go with me or wait here."

Turning away, Evadne left her and went to her room. Here the bed beckoned. She turned her back on it reluctantly. She must hurry if she was to get to the Tylers and the Dillards and back before the curfew. There was no time to change, she realized. Taking off the torn jacket, she put on her sealskin coat. In her closet she found a pair of old, sturdy walking shoes left over from her school days and managed to get them on her swollen feet. After a last, longing look at her bed, she went back downstairs.

"Well, Grace?" she asked.

"I can't walk another step," Grace declared.

"Then you will have to wait here. I will be gone as short a time as possible," Evadne added, not mentioning the curfew, not wanting to draw a fresh outburst from Grace.

She left quickly, before Grace could protest—and before her own courage failed. The smoke and fire seemed closer, but it had to be her imagination. Then, too, in front of houses she passed were small fires around which people clustered. She was puzzled at first, until she remembered the mayor's proclamation and the warning about cooking indoors. What these people were doing was cooking, she realized, as the aroma of roasting meat assailed her nostrils. The smell awakened pangs of hunger, along with the awareness that she had eaten nothing all day and had had little to eat the day before.

Crossing the street, Evadne glanced toward the Hopkins mansion. It was a hive of activity, with people rushing out with paintings and statues from the gallery and then scurrying back inside for more, leaving the treasures on the lawn. Some were being carted away; others were being taken to the Flood mansion and stacked on its lawn where there was more room. Evadne was stunned. She tried to tell herself that these people were acting out of panic, as she cut down the street toward the Tylers. It would be better to talk to them first, she had decided, much as she disliked the idea of being at the mercy of Mr. Tyler. Mr. Dillard would have his hands full with Lillie and her mother while Mr. Tyler had Paul to help him.

When she saw Mr. Tyler, however, pity overwhelmed her. He was sitting on a chair in front of the house, his head in his hands and his whole body sagging in utter dejection. His wife was beside him, her hands fluttering helplessly in the air. There was no sign of Paul.

Evadne hesitated, glancing next door. Mr. Dillard stood alone in front of his house, staring down the hill toward the fires. His shoulders, too, were sagging, but he seemed to be more in control of himself than Mr. Tyler.

Evadne hurried toward him. "Mr. Dillard," she called softly.

He turned. His gray hair was streaked with black from smoke and his face was lined with fatigue. "Evadne," he said in a tired yet firm voice, "are you all right? I heard about your parents. I *am* sorry," he added, as courteous as ever.

"I am fine. How are Lillie and Mrs. Dillard?" she asked.

"They are resting." He looked back at the city. "It is all gone," he said, as much to himself as to Evadne. "I watched it go—the Call Building, the Hearst Building, the Emporium, Mercantile Exchange, the banks, the Palace. Everything I own is either on fire or a mass of cinders . . . except this house." He shook his head, taking out a cigar and lighting it. "Do you know, yesterday I was worth a million dollars. By tomorrow . . . ? He shrugged.

"Lillie. . . ." Evadne began.

"Perhaps your parents were lucky, my dear, not to see this," Mr. Dillard mused. The sound of an explosion as another charge of dynamite went off made him smile. "It is hell," he said softly. "The soldiers, the fire department, they think they can blast the fire out. It has not worked—not without water to help. Soon it will be our turn."

"Oh, no!" The cry burst from Evadne's lips.

"I hope not, but I am afraid. . . . Do you know that I paid fifteen hundred dollars for Lillie's piano? Do you know what Emma paid for all that china she is so fond of? It means nothing now." He shook his head. "Nabobs, they used to call us. We are nabobs of nothing."

"I . . . I'd better go home, Mr. Dillard. Will you give my regards to Lillie and Mrs. Dillard?" Evadne edged away, not wanting to hear any more.

"Of course. I will tell them you called, Evadne." Mr. Dillard ground out his cigar. "I had better see what I can do for them," he added gently.

Evadne left, more dejected than she had been. Until this moment, hope had been alive. Passing the Tylers, she looked at the house. Paul had come out and was starting a cook fire, his back to the city in flames. As Evadne hesitated, he looked up and saw her.

Glancing at his parents, who were still in the same position as before, he left his attempts at a fire and came to her. "Vad, you're all right? I went by the house earlier and it was empty."

"Your father . . . he looks so—" Evadne began. "What is the matter with him? Did he get to the bank?"

Paul's mouth twisted. "The soldiers commandeered the car before we reached Union Square. They wanted me, too, but my father managed to prevent that. We had to walk to the bank. It's gone." He looked bewildered. "We did hire a dray to bring as many of the account books here as we could. The driver wanted a hundred dollars. Imagine, a hundred dollars to drive here!"

"At least you managed to save something," Evadne said.

"What good are the books without any money? God knows what is left in the vault. We are poor, Vad!" the young man cried.

Evadne looked at him, remembering how his father had broken the news to her of her parents' death and her poverty. "You are alive," she said shortly.

"Poor! I cannot believe it!" He shook his head, wrapped up in his own misery.

She wanted to ask him about William. She said as gently as possible, "It may not be as bad as you think. The fires will soon be extinguished—"

"Do you think so?" He grasped at the thought. "Maybe we can salvage something if they are."

Evadne pitied him. What a poor creature he was, she thought. Trying to be casual, she asked, "You didn't see William, did you?"

"Hopkins!" Paul snorted. "You don't mean to say that you are still interested in that—that bastard after what I told you? Forget him, Vad. He is probably a long way from here by now. That is," he added cruelly, "if he hasn't been killed by the fire or shot as a looter."

The reply was all that Evadne needed. Weariness washed over her and she was afraid that she was going to faint, but the idea of Paul having to care for her sent a rod of steel up her back.

"You had better see to your parents, Paul," she said and turned away.

"You're not going, are you?" He ran after her, grabbing her arm.

Evadne pulled free. "I told you once before not to touch me. Nothing has changed that. I must get home. The servants—" She didn't want him to know she was alone with Grace.

"Paul!" Mr. Tyler's voice rose thin and whining. "Paul, your mother and I need you. Don't go chasing after that—"

"You see, Paul?" Evadne said bitterly. "Your father does not want me to contaminate you." She recalled what Mr. Dillard had said. "Well, who knows? Tomorrow, we may be little better off than the people on Telegraph Hill we've always looked down on."

"Vad, don't go. Father did not mean—" He glanced over his shoulder at his father.

"Paul!" Again Mr. Tyler called his son, in a voice that was hardly recognizable. "You come here!"

"I have to go, Vad. I will try to come later," he promised.

"If you don't get shot for a looter on the way, you will not get in. The door," she added ironically since the door would not close, "is shut to you."

Not waiting for a reply, she stepped off the curb, hurrying across the street in front of a line of soldiers and drays. A big limousine passed her, and she saw Mayor Schmitz in back along with other city dignitaries. The sight struck her more forcefully than the lieutenant's words had, for it meant that the lower areas of the city had been given up for lost. The only place left, if Nob Hill went, was Golden Gate Park.

At the same time, Evadne felt a spark of hope. Even if Portsmouth Square had surrendered, there was still Union Square. The mayor's arrival could mean that William was on his way to her—maybe even waiting for her. The idea made her heart beat faster and sent new strength through her body. She forgot the tempting aromas of cooking food in her eagerness to get home.

"William," she whispered, "please be there."

At the corner, she paused, closing her eyes and crossing her fingers like a child as, once again, she said a silent prayer. The drive in front of the house, when she opened her eyes, was as empty as when she had left it, the door still standing half ajar. Her heart almost stopped, leaving her so weak that she could barely move. Surely if William were there he would be standing outside waiting for her. Still, she did not give up hope until she had actually reached the house. By then, darkness was beginning to fall, but it was an unreal darkness. Overhead the sky was dark, but the streets were brightly lit by fires that were so distant now. It would be possible to read a book by their light.

Grace was still sitting where Evadne had left her. Her first

words, when she saw her mistress, were: "I'm hungry, Miss
Vad, I ain't eaten all day. What we gonna do?"

The question, repeated once too often, made Evadne bite
her lip to keep from screaming. She was amazed at the change
in Grace, who had always seemed so self-sufficient. That
Grace who had once entered the worst dens on the Barbary
Coast in search of her father could now be so helpless while
she, Evadne Harper, pampered and spoiled from birth, could
manage—must manage—for them both was as unbelievable
as everything else about this topsy-turvy day.

"Well, Grace," she said, trying to sound more cheerful
than she felt, "I guess if we want to eat, we will have to go to
the kitchen and find out what we have there. Then we can
make a cook fire outside."

"Yes, Miss Vad." Grace got to her feet obediently, ready to
follow her mistress. Evadne looked at her and sighed.

They went to the kitchen. Evadne found some beef and
Grace turned up some vegetables. Since Evadne had gone to
Sonoma for Easter and Auntie was a light eater, the cook had
not bothered to stock the larder.

"Do you think we can make a stew?" Evadne suggested.

Grace was doubtful after turning on the water and discovering there was none. "What do we cook it in? You got to
have water."

Evadne frowned, feeling totally helpless in the face of such
facts of life as cooking. "Do we really need water?" she
asked.

"Oh, Miss Vad!" The question revived Grace as nothing
Evadne had said before had. "We got to have something wet
to make a stew." She looked around. "I know what we can
use!" she exclaimed.

"What?" Evadne asked, relieved that Grace seemed to
have recovered.

"Wine! There must be at least one bottle of wine left."
Grace disappeared into the wine cellar. She came back
shortly with several bottles. "See? We got plenty, enough for
a stew and to drink." She placed the bottles in a big iron pot,
along with the meat and vegetables, taking charge now.
"Now, you carry that, Miss Vad, while I get some wood." She
went to the woodbin by the range.

Out in the front yard, Grace set about making a fire in the
drive. Leaving Evadne to guard the fire and pare the carrots
and potatoes, after showing her how to go about it, Grace

went off to find a corkscrew and some dishes and table-ware. Soon, the stew was simmering away, giving off the most heavenly aroma that Evadne had ever smelled. Grace opened up another bottle of wine, pouring some into two glasses.

Evadne smiled at her. "Well, Grace, at least we have each other."

"Yes, Miss Vad, and—" the little maid smiled hesitantly "—I guess I owe you a lot. I mean, I don't know what I would have done without you." She took a big swallow of the wine. "You never did tell me how you got me home. I sure don't remember walkin'!"

"Someone . . . helped me carry you," Evadne said eva-sively.

"There's blood on the carpet. I seen it." Grace looked at her.

"It's over, Grace. We are home, and I do not want to talk about it," Evadne said firmly.

Grace knew she meant it. "Well, I just want to thank you for . . . for today—for everything. I've been an awful bur-den, I guess. I'll try to make it up to you from now on," she promised.

"That is all that matters. But, Grace," Evadne fingered her glass, "you know I cannot pay you any more."

"I know." Grace smiled sadly. "I guess we're all in the same boat now—you and me and a lot of other folks."

The two girls smiled at each other.

The night was as bright as day from the fires in the city and the wind whipped the cooking fire, causing the stew to bubble.

"Grace," Evadne asked suddenly, "do you think the stew is ready? I am so hungry!"

"Me too." Grace poked at the meat with a fork. "It's done, leastways, it's cooked." She took a ladle and spooned the stew out into heavy kitchen plates, handing one to Evadne.

She took it, too hungry to think about the niceties that were lacking—the shining silverware and damask napkins and glittering crystal. She picked up a kitchen spoon, dipping it into the stew, blowing on the spoonful before tasting it. "Oh, Grace, that's good!" she cried. "I have never tasted anything better in my life!"

"Me neither!" After her second spoonful, Grace was more critical. "There's too much wine," she decided.

"Who cares? It's food, and it is delicious." Evadne had

already finished and was ladling out some more. "We had better finish it up."

They did, to the last mouthful, finally sitting back to sip their wine. The cook fire had gone out, but the conflagration in the city seemed to blaze even brighter. Nob Hill, with its height, seemed an island of safety.

When Grace asked once more, "What we gonna do now, Miss Vad?" Evadne only smiled, saying, "I haven't the slightest idea, but I think we should get some sleep. It has been a long day."

Grace nodded, picking up the dishes and the pot. The kitchen, too, was lit by the light of the fires burning in the city. At Evadne's suggestion, they looked to see what other food they could find. All there was was a loaf of bread and a piece of corned beef.

Evadne looked at the meat. "I wonder how corned beef will taste cooked in wine?"

Grace giggled. "I don't rightly know, Miss Vad, but I guess we'll find out tomorrow. What are you doing?"

Evadne was poking around, opening chests. "Papa always had a good supply of *apollinaris* water, Grace. Where does cook keep it?"

"Why, I forgot it! You sure are smart to think of that, Miss Vad," Grace declared, admiringly.

Evadne smiled. "If I'm so smart, where is it? Where did Cook keep it, Grace? You know more about that than I do."

"It should be in the dining room, at least, a few bottles," Grace said thoughtfully. "There may be some in the wine cellar."

Evadne went down into the wine cellar, feeling around in the darkness. "Where?" she called.

"To the left, I think." Grace appeared in the doorway. "I can get a candle."

"No!" Evadne did not want to frighten Grace, but she had to impress on her the need to be careful. "We are not to light anything inside the house. Remember, there may be escaping gas from broken mains."

She discovered some bottles on the floor to the left of the wine cellar and returned to the kitchen with them. "Look, I found the *apollinaris*. Now, let's go look in the dining room."

In the sideboard were four more bottles. They carried them to the kitchen.

"We should get some sleep," Evadne said again. She didn't add that they didn't know what the next day would bring.

Grace shifted nervously. "I'm scared, Miss Vad. We could be burned up in our beds."

"If the fires get close, the soldiers will warn us." Evadne tried to sound reassuring, but she was just as reluctant to go to bed, tired as she was. "Let's open a bottle of water and have a drink. The wine made me thirsty."

Grace hunted around for the glasses they had used for the wine and they carried them outside.

The street was quiet. Once in a while, soldiers passed by, on their way to the Fairmont Hotel, but Nob Hill was too far to the northwest of Golden Gate Park for refugees to be using it. In the silence, each girl was lost in her own thoughts.

Evadne was thinking about William, torn between her heart and her head. Her heart longed for him, for his arms around her, his tender exploring hands arousing her, his mouth hungrily seeking hers. Her mind kept putting questions for which she had no answers: Where was William? Why hadn't he come back to the house as he had promised? If he had come back, why had he taken the car and gone? She tried to tell herself that he had gone searching for her, that he had been caught by the curfew. But there was that nagging fact that he had lied about who he was to the Tylers—and to her. Could Paul be right? Was William a fortune hunter? No, she refused to listen to that question, refused to hear it. Again, she forced all thoughts of William out of her mind.

Evadne sighed. It was true that right now she was no better off than Grace, that sooner or later she would have to face the fact that she must earn some kind of a living. The only other way out of her predicament was to marry someone like Paul. The very idea made her shudder. With a grim kind of humor she recalled then that Paul, for all his airs, was now no better off than she was. All that was left of his father's bank was the account books. He could call in all the mortgages and loans he wanted to but who would be able to pay?

Grace's thoughts were far different. She had had no doubts about her Ethan's love and she had worked at something or other all her life. As a result, there was only one thought uppermost in her mind, and she was forced to some to grips with it: Ethan was dead, killed either in the earthquake or in the fire that had followed.

"Miss Vad," she said tentatively, her hand unconsciously reaching out for Evadne's. "Miss Vad . . . ?"

Evadne wrenched her mind from her own gloomy

thoughts. "Yes, Grace?" She turned her head and, seeing the sorrow in Grace's face, squeezed the girl's hand comfortingly.

"He's gone—my Ethan, I mean. I ain't never gonna see him again, am I?"

Evadne took a deep breath. Although she wanted to be reassuring, she said frankly, "I don't know, Grace."

"Maybe Mr. William too," Grace added softly. "I guess all we got is each other now."

Evadne closed her eyes to stop her tears. "Grace," she said, "in the morning, I think you should leave, look for your family and friends—"

"Leave you!" Grace was horrified.

"I told you. I cannot pay you," Evadne said reasonably. "More than that, I don't know what I shall do, or where I will go."

"You're all I got, Miss Vad. My Ma's folks, all they ever saw in me was another mouth to feed. Once I came here, they kinda washed their hands a me. I got no place to go, 'cept with you. Why, you're my family now," the maid declared.

"You're sure, Grace?" Evadne asked anxiously. "It's not fair for me to ask you to stay, not when—"

"I'm sure," Grace said firmly. "Now that my Ethan's gone, well, if it weren't for you and all you did, I'd be gone, too, most likely."

"As long as you are sure, Grace, but any time you want to leave—"

"Miss Vad!" Grace cried and began to cry.

Evadne put her arm around her. "Then let's . . . well . . . let's be friends, Grace."

"Sure, Miss Vad," Grace said eagerly. "We'll be friends, and I'll make up for all you done for me today. I promise!"

"Then begin by not calling me Miss Vad any more." Evadne was thinking about Matt the sailor. Perhaps he would have tried to attack her anyway, even if she had not lived on Nob Hill, but Evadne could not be certain of that. She did know that it had not discouraged him. "It will be Grace and Vad from now on," she declared firmly.

"Miss Vad, I couldn't do that!" Grace was horrified.

"It has to be that way. How can we be friends if you go on calling me Miss Vad, treating me as your mistress? And we are friends, Grace," she squeezed the girl's hand, "especially after all we have been through since yesterday. And now," Evadne stood up, "I think we should go to bed. We are going to need all our strength in the morning."

They went inside. At the staircase, they hesitated a moment before climbing to the next floor. Even when they were in Evadne's room, neither wanted to lie down. A burst of fresh explosions from the northwest made them shiver.

"Maybe we shouldn't go to bed, I mean, *really* go to bed," Grace said. "There could be another quake."

"We have to get some sleep and the floor is too hard," Evadne pointed out.

"I know." Grace hesitated. "I was thinking, well, mebbe we could drag a couple of mattresses downstairs and sleep in the library for tonight. What do you think?"

"That is a good idea," Evadne responded, adding, "let's get some clean clothes, too, and take them downstairs with us."

While Grace went off to her own room to get her things, Evadne changed into her green suit. It was practical, and practicality had to come ahead of mourning. Later there would be time enough for black.

Once they were in the library, with the curtains drawn to keep out the light of the fires, Grace said softly, "I gotta say it again. I'm sorry about today. You know, I gave up the idea of ever seeing Ethan again a long time ago. When he came back, like out of the blue . . . well, I had just about gotten used to him being back and us actually getting married when I lost him again. I couldn't believe I'd gotten him back only to lose him, it seemed so . . . so cruel."

"I know, I understand," Evadne said.

Grace sighed. "Life sure ain't easy, is it Miss . . . Vad, I mean? Not for anyone. Look at you, you had everything— your Mama and Papa, all that money. . . ."

Evadne's eyes filled with tears. "And William," she added softly.

"And Mr. William too." Grace gave a sigh. "Why does it have to be this way? I mean, is it wrong to be happy? Pa always said God didn't make man to be happy, that we had to pay for our sins." She sighed again. "Maybe he was right. He sure did a lot of sinning, enough to know."

Evadne had to smile, glad for the darkness that hid her face. "If that is true, I guess the whole city must have sinned, Grace."

"Like Sodom and Gomorrah in the Bible, huh?" Grace asked, finding in that comparison the answer for which she had been searching, one that seemed to excuse all that had happened.

For Evadne there was little comfort in it. "In that case, Grace, we will just have to leave here and not look back. But let's not think about that now. For now, let's wait and see what tomorrow brings. Go to sleep."

Evadne heard Grace turn over. Soon, the maid's regular breathing told her that she was asleep. For her, sleep would not come. Every time she closed her eyes, she saw William's face. She had to force herself to close her eyes and keep them closed . . . until sleep overwhelmed her at last, relaxing her tired body and mind.

Chapter XI

THE FIRES DID NOT SLEEP. SOUTH OF THE SLOT AT LEAST TEN fires raged, burning to cinders most of the commercial and banking life of the city. Flames roared as high as two miles into the sky, the wind carrying sparks and flames leapfrogging from one building to another, from one street to the next.

Although the prevailing wind carried the paths of the fires west, one blaze roared east, toward Van Ness Street, started by a woman who had lit a fire in her kitchen to cook breakfast. The chimney had been plugged with debris from the earthquake, fulfilling the mayor's warning about not cooking indoors. North of Market, more fires raged, some of them set by the dynamite and black powder that was supposed to stop them, by creating a fire line that the fires could not jump over it.

The fire department struggled vainly, but from the firemen's hoses no water came, or only a meager stream from cisterns. The fires could only be left to burn themselves out, leaving behind them smoldering, charred ruins. Metal skeletons towered above blocks of less sturdy buildings, so totally incinerated that one street could not be distinguished from another. While Evadne and Grace slept, the fire surrounded Union Square; the intense heat set the interior of the St. Francis Hotel afire.

In the early morning, long before dawn, the fire department abandoned other fire lines and attempted to establish a new one at Powell Street, only a few blocks from the sleeping girls, the Fairmont Hotel, and the Hopkins mansion, where many works of art still lay on the ground outside. At the Harper house, the heavy drapes that shut out the light of the flames could not completely smother the sound of a fire engine clanging imperatively up Nob Hill. At first the clanging intermingled with the nightmare that Evadne was having.

She was on a ship in a storm, the decks pitching and heaving the way William's room at the St. Francis had at the height of the earthquake. She was hunting for William, who was just ahead of her, turning and beckoning as a wave crashed over the rail and he disappeared. At that moment, Evadne realized that she was naked, her body gleaming marble-white, though none of the other passengers seemed to notice as she dashed among them, now trying to find her cabin. At the same time, she became aware of being followed by someone who was just out of sight behind her, coming closer and closer. Then she saw William and dashed into his arms. As her lips eagerly sought his, she opened her eyes to see Matt the sailor leering at her, blood pouring from the wound in his head.

Evadne cried out in her sleep, the cry arousing her from the depths of slumber to the sound of clanging fire engines. Even so, it took a few seconds for her to recognize her surroundings. Her body was damp, not with spray from the ocean but from her own perspiration.

The clanging sounded closer, banishing the last of the dream. Seeing that Grace was still curled up asleep, holding the pillow for comfort, Evadne left her as she was for the moment. Recognizing the ominous clanging sound, she tried to tell herself that Nob Hill was safe, that no harm could possibly come to her in the safety of what had always been her home.

She struggled to her feet. The movement made every muscle in her body cry out in anguish, forcing her to sit down to massage her legs and her swollen feet before she tried to stand again. Even then, she hobbled painfully as she went to the door.

The sight that greeted her brought a moan of anguish and fear to her lips. The white Greek Revival tower of the Fairmont Hotel, which had been due to open that day, stood in pristine clarity against a smoky, flame-filled sky. To one

side she could see the filigreed turrets and towers of the Mark
Hopkins mansion. Although its high chimneys, along with a
few of the towers, had toppled during the earthquake, it was
still impressive. The rest was devastation.

Evadne felt curiously detached, as if she were watching
history that did not affect her. Then she saw the people.

Nob Hill had gone to sleep secure in the thought that the
fire would be halted at Union Square. Now its inhabitants had
been routed from their beds by the soldiers, forced out in
whatever garments they could hurriedly put on, and with only
those possessions they could carry or push or pull in any
vehicle at hand. A few were driving their own cars, those who
had not had the vehicles commandeered the previous day.
Evadne watched them and saw the same look of calm
resignation on their faces that she had seen on the faces of
refugees from the Barbary Coast and south of the Slot. The
world was upside down, with rich and poor alike accepting
the twist of fate that made all men equal.

A line of soldiers was advancing along the street, pounding
at doors with their rifle butts and warning people to evacuate.
At the sight, Evadne hurried back inside.

"Grace! Grace! Get up!" She shook her by the shoulder.
"Get up," she said again. "Go to the kitchen and put what
food and water you can into a basket."

Grace nodded, struggling to sit up, blinking owlishly, her
eyes heavy with sleep. As Evadne turned to leave, she
mumbled "What is it? Where are you goin', Vad?"

"I am going upstairs to get us some more clothing. We are
going to need it," Evadne said calmly. "Now, hurry, Grace!"

She went quickly to the stairs. Any hope that William
would appear to rescue her, like a prince on a white charger,
was gone now. Whether he had been killed in the fire, as poor
Ethan had undoubtedly been, or had returned to take the car
and desert her made little difference. From now on she would
have to rely on herself; she had only herself to look out for
her needs and safety. She also accepted the fact that Grace
was depending on her. Yet, instead of resenting it, she was
grateful. It was better than being alone and would give her
little time to think of—and feel sorry for—herself.

Sooner or later, Evadne decided, they would need money,
but there was little in the house. The Harpers, like the other
families on Nob Hill, did not deal in cash. Whatever they
wanted and wherever they went, they either signed for it, to
be billed later, or charged it. As a result, it was not money

that Evadne was after. She went first to her room for her pearls and then to her mother's jewel box, to take the few gold rings, earrings, and other pieces of jewelry that her mother had not taken with her and had not placed in the bank. What she found was less than she had hoped to find. Still, it was something. Evadne put the jewelry into a big reticule before going to her mother's closet. She had only time to pack a wool dress and take her mother's second fur coat for Grace before the soldiers' rifle butts beat a tattoo on the front door.

Grace, a basket over her arm, ran out of the kitchen, almost colliding with Evadne.

"What are they here for?" Grace asked. Taken by surprise, she began to shake with fear.

Evadne patted her shoulder comfortingly before answering the door. "Yes?"

"I'm sorry, Ma'am, we have to ask you to leave." The corporal's eyes were bloodshot, and he had a two-day growth of beard. His once trim uniform was stained and rumpled. The soldiers behind him looked no more respectable. All had their bayonets fixed and were holding their rifles ready, prepared for any and all kinds of trouble they might encounter.

"We will," Evadne promised. "I just want to get a few—"

"Sorry, Ma'am, orders is to get everyone out immediately. Who else is here?" He peered into the hall.

"No one. Just my—Grace and me," Evadne said.

"I'm afraid, a house as big as this, I gotta have a look." The corporal rubbed his cheek wearily.

"Very well." Evadne stepped aside.

"Wait a minute!" Grace puffed up angrily like a bantam hen. "You got no right to go poking around."

"Ma'am," the corporal told her, his voice flat with resignation, "the city's under martial law. The Army's in charge, and my orders is to search and make sure no one is left behind."

"He's right, Grace. Let him look." Evadne drew Grace aside, handing her the clothes she had taken from upstairs. "Is it all right for me to get my coat?" she asked the corporal. "It's in there." She nodded toward the library.

"Go ahead, Ma'am, as long you're ready to leave soon's I get back." The soldier eyed the staircase, seeing it as one more obstacle. His boots thudded heavily on the stairs, fatigue marking every step.

"Put this on, Grace." Evadne handed her her mother's coat. "I'll go and get mine."

In the library, Evadne arranged her clothing, donning first the suit jacket and then the sealskin coat. A stab of pain knifed through her heart as she did. The suit and coat could not help but remind her of William, of their first meeting at the Palace Hotel, now a pile of glowing coals, and the next day's excursion to Cliff House. Was it still standing, she wondered, or had it trembled and fallen into the sea?

The thud of the soldier's feet on the stairs again brought her back to the present. She took a last look at the room. It had always been a favorite, not only of hers but also of her parents. Her parents! How long had it been since she had had time to think of them . . . to grieve for them or for Auntie? Now was not the time either. She brushed the tears from her eyes and walked resolutely into the hall, determined to face whatever lay ahead as bravely as possible, as her parents would have expected her to do.

Grace was sitting on the bottom step of the staircase, tears running down her cheeks. "What we gonna do now? Where we gonna go?" she asked helplessly.

Evadne's resolution faltered. She realized that for all her brave thoughts she had given no consideration to what came next. "Yes, Sergeant," she said, the number of stripes on the noncommissioned officer's sleeve meaning nothing to her. "Where do we go?"

"I'm only a corporal, Ma'am," he admitted bashfully.

"Corporal, then. Where do we go?" insisted Evadne.

"That's not my business, Ma'am. All I know is that you gotta get outa here." He looked at the two girls, who were watching him hopefully. "You got friends or relatives west of here?"

"No . . . no, we don't," Evadne replied.

"Then the best place is Golden Gate Park. I hear they got soup kitchens there and a first-aid tent. You'd best go there."

"Very well. Come, Grace." Evadne shifted the reticule and a blanket she had picked up in the library to one arm, taking Grace's hand with her free one.

The two girls left the house, tears still running down Grace's face. At the end of the drive, the maid stopped to look back. The soldiers were already on their way to the next house, and Grace started to take a step in retreat.

Evadne sighed. Recalling their conversation the night

before, she said, "It's no good, Grace. We can't go back, so let's not look back . . . like Lot's wife."

Although the Biblical reference brought a fresh flow of tears, it did serve to hurry Grace down the street. At the corner, they had to stop to let several cars pass. The cars carried Mayor Schmitz and other members of the committee he had formed in the first hours of the earthquake. The soldiers had not been alarmists, after all, Evadne thought, recalling that the committee had already moved from City Hall to the Hall of Justice to Portsmouth Square to the Fairmont. It was not even dawn, and if the Fairmont was now being abandoned, too, little hope was left for Nob Hill.

After the motor caravan passed, followed by a company of soldiers and police on horseback, Evadne glanced down California Street. Flames were licking at the mansion that Mark Hopkins had built as his memorial to success and the success of the railroad he had helped found which had made San Francisco such a great and vital city. Soon it would be the turn of the Crocker and Huntington mansions. Just as the nabobs, who had made the city great and from whose often derogatory title Nob Hill had taken its name, were gone, so the houses that were supposed to last for centuries would soon be only a memory.

The girls went down California Street to Leavenworth, zigzagging their way toward Van Ness. Behind them, to the east, day was breaking unseen behind the clouds of smoke and new pillars of flames, although the first rays of the sun glinted on the buildings atop Russian Hill. At the corner of Bush and Hyde, they paused to catch their breath. No soldiers had yet come to evict the residents of this neighborhood, and a few were standing on the steps of their houses, watching the stream of refugees.

Evadne glanced up at a man standing at the top of a steep flight of steps. He was a big man, nearly bald, with a heavy gold watch chain draped across the vest he wore to conceal his paunch. He was in his shirtsleeves, but his collar was neatly fastened and his cravat tied. He looked like a merchant about to don his jacket and go to his store. A frown drew his thick eyebrows together. When he noticed Evadne watching him, he tried to smile, saying, "You're welcome to sit on the steps."

"Thank you." Evadne sat down, Grace beside her, with a sigh of relief.

The man came down the steps to join them, looking back at his house. It was a five-story frame building with a bay window, painted yellow with white gingerbread trim around the doors and windows and adorning the false front on the roof that gave the appearance of an extra story. Both yellow and white, however, were now streaked with smoke and soot.

"We just finished having the house painted," he said simply, "now we will have to have it painted all over again. From the looks of things, though, there will be plenty of people looking for work—and a lot of work to be done."

"Yes," Evadne nodded. "It's a pretty house," she offered.

"Thank you, Miss. My wife is very proud of it. She bought only the best—the best horsehair furniture for the front room and a Brussels carpet too. I told her not to spare any expense," he added.

His words reminded Evadne of Mrs. Tyler, with her imported furniture and carpets and conservatory. How she had bragged to Evadne's mother about how much everything had cost, saying, "Nothing but the best, I always say, Sally. Buy cheap, it looks cheap. If you want things to last, you must pay the price." Now the Tyler house and everything in it must be in flames—the Dillard house, too, along with Lillie's fifteen hundred dollar piano which she rarely played after her father had finally given into her tears and tantrums. Evadne wondered where the Dillards and Tylers had gone, if they, like Grace and herself, were on their way to Golden Gate Park with only what possessions they could carry.

"I understand they managed to stop the fire at Powell Street," the man was saying. "Thank God for that."

Evadne bit her lip, not wanting to destroy his hopes, yet not wanting to give him any false sense of security either. She lowered her eyes, wondering what to say.

Her silence alerted him. "I mean, they . . . they did stop it, didn't they—with all that dynamiting that was going on?"

Evadne raised her eyes, seeing the anxious look in his face. "No. No, they didn't." She got to her feet, pulling Grace up beside her. "Nob Hill's on fire," she explained. "We just came from there. The soldiers made us leave. I saw the Hopkins mansion catch on fire."

The man nodded, resignation in his face now. "I guess I knew that when I saw you, Miss." He was looking at her sealskin coat. "I just didn't want to believe it."

"We have to go now," Evadne said. "Thank you for letting us sit here."

The man nodded again, only half hearing her. "I don't think I'll tell my wife yet," he mused. "It will only worry her." He climbed slowly back up the steps.

A violent explosion, so near that it shook the ground under their feet, sent the remaining glass in the windows of the yellow and white house showering to the ground. Inside, a woman screamed, and the man hurried through the door.

The stream of refugees paused momentarily. Evadne, with Grace holding tightly to her arm, joined them, finding a kind of comfort in numbers. Just ahead was Van Ness Street, a wide boulevard that certainly should stop the fire.

Evadne had planned on taking Golden Gate Avenue to the park, the route she had taken with William. But a line of police barred the way, stopping the current of people like a dam in a stream. Grace sagged against her in fear.

Fear gripped Evadne too. The line of police, their nightsticks held in front of them, seemed somehow more frightening than the soldiers with their bayonets fixed. They were the first police Evadne had seen since the earthquake. Somehow, she had grown more used to the sight and appearance of the soldiers, day and night.

Her first thought was that the police were there to send them back into the red maw of the fire. Many of the other refugees evidently had the same idea. There was a sudden surge forward toward the police line. An officer, standing to one side, hastily drew his gun to fire into the air, halting the crowd.

"Listen, folks!" The policeman cupped his hands like a megaphone. "Listen to me now! You're to turn here—go west on Hyde," he added hurriedly as a cry of protest rose from the crowd.

"Why?" a man shouted. "California's closer."

"Ain't we walked enough," a woman complained, "that you gotta send us outta our way?"

"Please, folks!" the policeman pleaded. "Just do as we say. We don't want to hurt anyone—and we don't want anyone hurt." To emphasize his words, he motioned to the street behind the policemen.

Evadne was tall enough and close enough to see what lay ahead. The area south of Golden Gate Avenue was a smoky, blackened ruin. Here and there, a wall still stood, but most of the buildings had been made of wood, which had not been able to put up any kind of resistance to the fire started by the woman who had tried to cook breakfast. In some places, flames still licked hungrily at what remained to feed them; in others, smoldering coals sent plumes of smoke into the air. Coming north along Van Ness was a group of soldiers, preparing to set another charge of dynamite. It had been dynamite that had caused the earlier explosion.

There was no complaint, not even a sigh, as the first of the crowd moved west on Hyde Street. Evadne and Grace let themselves be carried along.

Evadne's feet were beginning to hurt again. To distract herself, she looked around at her companions. Most had had time to dress before the soldiers had routed them from their homes, unlike the refugees in front of City Hall and the Mechanics Pavilion yesterday, many of whom had been in nightdresses with only a shawl or a blanket to cover them. There were fewer belongings being abandoned too.

She recalled the trunks dragged with such effort into the streets around Union Square, only to be left when their owners could find no means of transporting them. It was not that these new refugees had had the forethought to take only what they could carry. It was that many of yesterday's refugees had been travelers and tourists staying in the hotels on Market Street and around Union Square. With a smile, she remembered the great Caruso sitting atop the garbage dray.

As she examined the faces, she began to look for familiar ones—Lillie and her family, and the Tylers. Even the sight of Paul would have been welcome just then, but she saw no one she knew and gradually gave up looking. There would be time enough for that at the park.

"We almost there?" Grace asked. "My feet sure do hurt."

"Soon, Grace." Evadne sighed. "My feet hurt too. Don't remind me!"

"What's at Golden Gate Park? Do you know, Vad?" Grace gave a rueful laugh. "Do you know, I never been there. Me and . . . and—" She swallowed hard, trying not to break down again. "Me and Ethan were gonna take the railway there an' have a picnic, maybe look at them Japanese gardens, when the weather got warmer."

Evadne knew all too well what it must have cost Grace to say Ethan's name, if her own thoughts and feelings about William were any example. Yet, what could she say to reassure Grace? There was little enough at the park, because that was all it was, really, a park.

"It's . . . well . . . it's a park, with grass and trees—" Evadne began.

"Like Union Square?" Grace interrupted with a frown, looking around at all the people. "What will we do?"

"Oh, it's much, much larger than Union Square!" Evadne replied quickly. "There are acres and acres of it, with plenty of room—"

"An' places to stay? I mean, like restaurants and such?" Grace was not reassured. "I don't much care for sleeping out in the open. I like a roof over my head."

"So do I, but we will just have to wait and see. The corporal said there was a first-aid station," Evadne offered.

"Well, we ain't sick or hurt," Grace pointed out. "What good's a first-aid station? Right now, after all this walking, I'm more interested in some food. I'm mighty thirsty, too."

A bitter taste rose in Evadne's throat. "But, Grace, when you went to the kitchen, you *did* take that corned beef and the *apollinaris* . . . ?"

Grace looked down at the basket dangling from her arm, as if seeing it for the first time. Her face reddened, crumpled into the by now familiar sign of an outburst of tears.

"Grace!" Evadne was hungry and thirsty too. "You did take the food and the water!"

Tears were beginning to roll down the girl's cheeks. "I started to. Honest I did. See?" Grace held up the basket. "I took the basket to pack it. Then them soldiers banged on the door and I ran out to see what it was—"

Evadne bit her tongue. It would do no good to lose her temper, no matter how much she wanted to.

"Miss Vad?" Grace's tears were spilling over. Shame made her revert to the old way of addressing Evadne. "Miss Vad?" she said again, as Evadne struggled to control herself.

Evadne's anger evaporated slightly at the pitiful note in Grace's voice. Exasperated, she said testily, "Grace, didn't I tell you not to call me Miss Vad anymore?"

"Yes . . . Vad," Grace said meekly. She knew Evadne's temper all too well.

"And don't ask me what we are going to do because I don't know any more than you do. I haven't the slightest idea," Evadne went on, "where we will sleep or what we will eat or drink or when. All I know is that we are alive and, somehow, some way, we will survive."

The moment she said it, Evadne felt better. Her fear was

gone. Once more she straightened her back, holding her head up proudly.

Her parents were gone. The wealth with which she had been brought up was gone. If the luxury in which she had lived all her life was not already gone, it soon would be. Much worse, she had lost William and the new-found ecstasy he had brought her. All she had was herself—her intelligence and ingenuity and, above all, her desire to live. If the worst had not already happened, she would manage to overcome what still lay ahead.

Chapter XII

EVADNE AND GRACE HAD STARTED THEIR JOURNEY IN STREETS lighted by the fires at their backs. As they reached Golden Gate Park, the sun pulled itself reluctantly above the horizon. The sight that greeted them was enough to make even Evadne falter, despite her new resolve.

People seemed to be everywhere. Some were huddling in groups around small fires; others were lying on the ground, trying to sleep with only the flimsiest of coverings. Bedsheets, blankets, shawls, coats and other garments had been pressed into service as both mattresses and bed coverings. Here and there a figure moved through the throng looking for a familiar face or a loved one.

The sight sent Grace to her knees, the courage that Evadne had infused in her gone. "Gawd," she moaned, "no matter what you say, Vad, the worse ain't behind us—it's ahead of us. This ain't no Golden Gate . . . it's Hell."

For a moment, Evadne felt dizzy. Taking a deep breath, she let it out slowly. She took a step forward, trying to peer deeper into the park. Surely, in a place so large, there was still room enough for the two of them.

"Oh, Miss Vad!" Grace scrambled to her feet in panic. "Don't leave me now!"

"I wasn't going to leave you, Grace." Evadne let the Miss

169

Vad pass. Actually, she had to smile as, for the first time, she paused to take in the sight of Grace in her mother's fur coat. Her mother, after all, had been almost as tall as Evadne while Grace was a good head shorter. The fur was red fox, and the full, silken hair made Grace appear even stockier than she was. The sleeves, moreover, were much too long, so long that nothing could be seen of Grace's hands. The hem that had been mid-calf on Sally Harper almost brushed the ground on Grace, giving the little maid the appearance of a chubby bear ready to hibernate for the winter. Evadne could not hold back the giggle that rose to her lips.

"Oh, Gawd, don't laugh! It ain't funny. Where we gonna go with all them people? There ain't no room for us. Golden Gate, huh!" Grace snorted in disgust.

Evadne patted the girl's shoulder, relieved at the way Grace had revived again and trying to smother the laughter that kept bubbling up in her.

"It's a big park," she managed to say, still smiling. "We will look around until we find a place for ourselves. That will give us a chance to look for anyone we know too. It would be good to find some friends. . . ."

"I'd sure like to find Cook," Grace said wistfully. "I bet she's got a big basket of food with her. She's not one to go hungry."

"Then let's start looking." Evadne took Grace's arm again, trying to take advantage of the girl's new optimism. "The longer we stand here, the more people there are going to be ahead of us."

Grace looked around doubtfully. "Where do we start? I've never seen so many people in one spot!"

"Let's walk toward the lake," suggested Evadne. "It's over there. You look to the left and I'll look to the right."

Once more, they started walking, the empty basket dangling from Grace's right arm. Evadne looked at her, feeling a little ashamed of having laughed at her. "Wait a minute, Grace." Like a mother with a child, she turned up the sleeves of the fox coat until Grace's hands could be seen. "Isn't that more comfortable?" Evadne asked.

"It sure is!" Grace wiggled her fingers, snuggling in the luxury of the fur. "You don't think your Ma'll mind me wearing her coat, do you?"

The words, innocent though they were, triggered a shiver of memory. Evadne felt cold and hot at the same time. "No," she finally managed to say. "No, Grace, I think Mama would like it. You need it more than she does now."

"Gawd, I'm sorry—I forgot! Your poor Ma and Pa. . . ." Grace started to take off the coat.

"No, Grace." Evadne stopped her. "The coat's yours. Now," she took a deep breath, "let's see if we can find anyone we know."

Most of the refugees at the eastern edge of the park must have been early arrivals from the city hall, Mechanics Pavilion, and Portsmouth Square, Evadne decided. They seemed to have had time to settle in, enough to erect makeshift tents of sheets and blankets and to improvise cooking arrangements. They had almost a festive air as they gathered around the iron pots over the small fires, giving them a stir now and then. A mixture of cooking odors drifted on the air. What destroyed the illusion of picnickers out for a lark was the comparative silence. Voices were low, hushed, like the wind in the trees, and the faces were resigned and tired. Even Grace lost the desire to talk, much less complain, as she and Evadne moved along, overwhelmed by the scene.

Regardless of all they had been through, neither girl had actually absorbed the fact that the entire southern part of the city—and much of the northeast—had been destroyed and lay in ruins. Evadne, moreover, had thought largely in terms of the business and commercial areas—of hotels like the Palace and St. Francis, of newspapers and stores burning—not of the hundreds of frame houses crowded together south of the Slot and in Chinatown and the Mission District. The homes that she knew were the fine houses on Nob Hill, stretching west to Van Ness. But there were thousands—perhaps hundreds of thousands—of people here now as homeless as she.

Women with careworn faces and red, chapped hands held children to their breasts, rocking them to the monotony of soothing whispers. Beside them sat women with unlined faces and manicured hands. Women in calico and shawls rubbed shoulders with women in silk nightdresses and expensive fur coats. Men, still dapper in black suits and bowlers, spoke in low voices to men in rough cotton shirts and denim pants. Here and there were Chinese from the Sansome Street area. Everyone had lost everything, and even the Chinese were being accepted as human. A little boy with blond curls in short pants and jacket and big tie was sitting playing with a pigtailed Chinese boy of about the same age, wearing a cotton quilted, high-necked jacket and black silk pants. Each boy had a serious expression on his face as the Chinese boy's carved wooden animals provided a cavalry of sorts for the blond boy's tin soldiers. Evadne smiled as she watched them, moving on again only when Grace tugged at her arm.

A man with a bloodstained handkerchief tied clumsily around his head was supporting another man whose right arm was held at an awkward angle and whose hands were badly burned.

"Excuse me, Miss," said the man with the bandaged head. "I heard there was an aid station somewhere—this way, they said. Do you know where it is?"

"No," Evadne answered, slightly sickened by the sight of the other man's burnt hands. But she looked around, shading her eyes. "It may be just ahead. At least, I see a tent with what looks like a Red Cross flag."

"Thanks, Miss." The man swayed as he tried to get a better grip on the man he was holding.

"Here, let us help you. We're going that way," Evadne offered impulsively. She went to his companion's other side, trying to hold him up and avoid touching the broken arm. "Wait a minute," she said. The reticule she was holding and the blanket were in her way. She handed them to Grace to carry and was able to get a better grip. Between them, Evadne and the man managed to get the more badly injured man to the aid tent. Relieved at last of his burden, the man with the bandaged head sighed with relief.

"It's a long walk from Portsmouth Square," he explained. "I didn't think we were going to make it."

"He must be a good friend of yours," Evadne said, admiring his courage and perseverance.

"Friend?" The man shook his head. "Miss, I never saw him before yesterday. He was in the room next to mine at a rooming house. I was lucky, just got knocked around a bit, but he was trapped when the building started to burn. I couldn't just leave him there, could I?" He looked inside the aid tent where a doctor was examining the other man's injuries. "I guess he's in good hands now. Goodbye, Miss, and thanks for your help."

As Evadne stared after him, astonished by his selflessness, the man disappeared into the crowd.

"Vad . . . ?" Grace's voice broke in on her thoughts. "I smell food."

A Red Cross worker heard her and said, "There's a soup

kitchen over there—where you see the people in line. The Army set it up."

"Thank you." Evadne took her reticule from Grace, leaving her the blanket to carry. Then, remembering how Grace had left the food behind, she took that from her too.

The line at the soup kitchen was long and more people were heading in its direction. Evadne took her place behind an ancient Chinese woman, with Grace behind her. As hungry as everyone was, there was no pushing or crowding. Even when the line stopped moving while another kettle of soup was warmed up, no one complained. A few people had cooking pots to carry food back to their families. Others carried plates, but most were as empty-handed as Evadne and Grace. As the line drew closer to the cook tent, Evadne noticed those people with nothing to eat out of were being given Army mess kits.

Finally it was their turn. An Army cook, bare-chested in the heat of the fire, glanced at them. Seeing that they had nothing in their hands, he filled two tin kits with a thin stew. Another man placed a slab of bread on the first kit and handed it to Evadne with a spoon.

"Hang on to the kit and the spoon," he advised. "We ain't got many more, and you're gonna need them."

Evadne thanked him, waiting for Grace. Carrying the kits carefully, the girls found a place by a nearby pond to sit and eat. The bread was coarsely textured and lumpy, as if it had not been given enough time to rise before being put in the oven and the stew was thin, a few pieces of unidentifiable meat and some vegetables drowned in broth. To Evadne, however, it was even more delicious then the stew Grace had made the day before. She soaked the bread in the broth in order not to waste a drop.

Grace tasted the stew and made a face. "I don't see how you can eat it," she declared, eyeing the meat suspiciously. "It may be dog, like them Chinese eat, or maybe even horse."

Evadne stared at her, totally exasperated. "If I can eat it," she said, thinking of the delicious meals shared with William —the oysters, the tender beef, the succulent lobsters and other delicacies, "you can too. And you had better eat it while it's hot," she told her bluntly. "It won't taste any better when it's cold."

Grace looked down at her plate, suddenly ashamed of herself. There had been a time in her life when she would have eaten the mess on her plate gratefully. And if Miss Vad could get it down, she could. She tore off a piece of the bread and soaked it in the broth, raising no more objections.

When they had finished, they rinsed the mess kits and spoons in the pond. Evadne put hers in her reticule and advised Grace to put hers in the empty basket she was carrying. "We don't want to lose them."

Her hunger abated, Evadne looked around. More refugees were gradually filling the area. "This is as good a place for us to stay as any, Grace," she decided. "What do you think?"

Grace looked around dubiously. "Where we going to sleep?" she asked.

"On the ground, I guess, like everybody else. We have the blanket and the fur coats. Perhaps we can make a tent using the blanket," Evadne suggested.

Grace regarded her with admiration, marveling at how Evadne seemed to take every new obstacle in stride. "Maybe we can," she agreed. "Anyway, we can't just keep walking around."

The mention of walking reminded Grace of her aching feet, and she took off her shoes. A blister had formed on her left heel. She looked at it in dismay. "I guess we gotta stay here, like it or not," she said.

Evadne took the blanket and spread it on the ground, marking off a little bit of territory for them, before taking off her fur coat to use as a pillow. "Let's try and get some sleep," she suggested. "A nap will do us both good."

She stretched out on the blanket, closing her eyes, and Grace lay down beside her. But Evadne's eyes refused to stay closed. Staring up at the blue sky, she began to think of William. Had he tried to go back and look for her? Had he, perhaps, died in the fire trying to get back to her? She shuddered at the thought. Or had he deserted her and the burning city, concerned only for his own safety . . . ? No, she couldn't believe that, not William. But, then, where—?

Grace, too, was wide-awake. "I keep thinking about my Ethan," she said softly. "I keep trying to tell myself he's gone, but my heart just won't let me believe it."

"I know," Evadne said. Her heart longed to tell Grace not to give up, that they might still find Ethan. But it was wrong to raise such false hopes.

She sat up and wrapped her arms around her knees, trying to think, to plan what they would do after the fires were out. Any plans for the future were useless at the moment. The city was still afire, pillars of smoke rising to unbelievable heights, and the soldiers and fire department were still using dynamite, by the sound of the explosions, in a futile effort to create a fire line, always retreating from a fresh onslaught of flame.

There was always Auntie's house in Sausalito, Evadne thought, if there was any way to get there. No, she remembered, that wouldn't do. Though Auntie had made out a new will, leaving everything to Evadne, she had not signed it, which meant the house and everything else would go to charity. Of course, Evadne could contest the old will, but that would take money, and she had no money. Still, the idea offered a ray of hope . . . a ray that dimmed when she remembered that she had put the unsigned will into the pocket of the black suit she had been wearing when William handed it to her. She had changed from that suit after the sailor had ripped it into her own green one. The will, like everything else on Nob Hill, was now ashes.

Evadne sighed. She looked over at Grace, who was studiously examining the blister on her heel, and suddenly wanted to be alone. "Grace, I want to look around," she said quickly. "I know you can't walk with that blister, and anyway someone should stay here and keep our place. I won't stay away long," she promised, seeing the look of alarm on Grace's face.

"How you gonna find me again?" Grace demanded, looking around at the throng surrounding them.

"As long as you stay where you are, it will be easy. I can always find the pond," Evadne pointed out.

"Well. . . ." Grace looked doubtful.

"Listen, Grace, we have to know where things are, like fresh water and . . . and—" Evadne was thinking of bathrooms, which were something that ladies did not discuss.

Grace giggled, understanding her immediately. "You're right, Miss . . . Vad. I guess you had better look around. I won't move till you get back," she promised. "Not that I could," she added wryly, looking again at her blistered heel.

"Good." Evadne rose, aware of her own aching feet and sore muscles, but she had to get away from Grace for awhile. She skirted the pond, heading for a stretch of open ground.

In one direction, the soldiers were erecting tents for the old and the very young and the ill. There were not enough tents for everyone in the park and would not be until emergency

supplies arrived from the other Army and Marine bases of the
Pacific region. Near the tents trenches were being dug that a
soldier, blushing, told her were for latrines.

Evadne nodded, equally embarrassed, and started in the
other direction. She saw an elegant brougham rising in lonely
splendor in the middle of a small group of people. The Tylers,
she thought, had had a carriage like that that Mrs. Tyler had
insisted on keeping even after her husband had bought their
automobile. She had, in fact, refused to ride in the car, which
she saw as a noisy and dangerous contraption: An automobile
was all right for insensitive masculine natures but completely
unfit for a sensitive woman like herself.

In the hope of finding someone she knew and learning news
about all her friends, Evadne hurried as quickly as she could
toward the carriage, avoiding the campsites set up in her
path. At the same time, she refused to let her hopes rise too
high, not wanting to be disappointed.

Then she saw Mr. Dillard placing a blanket over a horse
standing near the brougham, its head drooping to munch a
few clumps of grass. "Mr. Dillard!" she called, not pausing to
wonder what he was doing tending to the Tylers' carriage
horse.

He turned at the sound of his name, searching the faces
around him. When he saw Evadne, a smile spread over his
tired features. "Evadne!" he cried, and put his arm around
her to give her a hug. "How good to see you . . . alive."

Evadne hugged him back, looking around the little en-
campment. Lillie ran toward her from behind the carriage,
where she had been sitting in the shade. "Oh, Lillie!" Evadne
hugged her friend.

Over Lillie's head, she looked at Mr. Dillard, her lips
silently forming the words: The Tylers?

"Lillie, don't hug Evadne so. She won't be able to
breathe," Mr. Dillard said. He took Evadne by the hand,
leading her in the direction of the carriage. "Mrs. Dillard and
Mrs. Tyler are inside the carriage, resting. Lillie and I are
doing what we can."

Evadne glanced at him, surprised by his words and at the
change in him. Although he had always been pleasant to her,
she had never really been comfortable in his presence. Unlike
her own father, who had been a hearty, affectionate man, Mr.
Dillard had always seemed cold and distant. He had rarely
been at home, preferring to spend his time at his office or his
club. Instead of lavishing attention on his wife and daughter,

he had lavished it on the business of real estate. Not that he was ungenerous, quite the opposite. Whatever Mrs. Dillard or Lillie wanted, he had given them, regardless of the cost.

Still holding Evadne's hand, he stopped on the other side of the brougham. Henry Tyler was sitting on the ground, his back against the front wheel of the carriage, staring into space, totally withdrawn from his surroundings. His face was gray and his hands lay uselessly on his outstretched legs. He was muttering to himself.

"What—what is he saying?" Evadne asked, filled with pity, in spite of his callous treatment of her, at the sight of the man sunk to such depths of despair.

"Nothing that makes much sense." Mr. Dillard rubbed the stubble of beard on his cheeks. "He keeps blaming Vesuvius and the Italians for all this, saying we shouldn't be so generous with foreigners when we need the money more."

"He's not the only one saying it," Evadne said, thinking of Grace and Cook. "But when we raised the hundred thousand dollars for the relief of the victims of Vesuvius, how could we know?" Evadne shrugged.

"We would have lost the money anyway," Mr. Dillard said. "There can't be any paper money left in the city except what people have in their pockets. And who knows what has happened to the gold in the banks?"

"Surely Mr. Tyler must realize that!" Evadne said.

Mr. Dillard shook his head. "I don't think he even hears us when we talk to him, Lillie and I. Usually we just bring on a recital of all the assets in his bank. Mostly we just leave him be and try to get him to eat something now and then. It's all we can do."

Evadne was puzzled. "But the brougham, the horse . . . ? Someone had to think of that, harness the horse—"

"Father did, Evadne," Lillie said proudly. "He thought of everything—food, clothing. . . ."

Evadne looked at Mr. Dillard again. He smiled at her shyly. "Someone had to do something. I kept my eye on the Fairmont. From the top floor of the house I saw when the fire reached Powell Street. I came down and went over to the Tylers. When I saw the state Henry was in, well, I took charge."

"I got blankets and clothes together," Lillie added, "and Papa and I put all the food we could find into baskets. When the soldiers came, we were ready."

Mr. Dillard patted his daughter's shoulder in what was for

him a remarkable show of affection. "I don't know what I would have done without Lillie. She wanted to go and get you, but the soldiers refused to let anyone into your street."

"How did you get here?" Lillie asked Evadne.

"Walked!" Evadne laughed. "I have never done so much walking in my life."

"Alone?" Lillie was horrified.

"Grace was with me. We—we managed," Evadne said.

"You must stay with us," Lillie said. "Mustn't she, Father?"

"You're very welcome, Evadne. We don't have much," Mr. Dillard admitted, "but—"

"Vad!"

Evadne turned to see Paul Tyler coming toward them from the direction of the soup kitchen. It occurred to Evadne now that neither Lillie nor Mr. Dillard had mentioned him. She wondered why. The answer was not long in coming.

Lillie left Evadne's side to rush to Paul. She took his hand and led him forward. Paul's eyes were as feverish as his father's were dull, but there was the same slackness to his jaw. Where his father muttered dolefully to himself, Paul, Evadne discovered, chattered with the lively inconsequentiality of a child.

"Vad!" he cried. "I was wondering where you were. We're having a picnic, but how could it be a real picnic without you? I told Lillie that. She just wouldn't listen when I said you'd come."

"Paul. . . ." Evadne's heart twisted. She didn't know what to say.

"Your parents, they should be here, too. Are they coming later, Vad?" He shook free of Lillie and approached Evadne, grasping her hands. "You look so pretty in that green suit. Did you buy it because it matches your eyes?" He planted a wet kiss on her mouth. "We make such a handsome couple . . . don't we, Vad?"

"Paul." Lillie took his hand again. "Don't excite yourself so." She put an arm around him, as a mother would do with a child. "Sit down now and put your head in my lap. I'll shield your eyes so you can sleep," she told him, rocking him gently in her arms.

Evadne turned back to Mr. Dillard, who was watching his daughter thoughtfully. It amazed her that he could be so calm under the burden of caring for everyone. But the adversity that had shattered Mr. Tyler and Paul seemed to have given him new strength. Once again, Evadne looked at Paul in Lillie's arms. Poor Lillie! She had loved and wanted Paul so much for so many years, while Paul had pursued Evadne no matter how much she had tried to discourage him. Now Lillie had him—but in a way that no one could ever have imagined.

Mr. Dillard followed her gaze—and her thoughts. "Well, Evadne," he said softly, "what we hope for is not always what we want when we have it."

"Is there anything I can do?" she asked him.

He smiled. "No, my dear, except hope for the best, hope that Paul snaps out of this—this condition. His family is going to need him."

"I am sure he will," Evadne said with more confidence than she felt. "After all, he is young."

"And the young are more resilient?" Mr. Dillard patted her shoulder, studying her face when she turned to look at him. "What about you? You cannot stay alone. At the moment, everyone is calm, but that may not last. There are many . . . well . . . crude men here, Evadne. You could be in great danger."

"I have Grace to look after—and to look after me," she added hurriedly, so as not to worry the man. "I cannot leave her, Mr. Dillard, and it would not be fair to you—all of you here—for us to join you and add to the burdens you already have."

"You would be a great help, not a burden, Evadne. I always felt that you were the most sensible of Lillie's friends, headstrong though your father said you were." He smiled at her.

Evadne smiled too. The mention of her father somehow comforted her. Recent though her loss was, it now seemed to have happened in another life. "I am afraid that he knew me only too well, although I never meant to worry him."

"You never did. You were a source of great pleasure to him. He was headstrong too," Mr. Dillard reminded her. "Always ready to invest in new ventures, and with a zest for life that I envied."

"Then I could do worse than take after him," Evadne said.

"Yes, and you will need those qualities he passed on to you in the weeks to come." He looked toward the east and the burning city. "People like you and me—and there are many of us—may be defeated now, but we will win, Evadne. You will see. San Francisco will rise out of its ashes like a phoenix, more beautiful than ever."

For a moment, Evadne thought that perhaps Mr. Dillard had lost his senses too. No one seeing the pillars of smoke could possibly believe there would be anything left, much less any means to build it. "Do you really think so?" she asked doubtfully.

"I do." Mr. Dillard put his arm around her. "And if your father were here, he would say the same, Evadne."

"I'll remember that, Mr. Dillard, and . . . thank you. You have given me fresh courage." Impulsively, she kissed him on the cheek.

"Thank you, Evadne. If you need us, or want anything, come back." He kissed her forehead. "Always remember that you are your father's child."

"I will. Now, I must get back to Grace. Give my best to Mrs. Dillard and Mrs. Tyler. . . ."

She left him, walking slowly back in the direction from which she had come. Just before she reached the pond, she turned toward the Japanese Tea Garden, wanting a few more moments to herself. She had never realized that her father and Mr. Dillard had been such friends, although she had known that they often lunched together at the Bohemian Club. She knew, too, that Mr. Dillard was right, that her father would have found new courage and a fresh challenge in the destruction of the city. But . . . she was a woman. Even so, she could try to live up to Mr. Dillard's—and her father's—expectations of her.

At the top of the arch of the Japanese bridge, she stopped, staring down into the water. There was no sign of the carp that she had pointed out to William that day. Where the woman had walked with her little boy was a young couple, walking arm in arm, obviously in love. Nearby, another couple held hands as they sat on the ground talking, oblivious to everyone except themselves.

Tears rose to Evadne's eyes. Watching the couples enviously, she struggled to keep any thought of William out of her head. He was lost to her forever, she told herself. She must look to the future, not live in the past as Mr. Tyler and Paul were doing.

Another series of explosions from the city made her raise her head. All was not lost if the soldiers still had hopes of stopping the fire, she told herself. With that thought in mind, she retraced her steps to find Grace.

The girl greeted her with a cry of relief. "I was beginning to get worried, you were gone so long," she said.

"I'm sorry," Evadne apologized. She had decided not to tell Grace about the Tylers and the Dillards. She was afraid of bringing on a fresh wave of crying.

"I've been thinking," Grace said as Evadne sank down on the blanket beside her. "I've been nothing but a burden to you, and you've done nothing but care for me."

"Oh, Grace!" Evadne protested. "If you needed me, well, I needed you too. What would we each do alone?"

"That's just it. I haven't been doing my share, but things are going to be different from now on," Grace promised. She put on her shoes, wadding some grass in the back of the left one to cushion the blister.

Evadne watched her. "What are you going to do?"

"Go back to that soup kitchen for one thing. Give me that mess kit. Maybe I can find some fresh water too."

Evadne let her go, after first telling her about the latrines. As she watched Grace hobble off, she smiled. Now, this was the Grace she knew, and it was a relief to have her acting like her old self again. She thought of Mr. Tyler then and Paul. Perhaps they, too, would eventually recover from the shock of the disaster and become their old selves again.

She lay back on the blanket, stretching her body, relaxing muscles that ached and ached. Despite the smoke and fires, the sky above was a clear, brilliant blue . . . the same blue as William's eyes. She squeezed her eyes shut, refusing to think about him and succeeding only in seeing his face smiling at her, filled with love and desire. She sat up quickly—to find a man watching her speculatively with narrowed dark eyes. His hair was a curly ink-black, his lips full and rosy, and his skin was swarthy, reminding Evadne of the fishermen who manned the boats at Fisherman's Wharf though he wore a too-tight black business suit.

She averted her eyes, gazing in the direction of the soup kitchen, hoping to see Grace returning. Her mouth went dry with fear, and she tried to calm her wildly beating heart.

"A pretty young thing like you shouldn't be all alone," the man suggested in a soft, musical voice. Seeing Evadne press her lips together, still not looking at him, he went on, "There are all sorts of rough types around. You need a man to protect you." He took a step toward her.

She could see his black boots at the edge of the blanket. If she shrank back, it would only tell him how frightened she was, and if she stood, she would be in easy reach of him. All she could do was keep her place, maintaining a stony silence.

If she ignored him, he might go in search of more responsive company.

"I'm frightening you, aren't I? You shouldn't be afraid of me," he said. His voice had a sensuous quality that disturbed her. In spite of herself, she raised her eyes to his face, to the glittering eyes and slightly parted full lips that pursed to blow her a kiss. She began to tremble. "Please go away," she said in as firm a voice as she could manage. "I am waiting for someone who will be back at any moment."

"I know." He chuckled. "I saw her leave. A little thing like that isn't much protection."

Blood flamed in Evadne's face at the thought that this man had been watching her for some time. She began to wish that she had not been so quick to refuse Mr. Dillard's invitation to join them, now fully aware of how vulnerable she and Grace were.

"Please go away," she repeated, trying to keep her desperation out of her voice and not knowing what to do if he refused. Helplessly, she glanced around, looking for someone who might help her.

Nearest her were an elderly man and woman, fussing so ostentatiously with their few belongings that it was obvious that they could see what was happening and had no intention of getting involved, except to send sly, sidelong glances in Evadne's direction. If she screamed, someone might come to her assistance, but that person might be no better than this man who, at least, had not yet attempted to touch her.

He had observed her actions. Realizing that he had the upper hand, he took his time. "You surely do need the protection of a young, healthy man like me." When she kept silent, he went on, his voice taking on a harder edge. "There's plenty of time. Take all you want. It's not dark yet."

The last remark, instead of frightening Evadne, strengthened her courage. After all, it wasn't even noon yet. Darkness was hours away. Grace would be back soon and, seeing what was going on, would get help. In the meantime, Evadne was protected by the bright sunlight and open surroundings. She was not trapped in an empty house. This man could not attack her as the sailor, Matt, had done.

Ignoring him, she looked down at the ground again, studying the early spring blades of grass. They were a lovely green, still pale from the weak sunlight. . . .

"Vad!" Grace's cry, so close that it startled Evadne, made her tormentor jump back. Evadne took advantage of the man's surprise to scramble to her feet, ready to run. She stopped in shock. Coming toward her with Grace was a man with singed red hair and a freckled, smoke-smudged face. The too-large trousers he wore were held up by suspenders and the too-small white shirt bulged with the stress of his brawny arms and chest. Evadne stared incredulously, not only at him and Grace but also at the man walking slightly behind them.

Her heart pounded. He was big—broad-shouldered and deep-chested—deeply tanned with blond-streaked hair. Then, as quickly as the fire of desire inside her ignited, it died. Oh, how cruel—how closely the man resembled William . . . but he was a stranger.

Whoever he was, he assessed Evadne's predicament at a glance. He strode toward the man in the tight black suit, moving Evadne to one side with a touch of a big, calloused hand, confronting her tormentor.

"I was only talking to the lady," the man whined. He backed up from this stranger who towered a good head over him.

"It doesn't appear to me that the lady wanted to talk to you," the newcomer replied. "I'm not going to tell you twice to be on your way," he warned, obviously used to giving orders, "so you'd best leave now."

The other man did not bother to answer, but took to his heels with such speed that he almost tripped over his own feet.

Evadne looked at her rescuer more closely. Standing so near to her that she could almost touch him, his resemblance to William was even more striking. There were the same sun wrinkles at the corners of the eyes, the same broad cheekbones, the same firm mouth, but the nose was longer and slightly crooked, as if it had been broken. The eyes were brown, not blue, and more deeply set. What's more, it was a stern, humorless face. When he smiled, however, the smile softened the stern lines slightly.

"You must be Miss Evadne Harper," he said in a firm, slightly rough voice.

Evadne nodded, speechless, looking to Grace for help. Grace was all smiles, her round eyes sparkling. She stepped up to Evadne, dragging her oddly dressed companion with her. A broad grin split his grimy face. Though his fantastic appearance made him hard to recognize, he had to be Ethan, for only Ethan could have brought such joy to Grace's face.

"Vad!" Grace exclaimed, hugging Evadne with her arm. "I found him—I found my Ethan!"

"Oh, Grace, I'm so happy for you," Evadne told her, concealing her own disappointed hopes that had been raised by the stranger. She looked from Grace to Ethan to the stranger. "Where . . . how—?"

"It was a miracle, a true miracle," Grace exclaimed. "I went up to that soup kitchen—" She stopped, her face reddening. "Oh, Vad, I forgot all about the food!"

Evadne laughed. "It doesn't matter, Grace. Just don't keep me in suspense about this miracle."

"Well, first I looked at the people in the line, thinking mebbe Cook or someone might be there," Grace said. "I didn't see anyone I knew, so I got in the line, not paying any attention to anything except the smell of food, getting hungrier and hungrier—"

Ethan shook his head. "Sweetheart, let me tell the story." He put his arm around Grace. "I was on my way from the aid station when I saw the soup kitchen and was about to get in line. I was with Captain Nevis here." He nodded at the stranger. "The next thing I knowed, there was Grace, looking so patient. So, I just rushed over to her. She told us about you, and we came here." He grinned. "Just in time, I guess."

"I'm still confused," Evadne admitted. "Who is Captain Nevis?" She noticed then that the stranger was wearing a blue uniform jacket with brass buttons the kind the captains on her father's ships wore.

He took charge now. "I'm the captain of the whaling ship on which Ethan was second mate, Ma'am," he explained. "We were standing off in the Bay, taking on supplies, when the earthquake hit. Half my crew was caught ashore—we were due to sail today. I came looking for them as soon as I could. I knew Ethan hadn't signed on for another voyage, but I found him on Mission Street, wandering around in a daze in only his . . . his . . . ."

"My drawers, Miss Evadne," Ethan said, blushing furiously. "I don't recall anything, just that first shock, until the Cap'n found me. I wanted to go straightaway to find Grace, but first I had to get some clothes."

"There were crates of clothes for the Vesuvius refugees on the wharves, ready to be shipped to Naples," the captain went on. "They opened them up, which accounts for this scarecrow," he added with a smile, squeezing Ethan's shoulder. "By then, we couldn't get through the fires to Nob Hill.

All we could do was help keep the wharves dampened down, to save what we could."

"Finally, we managed to make our way to Telegraph Hill," Ethan took up the story, "and from there to Russian Hill. But everything between there and Nob Hill—" Ethan shrugged. "It was just one big wall of flame. There was soldiers all over, too, and they kept talking curfew. We had to wait till morning. Then we came here, following the crowd like everyone else. I was positive sure I had lost Grace forever, and then I saw her."

"And now?" Evadne looked at the hand-holding pair.

"We ain't had time to talk about that, Vad," Grace declared, "but I'm not leavin' you here." She turned to Ethan. "Vad saved my life, Ethan, and she's all alone now. All she's got is me!"

Evadne turned to the captain, not wanting to discuss her personal situation. "Captain . . . what did you say your name was?"

"Nevis, Ma'am. Samuel Nevis out of New Bedford." He was looking at her with open admiration. "I'm at your service, Ma'am. . . ."

Chapter XIII

EVADNE SMILED AT NEVIS, FINDING COMFORT IN HIS RESEM-
blance to William. "I think," she said softly, "we should
leave Grace and Ethan alone. They have a lot to talk about."

Nevis nodded, his brown eyes never leaving her face. "It
might be well to chart a course," he agreed enigmatically.

"Captain, I can't presume on you and your kindness,"
Evadne protested. "Now that Ethan is here, I'm sure that
Grace and I will be fine."

"Perhaps so. From what sense I managed to make out of
what Grace said, I gather you have been most capable," he
said. "At the same time, I also have no place to go."

"You are being most gallant, but you have your ship to
consider," Evadne said.

"My first mate is seeing to her. At any rate, I cannot reach
my ship—and I do not have a crew." He looked around.
"This may be the best place to find the men I need. In the
meantime, I suggest that we chart that course. We could all
use some food."

"We will have to go back to the soup kitchen," Evadne
said. "If only we had a cooking pot of some sort, it would be
so much simpler."

Nevis noticed the elderly couple watching them now with
open curiosity. Among their belongings was a large iron pot.

He smiled. "Let me see what I can do." With that remark, he approached the couple, buttoning his jacket formally and raising his hand in a salute.

At first, they shrank back in fear, intimidated by his size, but his manner and whatever he said to them won them over. They smiled tremulously, and the little old lady timidly held up the pot with a hand trembling with age.

Nevis returned with the pot, smiling. "I told them that we would get enough food for them too," he explained. He hefted the pot. "I don't know how they managed to carry it this far. I doubt either of them could manage it with food in it."

Evadne smiled. Anyone who could win the old couple over so quickly had to be trustworthy. He suggested that she take the basket for bread or any other food that might be available. They set off, Nevis holding the pot with one hand and guiding Evadne with the other. She found herself relaxing in his presence and in the relief of his taking command.

As they walked, Nevis asked, speaking in the precise tones of a native New Englander, "Grace is your maid, is she not?"

"Why do you say that?" Evadne hedged, not sure how to answer the question under the circumstances.

"In five years aboard ship, men get to learn a lot about one another. Since we left San Francisco five years ago, my crew has been to Hawaii and Alaska and Mexico, whaling, then back to Hawaii before returning to New Bedford and now San Francisco again. Once we sight a pod of whales, there is little time for talk, but it can be a long time between pods," he explained.

"And a long trip around the Horn too," said Evadne.

"True enough, Miss Harper. You are not ignorant of the sea then?" he asked, smiling.

"My father has—had," she corrected herself, "a fleet of ships engaged in the Hawaii and Far Eastern trade."

"So Ethan told me."

Evadne glanced sidewise at the big man in the blue uniform, studying the rugged profile and crooked nose, the firm line of the jaw. "It is all gone now, Captain," she told him in a tone as calm as his own. "My father wanted more ships and could borrow no more money in San Francisco. He went East with my mother to see the bankers there. They . . . they had an accident." She took a deep breath. "Even without the earthquake, I would have been . . . put on the street."

"I am sorry to hear that. Yet, Grace—?"

"She was my maid, yes, but she has been my friend too." The sigh that Evadne had been suppressing rose to her lips. She hastened to add, "She *is* my friend. She is also free to go with Ethan."

They had joined the line of refugees at the soup kitchen. To Evadne's eyes, more than a hundred people seemed to be ahead of them, none of them raising their heads any more at the sounds of dynamite and black powder exploding along Van Ness Street. Just as they had become inured to the sight of flame and smoke, so they had become used to the detonations.

"And you, what about you?" Nevis asked. "From what she said, Grace will not leave you—not even for Ethan."

"She must, mustn't she, Captain? You and I will have to see to that," declared Evadne. "Somehow, I will take care of myself."

Nevis nodded. "How, Miss Harper?" His hand turned her head to look at the flames still rising in the city. "I have no doubt that thirty-six hours ago you had friends who would have helped you. You may have been in love—"

"Please! I will be all right!" Evadne cried.

"Very well." Nevis didn't press her any further. "For myself, as soon as I can get a crew and back to my ship, I intend to sail to Hawaii. The climate is most amenable—especially after the New England winters," he added.

"You intend to stay there, then?" Evadne asked, looking at him curiously.

"I do, Miss Harper. I intend to convert my vessel for the island trade and eventually buy land there," he explained.

"It sounds so . . . so simple, Captain Nevis. It is—" she smiled at him "—a well-charted course."

"I hope so." The captain shifted the heavy pot to his other hand. "I have also been thinking about taking a wife—a wife who will be a help to me, able to keep accounts and care for my business while I am away."

A scream rose from the depths of Evadne's being. Desperately she looked around, hoping to find William—or for William to find her—as miraculously as Ethan had discovered Grace. She understood all too well why Nevis was speaking to her as he was.

"I would not want just any woman as my wife," he continued. "After all, I can always hire a bookkeeper. I would like a wife to be proud of, one who will be a friend and companion."

The line moved suddenly forward. A vagrant breeze wafted the odor of cooking meat and warm bread toward the line, evoking a sigh of hunger. Evadne tried to think. Even though Matt the sailor now seemed a bad dream, a nightmare, the memory of the man in the tight black suit, his feet planted firmly on the blanket, was not. Nor could she ignore the fact that she had no one whom she could go to for help. She could hardly turn to Mr. Dillard, even though she knew he would take her in. The poor man had enough to bear.

Once more, Evadne found herself studying the profile of the man beside her. It was a strong face, a face enough like William's that she found herself attracted to it. She straightened her back. William was gone, and Captain Nevis seemed a gentle man, a determined man, with a will that matched her father's. She could do worse.

A smile trembled on her lips as she looked up at him coquettishly from under lowered eyelids. "Captain Nevis, it almost sounds as if you are proposing to me."

A flush rose in the man's cheeks. "You are a beautiful woman, Miss Harper, so far above me in station," he declared in his old-fashioned manner, "that had I met you a few days ago, I would never have dared speak to you. Now, the world has turned upside down. Time has no meaning—"

"Yes," Evadne interrupted. "We have lived years in hours. I feel an old woman. I have seen a man killed . . . almost killed a man myself."

"That's why I said what I did," he replied calmly. "Think about it. There is time. It is difficult to say when we will be able to make our way through the city, and there is the matter of a crew."

"Grace and Ethan . . . what about them?" asked Evadne, her mind reeling with the thoughts that this man had sown in the fertile soil of her confusion about her present and concern for the future. "Ethan planned to make his home here."

"He has decided to sign on again as my second mate. He and Grace will be married as soon as possible, and the two will sail with me. Once we reach Honolulu, they will look around for a place to live. Island trading is profitable, and Ethan would be gone only a few weeks at a time instead of the years a whaler spends at sea." He paused a moment, then added, "At least, he had agreed to sign on and those are the plans . . . depending on you. Grace insists that she will not leave you unless you are safe and provided for."

"Captain Nevis, I . . . I am very confused," Evadne confessed. "You are being very kind—"

"And practical," he pointed out. "What I am offering is a solution to your problems. I am a God-fearing man, I might add. The Bible is . . . well . . . my bible. All I ask is that you think our conversation over."

The girl nodded. "I will, I promise you, but you have spoken of marriage and that's a big step even under these circumstances. I do not love you, after all. In fact, I have only just met you."

"I am aware of that," Nevis said solemnly. "I am looking for a wife—a helpmate, if you will, Miss Harper—who is willing to work alongside me as my mother did with my father. You have the intelligence and the other qualities that I seek. You are pure and you are beautiful . . . very beautiful. If it were any woman I wanted," he flushed slightly, betraying the strength of his New England upbringing, "I could find her in any port. I am not looking for company for the voyage."

It was Evadne's turn to blush, for that was just what she had been about to suggest. The captain's sharp eyes noticed her flushed cheeks. He concluded his recital primly: "I have many misgivings about women—even wives—aboard a working ship. If the situation were different, you and Grace would go by passenger ship. As it is, it is best for you to sail with me, but only if you are both properly wedded."

They were almost at the head of the line, to Evadne's relief. She decided to bring the disturbing conversation to a close. "I will think over what you have said, Captain. That is all I can promise for now."

"That is all I wish," Nevis declared, handing the iron pot over to an Army cook. "The fact that you did not—cannot— give me an immediate answer is in your favor. You rise even higher in my estimation."

"I will get the bread," Evadne said quickly, moving along the planks on sawhorses that had been set up to serve as a table.

When she explained that she needed food for six, a soldier filled her basket with coarse bread. "If any of you need any clothing," he told her, "the Red Cross has boxes over near the aid station. They were collected in Los Angeles for them Italians at Vesuvius, but the Red Cross sent 'em here instead. I guess they figured you people need them just as much, if not more," he added, glancing at the array of clothing on some of the refugees in the line.

"Thank you," Evadne told him and rejoined the captain.

Nevis, she was learning, was a man of few words. Having said what he had to say, he did not speak again until they had returned to Grace and Ethan. The couple were sitting on the blanket, staring at one another and holding hands.

"Miss Harper," Nevis said in a voice so low that Evadne barely heard him. "You are still young enough to be romantic. Marriage without love does not mean that love may not come afterward. You can be sure I will do all in my power to win your love, as well as your hand."

Evadne stared after him as he carried the food first to the elderly couple. They looked up at him with tears in their eyes when he ladled a generous share of the stew into their plates and gave them enough bread to last the day.

What was left, he divided equally among the four of them. As they ate, Evadne mentioned the clothing the soldier had told her about. Ethan grinned, looking down at the comic array he was wearing. After they had eaten and cleaned up, he went off with Nevis—Ethan wanted to see about other clothing while Nevis wanted to see if he could find any other members of his crew. At the captain's suggestion, the two girls joined the elderly couple. They would all be safer, Nevis pointed out, if they appeared to be a family group.

Comforted as much by the captain's old-fashioned, courtly manners as by his logic and the food, the old couple agreed to the proposal. They chattered aimlessly to the two girls. They were brother and sister; he had been a bank teller all his life while she had been a teacher and had kept house for the two of them. After their retirement, they had used their savings to buy a little house in the Mission District, taking in a few respectable roomers to supplement their meager income.

Evadne listened, filled with pity. They had worked so hard all their lives, caring for one another and obviously taking whatever came their way with no complaint. Now, everything they had worked for was gone. Yet, even in the recital of their woes, there was no complaint—they still had each other. Evadne wondered what would happen to them.

She was young and healthy. Even so, how much of a future did she have, Evadne wondered. She had no training with which she could make a living. She had always expected that she would marry, that when the time came she would learn to run her own house—with her mother's help. In the meantime, all she knew how to do was enjoy herself, flirting with the young men she knew, any one of them whom would have been happy to marry her.

Marriage with one of those young men was out of the question now. None would be in any position to take on the responsibility of a wife. Most, like Paul, had gone into business with their fathers, or had been set up in a law practice or in a physician's office. For a long time, their primary concern would be to save what could be saved and to reestablish themselves. A young wife would be an unwelcome burden.

No matter what Evadne had said so bravely to Mr. Dillard—and to Grace—about taking care of herself, she was ill-equipped even to protect herself. Looking at the elderly brother and sister, she realized just how alone she was, how helpless to take care of the necessities of life. She was useless, except as a decoration, and no one in San Francisco now would need a mere decoration.

Captain Nevis, however, did not consider her merely an ornament, she thought. What was it he had said about wanting a helpmate to work beside him? Could he have seen something in her that no one else—not even William—had seen? Moreover, he had called her intelligent. The idea was new to her, despite her having excelled at school. Granted, little of what she had learned—such as French and embroidery—would serve her in any productive capacity, but she had been good at the rudimentary mathematics taught. Surely she could learn to keep books with help and practice.

The proposal that had seemed so ridiculous in the line at the soup kitchen began to have some appeal—if only she could put aside her romantic notion about marrying for love. This was no time to think about love, Evadne thought, shuddering at the sound of another explosion from Van Ness. Listening, she began to think over seriously the strange conversation—and to think about the man himself.

Captain Nevis was obviously a serious, upright New Englander, sternly schooled in the precepts of the Bible and hard work. Evadne tried to imagine what life with him would be like. What she envisioned was not the kind of life she had been expected to lead. Instead of ball gowns, fitted to show off her breasts and narrow waist, there would be high-necked black dresses, cut to conceal and not reveal the body, like those worn by the missionaries in Union Square who exhorted passersby to sin no more. Instead of parties, there would be Sunday afternoons spent reading the Bible and praying. Instead of waltzes and lighthearted conversation, there would be hymns and prayer meetings. Nevis, Evadne suspected, was a man filled with high purpose and little humor . . . or joy of life.

If only she knew what had become of William, she was sure that she would be able to think more logically about the future—not that it made much difference whether he had lost his life or deserted her. The truth that she had to face and accept was that he was not there, that she must make up her own mind. Even Grace could not help her . . . most particularly not Grace in view of what Nevis had said about Grace's refusing to leave her. A heavy weight settled on Evadne's shoulders with the awareness of how many people's fate rested on her decision.

During a lull in the brother's and sister's chatter, Grace took Evadne's hand, whispering, "I wonder where my Ethan's gone? It's been an awful long time since they left."

The words relieved Evadne of the burden of thought for the moment. Glad of the interruption, she whispered back reassuringly, "He'll be back soon. He and Captain Nevis may have found someone they know."

"Sure," Grace agreed. "I guess I'm being silly. It's just that, after having found him," she smiled in embarrassment, "I don't like it when he's outta my sight for a minute."

"I know. I'd feel the same if—if. . . ." Evadne closed her eyes and swallowed hard, unable to say William's name.

"I just wish," Grace said, "that you was as happy as me, that you had someone too."

Evadne glanced at her thoughtfully. She couldn't possibly know about Captain Nevis's proposal . . . ? She said simply, "Well, who knows what may happen, Grace. Look at you and—"

"They're back!" Grace cried, scrambling to her feet and beginning to run.

Evadne's eyes followed her. Ethan was no more appropriately attired, in denim overalls and a work shirt, but at least the clothes fit better. He had managed to clean up too. His freckled face lit up at the sight of Grace running to him. Nevis nodded politely to Evadne, his face a mask hiding any feelings.

She studied that face, wondering what he was thinking. "Do you have any news?" she asked.

He drew her to one side, glancing at the others to make

sure they were out of hearing. "What news I have is not good," he stated. "I do not wish to worry the others—"

Evadne's lips twitched. "But it is all right to worry me?"

Nevis's face flushed. "I did not mean it that way. It is only that I feel you have the courage to bear up under it."

"In other words, we may not be safe even here," Evadne said, beginning to wonder how much she *could* bear as she looked toward the east at the thick clouds of smoke that hid the city more completely than the fog had ever done.

"I would not go so far as to say that." Nevis's voice was flat and unemotional. He was speaking carefully, choosing his words with deliberation.

Evadne looked at him in exasperation, wondering if he ever lost that iron control, or did he have it even . . . even in bed. "Then what would you say?" she demanded.

"The Mission District is still afire. It is all the fire department can do to contain it south of Dolores," he said.

"That's well south of here," she pointed out.

"It is north of there—along Van Ness—that the real danger lies. The Army is dynamiting the entire east side of the street. If the fire somehow manages to jump that avenue—"

"It will be the turn of the western addition, and Golden Gate Park isn't far away," she finished. "We would be trapped." When Nevis was silent, Evadne added optimistically, "Perhaps it will not come to that. Perhaps the dynamiting will be successful."

"Even if it is, it may not mean we are safe," Nevis went on in that impossibly calm manner.

"What do you mean?" Something in his voice warned her that the fire might not be the worst they had to fear.

"I do not like telling you this, Miss Harper, for you are a woman—a very young woman with little knowledge of the world. But I have no choice. Ethan is too much in love to be able to keep his thoughts to himself, and I fear Grace is more likely to panic—from what I have heard and observed—than you." Although the captain tried to smile as he paid her the compliment, his eyes betrayed his concern.

"Go on, Captain. I assure you I will not betray your confidence by having hysterics or fainting or otherwise acting like . . . like a woman," she finished, unable to resist a smile.

"It is nothing to laugh about." His eyes sought out the black pall over the city. "From what I have heard, the military and health authorities fear still another scourge—the plague and typhus spread by the rats driven from the wharves and warehouses by the fire."

For a moment, Evadne felt dizzy as the blood seemed to rush from her head. Her face ashen, she pressed her lips tightly together to keep from crying out and breathed deeply. "Dear God," she managed to say at last, "is there no end to what we must endure?"

"Perhaps we must endure these misfortunes as Job did, to prove we have not lost our faith."

Evadne realized that he truly believed what he was saying. She had been right about him. It showed in his face and in the flat tone of acceptance in his voice. He was a man who knew his Bible—and believed in it with all the evangelism of a missionary out to save the heathen.

"If the situation is so desperate, I wonder why you are telling me?" Evadne said slowly. "It does not seem in character to worry me unnecessarily."

"I have a plan, and its success may depend on your assistance," Nevis told her.

Evadne stared at him, anger at his self-confidence competing with admiration. He was, she decided, a most exasperating man. But in spite of this, she felt drawn to him.

"What is it?" she asked.

"Miss Harper, the Presidio and Fort Point are to the north of us, are they not?" he asked.

"Yes, the Presidio is a military base and Fort Point is an old fort at the narrows that we call Golden Gate. Why?" She was puzzled.

He smiled at her briefly. "When the fires broke out along the waterfront, though water was being pumped from the Bay to wet down the wharves, I moved my ship to a new anchorage west of Alcatraz Island. If we can get to the Presidio or the fort, it is possible that I can send a message to my mate to have one of the ship's boats pick us up," Nevis explained.

"You are sure that he has not taken advantage of your absence to make sail?" she suggested.

Nevis smiled, broadly this time. "Quite positive, Miss Harper. More than half the crew had been given shore leave and had not returned before the earthquake. Once the fires started and it became apparent that they could not get back through the flames, it was all the few of us left aboard could do to hoist enough sail to move the ship that short distance.

No matter how eager my mate may be to escape this inferno, it is impossible for him to put to sea with a skeleton crew. Otherwise, I would have been gone with the ship long ago," he pointed out matter-of-factly.

Evadne hesitated. "You still have no crew," she pointed out, "and you could make your way to the Presidio faster alone, unencumbered by Grace and me."

"There will be sailors stranded, like myself, at the harbor, but I will need your help to get there. My knowledge of San Francisco is confined mostly to the Bay area. I am taking it for granted that you are better acquainted with the area around the Presidio."

"A little," she admitted. "I have been to balls there at the officers' club, and my escorts have shown my around." She remembered what he had told her earlier. "Have you decided to take us—Grace and I—with you, in spite of your misgivings about women on a working ship?"

"I have," Nevis said flatly. "While it is true that your services as a guide will save time, I have another reason for my decision."

She looked at him questioningly.

"You, Miss Harper. I have asked you to be my wife, and your safety must come above any other consideration. I know that you would not leave Grace and so she will accompany us, and I will need Ethan, who would not desert her any more than you would," he finished, as unemotional as ever.

Evadne stared at him in amazement. Her inclination was to remind him that she had not, after all, accepted his proposal, but she had no chance to protest.

As if guessing her thoughts, he added calmly, "I realize that you have not had time to think over my proposal, but you are a sensible girl and I am sure that you will eventually accept. More than ever, I want you for my wife. You are the wife I need."

Her senses reeled. No one had ever spoken to her before with such arrogance, and it *was* arrogance for the captain to make such an assumption. Her temper rose, making her eyes flash dark green. How she longed to tell the presumptuous, conceited lout that she would not have him if he were the last man on earth. But the words died on her lips. He might, after all, hold her fate in his hands. Even so, his attitude demanded a protest of some sort. Somehow, she must assert herself.

"What about them?" She nodded toward the elderly brother and sister.

"They would make the trip to the Presidio more difficult since they cannot keep up with us—"

"Captain Nevis! They have been kind to us," Evadne protested.

"Please, Miss Harper!" Nevis raised his hand to pat her awkwardly on the shoulder. "Do not make me appear more hardhearted than I am. If they wish to come with us and take their chances, I will do whatever I can to see that they reach safety."

Evadne smiled then. Perhaps the captain was not as unemotional as she thought.

"From your smile, I assume that I may count on you?" he asked.

"Yes, Captain Nevis. I will do whatever I can and whatever you say," she assured him.

The delighted smile that appeared on his face at her statement drove a knife into Evadne's heart.

Walking back to where Ethan and Grace sat still engrossed in each other, Evadne found herself marveling at this man's self-confidence and perseverance. He was made of the stuff Mr. Dillard had been talking about. He might be forced into taking a detour, but nothing would prevent him from eventually reaching his goal. One day, she was sure, he would be a wealthy and important man, no matter what he chose to do. Life with him would be filled with work but crowned by success.

The pace of the dynamiting accelerated as night approached and attempts to contain the fire grew more desperate. The others seemed to recognize it, too, although they were silent. The brother and sister, a patchwork quilt under them and another over them, lay side by side, holding hands. Grace curled up in Ethan's arms and he caressed her, warming her against the evening chill.

Evadne sat to one side, her fur coat over her shoulders and her arms wrapped around her legs. Whenever she thought about trying to sleep on the cold ground with only the stars above her, her mind summoned up the night she had spent with William in the shed. The nakedness of their bodies, the desire the touch of his hands had stirred in her made her body ache with longing and would not let her rest.

A shadow falling over her made her look up. Nevis stood towering over her, his hands clasped behind his back. She shrank away, recalling the menacing man in the tight black suit warning her to wait until night. Had the fall of darkness brought out the same lust in this proper New Englander?

"Miss Harper, you cannot sit up all night. You need your rest," he said. "We have all had little enough sleep these past two nights."

Evadne rested her chin against her knees. Was it only two nights ago that she fled to William's arms—to the ecstasy they had shared, oh, so briefly? She shook her head slightly.

Nevis mistook the shake of her head, thinking it meant that she did not want to sleep. "You must sleep," he insisted. "With only a few hours sleep, you will be able to think more clearly. You need not worry for your safety. I will be here to protect you."

She had to smile at that. If William were here, her safety and protection would be the last thing in her mind. Luckily, the darkness hid her smile. "I am sure of that," she murmured.

"Then, come. Lie down on the blanket. It will not make the ground any softer, but it will provide a little protection from the cold." He drew her to her feet and led her back to the blanket.

Too tired suddenly to resist, Evadne lay down, half turning on her side to give what privacy she could to Ethan and Grace wrapped in each other's arms. To her surprise, the captain lay down beside her and took her in his arms. Her body recoiled in shock.

"Do not be afraid," Nevis told her. "I do not intend to—harm you, only to keep you warm. Whatever you may believe of me, I am not a man to take advantage of a woman, especially a woman as gently reared and pure as you."

His words brought little comfort to Evadne. Lying beside him, she saw herself in a high-necked, long-sleeved nightdress in a big four-poster bed—untouched, loved and yet unloved, never again knowing the ecstasy that William had aroused in her, never again rising to join a lover in shared passion, never again experiencing the sweet joy of total fulfillment. She sighed, shivering for what had once been known and was now lost forever.

Nevis thought she was cold. He held her more closely, first making sure her coat was between their bodies.

Evadne grew desperate now for sleep, for a sleep that would let her forget, would swallow her and give blessed relief from her thoughts. She closed her eyes and tried to force herself to relax. Gradually, Nevis's presence brought her that relief, a relief that vanished when she recalled what he had said: "A woman as . . . pure as you." He thought, she was sure, that she was a virgin. What would he do when he discovered that she was not? That she was not pure but as spoiled as the women whose company he so disdained?

Her last thought, as she gave in to fatigue at last, was that she must tell this man that, young as she was, she was no longer innocent, no longer what he supposed her to be. Yet . . . did he really have to know, she wondered . . . ? Sleep postponed the answer.

Chapter XIV

EVADNE DID NOT SLEEP FOR LONG. HER LEFT ARM WENT TO SLEEP under the weight of Nevis's body and this woke her.

She had been dreaming of William and, for a moment, befuddled by sleep, she thought it was William holding her. Moving cautiously, she tried to free her arm to avoid waking him. In the light of the stars, she noticed his eyelashes and thought how long they looked against his cheeks. She reached out to stroke his cheek lightly . . . and came fully awake, remembering where she was and who this was. She pulled her hand back quickly. When Nevis stirred, she tensed, afraid that he would wake too. Noting how deep and regular his breathing was, she let the air out of her lungs in relief. He had changed position slightly, although he was still holding her, and the shift allowed her to work her arm out from under him.

Pins and needles tingled along her arm, but she dared not rub it to restore circulation for fear of waking him. As a result, she lay quietly, the thoughts that had overwhelmed her as she had fallen asleep returning.

Nevis's face in sleep was as inscrutable as it was when he was awake. Was he really as unemotional as he had appeared to be, she wondered. Was he so in control of himself that the closeness and warmth of her body, the scent of her hair stirred no longing for her at all? As for herself, desire began to stir in her as she became more aware of his closeness, recalling the passion of William's embrace. She began to wish that Nevis *had* taken her, had forced her to submit to him. That would have been preferable to the cold calculation of his proposal.

But . . . would it have been? With the memory of William so strong—the ecstasy they had shared, the caresses that left her body, tingling with desire, burning for the release of her passion—wouldn't she have fought Nevis off with all her might? She could not answer with any certainty, for it would be all too easy to pretend that Samuel Nevis was William Hopkins. The physical resemblance was too strong for her not to feel attracted to the captain. Still, in every other way the two men were as different as the sun and the moon. William was the sun, warming her with the promise of life, and as unpredictable as the clouds that drifted across the sun to bring rain or pass on by. Nevis was the moon, cold no matter how full it might be and as predictable as its phases and the tides it ordained. William was the epitome of joy while Nevis was the personification of reason. She could have laughed once and been amused by the ponderous Nevis—there would have been no contest between him and William. But that was in another lifetime—a lifetime that had ended less than forty-eight hours ago. Now the world was upside down, and she had little choice.

Tears rose in Evadne's eyes, accompanied by the familiar ache of longing in her body. She *must* put William out of her mind. It did no good to cry for the past. She must, she thought with grim humor, burn her bridges behind her. Like Nevis, she must take account of the present and plan for the future.

Her prospects seemed more discouraging than ever. Granted, William had been trying to get some of the bankers, her father had owed money to to hold off calling in the loans and at least save the house on Nob Hill. That hope was futile now; the house was gone. In addition, her father's ships might well represent the only equity left on which the banks themselves could borrow money. No banker in his right mind would hesitate to take possession of them. As far as Auntie's money and property was concerned, she could not count on that—not with the unsigned will in ashes. No, she was destitute except for the few jewels in her reticule and her own ingenuity.

Nevis stirred again and Evadne studied him carefully. Despite his stern manner, he was a kind man—he had shown that in his willingness to take the elderly brother and sister to safety with them. She sighed, wishing that he had shown her some sign of affection, a light kiss, perhaps, when he had taken her in his arms to keep her warm against the night. But she might as well have been a doll or a puppet for all the emotion he had shown.

Could she live without affection? she asked herself. Both her parents had been openly loving with her and each other. William, too, had been loving. She had known nothing but love and warmth all her life.

Yet, if she refused Nevis, what could she do? Where could she go? She could not impose on friends, now as homeless and as destitute as she was. As far as supporting herself was concerned, she had no illusions—she had no training to do work of any kind. Besides, it would be months, if not longer, before there was any place to work in San Francisco.

For the first time, Evadne realized and accepted to what lengths she might be forced to go in order to live, without a man to protect her. Her only asset, she thought grimly, was her body—the body that William had awakened and taught her to enjoy and use for the rapture of love. Life with Nevis, as joyless as it might be, would still be better than that!

She tried to tell herself that it would have been better never to have known the rapture. She could not. She could accept the fact that William was lost to her forever, but she could not accept the idea that it would have been better not to have known him at all. The memory of their hours together, their mutual passion, their shared ecstasy, might be all she would have to comfort her in the years ahead.

With that understood, Evadne began seriously to consider Nevis. He had called her pure. She knew what that meant: He believed she was a virgin. What would he think—and do—when he discovered that she was not, that she had known another man before him, that she had broken one of the rules of the Bible by which he lived? She was not sure which would be worse—to have him turn her out or to have him set himself the task of saving her. A faint smile touched her lips. There was another chance, faint though it now seemed: that she could teach him the joy and ecstasy, the pleasure in his body that William had taught her.

In any case, she must delay his discovering the truth about

her as long as she could. And if they should have to flee the
city as precipitously as he had suggested, there surely would
be no opportunity for them to marry before they reached
Honolulu. If, though, San Francisco's fires were somehow put
out and Nevis insisted on marriage before the ship sailed,
somehow she would have to convince him to wait.

Her mind made up, Evadne closed her eyes again in
another attempt to sleep. She nestled against Nevis, matching
the curves of her body to his, pretending he was William. The
broad shoulders and deep chest reassured her as his arms
enveloped her. "William, oh William," she murmured as
sleep overcame her.

Sunlight filtering through her eyelids aroused Evadne
again. She stirred, reaching out for William, only to find that
she was alone. Startled, she opened her eyes, the sight of the
dreary, makeshift campsite bringing her to her senses. William was a dream, the park was reality. Sighing, she sat up,
looking around for the others.

Grace lay nearby, her eyes squeezed shut in an attempt to
sleep a little longer and put off the inevitability of another day
in this place. Just beyond Grace stood Ethan and Nevis, their
backs turned as they spoke together. Evadne wondered what
they were discussing, how much of his plan Nevis was
revealing to Ethan. Impulsively, she rose to her feet and
joined them.

"Good morning," she said. She noted the frown of disapproval on Nevis's face at the interruption, making her feel
like a child intruding on her elders. She flushed with anger.

"Is there something you want, Miss Harper?" Nevis asked.
Ethan looked embarrassed.

From the tone of his voice, it was obvious to Evadne that
she had better come up with a good reason for the interruption. She met his eyes levelly, willing herself not to be
intimidated. "I wondered if you had any news."

"If I did, I would certainly have awakened you. It is barely
daybreak. When the sun is a little higher in the sky, I will go
to the soup kitchen and learn what there is to know." He
turned back to Ethan.

The curt dismissal infuriated Evadne, but she controlled
herself, reluctant to antagonize him. Recalling her recent
decision, she went back to the blanket to reconsider it—try to
chart another course, as Nevis would have said.

Grace had given up trying to sleep and sat up, yawning. "You look as if you just touched a snake, Vad. What's wrong?"

"Nothing," Evadne said sharply.

"You don't really expect me to believe that," Grace told her. "I know you too well. When you get that look, someone's scratched that temper a yours."

"It's—" Evadne hesitated, but the need to talk to someone made her go on. "It's Captain Nevis. He's the most arrogant man I have ever met."

Grace giggled. "According to Ethan, he ain't so bad, 'cept for being a little too religious for Ethan's taste and too serious. Ethan likes a good laugh now and then. What's he done?"

"Asked me to marry him!" All the thoughts that had been going around in circles in Evadne's mind exploded at the question, like dynamite finally ignited by a slow-burning fuse.

Grace's jaw dropped. Whatever she had expected, it had not been that. "To—to marry him! Why, he's barely met you! That don't sound like him at all, 'cording to Ethan."

"Well, it's true," Evadne said curtly.

"When did he ask, last night when you two were . . . snuggling?" Grace's eyes were round with curiosity.

"He is not a man to—to snuggle. No, before." Suddenly, Evadne began to wonder what Grace had said to Nevis in the time between meeting Ethan and the captain and her return with him. "What ever did you tell him about me?"

Grace flushed. "I don't rightly remember, Vad. When I saw Ethen, I just, well, kinda went out of my mind. I hugged and hugged him. I guess I told him about you and me hunting for him and about how you brought me home and took care of me. . . ."

"Captain Nevis was there, listening?" Evadne demanded.

"Sure . . . I guess so. All I saw was Ethan, until I finally run down and Ethan introduced us. Matter a fact," Grace admitted sheepishly, "I forgot you was alone till then. Then I got awful worried and we hurried back here. But what does all that have to do with his askin' you to marry him? From all Ethan's said—and he's made two voyages with him—he ain't the type to fall in love at first sight."

"I doubt that love has anything to do with it. Your—your chatter seemed to have convinced him that I am the ideal helpmate. . . ." Evadne stopped as Grace burst into giggles that threatened to choke her. When the girl finally had control of herself again, Evadne went on, "Oh yes, Grace, that is exactly what he is looking for—a helpmate."

Grace, as suddenly serious as she had been amused a moment before, looked thoughtful. "Well, Vad, considering all that's happened, you could do worse. It ain't such a bad idea. As soon as he can, he's going to Hawaii. We could all go, and you and I'd be together, just like now."

"I have spent the night telling myself that." Evadne sighed.

"And he *is* an American," Grace pointed out triumphantly.

"We were all foreigners once," Evadne reminded her.

"Oh, sure, and my Ma and Pa were good folks. It was all right for them—being as they were both furriners—but for me I think it's best to marry a genuine American," Grace insisted.

"I believe you're prejudiced," Evadne said. Grace's words reminded her all too strongly of what the girl had said about William at first. "Yet, you did like . . . like William." She forced herself to say his name.

"They ain't all bad," admitted Grace, uneasy at the mention of the Australian. "It ain't that so much as, well, the captain's a good religious man . . . like my Pa. He'd be good to you, Vad, and, like I said, we'd be together."

"You shouldn't be thinking about me, Grace, but Ethan. Regardless of what I do, your place is with him," Evadne said.

"I ain't leaving you alone, no matter what you say. Not now," Grace said stubbornly. "What would you do by yourself, with no money, no place to live, and you used to the best of everything?"

"You must stop worrying about me," Evadne insisted. "You have almost lost Ethan twice. I will not have you lose him a third time because of me."

"I ain't leaving you here alone," Grace repeated. "I can't do that—not after the way you saved my life. If you stay, so do I. If Ethan wants to leave, well—" tears shone in Grace's eyes, "—that's just the way it's gotta be. I got along without him for five years. I can get along without him again." But the tears began to slide down her cheeks.

Seeing the stubborn set to Grace's jaw, Evadne knew it would do no good to argue any more. "We will see, Grace," she said, but she had made up her mind to find Mr. Dillard again and talk to him, hoping that he might be able to think of something that she had not. She must find a way of escaping Nevis for a while.

He himself provided the opportunity shortly afterward, when the elderly brother and sister awakened. The two were only too happy for Grace and Evadne's company again while Nevis and Ethan went to the soup kitchen for food. As soon as the men had disappeared from sight, Evadne rose to her feet.

"Where you going, Vad?" Grace asked suspiciously, noting the determined look on Evadne's face. "We're s'posed to wait here."

"I am going to see . . . if I can find the Tylers or the Dillards," Evadne said, remembering just in time that she had not told Grace of her earlier meeting with them. "You stay here. I won't be long."

"I don't like it, Vad—you wandering around alone. Who knows—?"

"Oh, Grace! I am a grown woman and quite capable of taking care of myself." Evadne put on her haughtiest manner and stalked off before Grace could say another word.

She retraced the route she had taken the day before, keeping an eye out for the brougham. To her dismay, however, the area was now filled with more people, many of whom had erected makeshift tents that made it difficult for her to spot the carriage. In addition, she had to pick her way among people sprawled on the ground, still sleeping or trying to sleep.

She had just about decided that it was foolish to go on—not only couldn't she see the brougham but she was in increasing danger of becoming lost—when a hand grasped her ankle, tripping her, and she fell heavily to the ground, narrowly missing an improvised blanket tent. Crouching over her, his head rudely bandaged, was Matt the sailor, an ugly leer on his face. Evadne's breath caught in her throat.

"Didn't expect to see you here, Miss High-and-Mighty. You and me, we got a score to settle," he said in a harsh whisper.

"The soldiers!" she gasped. "They let you go!"

He grunted what passed for a laugh. "Hardly that, Little Lady, but there ain't a brig built that can hold Matt—not when he wants to get out. There's a cop with a mighty sore head—even sorer than mine—back at that police station they brung me to."

Evadne struggled to get free, but he let her ankle go only after he had secured her hands with one of his. The other hand reached up under her skirt in spite of her attempts to kick him. Her efforts only made him grin. He fell on top of her, his weight forcing the air from her lungs, his parted lips close to hers. Her struggles were exciting him and his hand tore at her underclothing.

Evadne's gorge rose at the thought of his mouth on hers, his hand touching her where William—! Why, oh, why didn't someone come to her aid? Surely those around must see what was happening. She tried again to scream and only gurgled painfully for air. She was helpless beneath him. Worst of all, his manhood was large and pressing against her. She stared into bloodshot, red-rimmed eyes filled with lust. The smell of his rank breath filled her with new strength. She closed her eyes, waiting for the touch of his lips. At the moment their lips met, she bit—hard.

Caught by surprise, he let out a cry of pain. The grip on her wrists loosened. Evadne tore her hands free, clawing at his face until he was forced to raise his hands to protect his eyes. She wriggled to get free, but his weight was too much for her. She could not even scream with him on top of her, she could barely breathe.

Just as she felt that she could not resist him any longer, Matt's body was pulled off of her. Looking up through a red mist, her ears roaring, Evadne saw a stranger's face dancing in front of her eyes.

"Help—help me, please," she managed to whisper.

"Get him out of here," a man's voice said to someone she could not see. "We don't need his kind around here. If he tries anything—"

"I'll take care of him," another man said. "I hope he does try something. I'd like nothing better than to hurt him good, after the way he went after that poor lady."

Evadne struggled to sit up, her breath coming in gasps as her lungs gulped deep swallows of air. The roaring in her ears eased enough for her to hear her rescuer say: "You lie quiet a bit." An arm slipped under her head, raising it. "Drink this. It's only water, but it'll help." He held a tin cup to her lips. She drank gratefully.

"That's the girl," the man said, helping her now to sit up. "Do you feel better?"

Evadne nodded, blinking away the last of the red film to see the stranger. The man was perfectly ordinary, of no more than average height and weight. His face, though kind, was unremarkable.

"He didn't hurt you, did he? I mean, he only . . . well . . . scared you?" he asked anxiously.

Evadne nodded again. "Thank you. I—"

The man flushed in embarrassment. "Hell, Miss, I saw what he did—grabbing you like that. I wish I could have stopped him sooner, but I had to get help," he apologized.

He was, certainly, no match for the big, bull-like sailor physically.

"You were very brave," Evadne said.

"Me? Brave?" The man gave her a rueful smile. "You're sure he didn't hurt you?" he asked again.

Evadne looked at the red marks on her wrists, and became aware that her skirt was pulled up almost to her hips. Quickly, she pulled the skirt down. Her thighs stung from where Matt had clawed at her. Except for that she was unhurt.

"I'm all right," she assured her rescuer.

"You shouldn't be wandering around alone," he pointed out. "There aren't many like him around, thank God, but a beautiful young lady like you—"

"I was looking for some friends," Evadne explained weakly.

"Well, if you're feeling better, I'll go along with you, make sure you find them all right," offered the stranger.

Evadne shook her head. It was useless to try to find the Dillards and the Tylers. Without the brougham to guide her, she had no idea where to look. They might even have left the park, for all she knew.

"It's hopeless to think of finding anyone here, isn't it?" she said, looking at the mass of people.

"I'm afraid so, Miss. Do you have a place to go? You're welcome to stay with my friend and myself. You'll be safe with us," her rescuer added quickly.

Evadne looked at him gratefully, tears in her eyes. She wished she could stay with him, feeling more secure with him than she did with Grace and Nevis. He was only offering her his protection. He did not want to force her into making a decision that would change her life forever.

"Thank you," she said, "but I have friends waiting for me. I should get back before they start to worry."

"They should not have let you go off alone," the stranger remarked.

"It was my fault." Evadne forced a weak smile. "I thought I would be safe." She would have been, she thought, although she could not tell him that, if Matt had not seen her and decided to take revenge for what she had done to him.

When she got to her feet, her rescuer offered her his arm. "I will escort you," he declared. "I insist. Otherwise, I will worry for the rest of my life that I abandoned you, with no one to help you."

Evadne smiled. "I would not want you to have me on your conscience. It is this way." At the same time, she was wondering how she would explain this stranger to the others, especially Nevis. She was afraid that she had no choice but to accept the captain's proposal. She had glimpsed what her fate would be if she refused him. Next time there might not be a kind stranger willing to come to her assistance. Whatever life with Nevis might bring, it would at least offer more security than what was left for her in San Francisco.

As she reached the edge of the pond, she could see Grace sitting with the elderly couple on the other side. Grace, who had been looking anxiously in that direction saw her and waved. Evadne waved back.

She turned to her escort. "My friends are just over there. Would you mind if I thanked you again here? I don't want them to know . . . to worry," she explained, blushing.

"I understand," he said sympathetically. "Now that I see you will be safe, I can put my mind at ease."

"I don't know how to express my gratitude—" Evadne began.

"There is no need to say more." He dropped her arm. He looked around in amazement. "We have lost everything," he said, "yet we are still worried about the niceties of convention —of society. Don't you find that peculiar?"

"No, not after what you have done. Don't you see," Evadne said earnestly, "at least we have not lost our . . . our humanity. We have not become animals."

She did not wait for a response, but hurried toward Grace. Nevis and Ethan were returning, and she wanted to warn Grace not to mention her absence. When she did look back, the stranger had disappeared.

Chapter XV

NEVIS HAD GOOD NEWS, ENOUGH GOOD NEWS, IN FACT, TO distract Grace and the elderly couple and make them forget all about Evadne's having left them. The fire line had held at Van Ness. The fires were still burning and would have to burn themselves out, but the threat of their jumping the wide boulevard to set the houses on the western side alight had been stopped. The fires in the Mission District were also being brought under control.

"The city is saved then," the old man said eagerly.

Emotion played across Nevis's face, surprising Evadne. It was the first crack she had seen in the man's armor, and it gave her hope that he might not be invincible after all.

"I would not go quite that far," the captain replied carefully, not wanting to destroy all the old man's hopes. "The fires may be under control, but they are not out. The smoke over the city is still very thick. If anything is left, it will be in the northeastern section of the city, although I heard of fires there too."

When she could, Evadne drew Nevis to one side. "Will it be possible to leave soon?"

"That remains to be seen. A policeman I spoke to said that even when the fires are out, the coals will be hot. It is even possible, according to him, to read by the coals at night in some places—they are so bright. I do not mean to worry you, but it is better to face the truth, no matter how unpleasant," he added.

"Yes," she murmured, wondering how he would face the unpleasant truth that she was not the pure young girl he thought she was. His reaction was not something she wanted to risk, especially after what had happened with Matt the sailor, until they were safely in Hawaii. She simply had to find some way of preventing their marriage until then.

"Even an unpleasant truth is preferable to a lie, for whatever reason. The truth will always come out," Nevis went on sanctimoniously.

"Yes, of course," Evadne said slowly. His statement added to her burden. She had not lied to him. Granted, she had let him think that she was still a virgin, but then he had not asked her directly.

Fortunately, he did not pursue the conversation. Ethan was serving the food they had brought from the soup kitchen, and he called to them to come and eat while it was still hot. Fresh supplies had evidently arrived in the city; the stew was thick with meat and vegetables and the bread was finer than before.

Evadne ate slowly, trying to make the food last. Plain as it was, it was filling and that was what mattered.

Grace was eating slowly, too, but more from distaste for the monotony of the diet than anything else. "Oh my," she said longingly, "what I wouldn't give for a nice roast of beef, all pink inside and crunchy outside, with some of them pan-roasted potatoes that Cook used to make and spring peas and baby carrots with cream sauce. That's the first thing I want," she decided, "once this is all over. How 'bout you, Ethan?"

Ethan gave a sheepish grin. "All I've been thinking about is a cold beer, running over with foam and cold from the tap."

"A nice hot cup of tea and some homemade cake would just touch the spot," contributed the elderly sister. "What about you, brother?"

"Sunday breakfast," the old man announced, "with bacon and eggs, sausage, and your hot cakes with syrup. Now, that would taste good."

"How 'bout you, Vad?" Grace asked, sure she would mention oysters and champagne.

But Evadne laughed. "The very first thing I want is a good, hot bath." She sighed. "What a luxury that will be—to fill the tub with hot water and a bit of cologne, and just lie there.

How good it will be to be clean again!" She turned to Nevis. "What about you, Captain?" she asked, suddenly curious about what he would say.

He gave her a slight smile. "According to the Bible, cleanliness is next to Godliness, but my one desire is to feel a ship's deck rolling under my feet again, to see the sails billowing, white as birds, as they fill with the wind, to hear the creak of the timbers and taste the salt air."

Evadne put her plate down. "Why, Captain Nevis, that is very poetic," she exclaimed. "You make it sound very tempting."

"Aye," Ethan whispered. "That would be good. That would be the best of all."

"Ethan!" Grace protested. "You said you were done with the sea, that you want to settle down, do some fishing until we can put enough money by for a farm."

Ethan reddened. "Sure, Grace, I want that, too, but—" his eyes sought out the pall of smoke over the city "—but what I want first is a good ship, a fair wind, and a course to steer away from here."

"No, it ain't what you want first—it's what you want best of all, Ethan." Grace pouted. "Pa was right. He said never fall in love with a sailor, that sailors got sea water in their veins 'stead of blood."

"Grace, love!" Ethan tried to take her hand to reassure her. "Your pa could be plenty wrong some times, you know that."

"I know," Grace admitted, her eyes drinking in Ethan's face. "But he was a fair judge of men—especially sailors. They always come back from a voyage claiming it's their last one, he said, that they're gonna settle down. Afore you know it, they're down to their last cent and lookin' for a ship—if they ain't shanghaied first. Ain't that right, Captain?"

Nevis looked from Grace's stormy face to Ethan's pleading one. Evadne watched him carefully. Would he practice what he preached, she wondered, or would he lie to Grace to save her from worrying about the future.

What he said, soberly, was, "I am afraid that is true in all too many cases, Miss Jones. I have had men in my crew shake my hand and say goodbye, only to return and ask when I was sailing again and whether I needed a good man. I might add, I don't hold with shanghaiing. It is the curse of the waterfront and of any captain who must resort to such methods to fill his crew. Any man who sails with me signs sober and sails willingly."

This half answer did not satisfy Grace. "My Ethan," she asked boldly, "is he one of them who comes and asks to sail?"

"I cannot judge Ethan, nor will I," responded Nevis. "He has made only two voyages with me—the first when he met you and the second when he signed on as far as San Francisco. It is only because of this . . . this cataclysm, thinking you lost, that he asked to sail with me again. It is because of your safety that he still wishes to sail," declared the captain in a firm voice that forestalled any further discussion.

"What about you, Captain Nevis," Evadne asked softly. "In which category do you place yourself?"

"I make no pretense to be anything but a sea captain, Miss Harper. It is my profession," he said stiffly. "I do not think that I have led you to believe otherwise. It is true that I wish to end those voyages that can last years, but I do not intend to leave the sea. The time has come for me to take a wife, own my own land, and raise a family. Out of fairness, I must change the pattern of my life, but not my entire life."

She nodded, her eyes meeting his. "Then the woman you marry must share you with the sea?"

"Aye. I thought I had made that clear. Does that mean you now look with disfavor on me and my suit?"

"On the contrary, Captain Nevis. I understand your feelings and I hope you can understand my . . . my desire for clarification," replied Evadne.

"Aye. I respect your honesty, just as I hope you respect mine," declared Nevis, with an attempt at a smile.

Evadne also tried to smile. His statement about continuing in his profession relieved her of the worry of having to be constantly in his presence—in the presence of his righteousness. But his reference to her honesty recalled her other fears. She had not actually been dishonest with him, and she would never say that she loved him when she did not and could not. At the same time, how could she tell him that she had loved another man, that, in fact, she still loved him? The memory of William would always be a shadow between them. She knew that Nevis did not expect her to love him at first, but he did expect love between the two of them to grow. In that lay her only hope. When she accepted his proposal she would tell him, in all truth, what he wanted to hear. Now was the time to tell him, but she could not bring herself to the point of making the commitment until she had to . . . until circumstances forced her to.

Once more she thought about what life with him would be like, how different from the life she had been raised to lead. It was not that she would miss the balls and the gowns and the pampered existence. She had enjoyed the challenges that she had been forced to face these past days, as frightening as they had been at the time. No, what she would miss was the joy and love by which she had always been surrounded and the ecstasy that she had known with William. If only Nevis were . . . what? She smiled to herself, thinking that what she wanted him to be was—sinful!

Evadne picked up her plate. As she did, Nevis said, "There is a pump with fresh water not far from here."

"Good. Grace and I will wash the dishes," Evadne suggested, thinking that perhaps she could also manage to clean herself up a bit.

"I will help you," Nevis insisted. "The pot and dishes are much too heavy for you." He was already putting the dishes and utensils into the iron pot.

"I am sure that Grace and I can manage," Evadne protested.

"It is much too heavy for either of you," he repeated. He picked up the pot, giving Evadne no choice except to follow him.

Once they reached the pump, she was glad that he was there. It was difficult even for him to pump out enough water to fill the pot. Moreover, the pot had to be set on a nearby fire to heat the water. When the water was warm enough, Nevis moved the pot to one side, producing a sliver of soap that he had managed to get somewhere. Evadne washed the dishes awkwardly, with a clumsiness that betrayed her lack of skill, the clumsiness increasing with the realization that he was observing her. He said nothing then, or when he pumped more water to give her a chance to wash her face and neck with her handkerchief.

Only when they were on their way back to the others did he say, "I take it that you are not familiar with the kitchen, Miss Harper."

She flushed, biting her lip and wondering what to say.

"It is nothing to be ashamed of," he said calmly. "After all, you have been gently reared, although I would have thought a few domestic skills would have been included as part of your education."

Evadne's eyes flashed at the implied criticism, but her voice was steady when she replied, "My mother thought there was time. She had every intention of teaching me what I needed to know, once I decided to marry. Besides, Cook considered the kitchen her domain. She did not appreciate my mother's presence there, much less mine. Not," Evadne added, "that I am totally ignorant. I did help my mother plan menus."

"Miss Harper, I did not mean to criticize you, nor do I mean to confine you to the kitchen or household chores. As I told you, I want a helpmate. A cook can be hired, although I would have you learn enough to put together a simple meal in case of necessity."

The level tone, more than the words, made her temper rise. Did he never lose control, she wondered. Just once, she would like to see him angry. What added to her fury was his resemblance to William. Nevis had no right, she thought irrationally, tears rising in her eyes, to look so much like William and to be so unlike him! William would have laughed at her awkwardness and helped her. He would have given her a kiss and reassured her with his affection . . . just as last night he would have found some way of showing his love and desire for her, despite the nearness of so many other people.

Nevis, seeing her tears, did let some alarm show in his voice when he said, "I did not mean to hurt your feelings."

"Hurt my feelings?" She stopped, anger blazing out of her eyes now—anger at herself for letting him make her lose her temper and anger at him for misreading the tears. "You did not hurt me, Captain Nevis! As far as cooking or housework goes, you need have no fear—I am intelligent enough to learn. I *do* know how to read, and there are always cookbooks."

The captain's jaw dropped at the display of temper; it was obvious that he was not used to having anyone talking back to him.

His astonishment delighted Evadne. She decided to press her advantage. "You look surprised. I am glad to see you are human after all," she declared. "I was beginning to think you were a machine—incapable of emotion. Perhaps there is still hope for you."

Nevis shook his head. "Is that how you think of me?"

"What else am I to think? Despite your proposal, you have not shown the slightest hint of . . . of fondness. I am a woman—not a ledger showing assets and debits and profits and losses." Although she was not sure what the words meant, despite having heard them often enough from her father and from Paul Tyler, they sounded impressive.

"My dear Miss Harper!" Nevis put down the pot to take her hands. "I have never looked at you that way. From the first moment I met you, I have seen only a beautiful and very desirable—" he flushed at the word "—very desirable woman, whom I would never dare to pursue under other circumstances. If I have appeared calculating in any way, it was only because I did not think you would consider my suit otherwise. Remember," he added, "I have spent most of my life among men—not in the polite society of women. I beg your patience."

Evadne's temper vanished as quickly as it had appeared. She was charmed by the old-fashioned quaintness of apology. "You have made a good beginning, Captain. We will go on from there as the occasion arises." Impulsively, she kissed his cheek.

His sun-bronzed skin went a deep red. He dropped her hands and moved as if to embrace her, sending a shiver of anticipation through her.

"William. . . ." she whispered. The name was out before she could stop herself.

Nevis stepped back, the longing on his face wiped off as the inscrutable mask replaced it again. "We had best return to the others."

"Yes," Evadne agreed, ashamed by her lapse. Yet, she could not help wondering why he did not ask for an explanation, demand to know who William was? Unless Grace—? No, that was not like Grace. Besides, she had been much too excited at finding Ethan to think of Evadne and her loss. Evadne almost wished Captain Nevis had asked. Difficult as it would have been to tell him about William, she would have preferred that to seeing the mask drop again.

Trying to think of something to say, she looked around. The park was beginning to have the air of a more permanent site. A few ingenious refugees had even erected primitive fireplaces. One man had found some tin and made an oven, as if he expected to be there a long time. There were more real tents to be seen, too, and the flimsy, homemade tents of blankets and sheets had been set up more securely. People also seemed to have formed new attachments, grouping together and sharing what they had, giving an air of organization to the area that had been missing before.

The sight was encouraging. It meant that the panic was

over. At the same time, it meant that thousands of people had no place to go, even if they could. For months—perhaps longer, Evadne realized—hundreds of thousands would be homeless.

"What will happen to all these people?" she wondered out loud. "Will there ever be a San Francisco again?"

"Until the fires are put out and we can see what is left," Nevis said, "no one can answer those questions."

They had reached their own campsite. Ethan had been busy. With the thought of another night ahead, he had set up what shelter he could, using the blanket. He greeted them with a grin, eager to hear their comments on the lean-to he had erected. "It ain't much, but it's the best I could do," he said.

"It's—it's beautiful, Ethan," Evadne told him. "Look, Captain, at what else Ethan has done." She pointed to a carefully arranged circle of stones on which the pot could be placed to cook.

"Course, we need some fuel," the young man said, "and something to cook. But sooner or later—"

"I hope we won't be here much longer," Nevis said curtly. "I am getting anxious to return to my ship."

Evadne bit her lip angrily, seeing the way Ethan's face fell. She went over to the lean-to, sitting down beside Grace, feeling terribly tired and remembering suddenly that she had slept little. She yawned.

"I think I'll take a nap," she announced, lying down and using the lean-to to protect her eyes from the sun. Before she knew it, she was asleep . . . dreamlessly this time.

When Evadne awoke, the sun was low in the sky. She sat up, rubbing her eyes, to look around. Grace was sitting on the ground near her, her chin on her hand, staring thoughtfully into space. There was no sign of the men.

"Where did they go this time, Grace?" Evadne asked.

"Just wandering around, I guess, and to the soup kitchen." Grace looked at her. There were tears in her eyes. "I'm scared, Vad."

"There's nothing to be scared of," Evadne said patiently. "We're alive, and it won't be long before we are aboard Captain Nevis's ship."

"Then what?" Grace demanded. "I mean, who knows what this Hawaii is like . . . where we'll live, what we'll do when the men go off again? Ethan and I had it all planned!" Tears coursed down her cheeks.

Evadne sighed. "Please, Grace, nobody's going to leave us until we have a roof over our heads. You know Ethan better than that."

"Aren't you scared, too—just a little?" asked Grace.

Thinking the question over, Evadne realized then that she was more excited than frightened. "No," she said truthfully, "it will be a fresh start. There will be no memories there, nothing to remind me of Mama and Papa, Auntie, William. . . ." Even now she could not say the name without feeling a knife in her heart.

Grace's tears stopped then. "Vad, I'm sorry. I fergot—"

"Well, don't forget that you do have Ethan." Evadne stood up and walked to a spot from where she could see the men returning.

They were back shortly. The evening followed the same pattern as the night before. When they were finished eating, they stacked the plates and utensils in the pot to leave until morning. Too many people were already asleep, and it would be too easy to step on someone or stumble in the dark on the walk to the pump. When it was time to sleep, Grace snuggled in Ethan's arms under the fox coat while Evadne lay stiffly in the captain's arms under the sealskin coat. The lean-to, although it forced the two couples to lie close together, did protect them from the night breezes. Once the captain was asleep, Evadne managed to relax and fall asleep herself. Despite her nap, she was exhausted . . . too tired for her thoughts to waken her as they had the night before.

Saturday dawned with a bright sun in a clear blue sky. When they looked toward the city, the smoke did not seem as thick. For the first time, Evadne began to believe that the fires were actually being put out, despite the ominous scene to the northeast. She waited anxiously for news as Nevis and Ethan set out to wash the dishes and get on line at the soup kitchen to learn what they could.

Evadne tried to arrange her hair as best she could and straighten her clothing, looking ruefully at the green suit that she loved. The skirt was wrinkled and stained, and the braid on the jacket was ripped from her struggle with Matt. Well, it would have to do for the voyage to Hawaii.

"We sure look a sight, don't we, Vad?" Grace said with a grin, seeing her examine the suit and looking at her own clothing.

"No one else is much better off," Evadne had to admit. She sighed longingly. "If I ever get that bath, I'll never get out."

The captain and Ethan were soon back with plenty of food but little news. As a result, after Ethan and Grace had washed the dishes, the two men set out again to see if they could learn more.

Neither Evadne and Grace nor the elderly brother and sister were in a mood to talk. The old couple, in fact, had lain down after eating and were dozing off. Evadne and Grace sat watching passersby, nodding and saying, "Good morning," now and then. Though they said nothing, each was looking for a familiar face. There was none until they saw their two companions.

Captain Nevis sat down heavily, rubbing the stubble of dark beard on his face. "The firemen," he said, "are still trying to save Russian and Telegraph Hills. We were warned it is still too dangerous to pass through the city because of both the fires and the martial law."

"Your other plan?" Evadne asked softly.

"The rumors about plague and typhus were false, thank God. I will wait one more day. If we cannot get through the city tomorrow, we will try the other route. I am determined to get to my ship," he said firmly.

Evadne nodded. "Then you will want my decision in the morning?"

"I will." He stood up, looking down at her. "I will leave you alone to think it over," he stated, and walked off.

That Saturday was the longest day in Evadne's life. She kept looking at passersby, and finally realized that she was looking for William. Whenever someone stopped to ask her if she had seen a friend or relative of theirs, she in turn asked about William. Only when the sun began to go down and Nevis and Ethan went to the soup kitchen for the evening meal did she give up, accepting the decision she had already made with a lingering longing for what might have been. Even so, she resolved not to tell Nevis until the last possible moment. She did not expect a miracle, but she could not give up her last thoughts of those moments spent in William's arms.

Nevis did not press her, not even when she lay once more in his arms to sleep. She smiled sadly to herself. He told her that she had until morning, and he would wait for her word until then.

Evadne had no sooner fallen asleep when she awakened with a start. Rain was falling. Nevis had wakened, too, and the two sat up, huddling under the meager protection of the lean-to. Ethan and Grace joined them.

"If only we had had this rain Wednesday," Evadne mourned.

"It is God's will," Nevis stated. He stood up to look for more solid cover, but there was none. The blanket was now so sodden that it was worthless. All they could do was huddle together, hoping the long night would pass as quickly as possible. Evadne draped the sealskin coat over her head and the captain's, telling Grace and Ethan to do the same with the fox coat. The coats did protect them, but the fur was soon ruined under the steady rain.

Gradually, the rain abated. By then it was impossible to try to sleep on the wet ground. Cold and wet, Evadne drew closer to Nevis. She could feel his heart thudding in his chest as he held her. The man was not made of stone after all. She rested her head against his shoulder. His breath was soft on her cheek, a prelude to the kiss that softly brushed her forehead.

As soon as the sun rose, they gathered their few belongings together. Evadne picked up the blanket, spreading it out on the grass to dry, before turning to face Nevis. How absurd life was, she thought, laughter bubbling suddenly inside of her. Here they were, wet and cold and miserable, their clothes plastered to their bodies, their hair hanging in wet strings—it was hardly the time or place to consider a proposal of marriage.

She began to laugh, great whoops coming from deep inside her. Ethan and Grace stared at her. Nevis paled, his lips pressed firmly together. He turned to leave.

Evadne seized his arm. "Oh, Captain," she gasped helplessly. "Please . . . I am not laughing at you. It is only . . . look at us!" She sobered quickly then as the color came back into his face. "I will go with you. I will be—" She stopped, unable to say "your wife."

"I will be good to you," he promised.

Evadne lowered her head, tears now in her eyes. "I will leave the fur coat and blanket for them." She nodded toward the elderly brother and sister, still sunk in an exhausted sleep. "Let us go."

As Nevis took her arm, she raised her head proudly. It was

hardly the proposal she had imagined, marriage to a man whom she did not love and probably never would. Moreover, a man who would remind her constantly of the man she had loved . . . would love forever.

At the cook tent, fires were only beginning to be laid. Nearby, however, at a Red Cross tent, workers were setting out clean, dry clothing. Evadne and Grace went to the women's side.

A woman looked at them sympathetically, handing them some clothing to try on. Inside the tent, they took off their wet clothes, drying themselves with some towels lying there. Evadne picked up a calico housedress. Other than being too short, it was a good fit.

"Well, Grace," she said sadly, "we don't look much like brides, do we?"

"We sure don't." Grace gazed down at the cotton dress she had put on. "I hoped I'd be married in a pretty dress," she said with a sigh. "But I guess the dress isn't what makes a bride, is it? It's the spirit inside."

Evadne blinked back the tears that came to her eyes. If she didn't look like a bride, she felt like one even less. If she had never imagined such a proposal, she had also never imagined such a wedding. Sad as she felt, however, she had to smile when she and Grace rejoined Ethan and Nevis. Both men now wore denim work clothes, Nevis looking distinctly uncomfortable without his blue uniform.

At the cook tent, they managed to get some bread and canned meat to eat on the way. To the east was San Francisco proper. For the first time in four days, no flame or smoke rose into the sky. The black pall and the fire had been washed away by the rain. Wisps of steam rose from the smoldering embers. Evadne's step quickened as they walked along, but she drew to a stumbling halt at the top of O'Farrell Street.

Despite the fires that had raged, she had hoped to still see something she recognized. What she did see made her close her eyes in horror, her courage failing her at last. Nevis had to catch her to keep her from falling to the ground.

Grace, behind her, screamed, "Oh, my Gawd!" and crossed herself.

Evadne opened her eyes again, staring blankly at what was left of the city she had known and loved. Her mind still refused to take in what she saw, the destruction was so complete. Gradually, however, sights began to register.

Almost all the familiar landmarks were gone. The earthquake, fires, and dynamiting had all taken their toll. The towers and turrets of the Mark Hopkins mansion which had reared in lonely splendor on the height of Nob Hill before the Fairmont Hotel was built were gone. The mansion's glory was now no more than a crumbled mass of stone. The Fairmont still stood. Its white stone was black from the fire and smoke and its windows gaped vacantly. Here and there, steam rose as the still-hot coals condensed pools of rainwater. It was useless to hope that anything might have survived in the ruins of Nob Hill, to search for any possessions that might have escaped the flames.

Evadne forced her eyes from what was left of Nob Hill to Russian Hill. The buildings at the top of the hill, like those of Telegraph Hill beyond it, had somehow survived. From that distance, the shattered windows and fallen chimneys and masonry could not be seen, and the buildings looked as they always had. The fires had been stopped just short of them. To the east and south, nothing was recognizable. Even the streets were gone, filled with rubble and twisted girders. Where once cable-car tracks had pursued a straight line, a few people were weaving along, picking their way carefully over the broken streets between a few walls that still stood, the buildings behind them gone.

A line of soldiers passed the quartet, on their way to guard whatever was left and prevent looting. Evadne took a deep breath to steady herself. "Let us go, Captain Nevis. It does no good to stand here and look." She turned to Grace, who was still in shock at the sight of the acres of desolation. "Come, Grace," she said gently.

"There ain't nothin' left," Grace said, awed. She seemed paralyzed.

Evadne looked at Ethan. "You take one arm and I'll take the other, if we are ever to get to the ship."

"It's so quiet, ain't it?" Grace went on as they gently urged her forward. "And it's Sunday too. There should be church bells, an early Mass—"

Evadne recalled being awakened by the roar of the earthquake and then the wild ringing of church bells. Like everything else, the bell towers and steeples had fallen and the fire had undoubtedly melted the bells into shapeless lumps. Over Grace's head, she appealed to Ethan for help.

"Come, Grace, love," he said. "It's time to go, like Vad said."

"I want to go to church," Grace said unexpectedly. "We could find a priest or minister—someone to marry us."

"I doubt that there will be any services today, Grace. The priests and ministers had to leave the city, too, didn't they, Captain?"

Nevis was still standing staring at the destruction. Now he turned to Evadne. "Despite all I heard, I did not expect this. I cannot believe what I see," he said. "My father was with General Sherman on his march to the sea during the Civil War. The burning of Atlanta left more than what I see here." He shook his head.

Evadne looked angrily at all of them. She did not want to linger . . . she could not bear to.

"Are we going to stand here and wait for the city to rise again in front of our eyes? Do you expect a miracle?" she demanded. "You, Captain Nevis, I thought you were determined to get to your ship? Yet you stand here—"

The man shuddered. "You are quite right, Miss Harper." He looked down at the ruined city, suddenly lost. "I cannot see a street I recognize to tell how to proceed."

"Then we keep walking east, toward the Ferry Building. From what I can tell, I think the ferries are running." Evadne shaded her eyes with her hand as she looked into the sun. "But first, Captain, I must speak to you." She drew him aside.

"Yes, Miss Harper?"

Evadne studied him, knowing that she had him in a rare moment of weakness. It was not fair, perhaps, to take advantage of him, but she had little choice.

"It concerns your misgivings about women aboard your ship. Do you still insist on marriage? If so, we would be well advised to return to Golden Gate Park and try to find a minister."

Her words steadied him. "We have come this far. We will go on."

"Your misgivings?" Evadne pressed him.

"You are a stubborn woman. I have not lost them, if that is what you want to know. But your promise to wed me will have to serve. I could not leave you to . . . this." He waved at what was left of San Francisco.

Evadne suddenly felt ashamed. He was a good man, and she was not being fair to him. She seemed to hear her father saying: "Evadne, never give your word unless you mean to keep it and once you give it, never go back on it." What would he say if he knew she had given her word, secretly hoping she would never have to keep it?

Once more, they set out. The fires had not reached the area west of Van Ness, and the first few blocks were easy walking. After that they had to pick their way along slowly. Here and there, a path had been cleared, wide enough for the fire department and the Army to get their equipment through. Walking, nevertheless, was difficult. Sharp stones and glass were everywhere. Evadne winced as a careless step sent a sharp object cutting through the sole of her shoe.

The wooden houses and stone buildings, or what had once been wood and stone, gave way to brick and steel. A few more buildings were still standing, the brick having withstood the heat of the flames better than the stone. Many, however, were only girdered skeletons above the lower floors. In the eerie landscape, time and place lost its meaning. No one knew how far they had walked.

"Oh, wait!" Evadne cried. A familiar sight caught her eye above the destruction. Heedless of the rubble she had to climb over, she made her way toward it, leaving the others to follow or not.

Nevis, close behind, saw her stop and cover her face with her hands. "What is it?" he asked, looking around.

She raised her head, tears in her eyes. "I know where we are. It's Union Square. See? There's the Dewey Monument, with all the rubble around it. And that's the St. Francis," she said, pointing to a burnt-out hulk and thinking of William.

The St. Francis, blackened by the fire that had raged inside it, stood proudly on its corner. Across the square, the whole block was gone. What had not fallen into the street during the quake had been hurled into the park by the dynamiting. The park itself was no longer an oasis. Where walks had criss-crossed it in happier days and where the early refugees had swarmed for protection were only piles of rubble.

A man came toward them, carrying a camera on a tripod. He nodded politely as he adjusted the tripod and focused the camera. While Evadne watched, he took off his bowler to set it on the ground and put his head under the black cloth. After he had taken the picture, he mopped his face with a handkerchief.

Evadne went toward him impulsively. "Have you taken many pictures?" she asked.

"Quite a few since early this morning," he answered,

fanning himself with the bowler now. "I took the ferry from Oakland," he volunteered.

"The ferries are running then? What about any other boats?"

"The Bay is busy as a beehive. Fortunately, all the piers south of Telegraph Hill and the Ferry Building were saved by water from the Bay and fireboats. Is that where you are going?" He examined her curiously, noting the simple calico dress which was too short and totally inappropriate to her bearing and which did not match the expensive reticule she carried.

"Yes. If you came from there, perhaps you could tell us the best way to go. We would be grateful for your help," she added.

He thought for a moment. "Follow Geary to Market. Once you see Lotta's Fountain, you can easily find your way along Market. One side has been cleared for cars and other vehicles," he explained.

"Thank you. Good luck with your pictures." She smiled and returned to the others, telling them what she had learned. She led the way, the three following in her train.

With an aching heart, Evadne thought of the last time that she had walked this route, except that it had been in the other direction. She had been with William, that first afternoon when she had met him. He had pulled her to the safety of the fountain when she had stopped in the middle of the street, heedless of an approaching cable car. Just beyond was the Palace Hotel.

She paused at the fountain. Until now, they had passed few walkers like themselves. Market Street, however, had attracted a variety of people, mostly men, sightseers and also businessmen, on their way to estimate what they had lost. Little that was to be seen could be salvaged. Against her will, Evadne again began to examine faces, her heart pounding in her breast. Futile as the hope might be, there was still time to find William.

Her mouth went dry, as she gazed at the Palace, now as splendid a ruin as it had once been a hotel. The shell still stood, but that was all. As she glanced inside the carriage entrance, she saw that masonry and girders from the hotel filled the elegant court where the marble had cracked and heaved upward. Ahead, the Hearst and Call buildings also stood, lonely skeletal memorials to the once vital life of the city. Evadne began to be eager to reach the Ferry Building and quickened her step, though she could not keep from looking into the faces of the men coming toward her.

The Ferry Building was almost undamaged except for the clock tower. It still stood, the clock stopped at 5:15. The four halted near the entrance, finding a place to sit on an empty baggage wagon. Evadne had done all she could. She had led them here. Now she looked to Nevis.

"What now, Captain?"

He frowned. "We must find a boat of some sort to take us out to my ship."

Evadne smiled. "Then you will have to find it. I do not even know where to begin looking."

The captain spotted some men who were obviously sailors. "Wait here," he told her and the others.

Watching him go, Evadne was tempted to run away, while she still had time. Yet, where would she go? Even though Telegraph and Russian Hills had escaped the fire, they offered no haven to her, any more than Auntie's house in Sausalito.

Evadne sighed, and gave herself up to what must be her fate.

Chapter XVI

NEVIS CAME BACK SHORTLY WITH FIVE OF THE SAILORS HE HAD spotted. Four were brawny men with thick arms, souvenirs of their lives before the mast. The fifth was a short, reedy creature with long arms and big hands. All had red, sleepless eyes and gray faces. According to Nevis, they had spent the past four days pressed into service to fight the fires that had threatened to envelop the piers. Now they were eager to find a ship and put San Francisco behind them.

The short man, who said he was a ship's carpenter, said that they might be able to find a boat up toward Fisherman's Wharf. "Them fishermen were mighty busy the first day or so. Musta made a fortune, takin' folks across the bay, 'specially them with engines in their boats. I don't rightly think there's a boat with any gasoline left, but you might find one with a sail, ready and willing to take you if you got the money."

"I've money aboard ship," Nevis said.

"That may not be good enough, Cap'n," the little man said. "Them first days, they took whatever folks offered. Now it's ready cash."

Evadne clutched her reticule tightly. She had no intention of using the jewels she had saved except in an emergency. Not even Grace knew that she had them.

"We can try," she said. "We have managed so far."

"You are right, Miss Harper." Nevis regarded her thoughtfully. "I hate to ask you to walk any further."

Evadne stood, drawing herself to her full height. "Walking is the least of our trials. If walking could bring back what has been lost, I would willingly walk much farther."

"Oh, Vad!" Grace groaned. "I swear, once I get to that Hawaii, I'm never gonna walk again. You heed that, Ethan," she declared, getting to her feet, "and buy me a carriage."

They started north on East Street. Evadne marveled at the normalcy of the Bay. Ships still rode at anchor, more of them than usual since many had been moved away from the piers and wharves to keep them out of reach of the fire. Beyond the ships were the green hills of Goat Island and beyond that those of Marin County. Up ahead were the arms of the Golden Gate, out of sight at the moment.

At each pier, they stopped while Nevis asked about a boat. The discouragement he met only made him more determined. At Pier 39, one of the largest, he walked straight to the end of the pier. From there the Golden Gate was easily visible. More important to Nevis was the fact that he could see his ship. He came back, smiling broadly for once.

"She's there, the *Narragansett*." He turned to the five sailors. "There's a twenty dollar gold piece, once we get to my ship, to the first man to find us a boat—and jobs for all of you."

The little carpenter grinned. "I'll get ye a boat, Cap'n." He scurried off, followed by the others.

Evadne wondered at their ready acceptance of Nevis as the master of a vessel. In his work clothes, he looked far different from what he did in his uniform. Yet, something about him had persuaded these men to follow him, to take him at his word.

"Do we wait here, then, Captain?" Evadne asked.

"Yes. That's the best, I think. I'll return shortly." He went back to the end of the pier, unable to keep away from the sight of his ship.

On impulse, Evadne followed him. In the direction Nevis was looking only one ship rode at anchor, a broad-beamed, three-masted vessel with none of the sleek lines of the barkentines and schooners that Evadne's father put such stock in.

"That's your ship—the *Narragansett*, you called her?" she asked.

"Aye." He smiled like a proud parent. "She's a good,

sturdy ship, Miss Harper, not as fast as a clipper or a barkentine and she tends to wallow in heavy seas, but speed and looks are not the purpose of a whaler."

"I suppose not," Evadne agreed.

"It will be easy to convert her for the island trade. There's plenty of room in that solid hold for cargo instead of whale oil," he added.

Evadne nodded, only half listening as he spoke about taking out the boilers used to render the blubber into oil. Still, she was more interested than she wanted to admit. When the captain paused, she asked, "What will you carry for cargo? You keep talking about converting her for cargo, but you do not mention what the cargo is to be." She added, with a smile, "I did learn a little from listening to my father."

"You are indeed well suited to be my wife," Nevis told her admiringly. "It is my intention to carry supplies from Honolulu to the other islands, to the sugar and pineapple plantations where I hope to pick up cargo for transshipment to the United States. It may be," he said with a frown, "that I will have to carry passengers too. Most of the labor on the plantations is contract labor."

"Including women?" Evadne could not resist the question.

"If necessary." The admission was made reluctantly.

Before Evadne could say anything more, Ethan came running out on the pier. "Cap'n . . . Cap'n!" he called. "That sailor's back—and he's got Mr. Stevenson with him!"

"Stevenson! What—?" Nevis wheeled around and sprinted back down the pier, leaving Evadne behind with Ethan.

"Who is Stevenson?" she asked him, puzzled by the captain's reaction.

"The first mate. Seeing the fires was out, he took one of the ship's boats and came here looking for the Cap'n," Ethan explained.

"I see." Evadne walked slowly back along the pier to where Grace was waiting for them.

"Oh, Vad." Grace came up to her, her eyes large as saucers, as Ethan left them to join Captain Nevis. "We're really goin', ain't we? I'm scared out of my wits!"

"Now, Grace, what is there to be frightened of?" Evadne soothed her. "You have Ethan to take care of you."

"And you?" Grace clutched Evadne's hand. "You won't leave me, will you? I mean, we're goin' to be together?"

"Grace. . . ."

"I know—I got my Ethan." Grace sighed. "He's not the

same as you. He don't understand that I'm scared. I've never been on a ship before. Vad, I don't wanna go to a furrin country. I'm an American!"

"Hawaii *is* a part of the United States. It was annexed around the turn of the century. You'll find people are the same there as here," Evadne said, trying to reassure herself as much as Grace.

"Ethan says there's a lot of natives, and Chinese and Japanese too. It ain't like San Francisco at all. Oh, why does Ethan have to go to sea again? He promised when I said I'd marry him that he'd never go to sea anymore!"

Evadne was looking at Nevis, who was listening intently to what the man named Stevenson had to say. How strange, she thought, if either of them had a right to be frightened, it was she, not Grace. After all, Grace knew and loved Ethan while Nevis was little more than a stranger to Evadne—a humorless, stern, Bible-reading stranger.

He was striding toward them. "Ladies, with luck, we will be able to leave with the ship on the evening tide."

Evadne nodded. With Grace holding her hand, she followed Nevis to the next pier. Ethan had gone ahead to round up the other four sailors. There was plenty of room in the whaleboat for all of them. As the sailors Stevenson had brought with him from the ship manned the oars, sending the boat skimming through the waters of the Bay, Evadne turned back for one last look at San Francisco.

The fire-blackened ruins stood out sharply in the afternoon sunlight. Here and there a structure still stood, rearing in loneliness above the piles of rubble. Looking toward Nob Hill, whole blocks were leveled, razed by fire more than by dynamite. Whatever the life that lay ahead of her, Evadne thought, it could not be worse than the bare existence that lay behind her.

Reluctantly, Evadne tore her eyes from the wounded city and faced toward the prow of the boat. The *Narragansett* loomed ahead. Evadne could see the figurehead of an Indian brave holding a tomahawk under the bowsprit. How like Nevis, she thought, to use a brave instead of an Indian maiden for a figurehead. A maiden, to her mind, would have been a better omen.

A Jacob's ladder was hanging over the side of the ship. Nevis mounted it first, signaling Evadne to follow. She stared at the swinging rope ladder that seemed just out of reach, no matter how steady the oarsmen tried to hold the boat.

Finally, Ethan grasped the ladder with one hand, holding it as rigid as possible, and Evadne managed to grab hold. Closing her eyes, she groped for the lower rung with one foot. Finally, she started the climb, trembling every time the ladder swung under her weight and with the motion of the ship. After what seemed like an eternity, Nevis's hands grasped her and she stood on deck.

Then came Grace's turn. She refused even to try to climb the ladder. When Ethan tried to help her, she collapsed on the bottom of the boat, wailing so loudly that Ethan was forced to give up. The sailors that Nevis had found at the Ferry Building mounted the ladder agilely as did the oarsmen who shipped the oars after the boat was in the davits. The boat with Grace, Ethan, and one other sailor still aboard was raised to its place above the deck. Even then, Ethan had to pick Grace up in his arms and hand her over to Stevenson to get her out of the boat.

The moment Grace was put down, she stumbled into Evadne's arms. "I'm scared!" she cried, tears running down her cheeks. "I don't wanna go to no furrin place. Take me home!"

Evadne held her helplessly. Over her head, she saw Nevis watching them, his mouth a grim line as if Grace had fulfilled his misgivings about women aboard a working ship. Glaring at him angrily, Evadne said, "Hush, Grace. We have no home, don't you remember?"

The words silenced Grace, sending her into a kind of shock. Evadne looked at Nevis. "Well, Captain, are you going to send us back?"

"I am not such a monster as to do that. Just keep her quiet. Ethan?" He turned to the second mate. "Get them below. Take them to my cabin. I will move my things in with Stevenson later."

"Aye, aye, sir." Ethan gave him a quick salute.

Between the two of them, Ethan and Evadne managed to get Grace below. The captain's cabin was well forward in the ship, almost triangular in shape, with a bunk along one wall on which Ethan and Evadne laid Grace.

"Can you manage? I gotta go above," Ethan asked Evadne anxiously.

"Yes, of course. She'll be all right now," Evadne assured him.

"I sure hope so." Ethan sighed. "The cap'n ain't gonna like it much if she carries on that way all the way to Hawaii."

As soon as Ethan had gone, Evadne looked around for some brandy. There was no decanter or bottle of any kind in sight. Seeing a sea chest, Evadne knelt down by it, opening the lid.

"What are you doing?" The voice boomed at her from the doorway.

Evadne raised her head. Nevis, his face sterner than ever, was glowering at her, his brown eyes almost black. "I was hoping you might have some brandy I could give to Grace." Evadne met his look levelly.

"You will find none there," he told her.

She got to her feet. "Then what do you suggest? I doubt that you have smelling salts aboard."

Some of the sternness left his face. He appeared almost bewildered by the situation. "I—I have some rum locked in the lazaret."

"Will you get it?" Evadne held her ground. If she was to spend the rest of her life with this man, she must show him that she was not to be bullied or intimidated.

He turned on his heel, returning shortly with a bottle of New England rum that he placed on the table in the center of the cabin. "There are some glasses in the cabinet there."

Evadne took a glass out of the cabinet, noticing that he was kneeling at the sea chest, taking out a uniform. "I am sorry to inconvenience you," she apologized impulsively.

"I will get the rest of my things later." Nevis moved toward the door.

"Very well. Will we be sailing soon?" she asked, aware of a creaking sound on deck.

"The sails are being hoisted now. Shortly we will be raising anchor. If you wish to see the last of this fair city," he said, his voice far too flat for sarcasm, "you may come on deck then. Until then, however, stay below—where you will be out of the way."

"Rest assured," Evadne said spiritedly, "it is not my intention to get in the way. Now, I must see to Grace." She turned her back on the captain and moved to the bunk. She was holding the glass to Grace's lips when she heard the cabin door slam. She smiled in satisfaction, having once more discovered that Nevis was human after all.

The harsh rum made Grace cough, and she opened her eyes. "Oh, Vad!" she cried. "I'm seasick!"

"No, you aren't." Evadne was thoroughly exasperated with her. "Pull yourself together. I do not intend to hold your hand all the way to Hawaii." When Grace's lips parted to quiver, Evadne went on: "Listen to me, Grace. It is too late to go back, even if we had anything to go back to. We have made our choice, and we must do the best we can. We will be no good to one another, now or in the times that lie ahead, unless we are both strong."

A tear slid down Grace's right cheek, but her lips stopped trembling. She looked at Evadne and sighed. "You're right, Vad. I'm sorry. I promised not to be a burden and here I am, acting like a baby again—and I always thought I was so sensible. *You're* the one with the real head on your shoulders."

Evadne smiled at her. "We'll both need our heads—" She stopped, hearing the clank of a metal chain. "The anchor is being raised, do you want to go up on deck?"

"No," Grace said. "I seen enough. You go, though. I'll be all right." She settled back on the bunk, yawning, sleepy from the rum. "I might sleep. We ain't had much of that recently."

Evadne went up on deck. Sails cracking under a stiff breeze, the *Narragansett* was moving ponderously toward the Golden Gate. The city was shrouded in mist from the steam still rising from the hot embers. It looked ghostly. Evadne shivered, aware of the chill ocean breeze as the ship moved steadily, slowly toward the open sea. As they passed the Golden Gate, Evadne took one last look. Beyond Seal Rocks, Cliff House still stood. She smiled, and her gaze sought the rolling waves of the ocean in front of her. The ship was moving more swiftly now, but as Nevis had said she was not built for speed and there was a wallow to her motion.

With a sigh, Evadne looked around at the ship that was to be her home temporarily. Nevis stood on the foredeck with his two mates and a helmsman. Aft, the deck was wide, with six whaleboats slung in davits. To the stern was another companionway that probably led to the crew's quarters, behind a large metal tripod that must have something to do with rendering blubber, she decided. The sight was unprepossessing. It was every bit the working ship that Nevis called it.

Evadne returned below. Ethan visited her soon after to ask about Grace. The girl was sound asleep, snoring slightly.

Evadne smiled, seeing Ethan's relieved grin. "All she really needs is sleep. None of us have had much. Last night it was impossible to do more than doze in that rain."

"I hope that's it." The broad, freckled face wrinkled in a frown. "The way she carried on, I was afraid Cap'n Nevis might change his mind and send her ashore. Now, though, there ain't nothin' between here and Hawaii."

"We'll manage," Evadne assured him.

"At least you'll be comfortable here."

"Which reminds me, Ethan. There's only the one bunk for the two of us." Evadne sat down on a heavy chair by the table, waiting to see what Ethan had to suggest.

"I guess the captain didn't think of that," Ethan said, scratching his head. "We ain't got no cots. All I can think to do is sling a hammock in here."

Evadne tried to imagine herself sleeping in a hammock, not for a moment considering asking Grace to do it. She started to laugh, the laughter bubbling up out of her, bringing tears to eyes. Ethan, totally bewildered, watched her. At that moment, Nevis, whose knock on the door had gone unheard, opened the door. He, too, stared at her in bewilderment, afraid that she was as hysterical as Grace had been earlier.

Seeing Nevis's look, Evadne struggled to control her laughter. "I apologize, Ethan," she said at last. "Captain Nevis, I am not having hysterics, if that is what is on your mind. Ethan mentioned slinging a hammock in here, since there is only the one bunk, and I was trying to imagine myself sleeping in one. The picture. . . ." She shrugged helplessly.

Nevis went red under his tan. "I am afraid that is all we have to offer," he said stiffly. "Stevenson is also making do with a hammock," he added.

"Then a hammock it will have to be," Evadne announced.

"See to it, Mr. Morgan," the captain ordered.

Aboard ship, Nevis had dropped the familiarity that had permitted him to call his second mate by his first name while ashore. "Miss Harper, there is one more matter to discuss. Before I sailed from New Bedford, I was asked to bring some boxes of clothing for the church missions in Hawaii. I have ordered the boxes with women's clothing to be brought here for you and Miss Jones to sort over, in the hope that you may find additional clothing for the voyage."

"Thank you, Captain." Evadne smiled at him sadly, thinking of all the castoffs of her own that had gone to charity in the past. "I will never again be able to give a few cents or some clothing to charity without recalling how dependent I was, even for the food in my mouth, on others' generosity."

"When that day comes, I am sure you will not be ungenerous," Nevis replied.

She let the statement pass. To her relief, Nevis left as soon as the sailor had delivered the boxes of clothing. By then, Ethan was back with a hammock, which he put up and showed her how to get in.

Evadne watched dubiously, not daring to try it out in front of him. When she was alone again, she made sure that Grace was still sleeping soundly, then opened her reticule. She searched in the bottom, finding the jewelry, looking at it and wondering what it was worth, hope rising briefly that it might provide an escape from marriage to Nevis. Hope quickly faded and reality returned. Whatever money she might get from selling the jewelry would soon be gone, and what would she do then? Besides, she had promised. . . . She closed her eyes, too tired suddenly to think. The lack of sleep overwhelmed her—her body and limbs ached from walking and her mind reeled from the decisions of the past few days. Until the ship reached Hawaii, at any rate, she could do nothing. Evadne put the jewelry away and laid her head down on her arms on the table, joining Grace in sleep.

A heavy knocking awakened both girls and announced the arrival of a sailor with their dinner on a tray. The food, boiled corned beef with potatoes, cabbage, carrots, and onions, was simple, but it had both their mouths watering after the monotonous diet of indefinable stew. Best of all were the steaming mugs of coffee that accompanied the dinner. Afterward, Evadne and Grace sorted through the clothes in the charity boxes, each of them finding a few dresses that fit well enough to serve. In addition, there were nightdresses.

The prospect of sleep was dimmed only by the fact that one of them would have to sleep in the hammock. Grace offered to use it, climbing in one side only to fall out the other. Next, Evadne tried to get in, climbing gingerly over the side as Grace watched, giggling. Managing not to fall out, Evadne tried stretching and relaxing in it, and at last made herself comfortable with a pillow under her head and a blanket over her. The hammock swung with the motion of the ship, making her sleepy. Before long, Grace in the bunk and Evadne in the hammock were sound asleep.

In the days that followed, Nevis did what he could to insure their comfort—and their isolation from the crew. Their first morning at sea, for example, he ordered huge kettles, normally used for rendering whale oil, brought to their cabin and filled with hot water. Evadne was touched that he had remembered her longing for a bath. The girls took their time, luxuriating in washing themselves and their hair. It was not quite the same as a real bath, but neither of them minded. Afterward they dressed in clean clothes selected from the charity boxes.

The dresses told Evadne much about the women who had donated them and about the captain's background. They were uniformly high-necked and long-sleeved, of a heavy wool serge as timeless and long-wearing as the style, fitted to the waist with just enough fullness to permit comfort in walking. No attempt had been made to flatter the figure or trim the garments. Even the self-covered buttons were designed for practicality.

As the girls soon learned, however, it made little difference what they wore. Meals were served in their cabin, brought by the little carpenter who handed the trays to them in the doorway, following orders not to cross the threshold either then or when he returned to retrieve the trays again. Twice a day, once in the morning and again in the afternoon, Nevis and Ethan appeared to escort them to the deck for an hour's exercise promenade in the fresh air. Other than that, Captain Nevis made it clear that they were to stay in the cabin, passing the time as best they could.

Both girls soon chafed under the restraint, Evadne because she would have liked to spend more time on deck in the fresh air, observing the crew at their work, and Grace because she wanted to spend more time with Ethan.

On the third day, shortly before Ethan and Nevis were due, Grace complained to Evadne, "It ain't fair—it's like we're prisoners. What's wrong with Ethan 'n' me having a little time alone together?"

"Obviously the captain believes in avoiding temptation by keeping it out of sight," Evadne said tartly.

Grace giggled and looked at her slyly. "Do you think he's worryin' about Ethan an' me, or is he thinking about you an' him?"

"I have no idea how his mind works," Evadne declared. "But I am tired of being cooped up in here."

"Ethan 'n' me can't even talk with you and him following us." Grace sighed. "I ask you, what harm would it do for us to have just a little time alone?"

"I'll try and discuss it with him," Evadne said. "Don't raise your hopes, though, Grace," she added, seeing the sparkle in the girl's eyes. "I have my doubts that he will listen."

"But you'll try?" Grace asked eagerly.

"I'll try," Evadne promised.

With that promise in mind, as soon as they were on deck, Evadne put her hand on Nevis's arm, saying, "Can we stop here a moment, Captain? I would like to speak to you alone, and I know Grace and Ethan would like a few minutes alone too."

"Yes, Miss Harper?" Nevis paused, only half listening to her while his eyes followed the other couple.

Evadne tried to keep annoyance out of her voice. "Captain Nevis," she began as sweetly as possible, "would it not be possible for Grace and I to spend a little more time on deck? I find the work aboard ship fascinating and I would like to know more about—"

Ethan and Grace had stopped at the rail across the deck, in full view. His mind at ease, Nevis now gave his full attention to Evadne. "I beg your pardon?" he said, betraying the fact that he had not been listening.

Evadne bit her lip, annoyance giving way to anger, making her forget her resolve to be both pleasant and logical. "It is quite unfair of you," she said, "to keep us below decks in your cabin all the time, with nothing to do, when the weather is so fair—"

"It is for your own good," Nevis told her firmly.

"For our good?" Evadne was astonished. "Surely, fresh air and sunshine is better for us."

"It is quite impossible. I do not have the time to be with you. I must run the ship."

Evadne smiled tightly. "It is not necessary for you to be with me all the time. I can surely find a place where I will be out of the way. . . ." She paused, remembering her promise to Grace. "Besides, it would give Grace and Ethan a little more time together."

"You are fulfilling my misgivings about women aboard a working ship, Miss Harper." Nevis eyed her disapprovingly. "I will not have you disturbing my crew with your presence, and Mr. Morgan has certain duties to perform. If that is all, we will join the others and continue our walk." He took her arm.

"Then it is not my well-being you are thinking of, but what you consider to be the good of your ship and crew," Evadne charged angrily.

"You are a beautiful woman, a most tempting sight to any man," he said bluntly. "Any man might give less than his full attention to his duties with such a distraction."

"And Grace and Ethan?" she demanded.

The captain continued to lead her across the deck to where Ethan and Grace were standing hand in hand. "As the Bible says, 'Lead us not into temptation.'"

"'But deliver us from evil,'" finished Evadne stopping and turning to face him. "Are women really evil in your mind, Captain Nevis?"

"I am sure you are aware of what passed between Adam and Eve. If not, I suggest that you pass your time reading my Bible," Nevis told her.

Evadne flushed, furious now, and bit her tongue to avoid saying something that might result in Nevis's denying them even these brief turns about the deck. Still, she could not help but recoil from his touch when he took her arm again.

Nevis looked at her solemnly. "Miss Harper, I am not a cruel man. I admit I am a man of principles—perhaps of too high principles." His eyes darkened with emotion. "I find myself more tempted by the sight of you than I like to admit." He smiled slightly. "I will never forget the first time I saw you, in that green suit that matched your eyes with your hair aflame in the sun, setting my heart on fire."

This speech struck Evadne-dumb. She stared at him.

"Once we reach Hawaii," he went on, "I promise you that you will find me quite a different man, one who desires you and will do all in his power to make you happy. Until that time, you must allow me the principles that guide me as captain of my ship. I apologize for anything I have said that has made you angry, but you are a sore temptation to me."

Evadne shook her head, her expression half-puzzled, half-admiring. "You are a strange man, Captain. I do not understand you at all. Just when I am positive that you are cold and unreasonable, you surprise me with a very different side of your nature."

"Then you will abide by my wishes as long as we are aboard ship?" Nevis asked with a smile.

"Yes, of course. You give me no choice," responded Evadne.

For the rest of the voyage, she ignored Grace's pleas and grumbling, pointing out that she and Ethan would have the rest of their lives together and besides they would soon be in Hawaii.

As for herself, Evadne had more than enough to do to try to decide what her feelings were. The more she thought about Captain Nevis, the more he puzzled her—and the more of a puzzle he became, the more she found herself attracted to him, and not just because of his resemblance to William. She took advantage of every opportunity to study him, to try to draw him out again, but he never again went beyond the bounds of polite conversation. On Sunday, however, Nevis relaxed some of his restraints. In the morning, as soon as the sails were set, the crew—except for the helmsman—was assembled on the maindeck. With Evadne and Grace seated on the foredeck with Ethan and the first mate Stevenson, Captain Nevis took his place at the railing separating the raised foredeck from the maindeck, to hold a church service. To Evadne's surprise, it was brief, opening with the Twenty-third Psalm and closing with the Lord's Prayer, with no exhortation to avoid sin or temptation. The closest Nevis came to a sermon was a brief reading of the destruction of Sodom and Gomorrah—which he likened to San Francisco—cautioning his listeners to look to the future and not look back as Lot's wife had. Evadne wondered whether the last was for her benefit.

Nevis and Ethan joined the girls for dinner. Neither Ethan nor Grace spoke much during the meal, being content to look at each other and hold hands under the table. Nevis not being a man for idle conversation, the burden fell on Evadne. She cast about for a subject that might interest them all. The only possibility she could think of was Hawaii.

"Tell me, Captain, how soon do you think we will reach our destination?" she asked.

He looked up from his plate. "We have had a fair wind. If it continues, we should make our landfall by week's end," he said.

"It will be good to see land again, won't it, Grace?" Evadne asked.

"See it!" Grace exclaimed. "The day I set foot on land can't come soon enough."

Evadne smiled and looked back at Nevis. "What is it like really?"

"You will find the city of Honolulu quite civilized, although I hesitate to say too much out of fear of raising false expectations. Still, Honolulu has all the amenities you could wish for, and the climate is most pleasant," he told them.

"The Hawaiians themselves? What are they like?" she asked.

"Yeah," Grace put in, "they're Injuns, ain't they?"

"They are Polynesian, Miss Jones, a very gentle, unwarlike people. They are most hospitable—perhaps too hospitable for their own good," Nevis added with a frown.

"I don't understand," Evadne said.

"They welcomed outsiders with open arms, indeed, even accepting our God in place of their pagan ones. They seem childlike in many respects," continued Nevis, "but isolated as the islands are, they had had little previous contact with other people. They did not know disease as we know it. As a result, several years ago, they were almost killed off by the measles."

"Oh, no!" cried Evadne, dismayed not only by what Nevis had said but also at the unfortunate turn the conversation had taken. Her concern was justified.

"You expect me to live in such a place, Ethan!" Grace glowered at her fiancé. "Well, you got another think coming!"

"Now, Miss Jones," Nevis said quickly, "that was a long time ago. You will find Honolulu every bit as safe as San Francisco—" He stopped, remembering the ruin they had left behind them.

But his attempt to appease Grace pleased Evadne, and she smiled at him. "I for one, Captain, am eager to see Hawaii."

"I hope you will not be disappointed," he told her gravely, ending the conversation.

Once more, Evadne was left puzzled by the captain's behavior. Still, despite the attraction she was beginning to feel for Nevis, she was still determined to put off their marriage as long as possible, to give themselves a chance to get to know one another better. How she would manage that, if Nevis insisted on an immediate ceremony, she did not know. All she could do was hope for an excuse that would persuade him.

Evadne approached each day that brought them closer to Hawaii with a mixture of feelings—eagerness for the new life she would be starting and dread at the decision she must make. Her heart and mind were again at odds with each other. If she was attracted to Nevis, her heart told her she was not in love with him, but her mind told her that she had no choice but to keep her word—just as she had had no choice but to accept his protection in San Francisco. She began to wish for a tropical storm, or for the wind to fall, leaving them becalmed and delaying the inevitable. But the fair wind held and brought them closer each day to their destination and Evadne, to her fate.

She and Grace had barely finished dressing one morning when there was a knocking at the cabin door. Surprised that breakfast was there so early, Evadne opened the door to see Captain Nevis himself on the threshold.

"Why, Captain! Good morning," she said in surprise.

"We have sighted Hawaii, Miss Harper. Excuse my disturbing you, but I thought you might want to see your new home," he added in embarrassment.

"I do!" Excitement flooded her. Forgetting all about Grace, she hurried to the foredeck.

The sun had just risen over the bowsprit. In the distance was a range of purple mountains, behind which fluffy white clouds hovered, tinged a deep pink by the rising sun. Toward the north was a vast rocky prominence that appeared barren in contrast to the lush green everywhere else. Nestled at the foot of the mountains was Honolulu, sparkling white in the dewy freshness of the morning, seeming to rise out of the bluest water Evadne had ever seen . . . water as blue as William's eyes. Tears rose into her own. Unconsciously, she reached out to take Nevis's hand.

He gripped hers firmly. "There is your new home, Evadne," he said, using her given name for the first time. "What do you think of it?"

Evadne tried to smile. "It's . . . it's beautiful," she murmured. Indeed, it was. Perhaps it *would* be possible to make a fresh start in a place that looked like paradise and held no memories of the past.

Chapter XVII

THE *NARRAGANSETT* DROPPED ANCHOR IN THE ROADSTEAD OFF
Honolulu, much to Grace's disappointment. She had only
one thought in mind: to get off the ship as quickly as possible.
Nevis, however, insisted on going ashore first to arrange for a
place for the girls to stay. Leaving them in Ethan's care, he
had a boat lowered.

There had been a time when whaling ships were not
welcome at Honolulu. Their crews, after months at sea, had
too often indulged in a drunken orgy of rioting and rape.
Those days were long past. As far from the mainland as the
islands were, news of the disaster at San Francisco had
already reached there, and the harbormaster greeted Nevis
eagerly. So did Thomas MacMahon, a shipowner, who
happened to be in the harbormaster's office. He had known
and done business with Evadne's father. When he heard that
she was aboard the *Narragansett*, he insisted that Evadne and
Grace must stay at his house.

The invitation was met with both relief and misgivings by
Evadne, when Nevis returned to the ship—relief at having a
place to go and misgivings about what MacMahon's reactions
to her father's death and bankruptcy would be. Grace, too,
was less than enthusiastic.

"Vad, they're goin' to separate us, aren't they? I mean, it's gonna be 'Miss Vad,' again. We won't be friends any more," she said mournfully.

"No, Grace. I will insist that they do not separate us. More than ever, I will need a friend," Evadne responded.

"You may not have much say about it," Grace pointed out.

"Then Captain Nevis will have to find another place for us. We will just have to wait and see what happens." She sighed then. "But, oh, I hope they don't turn us out before I have a bath—a nice, long, hot bath."

To go ashore, they had to use the Jacob's ladder. Grace watched Ethan help Evadne onto the ladder while Nevis reached up from below to assist her down into the boat. Despite misgivings, this time Grace did not protest in her anxiety to be on land once more, though she alternately reviled all ships and prayed with each step down, making Evadne smile.

Ashore, Grace's worst fears returned again. "It's rockin'!" she screamed. "The island—it's rockin' under my feet!"

Nevis chuckled, a deep throaty sound that made Evadne stare in surprise. "No, Miss Jones," he said, "the island is steady as a rock. You're used to the ship. You have to get your land legs back."

"You're sure?" Grace asked suspiciously.

"Of course he is, Grace," Evadne told her, as a short, sturdy man about her father's age stepped forward. He was dressed in a white suit and carried a white straw hat.

After Nevis had introduced them, Thomas MacMahon bowed deeply to Evadne. "Your father and I were business acquaintants, Miss Harper. It is a pleasure to meet you, although I deeply regret the circumstances."

Evadne smiled hesitantly, not sure how much Nevis had told him. "Thank you, Mr. MacMahon," she replied.

"There will be plenty of time to talk later," MacMahon went on. "I have sent word to my wife, and I know she is waiting for you." He turned to Nevis. "You have my address, Captain Nevis. Perhaps you and Miss Jones's fiancé would join us for dinner?"

"It would be our pleasure, Mr. MacMahon," Nevis told him, as he helped escort the two girls to the carriage that MacMahon had waiting.

During the drive to the spacious, rambling house set amidst tropical gardens where he lived, MacMahon did not question Evadne. He said only, "I know you have been through a great deal, my dear. Naturally, I am eager to hear what has happened—all we have heard are rumors of the most dire sort—but first we must attend to your needs and comfort."

"I appreciate your consideration, Mr. MacMahon," Evadne said gratefully. "You have no idea how I have looked forward to a hot bath." She laughed. "Captain Nevis did his best, but the *Narragansett* was not built to accommodate passengers."

MacMahon smiled, glancing at the meager bundles the girls were carrying and taking note of the heavy wool dresses they were wearing. Both girls' faces gleamed with perspiration in the heat of the Hawaiian sun. "You will need more suitable clothing, too, but I am sure my wife will see to that."

His wife was waiting for them. She was a tall, statuesque woman—even taller than Evadne. Her dark complexion, black hair, and almond-shaped black eyes bespoke her native Hawaiian heritage. Grace stared at her, all her fears about Hawaii and Hawaiians personified in the woman's alien appearance. Ada MacMahon, however, took no notice. She swept both girls in her arms, clucking over them sympathetically, her expressive eyes filling with tears at the thought of what they had been through.

"Poor things," she wept. "You are safe now." Holding them to her, she almost carried them inside the large, cool house. Once there, she stood them at arms length to study them, tears running down her cheeks.

Her husband had followed them inside to make the introductions, adding, "I told you, my wife would be waiting for you. You are in her hands now, and I will return to my office. Ada," he said, "Miss Harper has mentioned her desire for a bath."

"She shall have it." Ada MacMahon kissed her husband goodbye, then took the girls by the hand and led them upstairs to a large room that faced the ocean. A cool breeze drifted through open French doors leading onto a balcony that surrounded the upper floor of the house.

"One of my girls will bring you some food and something cool to drink," Ada announced. "She will also draw a bath for you. In the meantime, I must get you something else to wear." She giggled. "You look like missionaries!"

As Ada continued to fuss about, turning back the covers on the beds, Evadne, overwhelmed by the woman's welcome, managed to say, "I don't know how to thank you, Mrs. MacMahon. To take in strangers—"

Ada laughed, a rich, wonderful, deep sound. "Hospitality

is the heritage of the islands—of my people. It is one custom
that the missionaries could not change. And you must not call
me 'Mrs. MacMahon.' No one does. It is Ada . . . or Aunt
Ada, if you prefer. You are my family now." A shadow
passed over her face. "It is my one regret that I have no
children, but you will be my daughters now." Her face
wreathed in smiles, she drew them into her arms again. "You
are little more than children, poor things."

Evadne gave in to the warmth of the embrace. For the first
time in weeks, she felt young again. Tears rose in her eyes and
she laid her head against the big woman's shoulder.

Ada gave them another hug. "Now, I must see where that
girl is."

As Ada MacMahon bustled out, Grace turned to Evadne in
amazement. "You think she really means it? I mean, what's
she goin' to think when she finds out I used to be your maid,
Vad?"

Evadne shook her head. "I doubt that it will make any
difference to her, Grace. Probably she already knows." She
sat down on the bed. "I think we are very lucky that Captain
Nevis happened to meet Mr. MacMahon." She glanced
around the lovely room.

The arrival of Ada's "girl" ended any further speculation.
She was a bright-eyed half Chinese, half Polynesian beauty,
who eyed Evadne and Grace curiously as she set down a tray
loaded with food—

"You want bath now or later?" she asked.

"Now," Evadne said eagerly.

The girl nodded and moved toward a connecting bathroom.
"I come back," she announced.

Evadne helped herself from the plates of fruit and cold
meats. Never had food tasted so delicious. She did not
recognize half of what she was eating, but all of it was
ambrosial.

Grace had taken off her heavy dress and stretched out on
one of the two beds with a grateful sigh. "I couldn't have
stood one more night in that bunk," she said, forgetting that
Evadne had had even less comfort in the hammock.

"Bath ready now," Ada's girl announced.

Evadne followed her into the bathroom and sank into a
steaming tub of water, to which the girl had added a generous
amount of scented oil. Evadne closed her eyes, inhaling the
musky scent. For a long time she lay without moving, letting
the water wash over her, letting it sink into every pore.

Finally, when it began to cool slightly, she scrubbed every inch of herself, starting with her toes, moving up along her thighs, across her flat stomach, up to her breasts, her shoulders, neck, and face, finally washing her hair. Reluctantly, then, she forced herself to get out of the tub.

As she dried herself off, Evadne examined her body critically. She half expected to see that it had aged overnight, but her breasts were still high and firm, her waist tiny, the thighs slender, and the muff of hair between them as red as ever. She ran her hands slowly over her body, rejoicing in the life that flowed through her at the touch. Sighing at the hunger rising inside her, she put on the flowered cotton wrapper the maid had laid out for her.

While Grace took her bath, Ada's girl, who said her name was May, combed out Evadne's red hair, admiring the color and the curls that sprang to life as it dried. When Grace reappeared, May offered to help her with her hair, too, but Grace was uneasy at being waited on. She shook her head, combing out her own hair, assailed by a twinge of jealousy as she watched May try out various hair styles on Evadne. That had, after all, been her job not so long ago.

After May left, the girls lay down on the beds. To Evadne, her spine still curved by the hammock, it was the utmost luxury to stretch out and roll over. The bed felt soft as a cloud, and despite returning fears of what might happen after she spoke to Mr. MacMahon, she found herself drifting off into a dreamless sleep.

They were awakened late in the afternoon by Ada. She entered the room, her arms loaded with dresses and other garments, giggling happily at the way the girls had made themselves at home. She hugged them both again and touched Evadne's now clean and shining hair with what amounted to awe. "You are most beautiful, child. That hair and those eyes! There was a time in the islands when you would have been worshiped as a goddess!"

Evadne smiled hesitantly, uncomfortable with such praise.

Ada, meanwhile, stepped back, her lips pursed, examining Evadne's figure. Without the slightest embarrassment, she stripped the wrapper off of her and handed her a thin undergarment. It fit perfectly and brought a satisfied nod from Ada.

"I did not have time to do much shopping, but I have had my girls busy altering a few things." She giggled again. "It is good that you are almost as tall as I am," she told Evadne, handing a dress and helping her put it on.

The dress was pale green, cut low over the bosom, with short sleeves. The waist fitted snugly and the skirt clung seductively to the girl's slender body. There were more dresses to be tried on. Evadne, her head spinning, put on one after another, drawing more giggles of pleased satisfaction from Ada.

Grace was just as closely scrutinized as Evadne, to her embarrassment. Blushing furiously, she tried on gown after gown too, all chosen with as much care for her coloring and figure as Evadne's.

Finally, Ada stepped back with a satisfied look that turned to dismay when she realized that the girls were barefoot. "Shoes!" she cried. "I have forgotten shoes! Never mind, I will get some from my girls. The Chinese slippers will fit."

Evadne studied the array of gowns strewn on the bed. "Mrs. MacMahon, surely these are not all for us . . . ?"

"What else?" Ada laughed. "Although, if you call me Mrs. MacMahon once more I may take all of them back."

"Aunt Ada, then." Evadne smiled. "But we cannot accept such a gift, and I cannot repay you—"

"My dears, I am not asking for repayment. Thomas and I are very happy," she said simply, "and we have more than enough for our needs. This is not charity—" she waved at the gowns, her mouth twisting sourly "—it is a gift. I am no missionary—I am Hawaiian." She looked at the pitiful bundle of belongings that the girls had brought with them with distaste. "You are my guests—my daughters—and I won't have you shaming me." She picked up the heavy serge dresses and coarse nightclothes and Evadne's reticule. "I will have these burned."

Evadne quickly took the reticule from Ada's grasp. "Please. . . ."

"Of course. It is yours. Now, get dressed. I will have May bring some shoes. Come downstairs when you are ready. Thomas is home and waiting to speak to you." She swept grandly from the room.

"My goodness," Grace said, "do you think she's crazy? Just look—ain't they grand?" She picked up one of the dresses, holding it in front of her. "Just wait until my Ethan sees me in this."

Evadne was slipping on the green dress that had been

Ada's first choice for her when May came with several pairs of slippers for them to try on. Evadne selected a pair and finished dressing. After a last look in the mirror, she turned to Grace, who was fussing with her hair. "I am going downstairs, Grace, take your time. I must talk to Mr. MacMahon alone for a few minutes."

Downstairs, Evadne found Mr. MacMahon sitting in a corner room that opened onto the first floor veranda. The windows were open to catch the evening breezes. Thomas MacMahon rose to his feet as Evadne entered, offering her a chair and a cool drink. Evadne accepted the seat, but refused the drink. Ada joined them now, taking a seat next to her husband, holding one of his hands in hers. The open gesture of affection reminded Evadne of her own parents and she blinked back sudden tears.

"Mr. MacMahon," she began, "I am afraid Grace and I are here under somewhat false pretenses."

MacMahon set down his glass with a frown. "Nevis said—"

Evadne continued hurriedly, "Whatever Captain Nevis told you was the truth—he is an honest man—but he could not have had time to tell you everything." She took a deep breath and told her story, beginning with the news of her father's death and his bankruptcy and continuing through the events that led to her arrival in Hawaii. The only thing she did not tell him about was William. "And so, you see, I am totally destitute. All I have is some jewelry of mine and my mother's that I managed to salvage."

MacMahon had listened calmly, only nodding once in a while. Ada, on the other hand, had displayed every emotion —from tears to admiration. Both were silent at the end of the recital, trying to absorb all that Evadne had told them.

Evadne smiled hesitantly. "You have been very kind to us. Still, I cannot stay under the circumstances."

"I admire your honesty, Evadne," MacMahon said. "But as far as your financial situation goes, I cannot say that I am surprised." Seeing Evadne's startled look, he added: "I am in the same business, and I had heard rumors."

"Then, why . . . ? I mean. . . ." Evadne looked at him, puzzled.

MacMahon smiled. "Why did I bring you here?" He glanced at his wife. "I knew Ada would never forgive me if I did not."

"Then . . . we are still welcome?" Evadne looked from husband to wife.

"Of course!" Ada declared. "More than ever after what you have just told us. Are they not, Thomas?"

MacMahon nodded. "You are a very brave girl, Evadne," he said admiringly.

"You and Grace have a home with us for as long as you need it," Ada said, "which won't be long as soon as the young men of Honolulu meet *you*." She beamed at Evadne.

"I have promised to wed Captain Nevis," Evadne said quietly. She saw their startled expressions, but the arrival of Nevis and Ethan put an end to any further conversation.

The captain and his mate were overwhelmed by the warmth of Ada's welcome. Evadne's fine gown and Grace's arrival on the scene in equally splendid clothing did not do much to put either man at his ease. Only gradually, over dinner, did Nevis recover his composure.

The meal was lavish, a combination of Chinese, Polynesian, and European dishes that intrigued Evadne. The first course was soup, a chicken broth with strands of egg. This was followed by fish, cooked whole, and accompanied by an assortment of fruits and vegetables. After that came a whole roast pig and something pastelike that Ada called poi. There were also various other meats and fish wrapped in leaves. Finally came dessert, a rich coconut custard, and, of course, fresh fruit.

Most of the conversation at the table was about the earthquake and fire. A few ships had arrived before the *Narragansett* with sketchy news of the disaster. They had left immediately when it appeared that the San Francisco waterfront might go up in flames. As a result, much of the news they brought consisted of wild tales of looting, murder, rape, and disease. As their four guests told about their narrow escapes and of their walk through the ruined city, MacMahon and Ada listened intently.

"Is there nothing left?" MacMahon asked in wonder. "The Palace Hotel—remember, Ada? We spent our honeymoon there!"

"Oh yes! And how often we planned to go back," Ada mourned, tears filling her eyes.

"Nob Hill! Surely that—why, the Hopkins mansion crowned it like a castle," recalled MacMahon.

"There is nothing left," Evadne told them. She sighed. "In a way, I am glad that my parents did not live to see it. A few houses on Russian and Telegraph Hills were still standing. That is all we could see. And Cliff House, of course."

"How did you escape from Nob Hill?" asked Ada.

"We walked. The Army commandeered all . . . all the cars." Her voice broke slightly as the sight of William as she had last seen him, a bayonet jabbing his arm, rose before her.

"We were lucky to save the clothes on our backs and what we could carry," she added quickly.

"Walked!" Ada was appalled.

"There was no other way," Evadne said.

Ada shook her head. "Oh, Thomas, remember those hills? How my feet hurt! I could never have managed."

Grace giggled. "Sure you could, if you had had Vad with you. If it hadn't a been for her, I wouldn't be here now."

"Truly?" Ada looked at Grace who had been silent until then.

"Truly," Grace affirmed. "I still don't know how she got me home that first day when we went looking for my Ethan here. Last thing I 'member is being in Union Square. The next thing I knew, I was on the couch in the library at the house."

"Oh, Grace! Let's not go into that again," Evadne put in hurriedly.

Ada glanced at her speculatively, hearing an anxious note in her voice.

"It was the fires then, not the earthquake, that did so much damage," said MacMahon. "How did they start?"

"The gas mains broke, sir," explained Nevis. "The fires seemed to spring up all over the place at once from any open flame. I was aboard my ship, and from there they looked like a chain of firecrackers going off. My first thought was to get my crew together and leave at once, but I was trapped ashore by the fires. That was when I found Mr. Morgan here."

"San Francisco had one of the finest fire departments in the world, from what I heard. Where were its men?" asked MacMahon.

"They did their best. The water mains broke along with the gas mains," Nevis said. He went on then to describe the dynamiting and how the fires were finally brought under control.

"Well," Ada got to her feet, "it is all beyond my imagination. Come, girls, let us leave the men to their brandy." She smiled. "Although it is not a custom I like, I know they must have things to discuss."

Evadne left the table unwillingly, for she knew what "things" Ada meant—the marriages of Ethan and Grace and

Evadne and Nevis. Ada seemed to guess what was going on in
Evadne's mind. As soon as they were in the room that opened
onto the ocean, she sat down facing the two girls.

"Grace," Ada said, "I understand that you and Ethan have
known each other for some time, and that you planned to
marry before this . . . this disaster?"

"Yes, Ma'am," replied Grace who could not bring herself
to call the woman Aunt Ada. "Me an' Ethan, we were gonna
get married as soon as Vad's folks got back."

"I see. And you, Evadne?"

Evadne, unable to meet the woman's scrutiny, looked out
at the vast Pacific, shining in the moonlight. "I have promised
to wed Captain Nevis," she told Ada again.

"So you said, child. Perhaps I am a prying old woman,
putting my nose where it does not belong, but I see in your
face none of the happiness of a woman in love that I see in
Grace's. Marriage is a serious business . . . for a lifetime,"
Ada pointed out gently.

"I am well aware of that," Evadne answered, her eyes still
on the moonlit ocean. "I made my decision of my own free
will."

"Then look at me and tell me that you love this man," Ada
insisted.

Evadne looked away from the ocean, but she still could not
meet Ada's eyes. "I would not be here, were it not for him. I
have given my word," she said softly. "He is a good man,
a . . . a righteous man."

Ada sighed, recognizing the stubbornness that drove
Evadne. "Let me tell you a story about these islands, my
dear. When the missionary societies from New England sent
the first missionaries here in the early eighteen hundreds,
they sent only married men with their wives. One reason, of
course," she said with a smile, "was to make sure the men did
not stray into temptation with our native girls. Many of those
missionaries married women they had never seen before their
wedding day. Some did learn to love one another.
Others . . ." She shrugged. "This Captain Nevis is like those
men, I believe, just as I believe that you do not love him.
Perhaps love will come, in which case I will be happy for you,
but you cannot know that, and you are far too beautiful and
intelligent to be trapped into a loveless marriage. I would not
see you wither and grow old before your time, see the spirit I
sense in you die."

"Aunt Ada, please!" cried Evadne. "It will do no good to

talk about it." She sprang to her feet and went to the open windows. The breeze was cool on her hot face, carrying with it the odor of sandalwood. Overhead the moon rode and the stars twinkled. It was a night made for love, for walking in the garden. . . . She clasped her arms around herself, trying to contain the memory of the ecstasy she had known with William that rose unwillingly at the portrait Ada had painted of life with Nevis.

Ada stepped up behind her and turned her around, forcing Evadne to meet her eyes. "I think I see love in your eyes now, and I do not think it is for Captain Nevis. Do you want to tell me about it?"

Evadne shook her head. "I cannot. It is over and . . . and I have given my word."

"Very well, but will you promise me to stay here, to postpone this marriage until you are absolutely sure?" Ada took her in her arms.

After all, it was what she had planned to do, if at all possible. "Yes, I will promise that," Evadne whispered. "But what will I say to him?"

Ada chuckled. "Leave that to me. All you must do is say that you need time to prepare for the wedding. After all, a girl only gets married once. Her wedding should be something she remembers for the rest of her life."

For the rest of the evening, Evadne clung to what Ada had said as she waited for Nevis to speak to her. She watched him uneasily, noticing how stern he looked, how cold and grim, as if whatever the men had discussed had not pleased him. As soon as he could, he took his leave of the MacMahons and Evadne, saying only that he would return the next afternoon to talk to Evadne. A reluctant Ethan left with him.

Shortly afterward, the household went to bed. Ada hugged the girls, telling them to sleep as late as they wished and to ring for breakfast whenever they were ready.

When they were alone in their room, Grace turned to Evadne. "That Ada's taken a shine to you."

"To both of us, Grace," Evadne replied, detecting a note of jealousy.

"I can't understand half what she's talking about sometimes, and all that hugging! It makes me nervous," Grace declared. "I'll be glad when Ethan an' me are married; and I can leave this place. Won't you?"

"It's Ada's way," Evadne said. "I like her."

"You ain't changed your mind!" Grace's eyes narrowed. "I mean, you and the cap'n an' me and Ethan, we're gonna get married together I thought."

"A double wedding?" Evadne, recalling what Ada had said, was noncommittal. "I don't know, Grace. A girl's wedding should be something she remembers for the rest of her life."

"I'll remember mine, all right." Grace giggled. "I can't wait for me and Ethan to be together. Why, we ain't been alone for weeks an' weeks—not since you went to Sonoma with that furriner."

Evadne winced. "It's different for you and Ethan, Grace. If you want to get married as soon as possible, go ahead. As for me, I want a real wedding, the kind I always dreamed about."

Grace frowned as she climbed into her bed. "Better be careful, Vad," she advised. "I ain't so sure Captain Nevis holds with that sort of display. Didn't you see the way he looked at you in that green dress?"

"What do you mean?" Evadne, in the process of getting into her own bed, paused to look at her.

"His eyes near popped outta his head. Why, he couldn't keep his eyes off your . . . your bosom." Grace giggled.

Evadne lay down, smiling slightly. "Well, he had better get used to it, because I don't intend to go around dressed like a—a mummy in this climate."

Grace yawned. "You know what I think, Vad? I think you might as well make the best of it. You can't stay here with *her* forever, and you've got no money."

Evadne turned her back on Grace, putting her arms around her pillow. She knew all too well that she had little choice and that Grace was right. Still, she had promised Ada to delay the marriage as long as possible, and she would try. It would take time for Nevis to find a place for them to live, to refit his ship and establish himself in the islands. In the meantime, he would have little time or thought for her.

But when the captain called on her the next day, Evadne was less confident. He greeted her formally, calling her "Miss Harper" again, and suggested that they walk in the garden. Ethan had already taken Grace off in the carriage in which he and Nevis had arrived at the MacMahons' to "show her the town," Ethan said. From the glint in his eyes, however, Evadne guessed that Grace wouldn't see much beyond the room he had rented ashore.

In the garden was a charming gazebo. As soon as they were seated in it, Nevis said, "You must obtain more suitable clothing."

"What's wrong with this?" Evadne glanced down at the dress she was wearing. It was a thin, flowered cotton, low-cut and ruffled at the neck with short sleeves. "It's cool and it's comfortable, suited to this climate."

"But hardly suited to a modest young woman who is about to be married," Nevis objected, eyeing the swell of her breasts.

Evadne smiled. "I see nothing immodest about this dress." She smoothed the skirt over her hips, noting the flush that rose in his bronzed cheeks. "This is not New England, Captain," she reminded him gently.

Nevis ignored the comment. "I have spoken to a minister in town. He has said that he will marry us this coming Sunday, after regular services. Ethan is willing to be married at the same time," he added.

Evadne stared at him in alarm, her heart pounding. "Have you given any thought as to where we will live?" she finally managed to say.

"I have taken rooms in a boardinghouse near the harbor. That will be convenient for my overseeing the refitting of the *Narragansett*. Ethan has taken rooms there, too, so you and Grace will not be lonely while we are busy. I might add that Mr. MacMahon has been most kind in putting the facilities of his shipyard at my disposal." He looked at Evadne expectantly, waiting for her approval of his plans.

"You have planned everything without once consulting me." She glared at him, her temper rising. "I am not a member of your crew to be ordered about."

"I—I assumed . . ." he began, bewildered, astonished by her anger.

"That it would be all right with me?" Evadne got to her feet. "Well, it is not, Captain Nevis. It is not all right at all!" She stamped her foot angrily, folding her arms across her breasts in such a way that the white mounds rose seductively higher.

"It—it was understood that we would marry when we reached Hawaii. Are you going back on your word?" he demanded.

Evadne raised her chin proudly. "I gave you my word, and I have every intention of keeping it." She took a deep breath, realizing that her temper was doing her more harm than good.

"Then we will be married on Sunday?" he asked.

Evadne exhaled slowly. "We will not," she said, calmer now. "We will marry in good time. I have always dreamed of a proper wedding," she added, "and I will not be denied it. Let Grace have her day and then I will have mine."

"Must I remind you that you are hardly in a position to make such demands?" Nevis was grim.

"I am well aware of my position, Captain, but . . . but we hardly know one another," she said in desperation, her courage flagging.

"There will be plenty of time for that after we are married, Miss Harper," he said stiffly.

"The least we could do is to begin by calling each other by our first names," begged Evadne, "or is it to be Captain Nevis and Miss Harper all our lives?"

"There will be plenty of time for that—" Nevis began again.

Evadne's green eyes flashed. "I know—*after* we are married!" she finished for him.

"Children! There you are, hiding from me!" Ada came toward them from out of nowhere, making Evadne wonder if she hadn't been nearby listening. Not that she cared, she was too relieved to see her.

Ada gave each of them a hug in her exuberant way. "Have you been talking about your wedding?" she asked. Giving neither of them a chance to answer, she went on, "Captain Nevis, I have been discussing your marriage with Thomas. We have decided that Evadne should have a wedding appropriate to her station in life, especially after all that she has been through. Perhaps, in some small way, it will make up for what she has lost—her home, her parents, her friends. What do you think?"

She looked so pleased with herself that Evadne could not keep from smiling. "A proper wedding," Evadne murmured, glancing at Nevis.

"I will not take no for an answer, Captain," Ada insisted. "Let us call it a wedding present, if you wish."

"I do not wish, Mrs. MacMahon," Nevis said flatly. "You are putting ideas into Miss Harper's head that are entirely unsuitable to her *new* station in life—the wife of a simple ship's captain."

Ada laughed. "You are a hard man, Captain Nevis. If you are to make your home here in Hawaii, you must learn that our different way of life has its own merits. A wife can do much to help you in your business."

"It is for that reason that I have asked Miss Harper to marry me. It may be a difficult life at first, but—"

"It need only be as difficult as you wish to make it," Ada interrupted him. "This island is a small place, but it is a big place too. Relationships are important. My husband is an influential man on this island—and on the other islands. We have many friends among the planters, all of whom would attend your wedding if we were to invite them." Although Ada's voice was playful, the implied threat was obvious: Thomas MacMahon—both MacMahons—could make or break Nevis in his new venture.

The captain flushed a dark red and his eyes looked almost black in his anger. His fists clenched as if to keep him from striking the woman who was smiling at him so innocently, an arm around Evadne's shoulders.

"Very well," Nevis said tightly. "I can see that I have no choice except to leave my wedding in your hands."

"Good!" Ada beamed at him. "Rest assured, that you *and* Evadne," she chided him gently, "will have a wedding that the islands will long remember."

"I must get back to my ship." Nevis gave them a curt bow and stalked off.

Ada waited until she was sure that he was out of hearing, then burst out laughing. "Forgive me, child. I suppose you know I was eavesdropping. As I said, I am a nosy, prying old lady, but it is too late for me to change."

Evadne sighed. "I'm glad that you did listen in, although it will change nothing. Sooner or later, we will marry."

Ada shrugged. "But in the meantime, the islands will have a chance to change him, soften him, while you have time to consider your decision under less trying circumstances."

"I cannot go back on my word," Evadne said. "He could have left me in San Francisco." She told Ada about Nevis's misgivings about women aboard a working ship, how he had broken his own rule for her—a rule his men were well aware of.

"Now, I understand—a little." Ada looked at Evadne soberly. "Very well, child. I will not attempt to prevent this marriage, loveless as it may be on your side." She hugged Evadne to her. "At least, you will have a friend to stand by you—two friends, Grace and me. In the meantime, it will do no harm to see what we can do to make that man more human. I suspect that there is more passion there than he is willing to admit to."

Evadne glanced around her at the lush, tropical garden filled with seductive scents, at the Pacific, deep blue and alluring. Overhead, the sun shone out of a cloudless blue sky. The Garden of Eden could not have been a more enticing paradise. If Captain Nevis had the slightest passion in his breast, Hawaii must awaken it. She smiled at Ada, saying, "I hope so" so fervently that Ada looked at her in startled surprise.

Chapter XVIII

OVER THE NEXT FEW DAYS, NEVIS KEPT HIS DISTANCE, THOUGH Ethan arrived at the MacMahons' regularly each afternoon to spend a few hours with Grace. He always gave Evadne Nevis's greetings, along with news on how the refitting of the *Narragansett* was proceeding. Ethan explained awkwardly that supervising the work was taking up all of the captain's time—from early in the morning until late at night.

Evadne and Grace, meanwhile, spent their time working with Ada and May on Grace's wedding gown and trousseau, for Ada was determined to give Grace as fine a wedding to remember as the limited time allowed. Grace, despite her distrust of "furriners," could not remain immune to Ada's bubbling good humor and openhanded generosity. On Wednesday, she had the first fitting, just before Ethan was due to arrive. By then the gown would be bundled out of sight. Both Ada and Grace were too superstitious about a fiancé seeing the bride in her wedding gown before the ceremony for them to permit Ethan the slightest glimpse of the dress, much less see Grace in it.

The gown was of white satin with a high-necked, demure bodice and long sleeves. Both bodice and sleeves were of lace. The skirt was fitted over the hips in front and slightly puffed into a bustle in back, from which fell a short train.

Grace stared at herself in the mirror as May pinned the back. "Oh my, Aunt Ada!" she cried, calling Ada MacMahon aunt for the first time. "I never dreamed I'd be married in such a proper gown. Just look at me! Ain't I beautiful? I have to pinch myself to make sure it ain't a dream!"

Ada laughed. "If you are happy, then I am happy, child."

"What I don't understand . . . I mean . . . why're you doing all this for me? I ain't nothing to you. I'm just a nobody. All I ever was was a maid, like May here," Grace added.

"Let's say that I'm an incurable romantic, Grace. One thing I love above all is weddings, though I always cry, as Thomas will tell you." Ada giggled. "As far as May goes, she will also have a fine wedding."

Grace sighed. "We sure was lucky your husband was at the harbor that day!"

"Yes," Evadne agreed. "And neither of us will ever forget what you have done for us, Aunt Ada."

Ada looked pensively at Evadne a moment before saying to Grace, "Come, child, off with that dress before your young man arrives."

May took the dress off carefully to avoid sticking Grace with pins.

"Ethan says he don't know how he can ever repay you for all you done for me," Grace said.

Ada chuckled. "You tell him for me that the only repayment I want is for him to be good to you—to make you as happy as Thomas has made me." She hugged Grace, then straightened the simple cotton gown that Grace had put on. "Go along now. Unless I'm mistaken, that's Ethan at the front door."

Grace hurried off. Soon they saw Grace and Ethan, their arms around each other, walking in the garden. Just before the couple passed out of sight, Ethan leaned down to kiss Grace.

Evadne watched them with tears in her eyes, thinking how lucky Grace was. The wedding was only part of it. Above all, she had the man she wanted while Evadne, sooner or later, would marry a man whom she might respect but would never truly love.

Ada, watching Evadne, waved May out of the room. Going to Evadne, she drew her to a seat beside her on the sofa.

"The time has come for you to tell me the rest of your story, if I am to help you. I saw how you looked now at Grace and Ethan. If you are so happy for them—and I know you are—why are there tears in your eyes?"

Evadne hesitated. Memories of William exploded in her head like a fireworks display. Tears poured down her cheeks, and she threw herself into Ada's arms.

"I am so sorry!" she sobbed.

"For what?" Ada patted her back comfortingly. "You have been strong long enough. It is time you had a good cry. Then perhaps you can tell me what is bothering you so."

"Is . . . is it so—so obvious?" Evadne raised her tear-stained face. "If you can see it, why—?"

"Why can't Captain Nevis?" Ada finished. She smiled. "He is a man, and not the right man, I suspect. Why you are so determined to go through with the marriage, I cannot and will not understand."

"He is a good man," Evadne repeated automatically.

"Oh, child!" Ada shook her head. "If that is so, why are you so unhappy? Why do those green eyes of yours darken like a forest in the rain?" She raised Evadne's face, staring deep into her eyes. "No, Evadne. I suspect there is another young man. Tell me about him. . . ."

And Evadne did, smiling sadly. "The first moment I saw him, I felt the earth move under my feet. I told Grace that, and she said it was bad luck. I guess she was right."

Ada chuckled. "I wouldn't say that. That was how I felt the first time I saw Thomas, and look at how happy we are! Tell me the rest, child."

"He (she could not bring herself to say William's name) . . . he had the bluest eyes—as blue as the Pacific out there," Evadne began, not noticing how Ada frowned at the use of the past tense. Now the words tumbled out of Evadne until she came to the trip to Sonoma and the drive back. "The car broke down," she managed to say.

"So, you spent the night together," Ada guessed.

"He said that . . . that he loved me and wanted to . . . to marry me, but that is no excuse, is it, Aunt Ada?" Evadne asked.

"What happened then?" Ada avoided the question for the moment. She listened, holding the girl tighter as Evadne told about arriving home to find Mr. Tyler waiting with the news about her parents' accident, about William's leaving and promising to return, and about what Paul had said.

"Did you see him again?" Ada pressed her when Evadne suddenly fell silent.

"Yes . . . I went to the St. Francis to—to talk to him, and . . . and I stayed. Then came the earthquake." Evadne finished the story quickly, saying, "Perhaps he was killed, or perhaps he came back to the house while we were gone and simply drove away. It doesn't matter now. He is gone forever."

"Poor child." Ada lowered her eyes, no longer able to look at the misery in the girl's face. "You met Captain Nevis shortly afterward?"

Evadne nodded. "You have no idea what it was like, how horrible!" She shuddered. Haltingly, she told about Matt, the sailor, and about finding the Tylers and the Dillards in Golden Gate Park. "Then Grace found Ethan and Captain Nevis. He offered me his protection when I had no one to turn to . . . nothing left."

"I am sure you were not the only woman in such straits, but that does not make it any easier," Ada observed.

"I—I made a promise." Evadne raised her head and gently released herself from Ada's embrace. "And it is not a promise that I could break with an easy conscience. I would not be here if it were not for Captain Nevis. It is not a debt that money could repay. How I wish it were!" she declared passionately.

"Nor would he take money, I am afraid," Ada said. "Well, all we can do for the moment is postpone this marriage for as long as possible in the hopes that he will change his mind —or that the islands will change him." She giggled, her natural optimism reasserting itself. "Neither is impossible, Evadne!"

"Do you think so?" Evadne turned to her. Hope made her green eyes sparkle. "He is so like William in looks that it would not be so difficult to . . . if only he were not so—so serious and uncompromising!"

"Evadne," Ada said slowly, suddenly struck by an idea, "does he know about you and . . . and this young man of yours?"

"That I am not a . . . a virgin?" Evadne shook her head. "How could I tell him that? He thinks I am pure—"

"What would he say—or do—if he found out you were not? Perhaps he would not want the marriage then." Ada shrugged. "It is only an idea, child, but it is something to consider if matters between you do not improve."

"I have thought of that too," Evadne admitted. "But though sometimes I think he would cast me aside, other times

I think he would insist on marrying me, to—to save my soul!"
She could not help but smile.

The return of Grace with Ethan put an end to the conversation. Ethan, as usual, greeted Evadne on behalf of Nevis. "He said to tell you that he'll see you at Grace's wedding. He's to be my best man."

Ada beamed. "And Thomas, of course, will give away the bride. Afterward, I thought that we would all come back here for a party, then off you two will go on your honeymoon!"

"Honeymoon, Mrs. MacMahon?" Ethan laughed. "Grace and me'll just go to our rooms. That'll do for us."

"Oh, no, it won't. You have not spoken to Thomas, young man. We have a little place in the hills where we go when we want to get away from Honolulu for a while to be alone. It is yours for as long as you want it."

Ethan glanced at Grace. "Mrs. MacMahon, we couldn't! You've done enough—more than enough—for Grace, and for me too."

"It won't do you any good to argue with me, Ethan. Haven't you learned that by now?" Ada laughed. "Don't you know I always get my way?"

The young man blushed. "I sure don't know what to say, Ma'am."

"There's nothing to say. You just have that talk with Thomas—and make sure you take good care of Grace," Ada warned.

"I'll do my best!" Ethan promised earnestly.

"Good. Get along now. We all have work to do if everything is to be ready by Sunday. Remember, you're coming to dinner on Saturday night, and make sure that best man of yours—" Ada's mouth twitched as if she were trying not to laugh "—comes with you! He's been neglecting us—all of us," she said firmly.

When Ethan had gone, the wedding gown was brought out again and May summoned.

"Is anything wrong?" Evadne asked, noticing that Ada was muttering to herself.

"I was scolding myself," Ada said. "All this fuss about the wedding dress and we still have no dress for you—the maid of honor. You and I must go shopping."

Evadne's protests that she could wear one of the dresses Ada had given her were rejected. As a result, in the morning, Ada and Evadne went into Honolulu with Mr. MacMahon, leaving Grace and May to work on the wedding gown and Grace's trousseau.

The first stop in Honolulu was to let Mr. MacMahon off at his office. Ada told him they would be back in time for him to take them to lunch. The next stop was at one of the big stores.

"It may not be much compared to San Francisco—" Ada broke off. "I shouldn't have said that, should I?"

"It's all right." Evadne smiled at her. "Somehow, here, I find it hard to believe that if I were to go back everything would not still be exactly the same as it used to be."

"Good girl," Ada said. She nodded to the store manager who had rushed up to greet her. "Now," she told him, "what I want is some silk, the best you have. Green, don't you think, child?"

Evadne stood by as Ada quickly found what she wanted, a pale green silk that shimmered in the light, and a creamy French lace to go with it. As the packages were stowed in the open carriage, Ada said to Evadne, "By the time we're finished, we'll see what kind of stuff Captain Nevis is made of. If he can resist you after what I have in mind, the man is made of stone!"

Evadne laughed. Ada's mood was infectious. "What now?" she asked. "It's too early for lunch."

"I thought we might drive around a bit and let Honolulu have a good look at you—especially the young men."

"What good will that do?" Evadne sighed, but she could not help but notice the admiring looks she received from passersby as the carriage proceeded slowly down the main street.

"Put that parasol up," Ada said, raising hers with a decisive snap. "You want to protect that pretty complexion of yours from the sun."

Evadne did as she was told. Looking around her as they rode along, she was struck by the ethnic mix of the people. White skins abounded in the main district, but there were also a number of Chinese and Japanese, as well as a few native Hawaiians. Many people, however, seemed to be a mixture of the white race and Hawaiian or Hawaiian and Chinese.

Ada was watching her, seeming to await her reaction. When Evadne made no comment, she said, "Quite a few of our leading businessmen and professional men are Chinese. The Japanese arrived more recently, as contract labor on the plantations on Oahu—this island—and on the other islands.

They are now sending their sons to the mainland to college. First it was the Haoles—the whites—who came here, then the Chinese, then the Japanese. One of these days, few Hawaiians like me will be left."

"Aunt Ada, I hope not. If all Hawaiians are like you—" Evadne began.

"Thank you, child." Ada patted her hand, at the same time nodding to two women in a passing carriage. "I think we can pick up Thomas now."

Mr. MacMahon was waiting for them. As he took his place in the carriage opposite them, he said, with a chuckle, "I am going to be the envy of every gentleman, escorting the two most beautiful ladies on the islands to lunch."

Evadne smiled at the compliment. How good she felt—dressed in fine clothes and going to a fine restaurant. A sense of excitement and anticipation filled her.

At the hotel, MacMahon was greeted with deference and they were shown to a table overlooking the harbor. No sooner were the three seated when people began stopping by the table to say hello. They looked curiously at Evadne as they awaited an introduction, and when they learned that she was from San Francisco, could not resist asking her about the earthquake. Evadne glowed under the attention, smiling with sparkling eyes, while Ada watched her proudly. Only when the waiter arrived with a tray did the visitors reluctantly take their leave.

MacMahon smiled as the waiter poured the wine. "I do not want to make you sad, Evadne, but how proud of you your parents must have been. I can well understand why your father's eyes always lit up when he mentioned you."

"Thank you." Evadne blinked back tears. She looked at Ada and her husband and said impulsively, "You are so like my parents. I mean, you are so in love with each other and with life—"

Ada blushed. "Thomas, you hear? We are not the only ones who married for love."

"No." MacMahon glanced at his wife. "There was only one subject more dear to Evadne's father than his daughter and that was his wife."

"I know." Evadne bit her lower lip and turned to gaze out at the ships lying at anchor in the roadstead. She was thinking of how she had always said that she would not marry unless she and the man she chose were as much in love as her parents.

The thought stayed with her the rest of that day and in the following days as preparations for Grace's wedding progressed. May's sister and mother were staying at the house to help with all the sewing. Her mother worked on Evadne's gown, following a sketch Ada had drawn. Ada saw no reason why the maid of honor should be as modest as the bride. The gown was cut low to display the creamy mounds of Evadne's breasts and closely fitted to take advantage of the girl's tiny waist. The lace sleeves barely covered her shoulders. Ada's black eyes glittered with excitement at the thought of Captain Nevis's reaction when he saw Evadne.

Evadne did not see how everything would be done by Saturday evening. Yet, by four o'clock that day, the finishing touches were being put on Evadne's gown and Grace's trousseau was being carefully in tissue in a small trunk to be taken on the honeymoon. Ada smiled with satisfaction. She shooed the girls off for a nap before dinner.

"Whew!" Grace flung herself down on her bed. "That woman sure can work miracles, can't she? I couldn't believe all them fine things would ever be ready."

Evadne laughed. "Ada says she always gets her way, and she does. Who could ever refuse her anything?"

"She never raises her voice neither," Grace marveled. She glanced around the room. "You know, Vad, I'm gonna miss all this—being treated like a lady 'n' all."

"You can always change your mind, Grace," Evadne said, teasing her.

"Not marry my Ethan? You must be crazy to think such a thing, Vad!" Grace popped up in bed. "All I mean is . . . well . . . it's been kinda like heaven here."

"Remember, Aunt Ada told you you'll always be welcome, that she expects you to call," Evadne reminded her.

"I know, and I will. I'm gonna miss you too. I mean, we'll still be friends, but it won't be the same. You'll be getting married next, and then we'll both be busy takin' care of our homes and our husbands." Grace sighed happily at the thought of keeping house for Ethan.

Evadne turned away, to keep Grace from seeing the tears in her eyes and spoiling her happiness. "Yes," she said quietly.

"An' having babies too." Grace yawned sleepily. "Ethan an' me want lotsa babies. How about you?"

"I haven't thought about it. I'm not even married yet." Evadne blanched at the thought of having a child by Nevis.

She could not even imagine him with his clothes off, much less touching her in the intimate places William had known and used to rouse her.

But the more she thought about it, the more the idea of going to bed with Nevis began to stir her curiosity. She looked at him with new eyes as they sat in the living room sipping sherry before dinner that evening, trying to determine if the islands had made any change in him during the past week. But he seemed as stiff and formal as ever in his heavy blue uniform, and he made it obvious that he had not forgiven Ada for her interference. He barely answered her when she spoke to him, although he was saying only enough not to be accused of outright rudeness. Ada took his behavior good-naturedly, pressing him at dinner to help himself to more of the lavish meal.

If Ada did not take offense, however, MacMahon did. As they left the dining room to go to the living room for coffee, he drew Evadne aside. "I suggest that you have a talk with Nevis," he said, keeping his voice low. "He is pushing the bounds of my hospitality a little too far."

Evadne, who had found her own temper rising, nodded. The opportunity to speak to Nevis came sooner than she thought it would. The coffee was not waiting for them in the living room, and Ada went off to find out what had happened.

Turning to Nevis, Evadne said, "Captain, it is such a pleasant evening. Why don't we go into the garden for a walk before coffee?"

"If you wish," he replied stiffly, having no choice except to follow her.

As soon as they were out of hearing of anyone in the house, Evadne stopped and turned to face him. "You have been very rude this evening, Captain," she told him bluntly. "I am not accustomed to such bad manners."

"And I am not used to forward women or to being threatened," he countered. "You are not learning any habits that will stand you in good stead, Miss Harper. It was a mistake to bring you to this house, though at the time I thought it would be best for your comfort."

"No one could have been kinder to me than Mrs. MacMahon has been," Evadne said. "And she has extended the same hospitality to Grace as she has to me. Ethan, instead of resenting it, seems grateful for all she has done."

"Ethan is not me. I do not hold with all this frivolity. Marriage is a serious business," Nevis declared.

Evadne shook her head, marveling at his stubbornness. "I quite agree, but surely you can see the wisdom of combining our wedding with business—the business you intend to do in the islands."

"Miss Harper—"

"Dear God," Evadne interrupted, "is it not about time that you began to call me by my first name? Evadne is my name, just as Samuel is yours."

A faint smile crossed his face. "In my mind, I think of you in no other way," he told her.

She stared at him in amazement. "Then why," she finally managed to say, "why can't you call me that, Samuel?"

"No one, since I was a lad, has called me Samuel," he said. His voice was rough with emotion.

"Well, you are Samuel to me from now on." She took his hand, holding it in her small, soft one. "Please, Samuel, for me . . . for my sake—our sakes if we are to live in these islands—do be pleasant to Aunt Ada."

"I will try," he promised.

"Thank you." Evadne kissed his cheek impulsively, her body brushing his like a whisper.

Overhead, the full moon sailed in the sky. The air around them was heavy with the scent of flowers. A breeze from the ocean carried with it the heady odor of sandalwood. Nevis shivered though the night was warm. His arms embraced her, holding her close to him, and his mouth sought hers. Through the heavy wool of his jacket, Evadne could feel his heart pounding. Her arms went around his neck, her body pressing against his, as her lips responded to his kisses. She could feel his manhood rising between his thighs and unconsciously her hips rotated in response.

Nevis shuddered. The arms embracing her let loose their hold and he forced himself away from her with a groan that filled Evadne with pity.

"Samuel," she whispered, feeling sorry for him and at the same time relieved that she had finally scratched his armor and released the spring of pent-up emotions inside him.

"Now you know why I wish to marry you as soon as possible . . . Evadne," he told her, his voice hoarse. "I cannot wait much longer to . . . to know you."

She smiled at his use of the biblical language. She took his hand. "It will not be much longer, Samuel. First, let us give Ethan and Grace their time in the sun. Then it will be our turn."

Nevis smiled at her. "Very well."

"Now, let us go back. And, please, Samuel—?"

"I will do my utmost for your sake to forget my feelings about that woman, though I believe she is a bad influence on you," he declared, his voice stern once more.

Evadne shook her head. It was not going to be easy to change him. Yet, here in this paradise, there was hope even for him. The islands had already started to change him as his embrace had proved. Between the islands and her, he might even become a man she could love.

Ada looked up from behind the silver coffeepot as they entered the living room. She smiled broadly at what she saw. "Captain Nevis!" she cried gaily. "How do you like your coffee? Come, you must tell us how the work on your ship is coming along."

Nevis accepted the coffee with as much of a smile as he could manage. "I—I was telling . . . Evadne," he said, after what was obviously a struggle, "that the ship will soon be back in the water, thanks to your husband."

Evadne smothered a smile at the lie. "Yes, Aunt Ada," she said demurely, knowing that Ada would understand the veiled meaning, "Samuel is most pleased with the progress."

"Good, good!" boomed Ada. "Now, let us attend to the matters at hand."

The talk turned then to Ethan and Grace's wedding, which was to be at noon the next day. Afterward, everyone was to come back to the house for a wedding luncheon, and then the MacMahon carriage would take the couple to the hideaway in the hills, picking them up a week later. When the honeymoon was mentioned, Ethan glanced uneasily at Nevis, who frowned and seemed about to protest.

Evadne realized then that it was the first time that Nevis had heard anything about the honeymoon. She laid her hand on the captain's arm. "Samuel," she whispered, "you only marry once."

He nodded and held his tongue. But when Ada sent the men off a little while later, Nevis said wryly to Evadne, "Life with you is going to be difficult. Don't expect too much of me."

"Or you of me," she replied soberly, wondering what he would say when he discovered that she was not as pure as he thought she was.

"Well," Ada said as soon as the door was shut after him, "I

don't know what you said to that man, Evadne, but you seem to have changed him for the better."

Evadne flushed. "I merely told him that he was being rude."

Ada did not miss the blush. She raised her eyebrows. "And, being a reasonable man, he immediately saw the error of his ways!" She laughed, hugging the girl. "I suspect that he is not such a man of stone as he would like us to think. Good for you, my dear. Now," she said, "to bed. Tomorrow will be a full day for all of us."

Grace climbed the stairs slowly, pausing at the top to look back. In their room, she said, "I keep thinkin', Vad, how different it's gonna be tomorrow when I leave here—from what it was when we left your house." She shuddered. "I keep thinking of them soldiers chasing us out with no chance to take anything and you with all those pretty dresses!"

"It's better not to think about that, Grace. It's over. We're here now with new lives ahead for both of us," Evadne pointed out.

"I know. Still—" Grace hesitated, looking closely at Evadne, who was beginning to undress. "Think you'll ever go back, Vad?"

Evadne looked up, totally startled by the question. "No . . . except perhaps to visit although," she added, "I'm not sure I want to go back at all. There are too many memories. I would rather remember the city and my life as it was. How about you?"

"I guess in a coupla years, if Ethan is willing, I'll be ready to go back. It's mighty pretty here—and there's you and Aunt Ada an' all—but it ain't home and never will be," Grace declared.

Evadne went to bed, thinking about what Grace had said. Going back to San Francisco had never occurred to her. She had said goodbye to the city and the past the moment the *Narragansett* had sailed through the Golden Gate out into the vast Pacific. There were too many memories that returning there would bring back—memories of her parents and Auntie and William that were better left buried in the city's ashes. This was her home now. She would make a life here with new friends to take the place of the old ones, friends like Lillie and Jack Dillard and Paul Tyler.

A shiver passed through her at the thought of Paul as she had last seen him. For Lillie's sake, she hoped that he would recover. She thought of poor Mr. Dillard, with the Tylers as well as his own family on his shoulders. Would she ever learn what happened to any of them? She sighed, closing her eyes and trying to summon sleep. One day she might meet someone from the Mainland who would know. She hoped so. In the meantime, she let the gentle breezes of the soft Hawaiian night wash over her . . . to sleep dreamlessly until she awakened at dawn.

Careful not to wake Grace, Evadne slipped out of bed. She went to the armoire in the corner where her clothes were. In the bottom, tucked at the back, was the reticule that she had carried from the house in San Francisco. Once more, she took out the jewelry, looking for the gold locket on the thin chain that was there. When she found it, she put the rest of the jewelry back. Still kneeling, she opened the locket. In one side was a picture of herself; in the other, a lock of her hair. Closing the locket, she rose to her feet and went to the dressing table where Grace's brush and hairpins were laid out. She placed the locket beside them and returned to bed.

Grace found the locket almost immediately as she sat down to brush her hair that morning before washing it. "Vad, what's this?"

"A locket of Mama's that I managed to save with a few other pieces of jewelry," Evadne told her. "It's not much of a wedding present, but I'd like you to have it . . . and I know Mama would want it too," she added.

Grace opened the locket. "Why, there's a picture of you and a lock of your hair. Oh, Vad!" She threw her arms around Evadne, crying against the girl's shoulder. "It's—it's beautiful. I ain't never had any real jewelry before."

"You can change the picture, maybe put Ethan's in it," Evadne said, touched by the girl's reaction.

"Never!" Grace protested. "I'll keep it always, just as it is, to remind me of you—the very best friend I ever had." The tears that had stopped temporarily began to fall again.

"Grace, stop crying or your eyes will be all red!" Evadne warned her. "You don't want to have red eyes on your wedding day."

Grace giggled, hiccuping a little as she swallowed her tears. "You're right. Oh, Vad! I'm sure gonna miss you!"

"I'm going to miss you too," Evadne said.

With that, Evadne sent Grace off to bathe. She had already bathed, while Grace was still sleeping, and washed her hair.

She brushed it now, trying to untangle the curls, staring at her reflection in the mirror. Happy as she was for Grace, she dreaded the day ahead. She knew that as soon as this wedding was over, the subject of her own would come up. Groaning, Evadne tried to put the thought out of her mind, as May entered the room to give the girls a hand with their dressing.

Once they were ready, May went off to fetch Ada MacMahon. Ada, wearing a pale blue dress and a bib of enormous rosy pearls, entered looking very much the mother of the bride. In her hands were two circlets of tropical flowers. Smiling broadly, she draped Grace's veil over the girl's head and shoulders, adjusting the circlet on top of it. As soon as she was satisfied with Grace's appearance, she fitted the other circlet on Evadne's head, saying, "It's an old Hawaiian custom."

Soon they were on their way, Grace nervously clutching a bouquet of flowers. "I just can't believe it," she told Evadne. "Only a month ago we were homeless with just the clothes on our backs and the whole world in flames. Now, I'm marrying my Ethan, wearing a real wedding gown and with a trunkful of more fine clothes than I ever dreamed I'd own in a lifetime. It's sure like a dream, Aunt Ada."

Ada responded with her rich laugh, but Mr. MacMahon said soberly, "It's not a dream, Grace. Both my wife and I want you to know that you can come to us if ever you need anything. I hope, however, that you will always be as happy as you are today."

"I know I will, Mr. MacMahon, now that I have my Ethan." Grace's eyes sparkled. "I ain't takin' no chances of losin' him for a third time. Soon as ever I can, I'm gonna get him to leave the sea forever," she said firmly.

"If he does," MacMahon promised, "I will do all I can to help him get started ashore."

Evadne, listening to the conversation, was struck by the contrast between Grace's hopes and her own. She had none of the other girl's certainty about the future, only a growing restlessness, a distraught feeling of unease that amounted to a premonition. No matter how hard she tried to put the feeling aside, it stayed with her.

The sight of Nevis, dressed in his best blue uniform, standing beside Ethan intensified the feeling. And suddenly she realized that regardless of any change the islands might bring about in him, she could only like and respect the man, never love him.

As a result, the ceremony, brief though it was, seemed interminable to Evadne. At last, however, Grace was in Ethan's arms. Then MacMahon, as father of the bride, claimed his kiss. Even Nevis kissed Grace awkwardly on the cheek, although his eyes were fastened on Evadne, in stern disapproval of the low-cut neckline of her gown. Meanwhile, the whole MacMahon household, plus May's mother and sister who had come to the wedding, hurried to get back to the house and set out the wedding luncheon. The others left more slowly. Grace and Ethan went in the carriage with the MacMahons, while Evadne followed with Nevis and the minister and his wife.

"Do you like my gown?" Evadne asked him coquettishly. Nevis swallowed uneasily, not wanting to risk her wrath yet unwilling to lie. "I—it—the color suits you, Evadne," he finally managed to say.

"Is that all?" she teased him. She preened a little and her bosom rose seductively.

"It is . . . well . . . a little daring for my taste, especially for a wedding," Nevis told her.

The minister, a Mainlander from Los Angeles, smiled slightly. "It is both beautiful and appropriate for this climate, Miss Harper. Is it not, my dear?" he asked his wife. Both were in their mid-forties and had lived in the islands for twenty years.

His wife, a handsome woman although rather gaunt, was wearing a tan dress with a rounded neckline, higher cut than Evadne's but still low. "Indeed it is. I wish I were young again, except I fear I never had your figure, my dear." She turned then to Nevis. "Captain, you know the early missionaries from New England insisted on wearing the same clothing here that they had worn in the cold and the snow. It was entirely unsuitable—dreadfully hot. Even worse, they tried to force it on the islanders. Thank goodness, we are not so rigid nowadays. If you had been at service earlier—and I do hope both of you will join our church—you would have noticed many of the young girls dressed like Miss Harper."

"It is quite a sight from the pulpit, Captain, I can tell you." The minister chuckled.

"You see, Samuel?" Evadne looked at him triumphantly. "The gown is not so daring after all."

"I must accede to the general opinion," he acknowledged generously, to Evadne's surprise, "but I will expect my wife to dress more modestly."

"That's right," said the minister. "You two are planning to marry. Will it be soon?"

Nevis's dark eyes held Evadne's. "Yes, sir, as soon as possible now that my mate and Miss Jones are wed. Is that not so, Evadne?"

Evadne flushed, well aware that she had brought this on herself. If she had embarrassed Nevis, he was now paying her back. She was saved from making any reply, however, by the arrival of the carriage at the MacMahon house.

The others were in the garden where a buffet had been set up. In the center of the table was a tiered wedding cake. Their work done, the household had been invited to mingle with the guests. May had lost no time singling out Nevis's first mate, Stevenson. He had been invited to both the wedding and the luncheon and was enthralled by the exotic beauty of the tiny half-Chinese, half-Hawaiian girl.

As soon as the champagne was poured, Mr. MacMahon held up his glass, signaling for silence. "I offer a toast to Grace and Ethan Morgan. May you live happily all your lives, may you have children, and may your fortunes prosper," he said.

Grace giggled happily, sipping the champagne after everyone had toasted her, wrinkling her nose at the bubbles. "It tickles, Vad," she whispered. "I ain't never had champagne before."

Evadne smiled. The premonitory uneasiness she had felt earlier had returned. She could not drink champagne without thinking about William, who had always ordered it for them. She set her glass down, shivering slightly, and went to the buffet table and helped herself to some of the marvelous food. No one seemed to notice or miss her, as holding her plate, she stood to one side watching the party, smiling now and then when someone glanced in her direction. Only Ada seemed to realize that something was amiss. When she looked at Evadne a worry line appeared between her eyes.

After the wedding cake was cut, Grace left to change from her wedding gown into a traveling dress. Evadne went with her to help. Grace was bubbling over, half with excitement and half with champagne. She changed clothes quickly. At the top of the stairs again, she hugged Evadne and insisted that she go downstairs to where other unmarried girls were gathered in the hallway. Holding her wedding bouquet high, Grace looked at Evadne before throwing it directly at her. Evadne caught it, staring at it with dull eyes. Then, Grace was running down the stairs into Ethan's arms. The two hurried to the waiting carriage amid a shower of rice.

The rest of the party gradually dispersed. Nevis signaled Stevenson to wait for him. "Just a moment, before you leave," he said to the minister and his wife. "I think we should discuss my marriage—rather, Miss Harper's and mine. Is that not right, Evadne?"

"Yes, Samuel." She looked to Ada, who was standing next to her, for support. "It will take time to prepare a trousseau—"

"And issue invitations in time for people to arrange to attend," continued Ada. "Remember, Captain Nevis, you intend to do business here."

"Granted, Mrs. MacMahon. We have discussed that before. However, as I have told Evadne and she has agreed, I would like to set a date. Evadne, what do you say?" Although his voice was soft, there was a hard note to it that brooked no more delay.

Evadne glanced down at the bridal bouquet. Unknowingly, as they talked, she had been tearing the petals from the flowers. They lay strewn at her feet. She knew if she put the wedding off too long, he would insist on marrying her that very moment, regardless of what she or Ada or Mr. MacMahon or anyone else said . . . especially after what had happened between them the night before.

"Well, Evadne, what do you say?" he repeated.

She raised her head, her eyes meeting his and her heart heavy. "A month from today. That will give me—us—time to . . . to get ready."

She expected him to insist on an earlier date. Instead, he asked Ada, "Is that agreeable with you, Mrs. MacMahon?"

"Yes." Ada put her arm around Evadne. "If it is agreeable with this child, it is agreeable with me."

"And with you, sir?" he asked the minister.

"As far as I can remember, my calendar is clear. I will check it and let you and Mrs. MacMahon know tomorrow," the minister said.

Nevis smiled. He took Evadne's face in his hands, leaning down to kiss her forehead. "A month from today then, my dear."

Evadne closed her eyes. At the touch of his lips, the premonition raised gooseflesh on her skin and the earth seemed to shake beneath her feet.

Chapter XIX

DURING THE DAYS FOLLOWING GRACE'S WEDDING, EVADNE made every excuse to be alone, claiming she was tired. At first, Ada sympathized and obliged her. After all, the desire was all too understandable, considering all that Evadne had been through, and now to lose Grace too. Pressing Evadne about her own wedding would only exacerbate those wounds. As far as Nevis was concerned, once he had wrenched the wedding date from the girl's lips, he seemed to lose interest in her, staying away from the MacMahon house as he had during the preparations for Grace's wedding.

But as time passed and Evadne showed little interest in her surroundings or in any outing that Ada suggested, the worry line appeared more and more frequently between Ada's eyes. Finally, one morning after she had had breakfast in bed as was her habit and had come downstairs to find Evadne standing on the porch circling the house staring out to sea, Ada had had enough. She suggested, "Let's drive into Honolulu and shop a bit. Thomas will be only too happy to take us to lunch."

"No, Aunt Ada, not today," Evadne replied, her eyes still on the ocean.

"Child, what is the matter? Do you miss Grace so much?" Ada asked, putting an arm around Evadne and hugging her.

"Oh no!" Evadne withdrew slightly from the embrace. "I am relieved and happy that Grace has her Ethan . . . that she is happy."

"Then what is it? I haven't seen you smile for days. I know you are not eager to marry Nevis, but—"

"Aunt Ada!" Evadne cried then, "I don't know what is the matter with me. I have had the strangest feeling—almost like a premonition—ever since the day of Grace's wedding. I simply cannot get rid of it."

"I see," Ada replied thoughtfully. "Have you ever had this feeling before?"

"Never—not like this. I feel as if my skin were crawling and then I get so cold. It's . . . it's so silly. I keep telling myself that, but it doesn't help." She shook her head helplessly. "Have you ever felt like that?"

"No." Ada shook her head.

"What should I do? I cannot go on this way," Evadne added miserably. "There is so much to do for my wedding—"

"My dear, you are a strong young woman. I am not sure that I could have stood up under the burdens you have had to bear and the decisions you have had to make. I look at you," Ada smiled, shaking her head again, "and I am glad that I was never put to the tests you have been."

"But I have so much to be grateful for, too." Evadne smiled back at her, the smile lightening her eyes for the first time in days. "Especially for you. Oh, Aunt Ada. I don't know what I would have done, if Mr. MacMahon had not insisted on bringing us here." She threw her arms around Ada, resting her head against the woman's shoulder. "You are like my own mother."

Ada was touched. "Enough, child, although if I had ever had a daughter, I would have wanted her to be like you—not that she could have had that hair of yours." She stroked Evadne's flaming hair.

"I have been so ungrateful the past few days. Well," Evadne raised her head, her eyes shining with new courage, "I cannot go on that way. Thank you for talking to me, for not thinking me silly or childish."

"Oh, you must come to me any time, not that I may always be of much help. I certainly cannot explain this strange feeling of yours, but just talking can help sometimes. And so," she declared, laughing, "can a little shopping. We must get those invitations ordered, get some fabrics—" She sighed.

"It will be a wedding the islands will long remember, if I have my say."

Evadne found herself smiling against her will. "Let's go into town as you suggested."

"And have lunch with Thomas!" Ada clapped her hands like a little girl. "He will be so pleased to see you smiling again too."

"I'll go and change." Evadne looked down at the simple sheer cotton she was wearing. "If we are meeting Mr. MacMahon, I want him to be proud of me."

"I know what would please him more than anything," Ada said slyly.

"What is that, Aunt Ada?" Evadne stopped in the doorway to look back.

"If you were to call him Uncle Thomas. I know he will never ask, but he loves you as much as I do, child." Ada smiled, her teeth sparkling in her dark face.

Evadne nodded and smiled back. "Should I ask him first?"

Ada giggled. "Just call him Uncle Thomas. I want to see his face."

When they arrived at his office, MacMahon was only too happy to escort them to lunch. In the carriage, he glanced curiously from Ada to Evadne. Ada was beaming while Evadne was positively coquettish. He did not question them, knowing too well that Ada could not keep a secret for long and laying her good mood to the revival of Evadne's spirits. He, too, was glad to see the girl acting more like herself.

At the hotel, they were led to MacMahon's usual table by the window. As soon as they were seated, he asked. "Now, ladies, what is your pleasure?"

With Ada nudging her, Evadne said, "What would you suggest . . . Uncle Thomas?"

The smile on MacMahon's face widened. His eyes wrinkled with delight. "Thank you, Evadne. You have made me the happiest man in Hawaii."

She flushed, surprised at the joy such a little thing gave her benefactor. To cover her embarrassment, she picked up the menu.

MacMahon regarded her thoughtfully. "Captain Nevis was in to see me this morning," he said. "I must give the man credit for his labors. He has somehow managed to complete the refitting of the *Narragansett* in half the time I expected it would take. Unless there is an unexpected delay, he plans to take the ship out of drydock tomorrow."

"At least, he has something to show for his neglect of this child," Ada said. "If he is so eager to marry her, would you not expect him to call on her once in a while?"

"I admit that puzzles me, for he never fails to ask about her, and the expression on his face is one of adoration when he mentions her name," MacMahon replied. "Be that as it may, I invited him to dinner on Sunday."

"Good!" Ada said. "It will give me a chance to talk to him."

MacMahon shook his head. "No, it won't, Ada. He won't be there. He intends to take the ship on a shakedown cruise to the Big Island."

"You can't mean that he intends to leave without seeing Evadne?" Ada was shocked at such callous behavior.

"No, not that." Her husband gave a helpless shrug. "He asked me to ask you whether it would be convenient for him to call tomorrow evening for a short time. By then the ship will be in the water."

"He will come to dinner, naturally," Ada insisted.

"I suggested that, but he said that he could not promise what time he would be free. Still, Evadne," he turned to her, "he is most anxious to see you."

Evadne smiled. "Thank you for the message, Uncle Thomas."

"What a strange man he is," Ada murmured. "If he has so little time for the poor child before they are married, when he should be the ardent suitor, what will her life with him afterward be like?"

Evadne recalled how he had held her that night in the garden, the way his manhood had sprung to life against her thigh. "I am sure he will be a most devoted husband," she said.

Ada was still grumbling and shaking her head the next evening when Nevis called just as they were finishing dinner.

"I apologize for arriving at this hour," he told Evadne, when they were alone, "but it took longer to tow the ship to a dock and moor her than I expected."

"When do you plan to sail?" Evadne asked, expecting him to say in a few days, after Ethan and Grace returned from their honeymoon.

"With the morning tide. The crew is due aboard tonight," he said.

Evadne stared at him in surprise. "As soon as that?"

"I realize that I have neglected you," Nevis apologized.

"Please be patient, Evadne. Once this short voyage is over, you can rest assured that you will have my complete attention."

"But Ethan and Grace will not be back from their honeymoon until the day after tomorrow. Surely, you are not relieving Ethan as second mate." Evadne turned worried eyes on him, her first thought for Grace and what would happen to her. She knew that Ethan was counting on staying with Nevis, for a while anyway.

"There is no cause for alarm. For such a short voyage, my first mate Stevenson is enough, since we will be carrying only a crew—no cargo or passengers. My original thought was to wait," Nevis added, "but such a delay would prevent my giving you my attention even longer. Besides, it will give Ethan and Grace time to fix up their quarters."

"Very well, Samuel. I am sure you are right." Evadne sighed. "When do you expect to return?"

"In a week—ten days at the most." He rose to his feet. "Now, I must leave. Although Stevenson is aboard, my presence is required too."

"I will see you out." Evadne stood up, going with him to the door.

As they stood on the porch, Nevis hesitated, glancing at the carriage that was waiting for him. "Evadne, my dear," he began, "I hope you understand my reasons for not having called sooner, or more often. If the *Narragansett* is to provide our livelihood, it was imperative that she come first."

"Yes, I—I understand," she murmured.

"It is not that I have not thought of you. On the contrary, you have been in my thoughts constantly. It is because of you that I have pressed forward with such speed on the refitting, so that we can be together." He kissed her forehead, holding himself stiffly to avoid any additional contact with her.

Evadne ached for him to embrace her, to show her with his body the love he expressed so poorly in words. "Samuel," she whispered, "will you not hold me close? Will you not tell me," she took a deep breath, "that you love me?"

"Have I not proved my love for you time and time again?" he asked uncomfortably, but he did take her into his arms.

Evadne's mouth eagerly sought his. She pressed against him. Nevis seemed to shudder and pulled back.

"The driver is waiting," he muttered, releasing her.

Evadne moved away from him, quivering inside with the passion that longed to escape. "Go then, Samuel," she told him in a shaking voice. "I would not keep you from your duties."

"Evadne. . . ." He had not missed the sarcasm in her voice. "It is all for you. From the first time I saw you—"

Leaning against a pillar, Evadne rested her forehead on the cool wood, trying to regain her composure. She felt him come up behind her and caught her breath, thinking he was going to take her in his arms. Instead, he patted her shoulder awkwardly. Then his feet crunched on the gravel of the drive. There was the crack of a whip before the carriage moved off.

Evadne closed her eyes, waiting to make sure the carriage was gone before returning to the house. Ada looked at her as she came in and shook her head.

"What a strange man," Ada said.

"Nevertheless, he will do well here," MacMahon said. "Everyone who has had any dealings with him has nothing but good to say of him. You must be patient with him a while longer, Evadne. He is an ambitious man," he added kindly, in an attempt to reassure the girl.

She nodded, the premonition she had managed to ignore for a day returning. Vaguely, she wondered if it had anything to do with Nevis, a warning of danger to him and his ship that might lie ahead on the voyage to the Big Island of Hawaii itself.

The next day, although the morning dawned bright and clear, by noon black clouds had boiled across the Pali, and the air was still and heavy. Ada was as restless as Evadne, going periodically to the windows to look out.

"If it would only rain and clear the air." Ada sighed. "I hate days like these."

"Do they happen often?" Evadne asked, using a handkerchief to wipe her face. As thin as the pale green dress was that she was wearing, she was uncomfortably hot.

"Rarely at this time of year, more often in October." Ada mopped her face too.

"I wonder if Samuel was able to sail," Evadne said. "There is not a breath of air stirring."

Ada shrugged. "If he sailed early enough, he may have caught the morning breezes. Otherwise," she gave a short laugh, "he is probably pacing the deck—waiting. It would never occur to that man to take advantage of the situation and visit you, I suppose. What do you think?"

Evadne smiled sadly. "No," she said, "I doubt he would."

No sooner had she spoken than lightning flashed across the sky, followed almost immediately by a crack of thunder as a sheet of rain advanced in front of a gust of wind. The curtains at the French windows blew almost straight into the room. Ada hurried to the windows. As she did, she paused, peering into the rain.

"Perhaps I misjudged your captain. There is a rented carriage turning into the drive," she called.

Evadne went to a French window that still stood open. The wind had dropped after the first violent gust and the porch protected the interior of the house from the steady rain. The carriage had drawn up before the front door and a man was getting out.

"Well, well," Ada marveled. "It is your captain after all."

Evadne stared at the man. The dark suit he was wearing did look like a uniform, but when he raised his head to shake back his rain-wet hair in an inimitable, expressive gesture, her heart stopped and ground moved beneath her feet, and fire burned in her loins.

"William! It's William!" Evadne cried, running out on the porch.

Ada stared after her in amazement, not knowing who William was. Only when she saw Evadne throw herself into the man's arms did she realize that here was the man Evadne had told her about, the lover whose name she could not bring herself to say.

"Oh, William, William!" Evadne cried, her tears mingling with the rain on her cheeks. His arms circled her, holding her close, and his eager mouth kissed her so passionately that he bit her lip.

The taste of blood reminded them of where they were—and of the rain. "Oh, my love, you're soaking wet!" William said, drawing her under the protection of the porch roof, his arms still around her as if he would never let her go.

He kissed her hungrily again, unable to release her any more than she wanted to let him go. Her arms had circled his neck, and her body clung to his. She had forgotten Ada, forgotten everything in her desire for William. It was William who first became aware of Ada, who had come out on the porch and was watching them, a broad smile on her dark face.

"We have company, my love," William whispered, still holding Evadne.

Evadne laughed then, twisting around in his arms to see

Ada. "It's Aunt Ada. Come, William," she let him go, although she seized his hand, gripping it as if she expected him to disappear again. "You must meet her."

As the two walked toward Ada, the clouds broke and the rain stopped. Sunlight, like an omen, sparkled on the raindrops on the flowers. It struck the girl's red hair, setting it afire.

"Come in, come in," Ada invited, heedless of the water dripping off the two, "and tell me who this gentleman is, child."

"William Hopkins, Ma'am," William said, bowing slightly and raising Ada's hand to his lips. "You can only be Mrs. MacMahon."

"How would you know that?" Ada studied him, marveling at the resemblance to Nevis, although this man was not as broad through the shoulders and chest. His face, too, was not as heavy, and he had eyes of a magnificent blue that immediately won Ada's admiration.

Evadne had questions too. "What are you doing here? How did you find me? I thought you were—were—" The words tumbled out as her surprise gave way to curiosity.

"I don't know where to begin, my love." William's eyes focused on her face, feasting on her so openly she had to drop her gaze.

"Oh, William!" Tears of relief and shock suddenly ran down her cheeks. "I thought I had lost you forever. You never came back . . . your car was gone—" A shudder at the agony she had endured shook her.

Ada immediately stepped forward to take Evadne in her arms and draw her to a sofa. She sat down, holding the girl protectively. "Why are you here, Mr. Hopkins?" she asked, her voice wary.

"Not to harm Evadne." He brushed his wet hair back from his forehead. "I have spoken to your husband, Mrs. MacMahon. He told me that Evadne is to be married in a few weeks' time. Perhaps I should have left then but—" his blue eyes flashed and his jaw tightened "—I had to hear from Evadne that she is happy." He smiled grimly. "Whether she can still believe me or not—whether you can—I love her."

Evadne straightened, raising her head proudly. Clasping her hands on her lap, she looked at William steadily, green eyes darkened by the emotions tormenting her. Her desire for William, her love for him, fought with her gratitude to Nevis,

to whom she owed a debt she could repay in only one way.
"Do you really, William?"

In answer, William went to her, standing over her and
pulling her head against his body to stroke her hair. Finally,
he raised her face with his hands, holding it so that she had to
look into his eyes. "I love you, my darling, my beautiful
Evadne. All that has kept me going is the memory of you, of
those precious hours we—" he glanced at Ada "—when I
held you in my arms. If I did not love you," he added softly,
"would I have come here, after I had learned you are to
marry another man, to hear from your own lips that you no
longer love me?"

"True," Ada agreed, studying him.

"I did not leave you willingly, my love, you know that."
William sank down in a nearby chair, as if suddenly very
tired.

"I know. That soldier had a gun, a bayonet at your back—"

"The Army," William said grimly, "was not particularly
sympathetic to my pleas that I had two helpless young women
to protect, no matter how and to whom I protested. I suppose
I cannot blame them. They had quite a job to do. I don't
know how many times I drove between Portsmouth Square
and Fort Mason and the Presidio before the car ran out of
gasoline and they let me go. By then, they were evacuating
the Hall of Justice and moving the safety committee headquarters to the Fairmont. I made the mistake," he smiled
sadly, "of thinking that if they were moving the headquarters
there, Nob Hill was safe and so were you."

"If they didn't need you any more . . . ?" Evadne shook
her head in confusion.

"The fire was spreading rapidly. I tried to get south and
then north in the direction of the fire line. If fires did not bar
my way, the soldiers did. I had no choice except to make my
way back to Portsmouth Square. It was dark by then, and the
soldiers were enforcing the curfew to the letter. It was
impossible to leave without the strong certainty of being shot
as a looter. The smoke was so dense that no one could see
what was happening. By the time I managed to get near Nob
Hill, it was in flames."

"What did you do?" Evadne whispered.

"The soldiers suggested I go to Golden Gate Park, but I
couldn't get there from where I was because of the blasting.
The best solution, or so I thought," he grimaced, "was to go

to Telegraph Hill. Here I hoped to find someone with a boat who would take me to the Presidio and then I could make my way to the park from there. By the time I reached Telegraph Hill, the fires were spreading in that direction." William shook his head. "Everyone was too busy trying to save their homes to listen to me. There was a cistern that had some water, and the people were bringing out all the homemade wine from their houses. I swear we put the fires out with wine. Even though we were forced back block by block, we did save some of the hill." He stopped.

Ada glanced from one to the other of them. William was pale; Evadne, flushed, though the girl's hands were clasped so tightly that the knuckles were white. "Please go on, Mr. Hopkins," Ada urged.

"I honestly don't know quite what happened next, Mrs. MacMahon. I remember going into a burning house an old lady refused to leave and picking her up. I was told later that, just as I was leaving the house, a beam fell on me. Some men managed to drag me out along with the old woman." He rubbed his forehead. "I have no idea when that was, not even what day. The next thing I remember is awaking in bed in someone's house. It was Sunday and it was raining. The people wouldn't let me leave without my eating something."

"Sunday . . . we left on Sunday," Evadne murmured.

"I know, my love. I finally reached Golden Gate Park and, well, you know how crowded it was. But when I described you," he smiled, "a lot of people remembered seeing a tall, red-haired girl in a green suit."

Ada gave a hoot of laughter. "I'm sorry. I know it's not funny, but you do stand out, child, luckily as it turns out."

William smiled briefly and went on. "Finally, I happened on the Tylers and the Dillards. Mr. Dillard said he had seen you—"

"How were they?" Evadne asked eagerly.

William looked at her thoughtfully. "If you saw them . . . ?"

"I know," she sighed. "I only hoped that Mr. Tyler and Paul may have recovered a little, that's all. Mr. Dillard . . . ?"

"He was splendid. He had organized the people around them into a kind of camp, assigning chores to everyone," William told her. "He told me he thought you and Grace were near a pond. It was Tuesday when I found a little old lady sleeping by a pond under your sealskin coat." He grinned. "She and her brother told me about you, Grace and Ethan—and a Captain Nevis. The rest was easy, so to speak. Down at the Bay, I asked about Nevis and learned his ship was the *Narragansett*, bound for Hawaii. The next step was to find another ship bound here. I finally did." He laughed aloud now.

"Mrs. MacMahon, you would have had to have been there to understand." He turned to Evadne. "I still had my letter of credit, but it was worthless, with Tyler's bank burned to the ground. No one had any money. It was all barter. I even tried to ship out as a seaman, but there were too many sailors with experience looking for berths, regardless of where the ships were sailing. Eventually, however, I located an Australian ship that was sailing for Honolulu. Fortunately, the captain recognized my name and was willing to take my word until we reached here. We anchored in the roadstead last night. First thing this morning the captain escorted me ashore to the bank."

William laughed aloud again. "Considering what I was wearing then—a pair of seaman's trousers and a striped jersey—it seemed best I get a suit. I did not want to get thrown out of Honolulu before I had an opportunity to ask about you." He shook his head in admiration. "I must say, my love, for the few weeks you have been here, you have certainly made an impression."

Evadne blushed, and Ada laughed again. She said, "You went to the harbor to ask after the *Narragansett?*"

"It wasn't necessary, Mrs. MacMahon. After I was properly dressed, I asked about Evadne—it seemed second nature by then to ask everyone I saw. It seems that you are one of the store's best customers, and the manager told me to talk to your husband. I did, and here I am, in the first carriage I could find for hire."

"Oh, William!" Evadne went to him, kneeling on the floor beside him and resting her head in his lap.

"You are not going to marry this man, are you, my love?" William asked.

Evadne closed her eyes. "Yes, William. I must. I have given my word. It is, in fact, only luck that I am not already married."

"I will not let you, Vad. If I have to stand up in church when the minister asks if anyone knows any reason why you should not be wed—"

"You cannot—you would not—do that!" Evadne looked at him in horror.

"Only if you force me to . . . or," he looked into her eyes, "do you really love this man? If so, if you tell me you do, I will say goodbye and leave now."

Evadne turned her head away, unable to meet his gaze. "Aunt Ada, tell William. . . ."

"Only you know what is in your heart, child, just as only I know what is in mine." She chuckled, her eyes on the pair of them. "I must say, you are a very impetuous young man. So, from the depths of my experience," she chuckled again, "I have a suggestion to make."

"Yes?" William's face was grim.

"Now, don't look at me so threateningly," Ada said, "or I will not continue."

"I apologize. After all you have done for Evadne, taking her into your home, I have no right to be angry with you." He stroked the girl's hair lovingly.

Ada nodded approvingly at him. "I like you, William—I'm sorry, I cannot think of you as Mr. Hopkins. I hope you don't mind? What I have to suggest is this: that you stay a few days with us. Your arrival, without any notice, has been a shock to Evadne, as you must know."

"Yes, of course. How could she know I was alive, much less looking for her?" His blue eyes twinkled in a way that endeared him to Ada. "I accept your invitation."

"I will have a room prepared for you." Ada stood up before Evadne could agree or protest. "Off to your room with you, child. You are soaking wet. I must be getting old. In all the excitement—" She shook her head. "You, William, go to town in the carriage waiting for you to get your things. You may come back with my husband. How does that sound?"

Both agreed to Ada's proposal, although Evadne went reluctantly to the door with William. "You *will* come back, won't you?"

"I warn you, Evadne, now that I have found you again, I will never leave you." He kissed her gently. "I will be back before you have had time to miss me, my love."

Evadne watched him go, waving until the carriage was out of sight. "Aunt Ada, he will be back with Uncle Thomas, won't he?" she asked anxiously.

Ada smiled. "If I am any judge of men at all, he most certainly will."

Chapter XX

WILLIAM WAS AS GOOD AS HIS WORD. HE RETURNED, CARRYING A valise, with Thomas MacMahon, in time for dinner. He had already recounted his adventures to MacMahon. Now he was interested in Evadne. Over dinner and during the rest of the evening, he listened to what she had to say. Together, they pieced a collective and broader view of the destruction in San Francisco, which was greater than anyone there had guessed. Ada finally had to chase everyone to bed.

William's bedroom was in the opposite wing from Evadne's. At the head of the stairs, with Thomas and Ada watching, he took Evadne's face gently in his hands to kiss her goodnight.

"How beautiful you are, my love," he whispered, brushing her lips with his.

"Goodnight, William." She smiled at him, touching his cheek lightly. "I'll see you in the morning," she added quickly, resisting the temptation to put her arms around him. Her body was afire with the nearness of him, and she had to break away before she lost control of herself.

In her room, Evadne undressed slowly. Her mind was reeling with the events of the day. The premonition that had seized her on the morning of Grace's wedding was gone, fulfilled by William's return, but her mind was no easier. In fact, her world, which had begun turning upside down with the news of her parents' death was now revolving wildly again. In these past days, she had accepted the inevitability of the consequences of her promise to Nevis—a promise made of her own free will. She knew what it had cost him to compromise his principles and take her and Grace aboard his ship. It was because of Grace, too, that she felt she must keep her word. But now, with William back, with her body still hungry for his touch and her mouth burning from his kiss, she began to waver again. Could she go through with it now? Must she . . . ?

She sighed, running her hands over her slender body, studying herself in the mirror. With what tender passion had William caressed her firm breasts and the smooth skin inside her thighs, had touched her most intimate parts, spreading them apart to receive him . . . and how eagerly had she received the throbbing strength of his manhood. Evadne shivered and reached for her nightgown, pulling it on hastily and concealing her body. She slipped into the narrow bed, closing her eyes against the moonlight bright on the carpet— the same moonlight that was shining on Nevis's ship and on William's room too.

There was no sense worrying, she decided. Each time it seemed that her life was on a steady course, it veered in a new direction. She would have to wait and see what the morrow brought. With that thought in mind, she fell into a deep sleep, exhausted by all that had happened that day.

Evadne was awakened by May bringing a tray with her breakfast. The maid's almond eyes were alight with curiosity. She cast sidelong glances at Evadne as she set the tray down and poured the coffee. Evadne, who had never had breakfast in bed before coming to Honolulu, had fallen into the habit because of Ada. Although Mr. MacMahon had his breakfast served in the dining room, it had seemed simpler to Evadne to have a tray brought to her, as Ada did. She smiled at May, well understanding the reason for her scrutiny. All the servants, in fact, must be curious about the identity of the new guest in the house. Where Grace would have asked questions, however, May said nothing.

The comparison with Grace reminded Evadne that the newlyweds were due back that day. She almost groaned, thinking about what Grace would say when she saw William. All of Grace's original dislike of William had come back after they met Captain Nevis. She had never stopped comparing his goodness with William's desertion of them. Nothing Evadne said could persuade her that he might not have had any choice.

As soon as she had eaten, Evadne began to dress. For the first time, since the earthquake, she studied her wardrobe, trying to decide what to wear. Finally, she chose the yellow dress that she had worn for lunch at the hotel. May helped her into it, surprised at the choice. Usually Evadne preferred a more simple frock. This morning, too, Evadne fussed with her hair, holding it up and then letting it hang down her back. May waited patiently, more curious than ever, never having seen Evadne take so long over her toilette. At last, Evadne sighed. "Just tie it back, I think, May, with a yellow ribbon to match the dress."

"Yes, Ma'am." May picked up the brush, stroking Evadne's hair vigorously, fascinated as always by the rich color and the curls, so different from her own straight black hair.

Evadne smiled at her in the mirror. The girl who never seemed to tire of the brushing, seemed prepared to continue it all day. "Enough!" Evadne cried at last.

May giggled. She picked up the ribbon, tying Evadne's hair back with a flourish.

After taking a last look at herself in the mirror, Evadne went downstairs to the large corner room that was her favorite as well as Ada's. The windows were thrown open to let in the fresh air. Never had the flowers seemed so fragrant as they did that morning, Evadne thought, seeing William standing by one of the windows, smoking a cigar.

"Good morning, William," she called, her step light and her body swaying at the sight of him.

"Good morning, my love." He put the cigar in an ashtray, holding his arms out to her. His smile was eager and his blue eyes bright. "I thought you were never going to get up."

He had time only for a quick embrace before Ada walked into the room. "Children!" she cried. "Isn't it a glorious day after that rain yesterday?"

The couple moved apart. Evadne noticed the worry line present between Ada's eyes despite her laughter and broad smile. Guiltily, Evadne realized that she was the cause of that worry, that Ada was not sure if she had done the right thing, inviting William to stay and possibly leading Evadne into a temptation that might complicate her life even more.

Before anyone had a chance to say anything else, a carriage turned into the drive. Evadne looked out the window to see Grace and Ethan. "It's the two lovers, Aunt Ada," she said.

"So early?" Ada remarked, although it was already eleven and the carriage had left soon after daybreak to go to the house in the hills and fetch the couple.

Ethan and Grace burst into the room. Their faces were shining, and Grace was grinning happily. "Aunt Ada—" She stopped, seeing William. Her face darkened, anger and confusion spreading over her features. She grasped at the first thing that came to mind: "Where is Captain Nevis?" she demanded.

The unexpected question made Evadne catch her breath, leaving her speechless, and suddenly she was furious with Grace.

William ignored the rudeness. "Hello, Grace," he said cordially. "May I offer you my best wishes . . . and you, Morgan, my congratulations? Evadne has told me about your marriage."

"Thank you, sir." Ethan, though he had met William only briefly at the ferry that one time, still recognized him, but he was bewildered by Grace's attitude.

"Thank you," Grace said primly, her face grim. "Where's the captain?" she asked again. "Vad, it ain't right—"

"Samuel left yesterday on a cruise to the Big Island. He said to tell you, Ethan," Evadne turned to him, her eyes flashing and her temper rising at Grace's behavior, "that you are still his second mate but that he was eager to try out the ship."

"I know he sure was." Ethan was not at all disturbed. Instead, he seemed happy at being left behind. "That'll give me and Grace time to settle in, won't it, sweetheart?"

"It seems mighty funny," Grace sniffed, "no sooner'n the cap'n goes off than *he* shows his face again." It was obvious who he was.

"Come outside, Grace. I want to talk to you!" Evadne, in her anger, was using her most superior tone—the tone of a mistress to a servant that brooked no refusal—and the way Evadne walked toward the windows and out onto the garden left Grace no choice but to follow.

As soon as they were alone, Grace said, "Vad, what's gotten into you? You ain't talked to me like that since—I mean—ain't we friends no more?"

"That is up to you," Evadne told her haughtily.

"Well, you gotta admit it was an awful shock to see *him* in there," Grace insisted stubbornly, "makin' himself at home. What's Cap'n Nevis gonna say?"

"It is not his affair—not at all," Evadne said. "William was invited to stay by Aunt Ada. He is a guest here."

Grace shook her head, disapprovingly. "It's no good, you and that furriner staying in the same house. You made a promise—"

"No one knows that better than I do!" Evadne snapped.

"Then, what are you gonna do? Oh, Vad, you're the only real friend I ever had. I just gotta speak my mind. That man in there's trouble. He has been from the first time you met him. I ain't forgot what you said about the earth shaking; and just look what happened!" Grace shivered superstitiously.

"Oh, Grace, for heaven's sake, don't be so silly. It was just a . . . a figure of speech." Evadne's voice rose in exasperation.

"You send him on his way," Grace warned, "or somethin' else terrible is gonna happen."

"That's enough of that," Evadne said sharply. "I suggest that you remember your manners—for Aunt Ada's sake, if not mine." She started back toward the house, ignoring Grace's plea to wait.

Grace caught up with her at the steps to the porch. "All right, Vad, I'll be polite. We're still friends, ain't we?"

Evadne looked at her helplessly. "I want to be friends—we've been through so much. Oh, Grace," she took the girl in her arms, "let's not talk about it any more. You must tell me about the house in the hills."

"Vad, it was so lovely." Grace linked her arm through Evadne's. "There's a waterfall nearby an' all sorts of strange flowers an' trees. It was like—like the Garden of Eden," she exclaimed. "Just my Ethan an' me in paradise."

Evadne laughed, her good humor recovered, to the relief of Ada who was babbling away, trying to put the men at their ease. "A Garden of Eden, eh, Grace?" she said slyly. "With or without the fig leaves?"

"Aunt Ada!" Grace blushed furiously. So did Ethan.

Shortly afterward, the couple left. Evadné turned to William. "I'm sorry about Grace. You know how she feels—"

"About 'furriners'? I do, indeed!" William smiled ruefully.

"It took her a while to accept me," Ada told him. "I guess that puts us in the same category."

"Well, I don't propose to let Grace spoil such a beautiful

day," he said. He glanced at Evadne. "I say, Mrs. MacMahon, when the carriage gets back, would you mind if Evadne and I went for a drive?"

"Not at all. In fact, I think it's a fine idea." Ada beamed enthusiastically. "It will give the two of you a chance to talk. But you don't have to wait," she said, "you can take the other carriage."

"Would you like to go for a ride?" William asked softly.

Evadne hesitated only a moment. Sooner or later, she would have to talk to William and try to explain things. It would be better to do it now, before Samuel Nevis returned. "Very well."

"Good, good!" Ada said. "Why not drive past Diamond Head, toward Koko Head? It's a lovely drive. I'll have a lunch packed for you."

They left soon afterward in the small open carriage with William taking the reigns of a spirited bay. Palms arched in places over the road they followed, the fronds waving in the light breeze from the ocean. Alongside the road was a profusion of tropical growth, of ferns and exotic flowers, a dense and seemingly impenetrable jungle. A little past Diamond Head the road dipped toward a beach, the sand golden in the sun.

Evadne had given up trying to think. The day was much too lovely and the scenes were new to her. With William beside her, she forgot her argument with Grace, the promise she must keep, and simply enjoyed the sight of the beach and the sparkling blue Pacific. Her spirits rose.

William, too, was silent until they reached a trail, wide enough for the carriage, that led down to the beach. "What do you say that we stop here? There's shade for the horse—for us, too, if we want it, and we can walk along the beach."

"It sounds perfect," Evadne said.

He smiled at her and urged the horse down the narrow trail, reining it in at a shady spot out of sight of the road. He dismounted, looping the reins over a fallen tree, before going to where Evadne sat in the carriage. He held up his arms and swept her into them. Still holding her, he kissed her lightly before setting her down on her feet on the sand.

The soft sand sifted into her shoes. Evadne leaned against the carriage to take off a shoe and shake it out.

William's lips twitched. "Have you ever walked barefoot in the sand, my love?" When she shook her head, he said, "Why don't you take those slippers and your stockings off? You'll be much more comfortable."

"I don't know. . . ." She hesitated, the idea seemed daring.

"Well, I do!" William was quickly barefoot and wriggling his toes in the sand in invitation.

Evadne laughed. "Looking at you, it does seem sensible."

Soon, both were barefoot and walking hand in hand along the beach. On impulse, Evadne untied her ribbon and let her hair blow in the wind. She felt freer than she had ever felt before in her life. Dropping William's hand, she ran toward the ocean, letting the waves wash over her feet as she held her skirt high to protect it.

At a spot where the surf was calmer, William spread a blanket. "Lunch time?"

"I'm starving." Evadne looked around the idyllic spot—at the tropical foliage, the sand, the ocean. "It is beautiful, isn't it?"

William smiled. His blue eyes were filled with longing. "Evadne, my love. . . ."

Her heart was pounding and her breasts heaved. "Do you remember the picnic . . . ?"

"In the valley? I haven't forgotten."

"Nor have I." Evadne looked away from him, toward the ocean, the memory of their love-making on the bed of hay sending her blood pounding. A different hunger filled her now. If only they were not out in the open, sitting on the beach under a cloudless sky. She sighed.

"You're perspiring." William touched her cheek. "A swim would cool you off."

"A swim? I don't have anything to wear. Besides, I don't know how." She looked at him, startled by the suggestion.

"I will teach you." He began to undo the buttons at the back of her dress.

A protest died on her lips at his touch. She said weakly, "People will see us."

"Not here, my love. Look around you. We're well out of sight of the road, and I don't see anyone else around, do you? You'll have to get up to take off that dress."

Seeing him start to unbutton his shirt, Evadne sprang to her feet, her dress falling to the sand. His upper body was bare, the brown hair curly on his deep chest. His eyes were on her as he unfastened his trousers. She did not look away from him as she drew her chemise off over her head and dropped her petticoat and underclothing. They stood facing one another, their eyes drinking in each other's nakedness. Cautiously, Evadne reached out to touch his manhood, small and soft in the thatch of hair between his thighs. At her touch, strength surged through it.

William grinned, drawing her close to him. Slowly, they sank down on the sand. He lay half on top of her to kiss her eyes and her mouth as her arms circled his neck and her lips responded urgently. Their tongues met, and desire consumed her. Her hips moved, vibrating against his body. William lowered his head to kiss her breasts and rosy nipples while one hand caressed the inside of her thighs, moving higher and higher until it reached the red muff. She moaned softly, throbbing with pleasure and excitement at his kisses and the touch of his hand, her own hand dropping to slide between their bodies and seek out his manhood. It was strong and large now, surging with new power as she stroked it.

"My love." William raised his head, looking at her, at her half-closed eyes and slightly parted lips.

"My love," she answered, flushed with passion, waiting for him to enter her.

He moved slightly. For a moment, she thought he was going to leave her like that. Fury fueled her passion, and she reached out for him. Then his lips were kissing her thighs, his tongue fondling the softness of her until her body arched in ecstasy. It was the moment he was waiting for. His hands slipped under her hips, and he rose up to drive his manhood deep inside her, anticipating her cry of pleasure and the union of their bodies in glorious embrace.

Her body and her being were a part of William, responding passionately to every stroke of his manhood, filling her with the wet warmth of the life of her, exciting and arousing him. She had forgotten where she was—the bright sun in the cloudless sky, the gritty softness of the sand beneath her. All that mattered was William, the joining of their bodies as one, as he moved faster and faster, his breath hot on her cheek until his life exploded inside of her. She held him close, savoring the moment. Only when his manhood fell limply from her did he move slightly, separating them although he still held her, to look into her face.

"William, William," she murmured, closing her eyes against the intensity of his gaze. She drew his head toward her, to press her cheek to his. Hot tears burned her eyelids.

"Now, tell me," he whispered, "that you do not love me, that you intend to marry another man, my love."

"I love you, William." She sighed, avoiding the second question.

Apparently satisfied with her answer, he stood, stretching his body and gazing down at her nakedness. Evadne rose to stand beside him, raising her arms as if reaching for the sun, her breasts still swollen with passion.

"You witch. You will have me ready to take you again if you are not careful. Would you like that?" he asked, picking her up in his arms.

"Yes . . . yes, I think I would," she replied seriously. As he started to carry her toward the water, she cried out, "Where are you taking me?"

"To cool you off before you wear me out with your passion." He grinned.

"I told you, I can't swim." She clutched his neck in alarm.

"I can. Don't worry. Relax, my love, or you will drown the both of us," he said, going into the ocean.

With the waves washing over them, Evadne did relax, giving herself up to the sea's salty freshness. New life seemed to flow through her. The water was cool, but it did not cool the heat of her body and her longing. If William had not started back to shore, she could have floated there forever in the water with his arms around her.

He carried her back to the beach, setting her on her feet. They walked slowly, hand in hand, back to the blanket, letting the sun and the breeze dry them off. Still naked, they ate the lunch that Ada had had packed for them, licking their fingers and forgetting about the juices that dripped from the chicken and the leaf-wrapped chopped meat and fresh pineapple chunks. Finally, they sat back, satisfied, and William took her in his arms again. There was no need to talk. Everything had been said with their bodies. Evadne rested her head on his shoulder, closing her eyes and starting to doze off.

"How about another swim?" William asked. "Then you must put your clothes on." He stroked her gently. "I don't want that beautiful, loving body of yours burned by the sun—at least, not the first day."

Once again, he picked her up and carried her into the water. This time she was entirely relaxed, giving herself over to the enjoyment of the ocean.

After the sun had dried them off again, they got back into

their clothes. Evadne watched him dress as she put on her undergarments and dropped her gown over her head, waiting for him to button her dress up the back. When he did, he paused to stroke her hair.

"It will take a while for your hair to dry," he remarked.

For the first time, embarrassment replaced the flush of happiness in her face. She began to wonder what Ada would think if she returned with her hair still wet. "Can't we drive a little farther before we go back? My hair will dry quickly in the air."

"Very well, although I suspect that Ada had a swim in mind when she suggested this route." William grinned. "What do you think?"

"Perhaps." Evadne thought about it as she repacked the basket for William to carry to the carriage, where the horse was waiting patiently for them.

With Evadne beside him, William led the horse to the road, afraid that, in turning, the carriage might sink too deep into the sand. At the road, he helped Evadne into the carriage. Only later, when they were returning to the MacMahons, did William speak again. "Ada's quite a woman."

"I know." Evadne giggled. "You should have seen Grace and me when we arrived in Honolulu. The only clothes we had came out of some boxes of clothing from New England that Sam—Captain Nevis—was bringing for the missionaries. They were black serge, very scratchy and heavy. Before we knew it, Ada had clothes fit for a princess for both of us."

"I'm not surprised," he smiled, "but I had something else in mind. Don't you wonder why she invited me to stay?"

Evadne flushed. "William, I—I told her about you, not your name, but when I saw you and ran into your arms, she guessed."

William laughed aloud. "I think I like Ada more and more. No one else would have sent us off alone like this, knowing that."

The comment made Evadne smile, but it also worried her. She wondered what Ada's intentions were.

When the carriage rolled into the drive, Ada greeted them with her normal exuberance. If she noticed that Evadne's hair was snarled and slightly damp, she did not mention it.

"Well, children," she beamed, "I can see by your faces that you had a good time. You should have used your parasol, Evadne." She clucked disapprovingly. "You will ruin that lovely complexion of yours in this sun if you do not."

"I will soon have her looking as healthy as you, Mrs. MacMahon," William said. "It would flatter her, I think."

Ada laughed and then said pointedly, "I think it's what her future husband would think that matters."

Evadne looked at the two of them and suddenly tossed her head stubbornly. "I think," she declared, "that he has little say about it. I shall do what I—what I want."

The worry line appeared between Ada's eyes. "I hope so, child," she said softly.

Evadne flushed. Despite her brave words, she knew she was not free to do what she wanted—which, at that moment, was to run away with William. That would do no good, however. Even if Nevis did not come after her, she could not do that to him. She must pay back the debt she owed him even at the cost of her own happiness. Yet, as she looked at William, she knew she could not easily say goodbye. . . .

Ada patted her shoulder. "It will soon be time for dinner. Why don't you go and change before Thomas arrives?"

Chapter XXI

DURING THE NEXT FEW DAYS, EVADNE TRIED NOT TO THINK about the decision that was rapidly approaching. She gave herself up to living each day for itself, but she refused to try on the wedding dress though it was ready for the first fitting. Ada did not press her, but the worry line between her eyes deepened whenever she looked at Evadne and William together.

The two young people spent a great deal of time together, though each morning William drove into Honolulu with MacMahon to renew contacts he had made on his way out from Australia to San Francisco, and to take advantage of his stay to investigate trade possibilities. Though the earthquake had shortened his stay in California, he was still interested in buying grape vine cuttings from Di Corso, and accepted MacMahon's offer of the use of his office and employees to correspond with Di Corso. William was also interested in the pineapple plantations which were just becoming established in Hawaii and wanted to visit one. So it was that just before Nevis was due to return, William left one morning to visit a pineapple plantation, planning to spend the night there and return the next day. Although Evadne was disappointed, she was also relieved. It would give her time to think—something which was impossible in William's presence. He did not have to touch her, only look at her, for her heart to beat wildly and for the blood pound in her veins. She wished they could go to the beach again, but something always happened to prevent another such excursion.

In the afternoon of the day William left, Evadne was sitting in the gazebo with Ada, sewing on her trousseau. Evadne was working on a thin crepe de Chine wrapper. With a sigh, she put it down.

"Aunt Ada," she said stroking the silk material, "what is the use of this? Samuel will never let me wear it."

"I was wondering when you were going to mention him." Ada put her own sewing aside to take one of Evadne's hands. "You are still determined to marry him?"

"I have promised. We have set the date," Evadne said grimly.

"Engagements have been broken before," Ada said gently.

"I know, and in the normal course of things. . . ." Evadne shook her head. "That's just the trouble, nothing is normal any more. If it were—"

"William would have spoken to your father and you would be marrying him," Ada broke in. "I cannot help but think that William also has a claim on you, child."

"I know," Evadne said. "There is so much I know, and yet nothing makes any sense. Even my heart does not tell me the same thing twice."

"Well, I cannot help you there," Ada said. "I wish I could read your heart as well as I can your face at times. When you look at William—" Ada heaved a sigh that shook her big frame.

"Is it as obvious as that? I did not know." Evadne shook her head.

"Yes, child. Thomas has spoken of it too," Ada answered gently. "Speaking of Thomas—" she raised her head "—that sounds like his carriage. What is he doing home at this hour?" It was mid-afternoon, and Thomas MacMahon was never home before six.

Ada got to her feet, but as she started toward the house, her husband came out to join them. His expression was sober, his brows drawn together, giving him a solemn air that was unusual for him. Seeing his wife's worried look, he gave her a brief, reassuring smile.

"Evadne. . . ." He came to her and took her hands. "I have news for you: The *Narragansett* has just anchored in the roads. Captain Nevis sent me word that he will be here to call on you as soon as he has had a chance to clean up."

"I see." Evadne went pale. "I—I had not expected him quite so soon."

"Nor I," admitted MacMahon. "His message sounded as if he were eager to see you, which is why I felt I should come here first myself."

"Thank you, Uncle Thomas." Evadne turned back to gather her sewing together.

"I will take care of that," Ada told her. "Do you want to change?"

Evadne was wearing a simple lawn dress in a pale green plaid that was rather casual for receiving callers. "No, would you—" she took a deep breath "—would you send him to me here when he arrives?"

"Of course. Come, Thomas," Ada said, handing her husband half the sewing and hurrying him off. "If you need me," she called back over her shoulder, "I will be nearby."

Evadne gazed out at the blue Pacific on the horizon, unaware of what she was looking at. The idyll with William was over; it was time for her to face a future that would no longer wait. The thought that perhaps Nevis may have changed his mind about marrying her passed fleetingly and hopefully through her mind, but it was gone almost before she was aware of it. Whatever it was that brought him here so soon after his arrival, it was not that.

"Evadne!"

She turned at the sound of her name. Nevis was there, walking toward her with a smile on his face, his arms held out to her.

"Samuel, what a surprise. We did not expect you so soon," Evadne said quickly. "I hope nothing went wrong during the voyage?"

"No, it went even better than I hoped." He took her in his arms, kissing her on the cheek. "All I have thought about is you—how unfair I have been, neglecting you."

Evadne looked at him. His face was shining, alight with emotion as she had never before seen it. Her heart stopped for a moment and pity flowed through her mixed with regret. Now that he had found happiness, she was about to lose hers. She rested her head against his shoulder, neither resisting his embrace nor encouraging it.

He dropped his arms and stepped back, noticing her lack of

response and puzzled by it. "Is anything wrong? You look so—so pale."

"Samuel," her voice was low, almost a whisper. "I—I must talk to you. There is something you must know," she said firmly, raising her eyes to meet his, her decision made.

His face darkened, setting in the stern lines she knew so well. "If it is about the wedding, that you wish to postpone it again—"

"No. Sit down, Samuel," she urged. When he had seated himself in the gazebo, she took the seat opposite him. Clasping her hands in her lap, she faced him, not giving in to the urge to look away—much less to run away into Ada's comforting arms. "What I have to tell you is not easy. Please be patient with me," she begged, "as patient as you are with the *Narragansett*."

"Very well, although what you can possibly have to say that is so serious—unless it concerns our wedding—I cannot imagine." His brows had drawn together in a frown.

"It does, in a way. Wait!" she cried when he opened his mouth to protest. She breathed deeply, the scent of the tropical flowers strong in her nostrils. "Samuel, do you remember when you . . . proposed to me, how you mentioned my beauty and . . . and purity?"

"Of course. It was your purity, your innocence, that made me aware that I could not leave you to the fate that undoubtedly lay before you in that Sodom and Gomorrah," he declared fervently.

"That is the problem. I cannot marry you letting you go on thinking—" she stood, drawing herself to her full height, her head high. "I am neither innocent nor pure. Before I met you, there was another."

"Evadne. . . ." He smiled, the frown disappearing. "Of course I knew I was not the first man to love you. You are far too beautiful. Many men, all far more eligible than I, must have been attracted to you."

"You do not understand what I mean." Now that she had made up her mind to tell him, she was annoyed with his slowness.

"Then, what—?" He shook his head, totally puzzled.

"You amaze me, Samuel," she said honestly. "It is you who are the innocent. What I am trying to say is that I am not—am not a virgin. I am neither innocent nor pure." The words came out more harshly than she had intended.

The color drained from his face. His head snapped back as sharply as if she had struck him. He stared at her, stunned, in shock, trying to grasp what she had just said.

"I am sorry. I should have told you before—in the beginning—but I was afraid that if you did not take me with you, then Grace would not have gone with Ethan. You remember how she insisted that she owed her life to me and would stay with me forever," Evadne explained hurriedly.

The explanation did not seem to penetrate the state of shock he was in. Evadne sighed. "Samuel, please. . . ."

At the sound of his name, his color gradually returned. "This is the truth?" he demanded. "If so, how often did you . . . did you make free with—?"

Evadne flushed. "If you mean with how many men, there was only one—and we planned to marry." What an aggravating man he was, she thought, having no intention of telling him how many times, if that was what he meant by "how many."

"And then he left you!" His dark eyes blazed. "You poor little fool. You are more ignorant than I thought of the ways of the world. There are too many men eager to take advantage of such innocence, men who will lie about love and marriage." He took her hand, and, to her horror, knelt in front of her. "I admit that I am shocked by what you have told me. I had wanted to be the first to . . . to—" Color rose in his cheeks. "It changes nothing. More than ever do I wish to marry you. How brave you are," he marveled. "What courage it must have taken to tell me this!"

If Nevis had paled before, Evadne now went ashen as she listened to him. "You do not understand!" she cried. "I cannot be your wife . . . !"

"Dear Evadne, you are simply upset. The strain. . . ." He rose to his feet, patting her affectionately and clumsily on the shoulder. "I will send Mrs. MacMahon out to you. You need a woman right now. I will return tomorrow, after you have had a chance to rest." He kissed her gently on the forehead before striding off toward the house with the slightly rolling walk of a sailor.

Evadne leaned back against her seat, too weak to move. What more could she say to him, she wondered. What would she say to him tomorrow, when William would have returned? What, for that matter, was she going to say to William?

She looked up and saw Ada hurrying toward her, worry in her face. "Child, what is it? Nevis said you needed me, that you were in trouble—?"

Evadne began to laugh hysterically. "In trouble?" That was really too much and so like the man! "I am sorry, Aunt Ada. It is not funny, but—" Still laughing, she let Ada take her in her arms. Gradually, she calmed down and related what had happened, how Nevis had not even understood at first what she was talking about, but then. . . . "And so," she concluded, shaking her head wonderingly, "he insists on marrying me because I really am innocent. What am I to do?"

"I haven't the slightest idea," Ada answered in all honesty. "I was sure that he would refuse to marry you when he heard what you had to say. Does he know that William is here?"

"No." Evadne shook her head. "He gave me no time to tell him. When he finally understood what I was saying, he refused to let me say another word."

"I won't ask you what you are going to do about William," Ada said.

"If you did, I couldn't answer. I don't know myself," Evadne admitted. "But I will have to talk to Samuel again tomorrow . . . and to William."

The two women returned to the house where Thomas was waiting for them. He was too wise to ask any questions when he saw the expressions on their faces, deciding instead to go back to his office.

No sooner had Thomas MacMahon left when Grace arrived. Nevis had stopped at the rooms Ethan had taken for them to tell her that Evadne needed her. Her moon face filled with concern, she bustled into the room where Evadne and Ada were sitting, each lost in her own thoughts.

After hearing what had happened, Grace settled herself in a chair, a pleased look on her face. "There, you see, Vad?" she exclaimed. "It shows what a fine man the cap'n is. You couldn't ask for a finer gentleman. Now you ain't got a thing to worry about. You can marry him with a clear conscience. How brave you are—and him too!"

"If one more person tells me I am brave, I shall scream," announced Evadne. "I wasn't being brave, I was being cowardly, trying to let someone else decide for me what to do."

Grace's jaw dropped. "You got no choice. You gotta marry him now, Vad. You promised!"

"No." Ada stood up then. "Engagements have been broken before. It is still Evadne's decision, Grace. All Nevis has done is make it more difficult for her."

"That William ain't nothing but trouble, Aunt Ada," Grace insisted. "After the way he went off and left her all alone—"

"It wasn't his fault, Grace," Evadne objected. "You know that, you were there."

Grace looked as if she knew no such thing.

"Grace," Ada went to her, "I don't think either one of us should try to influence Evadne's decision. We can come up with reasons in favor of either man—reasons Evadne is well aware of. If we are her friends," Ada said kindly, "we will give her our support, whatever she decides."

Grace sighed and nodded. "You're right, Aunt Ada. Well, I suppose I better get home and cook Ethan's supper. He went off to the ship with the cap'n, and the cap'n may come back to supper with him." She hesitated, looking at Evadne. "Want me to talk to the cap'n, Vad?"

"No!" Evadne spoke more sharply than she had intended to. "You mean well, Grace, but I am the only one who can say anything to him now, and I must have time to think."

"Whatever you say, Vad. We're friends, ain't we?" Grace smiled then. "I'll stick by you, no matter what you do."

After Grace had gone, Ada said, with smile, "She's right about one thing, child, you do have friends."

"I know, and I appreciate it more than I can say."

She was thinking of how many good friends she had that night as she went to bed. Lying beneath the light cover, she watched the moonlight spilling in a wave across the carpet. The breezes rustled the trees in the garden in a lullaby of sound. Before long, she drifted into a light sleep.

A sound awakened her. She raised her head, listening. Someone was in her room. She opened her mouth to cry out, but before she could a hand closed gently across her mouth and William's face, smiling at her, leaned over her.

"Shhh," he whispered, removing his hand.

"William! What are you doing here?" she gasped.

He sat down beside her on the bed, one hand brushing her hair back. "I kept thinking of the last time I left you and I had to see your face again—to be sure that I had found you. So, after dinner at the plantation, I made my excuses, explaining that I had to come back. I saddled my horse and here I am."

"You can't stay here," she protested. "Aunt Ada

. . Uncle Thomas—" His hand slid down to her breasts, ondling them. She squirmed with desire.

"Why not? They don't know I am here. Besides they are in he other wing," William reminded her, his lips silencing her protests with a kiss.

Evadne's arms went around his neck. It was the second ime that day that someone had missed her so much he had changed his plans to be with her. Her mind told her to tell him hat Samuel was back, but her heart told her: "One more ime, once more. . . ." She held him close, her body on fire rom his touch.

William freed himself, pulling back the light cover. "Take hat nightdress off, my love." He was starting to remove his acket and unbutton his shirt.

Evadne slid out of bed, eager to obey him, and hesitated. It vould not be fair. If she had avoided telling Samuel the truth about herself, she had also avoided discussing her marriage with William. "William . . . ?"

"Aren't you out of that damned thing yet?" He was starting to undo his trousers.

"Samuel is back," she said.

"I see." William had sat down on the bed. "What did you ell him?"

"That . . . that I was not innocent, not a virgin."

"And he still wants to marry you?" William stood up, his body gleaming like gold in the moonlight. He took hold of her nightdress and pulled it over her head.

"Yes . . . more than ever."

"Good for him. It shows he is a gentleman." He seemed totally unconcerned as he threw the nightdress to the floor.

Evadne stared at him. "Is—is that all you can say?" she stuttered, and suddenly she was pounding his chest with her fists, furious with him, outraged because of his complacency.

William laughed, seizing her wrists. "What do you expect me to say?"

"You—you beast. Let me go! If you loved me—"

"I do, my love, and I am about to prove it to you," he said, he laughter disappearing. He pushed her gently down on the bed. "As for Samuel, I have no intention of letting him—or anyone else—marry you."

Evadne stared at him, any further protest smothered by his mouth on hers. He released her wrists, the weight of his body on hers preventing her from moving.

"You devil . . . you beautiful devil," he muttered, his

hands fondling her, arousing her more patiently than ever, his
mouth lingering on her mouth and breasts, teasing her thigh
into parting, until he had her panting for breath and her body
vibrating with a life of its own.

"Take me, my love," he whispered. "Put me inside you
when you want me!"

Her hand reached out, trembling in her eagerness to grasp
his manhood and guide it into her, to feel the strength of him
driving deeply, raising her to new ecstasy until she thought
she could bear it no longer. She moaned as he brought them
to climax, then held him close as he lay half on top of her,
luxuriating in the fullfillment of her desire.

Her hand stroked his hair gently.

"Oh, William," she sighed, closing her eyes and nestling
her body into the curve of his, as sleep overwhelmed her.

When Evadne woke, it was not yet dawn. William was
trying to slip from her arms without rousing her. "Let me go,
my love," he whispered. "It would not do for us to be found
like this."

"What will you do?" She watched him as he searched for
his clothes in the dimness.

"Go to town, have some breakfast, wait until a decent hour
to arrive here." He grinned, his teeth white in the pre-dawn
dark.

"You . . . you will come back?" She slipped out of bed to
kiss him.

"After last night, need you ask?" He put his arms around
her. "You still have a lot to learn, my love, and I do not
intend to let anyone else teach you." He kissed her lightly,
carrying his boots as he walked to the French window leading
to the balcony.

Evadne waited, listening for his steps in the distance before
getting back into bed. She curled up, holding the pillow in her
arms, and fell asleep almost immediately. Only when May
awakened her by knocking on the door with the breakfast tray
did Evadne realize that she was still naked, the nightdress
lying on the floor where William had thrown it. Calling out to
May to wait a moment, she quickly pulled the nightdress on
and crawled back into bed.

She hurried through breakfast and dressed just as hurriedly. Much as she dreaded the day ahead, she had no
intention of letting William and Samuel meet without her
being there. If she feared facing the two of them together, she

was even more afraid of what might happen if they met accidentally without her.

Ada had had the same thought, although of course she did not know that William had already returned. The two women met in the corner room. Ada glanced anxiously at Evadne, who was too restless to stand or sit in one spot for long. "I wish Thomas were here," Ada admitted.

Evadne had turned to reassure her when she heard horse's hooves clattering on the gravel. That would be William since Samuel always took a carriage to the house.

She greeted William with a kiss. He had obviously bathed and changed his shirt, for his cheeks were smooth-shaven and the shirt was unwrinkled. "Did you have a good trip?" she asked politely.

William had no time to answer. A carriage had entered the drive. Evadne glanced at Ada, her heart pounding. "That will be Samuel," she said calmly.

A moment later, Nevis was in the room. The two men acknowledged the introductions politely. Ada looked on helplessly, wondering what Evadne was going to do. Nervously, Ada asked, "May I offer you gentlemen coffee? It won't take a moment."

"Thank you, Aunt Ada," Evadne said brightly. "I think that our guests would appreciate some refreshment. Would you . . . ?"

Ada left the room reluctantly, regretting her offer. She glanced back from the doorway, not wanting to leave Evadne alone, but the girl smiled at her reassuringly.

With Ada gone, Evadne turned to face the two men. For all her apparent confidence, she did not have the slightest idea of what to do or say.

"Are you here on business, Mr. Hopkins?" Nevis asked innocently, assuming that William was a friend of the Mac-Mahons.

"You could say that," William replied agreeably.

"Are you going to be here long?" Nevis looked at Evadne for support.

She smiled at him, deciding the best thing to do for the moment was to leave the men alone. Calmly, she seated herself in a chair to watch.

"Long enough." William was as noncommittal as he was inscrutable.

"Then you must come to our wedding. I assume that the

MacMahons have told you that Miss Harper and I are to be married in a fortnight," said Nevis.

William laughed loudly. "If Evadne is going to marry anyone, it will be me."

Evadne sprang to her feet, shocked by William's bluntness.

"What? Explain yourself, sir!" Nevis, who had been sitting down, rose to his feet, his hands balling into fists.

"William! Samuel!" Evadne stepped between them.

"Stay out of this, my love." William pushed her gently to one side, as Ada returned.

"Aunt Ada!" Evadne ran to the woman's side.

William took a deep breath. He had no intention of being drawn into losing his temper. "I want to thank you for all you have done for Evadne, Captain Nevis. She has told me how—how kind you have been to her."

"I do not know who you are, but I suggest that you leave," Nevis said. "Who is this man, Evadne?"

"I am the man she intended to marry before you met her," William announced. "We were unfortunately separated during the earthquake in San Francisco, but now I have come to claim her."

"To—to claim her!" Nevis exploded. "Then you are the man who betrayed her innocence with false promises, the man who . . . who seduced her." He raised his fists. "You will never have her, and you will never have another chance to harm her." He started toward Evadne.

"Touch her and I will kill you!" All amiability vanished from William.

Nevis ignored him, stalking past him toward Evadne, only to find William, quick as a cat, barring his way.

"Get out of here," snarled Nevis.

Evadne stared at them, seeing two strangers. They stood facing one another with fists raised, fury in both their faces. They looked willing to kill each other—and capable of it.

"Damn both of you!" Evadne slipped away from Ada's restraining hand and stepped boldly between them. "Stop it. This has gone far enough. It is all my fault—"

"Let us settle it, Evadne," William said, his face eager for a fight.

"I can see how you will settle it!" Evadne glared at each of them in turn. "Well, go ahead, but first let me warn you. I have tried to reason with both of you, and neither of you will listen to me. You are determined to have your way without asking me what I want. Go ahead—kill each other!"

"Evadne," protested Nevis. "Your honor is at stake—and mine too. If I do not avenge the wrong that this man—"

"Oh, shut up!" Evadne stamped her foot angrily. "This is nineteen-oh-six, not the nineteenth century when men settled everything with a duel. But if that is what you want, well, go ahead." She turned away, going back to Ada. The two men stared after her in amazement. "As of this moment, I have no intention of marrying either of you," she announced, "since I certainly cannot marry one of you with the other's blood on his hands."

"Bravo," murmured Ada.

William began to laugh then. His anger vanished.

Evadne stared at him. "Do you think that I am joking?"

"No." William shook his head. "Knowing you, you are quite serious. If we fight and I kill Nevis, you could never look at me again without remembering what I have done—even though it was done for you and providing I managed to escape the hangman's noose. And if Nevis kills me—" He shook his head. "I admire your cleverness, Evadne. Don't you, Nevis?"

"I would call it courage," Nevis replied stiffly, dropping his hands. "It seems that neither of us can win."

"Neither can Evadne, can you, my love?" William looked at her sadly. "You should have let us fight it out. Now it is up to you to decide."

Evadne took a deep breath. "William. . . ." She looked at him with eyes dark green with passion—and shining with tears. She turned her back on him, facing Nevis, holding her head held high.

William caught his breath. His eyes met Ada's and he saw the tears in the woman's eyes. "Evadne. . . ." her name caught in his throat.

"Samuel." Evadne took a step toward Nevis, pride and dignity in every inch of her, despite the tears on her cheeks. "I have given you my word. . . ."

Nevis stepped toward her. Taking her face between his hands, he said, in a voice rough with emotion, "Do you love this man?"

"Yes, Samuel. I cannot and will not lie about that. You must know that I will always love William, that no matter how much I may learn to care for you—even love you—I will never forget him or love you as I do him," Evadne said quietly, her voice steady.

Nevis's arm went around her protectively. "I love you, my

dear. I fear I never told you that. It would be easy to keep you to your word, the word you have given in front of witnesses and God. If I do that, however, I will have committed a far greater sin." His arm still around Evadne, he turned to William. "I do not condone what you did. I have no doubt that you took advantage of her, but you must love her or you would not have been so willing to fight me for her."

"Nevis—" William took a step toward the man.

"You said you came to claim her. Do you mean to marry her?" Nevis demanded in a stern voice.

"Yes. It is all I have thought of. It is why I came here to find her." William met the other man's dark gaze.

"If you do not, if you only intend to use her and cast her aside, I will find you—wherever you hide—and kill you," Nevis said grimly. He kissed Evadne on the forehead, dropping his arm from around her. "Goodbye, my dear. I must return to my ship." With that, he turned and swiftly left the room.

Evadne ran to the window, watching him get into his carriage. He saw her and gave her a half salute, then the carriage moved down the drive. When Evadne turned around, Ada had vanished. "William . . . ?"

"You would have married him, my love, even after—after last night?" His blue eyes were dark and his expression more serious than she had ever seen it.

"Yes, William. Perhaps Samuel and I are not so different after all. I kept hearing my father saying 'never give your word unless you mean to keep it, and once you give it, never go back on it' . . . do you understand?"

"Not quite, my love." He smiled. "But it doesn't matter. If I loved you before, I love you even more now." He took her face in his hands. "It is still not too late to follow him. He was right, you know. I did seduce you, and I came back last night to seduce you again. The plantation overseer returned from town and mentioned at dinner that the *Narragansett* had returned. . . ."

Evadne chuckled and slipped her arms around his neck. "Well, then, we had better wed as soon as possible, because you will not seduce me again—until we are married!"

Dear Reader:

Would you take a few moments to fill out this questionnaire and mail it to:

Richard Gallen Books/Questionnaire
8-10 West 36th St., New York, N.Y. 10018

1. What rating would you give *The Firebird?*
   ☐ excellent ☐ very good ☐ fair ☐ poor

2. What prompted you to buy this book? ☐ title
   ☐ front cover ☐ back cover ☐ friend's recommendation ☐ other (please specify) _____

3. Check off the elements you liked best:
   ☐ hero ☐ heroine ☐ other characters ☐ story
   ☐ setting ☐ ending ☐ love scenes

4. Were the love scenes ☐ too explicit
   ☐ not explicit enough ☐ just right

5. Any additional comments about the book?
   _____

6. Would you recommend this book to friends?
   ☐ yes ☐ no

7. Have you read other Richard Gallen
   romances? ☐ yes ☐ no

8. Do you plan to buy other Richard Gallen
   romances? ☐ yes ☐ no

9. What kind of romances do you enjoy reading?
   ☐ historical romance ☐ contemporary romance
   ☐ Regency romance ☐ light modern romance
   ☐ Gothic romance

10. Please check your general age group:
    ☐ under 25 ☐ 25-35 ☐ 35-45 ☐ 45-55 ☐ over 55

11. If you would like to receive a romance
    newsletter please fill in your name and
    address:
    _____
    _____
    _____